I0819777

THE PAPER CRANE

AND OTHER STORIES

OBED OLIVARRÍA

metamorphosis
PUBLISHERS

THE PAPER CRANE AND OTHER STORIES

Names: Olivarría, Obed, author.
Title: The paper crane and other stories / Obed Olivarría
Description: Metamorphosis Publishing
Subjects: Fantasy | Short Stories | Collection.

For information contact:
http://www.obedolivarria.com

Print ISBN: 978-1-966179-05-4
eBook ISBN: 978-1-966179-06-1
Library of Congress Control Number: 2025911939

First Edition.

Book interior, cover design, and artwork by Obed Olivarría.

Printed in the United States.

OTHER TITLES BY OBED OLIVARRÍA

THEORY OF MIND AND OTHER STORIES

THE MESSAGE IN THE PAINTING AND OTHER STORIES

DREAMS OF GOLD AND BLOOD AND OTHER STORIES

THE FLIGHT OF THE BUTTERFLY

BROKEN

SCARS

DILUTED PUPILS

DEDICATION

For Letty, the best mother one could've ever asked for.

Thank you for giving me life. Thank you for setting me free.
Thank you for being my rock. Thank you for being the best.

CONTENTS

PREFACE

From an early age, I've enjoyed both, writing and reading fiction. I have to confess, however, that I have a particular love for short stories and novelettes. This is due, possibly, to my short attention span. They're perfect for me! It's no secret that our attention span as a society is also shrinking. (You can thank the nature of modern media for that.) Therefore, I believe that short stories are the perfect answer to that dwindling attention time in our individual and collective minds.

Nonetheless, short stories are not anything new. In fact, short stories have existed as long as humanity has been around. And very likely even prior to that, if we are honest. The truth is that condensing a message or narrative into short form can pack an extra punch that even the most distracted, media-saturated Zoomer might remember.

Though I tend to read long fiction – novels – significantly more often than I do short stories, novelettes, or novellas, the reality is that in the end, I've still read way more short stories than novels. Their brevity allows for any reader to cruise through them much quicker and move on to other things. The same is true with writing them. You see, I have constant ideas for stories – in multiple genres.

Unfortunately, however, I don't have the time (or patience) to develop all of these into full length novels, and I must become very selective. So, writing short stories and novelettes become the perfect answer to this dilemma.

Choosing stories for this, my second collection, proved easier than the first time around. On *Theory of Mind and Other Stories*, my first short-story collection, I decided to stick to sci-fi narratives. That was the plan from the very beginning. On this compilation, however, I wanted to pursue the low fantasy route – whether that was urban fantasy, magical realism, science fantasy, or horror fantasy. And I opted for selecting stories that had impacted me in one way or another when I'd written them. *The Paper Crane and Other Stories* is therefore an eclectic approach to all things fantasy.

Once again, it is my hope that you, as the reader, have as much fun reading my stories as I had when writing them. May these stories provide an opportunity to have something to talk about, or, at the very least, be an escapade for your daily routine.

Happy readings!

THE PAPER CRANE

AND OTHER STORIES

THE COSTUME CONTEST

"So what are you gonna wear tomorrow night?"

"I don't think I'm going," she said.

"What?!" I replied instantly. "Norma, you *have* to go!"

"I don't *have* to go. And, anyway, I want to be home so I can pass out candy to the trick-or-treaters from my neighborhood."

"Come on! Forget the kids!"

She gave me a look. It was not a good one.

"Okay, that came out wrong. But listen, Norma, it'll be fun. Reddy rented out the whole ship, for Christ's sake."

"Yeah, I know. But these parties are always so tedious and uptight. It's like we're still at work, just with light drinking and small talk."

At that moment, Reddy himself, our boss, emerged from his office. His real name is David Reedy, but myself and a few other agents like to call him Reddy after the color his face gets when his famous temper flares up.

"Can I get everyone's attention please?" he asks, yelling across the office. "I hope you all have big plans for your costumes tomorrow; and if you don't, then perhaps I can provide a little incentive. There will be a costume contest. But wait, there is more...the winner will have their Christmas bonus doubled!"

The office sat in stunned silence for a brief moment, then a couple of them yelled back to him.

"But David, I have to trick-or-treat with my kids."

"Yeah, that's not fair, Mr. Reedy! I had plans already too!"

As he listened, his face began turning his characteristic tomato color, and Reddy emerged.

"I don't care!" he yelled. He heaved a hefty sigh. "Look, everyone. The truth is that I don't care what your plans are. All I am saying is that if you want a shot at a bigger Christmas bonus, then come tomorrow night, and come dressed to impress. If you miss it, that's on you." With that, he went back into his office and slammed the door.

The few employees who weren't planning on going sat looking indignant, while there was an air of excitement surrounding those of us who were already planning on going.

I looked at Norma. "Well?"

"What?"

"Surely you're coming now."

She thought for a second. "I don't think so."

"Oh, come on!" As I said that, Andrew came up behind me and slapped me on the back.

"Hey, fool!"

But I was too busy staring at Norma's exquisite face.

"Yo, Leandro! Can you believe that?" Andrew said again, this time fully gaining my attention.

I turned to him. "Andy, you're going to the party, right?"

"Of course. Zoila and I wouldn't miss it."

"Norma doesn't want to go," I told him while looking at her.

"What?" He turned to face her as well.

Norma looked playfully annoyed. "You guys, I just don't feel like it."

"We can all go together!" said Andrew.

I looked at her. "Yes! I'll pick you up. And we can spend the whole night making fun of other people's costumes."

She rolled her eyes. "Okay, *fine*. I'll go. I mean, I guess." She smiled.

"Yes!" I high-fived Andrew.

"I'll pick you up at eight."

* * *

The following night, I parked outside her apartment, walked up to the door, and rang the bell. I heard her moving around inside for a minute before opening the door.

"Woah," I said, looking at her. "I'm sorry, I thought Norma Vern lived here, not an absolutely beautiful vampire." And I meant it. She looked gorgeous, even as a vampire.

The sight of her in a sexy vampire costume made me stand in awe like an eager teenager.

Even through the makeup, she blushed. "Hi. Sorry, Mr. Creepy Sherlock Holmes, but I can't talk long. I'm waiting to be picked up by my friend Leandro Barón," she said with a wry smile.

"Ha-ha. I'm actually Hercule Poirot," I replied.

"Who?"

"He's the detective from Agatha Christie's books."

"Nerd," she said, smiling at me.

I felt butterflies in my stomach and smiled back at her. Our first date was already going well.

"All right, let's go, then! Or we'll be late." she said excitedly. "We don't want to miss the all-important costume contest."

We arrived at the port in Long Beach and parked, blown away by the size of the ship docked in the harbor. I'd seen it several times before, but I'd never been on it. I was excited.

"The *Queen Mary*," said Andrew, waiting for us by the dock with Zoila on his arm. "Once a luxury cruise ship, hotel, and casino."

He was dressed as an old-school Italian mobster: hair slicked back under a vintage fedora, smooth black blazer with pants to match, and a fat cigar hanging out the edge of his mouth. It was seriously cool.

"I can't believe Reddy actually rented this thing out," said Zoila, dressed as a Wonder-Woman style Amazonian heroine: a golden headband, which went well with her long raven hair, skin-tight sleeveless dress, and boots up to her knees. She looked great too.

If I say so myself, we had quite a good-looking crew as we crossed the gangplank and entered the boat, the sound of music slowly building as we got closer and closer.

Much to my pleasant surprise, we entered the ship to see that this was no ordinary office party; there was no gross fluorescent lighting, cheap drinks, or quiet music.

No, this was a *real* party. Finally!

We walked past a ghoul working the coat check, then entered the ballroom, which was located in the heart of the ship. The lights were dimmed, and lots of people were there already, being served catered food by skeletons, getting drinks from an open bar staffed by three goblins, and dancing to the music coming from a pretty good band made up of ghosts and monsters. They were playing classic rock songs, which only made the ambiance better.

"Woah," we all said in unison. This bash actually looked fun!

I turned to Norma. "Glad you came now?"

She smiled and nodded, flashing her fangs at me.

I laughed.

"Reddy really kicked it up a notch for this party," said Andrew.

As if in cue, Reddy appeared out of nowhere. Or should I say, a very extravagantly dressed Viking who looked like Reddy. He had on a helmet and form-fitting armor covered in fur. He was clutching a huge plastic battle ax.

"Kids," he said in a shitty Norse accent.

"Hey, Mr. Reedy," said Norma.

"What's up, Reddy?" I said, and Norma stepped on my foot and gave me a look, though he didn't seem to notice, most likely due to the loud music.

He looked us all up and down.

"Looking good," he said, in a voice of approval that was rarely heard at work. He strode off to judge the costumes of more newcomers and we sighed in relief.

We went to go get some food—and drinks— and the night commenced.

We danced, we drank, we laughed, and had a blast. This was the first genuinely fun office party I'd been to. It felt great to interact with all these people and not talk about insurance policies or needy clients.

But I couldn't keep my eyes of the sexy vampire next to me.

We spent a while dancing to the music played by the monster band – they played all kinds of classic anthems and party hits, and everyone in the party sang along and danced together. As the night went on and the drinks kept flowing, the music only got better. Of course, they would never forget to play "Monster Mash" or "Thriller."

While they played our favorites, Andrew, Zoila, Norma and I circled up and drunkenly belted out the words together, laughing and having the time of our lives.

As the night went on, Andrew and Zoila drifted off to be together, leaving Norma and I dancing alone. I appreciated as Andy winked at me from a distance.

The monster band started playing a slow song, and I took off my beret and made a big show of asking her for a dance, outstretching my hand and putting on my best British accent. Yeah, I know Hercule Poirot was actually Belgian, but I have no idea how to imitate that accent. Besides, my sexy vampire wouldn't even know.

She graciously accepted by biting my hand, claiming she was "thirsty." My heart pumped harder at her words.

I held her close and we danced, staring into each other's eyes. When she leaned her head against my chest, I looked out the tall windows at the view of downtown Long Beach. It felt like that dance lasted for eternity, and there was no way I would rather have it.

However, even eternity ends, and eventually we found ourselves on the upper deck of the ship with Andrew and Zoila, nursing drinks and enjoying the view.

The party was winding down, and Andrew was drunkenly holding court with the girls, while I just smiled and looked out on the water.

What a perfect night, I thought. A beautiful girl, great music, and good friends.

"Oh, we should get back to the ballroom," said Zoila, looking at her phone. "It's midnight, the costume contest is happening soon!"

At just that moment, we felt the ship start to rumble. It started out soft, but quickly grew to the point where I was worried we could fall off the ship and into the harbor.

I grabbed Norma right as a blinding flash of white light illuminated the ship.

Then, everything went dark.

***

It took me a second after waking up to remember where I was. I looked around, bewildered and groggy, before seeing Norma before me.

The Halloween Party. The *Queen Mary*. It all came rushing back. By the looks on their faces, Andrew, Zoila, and Norma were experiencing similar things.

"What just happened?" yelled Zoila.

"I feel weird," said Norma.

"Guys," said Andrew, looking out over the water. We all looked out over the side of the ship and gasped.

We were no longer docked in the harbor. We were at least a mile out to sea. The lights of Long Beach shone off in the distance, dimly illuminating huge waves that were lapping against the side of the ship.

"What the hell?" I said, shocked. I reached into my pocket to grab my phone and see if an earthquake had hit LA, but instead of my phone, I had a handful of objects I didn't own.

There was a book of matches and a rugged leather pouch filled with tobacco.

Confused, I reached into my other pocket, where I had stashed my fake pipe. It felt heavier, sturdier than before. My cheap plastic pipe had been replaced by an ornately carved, rather expensive looking real pipe.

"You guys," I said, looking up to them. "My phone is gone, and I've got stuff in my pockets that doesn't belong to me."

They all reached into their pockets.

"Oh my God," said Andrew, slowly pulling something out of his pocket. It was dark, but the moonlight dimly reflected off the dull metal.

It was a handgun.

"Is that real?" asked Zoila in a hushed tone.

"Let's not test it out!" said Norma quickly.

Andrew's eyes grew wide, and he shoved it back in his pocket.

What is going on?

"My fangs!" said Norma, touching her teeth and starting to hyperventilate. "I can't take them off!"

"What?" said Andrew.

I went over to her and looked in her mouth. Sure enough, her plastic fangs were no longer there. In their place were what I can only describe as real fangs.

At that moment, Reddy burst out the door leading to the deck and marched over to us.

"Oh my God," said Norma as he approached. He was no longer out-of-shape, beer-belly Reddy. Now, he was huge, his muscles rippled as he walked. His beard was real.

He swung a great battle ax encrusted in various fine jewels as he walked, or should I say, stormed, toward us.

But, by far the most shocking, craziest thing about him: his usual shiny bald head was covered by the most glorious head of straw-blond hair I'd ever seen. It flowed out of his helmet, with various braids and baubles woven into it.

The only thing that hadn't changed about him was his face—it was as bright red as ever.

"What happened?" he yelled as he came up to us. "What is going on?"

Andrew was so shocked that he seemed to forget the gun in his pocket for a moment. "Holy cow, Mr. Reedy, have you been working out?"

"No, I haven't!" he roared back. Andrew wavered in fear at the great Viking warrior before him.

"What have you kids done? My battle ax is all... different now, and I was just hit in the head by Nichols with a bone!"

"A bone?" said Norma. "Wait, Mr. Reedy, what was Nichols dressed as?"

"A neanderthal. And a half-assed one at that. He doesn't stand a chance in the costume contest."

"Oh my God," said Norma again, eyes wide and darting left and right.

"What?" I asked her.

"Come with me," she said, and grabbed my hand. She began leading me, and I beckoned for Andrew and Zoila to come along, leaving our angry Viking of a boss alone on the deck.

***

Norma led us inside the ballroom, where it looked like a scene from a bizarre horror movie.

On the stage, grotesque monsters fumbled around among the instruments. Joe from HR bumped into me, and I immediately recoiled. He was dressed as the most realistic zombie I'd ever seen—he had fake blood coming from his mouth, tattered clothes, pale white skin, and dark yellow eyes. And the smell! He absolutely reeked.

We saw a princess, an alien, a cop, an angel, a robot, a cowboy and cowgirl. All were in absolutely incredible costumes. How did I not notice these before? I thought to myself. Everyone looked so legit!

It felt like a haunted dream as we walked deeper into the ballroom.

Then, we both stopped when we heard this great roar. We looked to our left to see a huge grizzly bear towering over us. We screamed for our lives and ran.

We got to the other side of the room before turning; the bear hadn't followed us and was just padding around the room, looking shy and bashful, almost apologetic it had scared us.

We had lost Andrew and Zoila in the mayhem. I turned to Norma, my heart racing. For some reason I was extremely attracted to her in this moment. I took a long look at her, and realized that something felt off.

"Leandro?" she said, sounding and looking panicked.

She looked different—a little paler, yet somehow a little more luminous.

"Leandro," she said again, more urgently this time.

"What?" I said absentmindedly as I looked at her, bewildered, playing with my curled mustache.

Her costume—it looked so much more vintage, real, authentic.

"Do you realize what has happened?" she asked me.

I did. Of course I did. But sometimes things that happen are so unbelievable that your brain refuses to believe them, makes up any alternative explanation just to avoid having to accept what is right in front of you.

"Someone let a bear into the party?" I said like an idiot. "A real freaking bear?"

"No they didn't, Leandro."

And then it hit me. Like a rush of adrenaline, my mind became hyper-focused, and began sifting through the evidence that was right before me, rapidly sorting, arranging, connecting information, drafting conclusions and hypotheses that suddenly became clear as day.

For that moment, I no longer felt like Leandro Barón. I felt like a detective, like… Hercule Poirot.

I returned to Norma. "Holy shit!"

She nodded. "Holy shit, indeed!"

"How is this possible?" I asked.

"I have no idea," she replied while feeling her body.

"Have you ever heard of people turning into their costumes before?"

"Obviously no!"

As the mystery of our circumstances became clear, Poirot emerged once more. I felt the high of doing what Poirot was put on this Earth to do: solve mysteries. It was the most incredible feeling I had ever felt.

At that moment, Andrew and Zoila emerged out of nowhere.

"There you guys are!" said Andrew. "You have to see this!"

They led us out of the ballroom and back to the deck. We heard the shouting before we even got out there.

Everyone was gathered in a big crowd. We pushed our way through to see what they were gathered around. We got to the inside to see a Mexican luchador on one end of the circle, looking angry and breathing heavy.

And Reddy on the other end, being held back by a Roman gladiator and an Aztec warrior.

"What happened?" Zoila asked an astronaut to our right.

"Mr. Reedy went crazy and tried to attack Jorge."

"I'm sorry, I'm sorry," we could hear Reddy saying. "I don't know what came over me, but I'm better now, I promise."

They released their grip on him. He shook his head, acting like a tired driver trying to stay awake at the wheel.

Then he looked at me, and I saw him change. A look of pure anger, utter rage. The look of a Viking as he goes berserk.

A fire ignited in his eyes, and he yelled and ran at me.

But the gladiator was ready and grabbed him, holding him back. "Woah!" he yelled as Reddy fought against him with all his strength.

I ran back, scared, but as I did, I noticed the lights of downtown Long Beach in the distance. I felt Poirot return within me, and I had an idea.

I took one cautionary look towards Reddy, but he was well-restrained. So, I turned to my friends and told them to follow me.

We arrived at the bridge of the ship to find a group of very confused sailors milling about.

They looked relieved when we entered, but also worried.

"Where's the captain?" I asked authoritatively.

"I'm the captain," said a man, stepping forward. He was elegantly dressed, with a very fine looking hat, robes over a pair of tight knickers, and an archaic-looking compass hanging around his neck.

"Captain, do you know how we ended up this far out to sea? Weren't we docked before? I was under the impression that the *Queen Mary* no longer sailed."

"I have no idea how it happened, detective," he said, genuinely confused. "Midnight struck, and there was a flash of light, and we suddenly were out here!"

"I see." I took out my pipe and put it in my mouth. "Well, can you take us back?"

"That's the thing. I don't know how!"

"What do you mean?" asked Zoila.

"I don't know how to sail this ship! The controls, these buttons, everything is so foreign to me. I have no idea what any of it does!"

"Wait," said Norma, eyes narrowing. "Captain, what did you dress as tonight?"

"Christopher Columbus."

Norma looked to his crew. "And them?"

"They dressed as my crew, of course!"

"Oh, crap," I said.

"What?" asked Andrew and Zoila in unison.

Norma and I looked at each other.

"We're stranded out here."

***

After explaining the situation to Andrew and Zoila, and the concept of electricity to the captain and his crew, we set to work trying to think of a plan. What had happened? And how could we get back to LA?

As we talked, the captain began rummaging through the cabinet, opening every compartment and hatch he could find, digging through them in the hopes that something might jog his memory as to how to sail a modern ship.

As the four of us were huddled together talking, we heard a loud crash, and turned to see him among a pile of assorted papers.

"Sorry about that, gentlefolk," he said clumsily.

But I wasn't listening. Nestled among the papers was a notebook. An old, ornate, aging notebook, one that contained great secrets and antiquated tales; the detective in me could just tell.

I rushed over and picked it up. Inside the cover it said:

Property of Hattie Weaver

"Guys, come look at this," I said to the others.

They gathered around. I flipped through the first few pages—they were filled with scribbles, doodles, and seemingly meaningless drawings.

But then, I soon came upon a dog-eared page—on the top it said October 31, 1932.

"Halloween 1932," said Norma. "That was exactly a hundred years ago."

I started to read from the page.

Something horrible and dreadful has happened tonight. We were all here, on the Queen Mary, to celebrate All Hallow's Eve. We were having a lovely time. Everyone dressed in their best costumes. Jim and I dressed as Beauty and the Beast—it was a wonderful success, and Jim spent oh-so-long on that beast costume.

But, at the stroke of midnight, right as we were all planning to go home, the boat began to tremble and quake. And with a flash, my Jim was gone, and replaced by a real-life beast!

It was horrible. He couldn't talk, only growl and roar. And yet, he still seemed to be in there, somehow stuck in the new form. And now the ship is out on open ocean, and we can't seem to get back to shore. I'm so scared.

"The Queen Mary Disaster of 1932," murmured the captain.

"What?" asked Zoila.

"The Disaster of 1932. It's famous. I heard of it before. The story goes that there was a party here. It went late into the night. The next morning, everyone had vanished. Not a trace to be seen. Nobody knows what happened to them. People assumed that everyone on the ship jumped overboard, into the harbor, their bodies washed out to sea. They had no idea why. The bodies were never found. A few years later the ship was docked here, never to be used again."

We all sat in grim silence for a long while. I flicked the page of the journal.

"It continues," I said, then began to read.

> ***A few hours have passed with Jim as that dreadful beast. It appears that what happened to him has happened to us all. I looked in the looking glass, and I truly am a beauty now! For a second I even forgot what was happening, I was that beautiful.***
>
> ***At first, it appeared as if it were Jim in the beast's body. He was gentle and kind, as my Jim is. (Or should I say was? No, it makes me too sad to think about that.) But lately he seems to be changing. He's having these violent outbursts. It almost seems as if he's becoming more of the beast and less of Jim.***

I'm afraid I feel it too. There are moments where I find myself forgetting who I was before, just thinking I am truly Beauty, and gazing longingly at my beast; not Jim, but the Beast himself.

"Reddy," said Andrew. We all looked at him. "Reddy was getting violent. Almost like he was becoming a Viking. A real one."

I thought back to the bear in the ballroom and nodded.

I turned the page. It continued.

Things have turned bad. As the night progresses, it seems that everyone is becoming more and more–

My reading was cut off by a scream from the deck. We looked at each other, then rushed out to see what it was.

We arrived on the deck to see it in a state of complete chaos. Animals, monsters, ghouls and goblins, ninjas and fairies, pimps, nuns, and sexy nurses were running around aimlessly. And Reddy, looking angry and mean, was on one side. He appeared to have assembled a small cadre of soldiers, and they were taking prisoners.

Remembering the way he had looked at me before, I grabbed the others and we ducked behind a wall. "Things are turning bad," I said. "We are becoming…our costumes. Real."

We heard Reddy yell, and a woman scream. We ran back to the bridge, and I opened back up Hattie's journal.

> ***Things have turned bad. As the night progresses, it seems that everyone is becoming more and more of their characters, and less of themselves. They're forgetting who they are, devolving into beasts of the earth or fantastical creatures. Even I have to keep looking at my journal to remember I'm Hattie.***
>
> ***Madam Marjorie just had an episode. She came to the gala tonight dressed as a witch doctor. And she just seemed to be...possessed by some magical energy. She began doing these chants, and then speaking these words:***
>
>> **The Queen Mary is overrun with dark energy, and the tendrils of the night are the only thing preserving little bits of our true characters. By the time the sun rises over the starboard edge, we will be forever trapped as who we pretend to be, and no longer will a drop remain of who we are.**
>
> ***I ran to her and grabbed her, asking her why she was saying this. But it seemed that, at that moment, Ms. Marjorie returned, and she seemed***

altogether confused as to what I was talking about. But then, a moment later, the witch doctor returned and, with eyes glazed over and voice deepened, began to speak once more:

Our only hope lies in a hundred drams of seawater, the spittle of a lowly beast, an otherworldly substance, the sweat of a worthy warrior, a strand of hair from an angry heathen, and finally the b–

They looked at me. "Keep going!" said Andrew.

"That's it. It cuts off there."

"What do you mean? It ends?"

"No, the page is torn. And that's as far as it gets."

I read it again, and this time as I read I felt Poirot emerge from within me. I began reading the words as if they were through a kaleidoscope: they merged and collided, broke apart and formed anew. I understood what I had to do.

"It's a potion," I said. They just looked blankly at me. "These things, together, they'll form a potion that, when we drink it, will turn us back."

"And we need to drink it before daylight comes," said Zoila.

"That's right," I said.

"But we don' know what the last ingredien' is!" said Andrew, sounding like Marlon Brando as the Godfather.

Zoila looked at him with passion and lust.

"Andy, if we get through this, I want you to work on your mobster accent," she said. "*For the bedroom*," she added with a whisper.

"Well," I said, ignoring their little aside. "We'll have to cross that bridge when we get there. At least we know the last ingredient starts with a B."

"So, what should we find first?" asked Norma.

"We need a hundred drams o' seawater," I replied as I finally lit my pipe.

"We can get you seawater," said the captain, and he and his crew promptly sped out of the room.

"Great," I said in between coughs. "So, we could try to get the spittle of a lowly beast?"

"If only Hattie and Jim were here," said Zoila. "Then we'd have a beast."

Norma and I looked at each other. The bear!

***

As we were making our way to the ballroom, the captain appeared out of nowhere, clutching a big jug of salty seawater.

"How did you get this so fast?" I asked him.

"This's my ship, mate. I may not remember how to sail it, but I remember my way around."

"All right," I said, starting to really like the old sailor. "Okay, come on guys."

We emerged onto the deck to see that the situation had only gotten worse. Factions had emerged, with a tribe of monsters and ghouls squaring off against a group of cartoon characters and sexy nurses that had captured and trained a gorilla, dog, and yeti to defend them. There was a small group of pirates running aimlessly around the boat, laughing.

A princess stood atop a higher deck, screaming to be saved from a killer clown that was working its way up to her, while a cowboy yelled that he would save her and sprang into action, jumping on his horse. A real horse.

As he galloped past us, we saw the scariest scene of all: Reddy, looking angry and sick, ruling over a small group of warriors and enslaved creatures. He had a guard consisting of the Aztec warrior and Roman gladiator. They looked formidable as they guarded over various animals, movie stars, and a pharaoh, all of whom Reddy had taken captive. An angel flew around overhead, trying to bring some semblance of order to the chaos, but she was wholly unsuccessful.

"*Rotzooi! Het is allemaal onzin,*" I said, wondering if we could even *survive* till daybreak, let alone create the potion by then.

"What did you say?" Norma asked.

"Oh, sorry," I replied without missing a beat. "I meant to say that it's all shit. Complete chaos."

She just stared at me.

"It's Dutch. Don't ask me how I know," I whispered as I shrugged.

We kept moving, keeping low and out of sight, and slipped into the ballroom. The bear was rampaging around, flipping tables and chairs and letting out a bone-chilling roar. A sexy bunny cowered under a table in the corner.

"Ok, we just need his spit," I said.

As we stood pondering how to get it, the bear noticed us and began making his way toward us, clumsily knocking over tables on his way. We got scared and began backing up.

"What do we do?" asked Norma, voice high-pitched and frightened. The bear seemed fixated on her.

Andrew and Zoila slipped away, while Norma and I kept retreating to the wall.

When the bear was halfway across the room from us, it stopped and reared up on its hind legs, standing over ten feet tall. It let out the most fearsome roar I'd ever heard, and we froze, paralyzed by fear. Then he started to charge. We screamed and tried to run for the door, but it was too far away at this point. We stood with our backs to the wall as it got closer and closer, until finally it was upon us.

We closed our eyes and braced, but right as it should've been on us, we heard it let out a pained roar.

I opened my eyes to see it off to the side, bowled over by a table, and Andrew and Zoila standing next to us, having done the bowling. They smiled at us.

The bear struggled under the table and chairs that surrounded it, and while doing so opened its mouth and let out one last roar. As it did, its spit and fluids flew through the air and hit us.

Disgusted, we wiped ourselves off as we turned to run away. But I then noticed the seawater I was holding starting to bubble and change color, to a light yellow. Some of the spit had gotten in there!

Once we got out of the ballroom, I told them about the potion, but Zoila didn't seem to hear. She got a strange look in her eyes as she looked out on the deck. She adopted a brave stance, the stance of an Amazonian heroine. Then she ran off. Andrew looked at us then ran off after her, concerned.

"Looks like it's just us now," I said to Norma. "Now we need an otherworldly substance."

She thought for a moment before saying, "Wasn't Richards dressed as an alien tonight?"

"You're right, my dear. We shall look for him at this instant," I said noticing my own accent and choice of words.

We searched for a while before eventually coming to the casino, where we saw a strange, garbled, blue-green creature sitting alone at the blackjack table. It seemed to be trying to learn about human culture by putting a deck of cards in one of its many mouths.

It turned and looked at us with its one eye, but evidently wasn't interested and turned back to its oral examination of the Queen of Spades.

"Poor Richards," I said. "How do we get a substance from him?"

That was when Norma noticed something oozing out from his back; or at least what seemed like his back.

"There!" she said pointing.

I looked, appalled, but quickly went over and examined it. Whatever it was, it was definitely otherworldly. He didn't seem to care as I scraped a little off his back with the craps stick and put it in the potion. It bubbled and hissed, once more changing color, this time to a deep purple.

I ran back to Norma, and we left Richards, or what remained of him, alone with his cards.

We returned to the deck, the scene of anarchy, the polar opposite of the tranquility of the casino.

"Now we need the sweat of a worthy warrior," I reminded her.

"Well," said Norma, "Reddy has a little gang of warriors; I don't know if I would call them worthy, though."

Then I thought of something. I grabbed Norma and pulled her into the fray. We ran across the deck, my keen eyes quickly searching through the crowd. Then I saw her. We ran up to Zoila, who was rescuing one of the cartoon characters from a zombie.

I felt her skin: bone dry. I looked around, then saw what I needed. I got Zoila's attention.

"Excuse me, madame heroine."

She looked at me, stoic and brave. I pointed to where the Aztec warrior was guarding over a steampunk couple with automata limbs, who looked terrified.

"These innocent people need your help!"

Zoila, the Amazonian warrior, rushed to their aid. We followed her as she brandished her spear, ready to free the gentle people.

She pounced on the Aztec warrior, who collapsed under her weight. But he pulled out a wooden sword studded with obsidian and clubbed her with it, knocking her back. They began a fierce battle. The Aztec would swing his club, and Zoila would deftly avoid his blows, sneaking in stabs with her spear as she did.

She got him in the shoulder, and he cried out in pain and began a frenzied round of swings and stabs at her. She parried and blocked them, but was clearly strained under his strength.

I saw my opportunity; as she fought back his blows, I went up behind her and wiped her shoulder. She was glistening in sweat.

I dripped some of it into the potion, and it began foaming and turned a greenish-yellow color. I grabbed Norma and tried to leave, but she stopped me.

"We can't leave Zoila!"

"We have to!" I said, looking at Hattie's journal. "We still need a couple more things, and daybreak isn't far off!"

At the mention of daybreak, Norma's eyes turned blood red, and her inner vampire emerged. She looked at me with an expression of primal fear, then turned and sprinted off, towards the interior of the ship.

I tried to chase her, but couldn't maneuver through the mangled crowd of people, and was forced to let her go. I wanted to go find her, but I knew that I had to keep going, keep making the potion, if we wanted any hope of making it out of this.

I ran back and found Andrew, still watching Zoila fight the Aztec. Zoila was gaining the upper hand.

A strand of hair from an angry heathen.

How would I get that? My mind raced and tumbled as I considered all I had taken in that night, combining and pulling apart all the people, characters, dreadful and fantastic things. I dug as deep as I could, then finally had it. I looked at Andrew, and silently asked him to forgive me.

I went up behind Zoila, locked in the heat of battle. I grabbed a monster who was pulsating nearby, and waited for my opportunity. When Zoila and the Aztec came by, I pushed the monster behind Zoila, tripping her and sending her sprawling on the ground.

The Aztec took his chance, kicking the spear out of Zoila's hand. He grabbed her and restrained her, a look of sick pleasure in his eyes. He tied her up and threw her with the other prisoners.

I looked to Andrew; fury burned in his eyes. The inner mobster emerged, but it wasn't enough to obscure his love for Zoila. He felt the passion of a gangster and the fire of loyalty to the woman he loved, and immediately marched over to the Aztec warrior.

"Ay!" he shouted in a full New York Italian accent. "You let 'er go!"

The Aztec just looked at him mockingly.

"Did you 'ear me? I said let her go!"

Reddy and the gladiator noticed what was going on and came over. Andrew pulled out his handgun and pointed it at the Aztec.

Reddy laughed at him. "You listen here, weakling. She's our prisoner now, and there's nothing you and your tiny little sword can do about it."

He and his gang of pre-gunpowder tyrants laughed at Andrew.

Andrew shot the gladiator in the foot, who fell over and began howling in pain. Their laughter stopped, and they looked at Andrew, confused and scared by his magic weapon.

"Listen heuh, Reddy," said Andrew. "I'll make ya an offa you can't refuse. You let my sweet lady go, and I won't blow ya brains out. Capisce?"

Reddy just stared defiantly at him for a moment. Then he opened his mouth and let out a scream, charging at Andrew, battle-ax raised above his head, ready to strike.

Andrew coolly shot at the blade of the ax, the force of the bullet sending it flying out of Reddy's hand, off the deck, and into the ocean below. He then strode forward and pressed the gun against Reddy's chest.

Reddy cowered in fear, and the Aztec quickly untied Zoila and let her go. Meanwhile, I ran behind Reddy and grabbed a strand of his hair while he was distracted and defenseless. I put it in the potion, which really began to bubble and pop, turning a dark green.

I ran off to try to find the last ingredient, but stopped as I looked at the horizon over the edge of the ship. It had that soft glow of early morning, the beginnings of dawn. The sun would rise within the next twenty minutes. There was no way I had time to figure out the last ingredient.

I was too late.

***

I entered the interior of the ship, looking for Norma. If I were to spend my last moments with anyone on that ship, I'd want to spend them with her.

She emerged from a room a ways down the hall.

"Oh, Norma, I was just looking for you. I have terrible news."

She said nothing, just gazed at me with a peculiar, lusty look, and strode towards me in a really sexy way. I was instantly entranced. She smiled at me and bared her fangs. She leaned in to kiss me, and at the last moment bore down, plunging her fangs into my neck.

I screamed and told her to stop, but she held on.

A bit of blood dripped from her mouth and fell into the potion I held. I finally managed to shove her off, and looked at her, terrified.

Then I noticed the potion bubbling like it had never before, turning a deep scarlet.

That was it!

The potion was complete. I just knew it. B was for blood. It had to be. I took a sip of it and felt the transformation within me.

I looked at Norma, who was still basking in the taste of my blood. I was suddenly ecstatic. I rushed over to her and poured a bit of the potion into her mouth. She smelled it and saw it looked like blood, welcoming my offering. As she drank some, she gagged, but it went down. Immediately, she began changing before my eyes. I saw her costume become fake leather and cheap velvet once more, her fangs become plastic and removable.

And then Norma was before me. Real Norma. I was so relieved I kissed her, and she kissed me back. We embraced each other for a long moment, before pulling apart and looking at each other sternly. We still had work to do, and not long to do it.

***

Getting everyone on the *Queen Mary* to drink the potion wasn't easy, but we managed to get everybody back to normal in those twenty minutes before daybreak. Some superheroes helped with the process. Yes, there were some injuries, like the stab wound in Bill from accounting—the Aztec warrior—and the bullet in our VP, Joe—the gladiator. And of course my neck wound. But they were nothing modern medicine couldn't handle.

Other than that, nothing too serious or lasting. Only strange, magical memories.

Columbus, turned back into a modern-day captain, brought us back to port as the sun rose over the city. Andrew, Zoila, Norma, and I disembarked in the early morning light, exhausted and weary, but relieved.

As we left, the captain found me and handed me a piece of paper. It was the missing piece of Hattie's journal. The last ingredient?

Blood of a true love.

HUNTERS

February 1, 1883

Pennsylvania Forest

"Outrageous, is what it is. No president should ever have established the hunters," he told me.

I shrugged and wrapped my coat around my body tightly. "I mean, you can't blame him. Some of these magical creatures are dangerous, Professor Rose," I said disinterestedly.

That was what everyone talked about these days—the magical creatures and the hunters. Truthfully, I didn't care much for any of it. The only thing that plagued my mind—and the only thing that should—was my studies.

"We're not in the university, Maggie. Just call me Dad," my father said with a roll of his eyes. "And I can't believe my only daughter isn't taking my side."

"There are no sides, Dad. Just the government going about their job. The nineteenth century is almost over, and change is bound to happen," I told him as we both continued our walk through the forest, hoping he would drop the topic.

Dad, apparently, wasn't ready to drop it. Though, it wasn't entirely unexpected. After all, he was a professor of the Magical Arts at Penn State University back in our hometown of Philadelphia, where I also studied. According to him, he'd been in love with all things magical since childhood.

"Do you know who you sound like?," he asked me. "That oaf of a politician who's always saying all mythological creatures should be wiped off the surface of the earth. We just concluded the civil war, what—two decades ago? And now, there's another war against enchanted creatures. The same enchanted beings that helped in our fight for freedom against the Europeans not long before," he explained. "I say that's bull crap."

A sigh escaped my lips. "Fine. You're right, Dad. Witches lives matter," I managed to say with a healthy dose of sarcasm. One which Dad clearly didn't appreciate.

The mustached, dark-haired professor shrugged and gave me a look that said, "This discussion is not over."

If there was one thing I knew about my father, it was that he would never stop until he proved his point. But that stubborn attitude was also passed down to me. So, he would have a really hard time with his only child.

To tell the truth, it wasn't as if I hated magical creatures. Some of them I found actually really cool. Though not most of them. Overall they caused more damage than good. Nonetheless, they were far from the last things on my mind at the moment.

"What again are we looking for in this creepy forest?" I asked. The morning fog had settled in the trees, limiting our vision to a few feet in front of us.

"A pixie hive," Dad finally said.

A less than pleased look claimed my face. "Wow! Very exciting. Aren't pixies like…pests? What do we need them for?"

"Pixies are far from pests, young lady. They have a community that supersedes any human civilization in terms of social hierarchy and relations. Like bees," Dad explained. "There's a hive in this forest. A kind of capital hive where the queen pixie lives."

"Not exciting," I informed him. "Just a few days back, a pixie stole my lunch at the university." That wasn't exactly the annoying part of the ordeal. It was that the chauvinistic Jason Brown was there to witness it, and he made a comment about how women who can't handle pixies shouldn't be in the university in the first place. Of course, I didn't tell Dad all that. He had a tendency to go to the dean to complain. He hated how few women were students in the university, and virtually zero staff. But no one hated it more than Mom. Had she been there, she probably would have done something Jason would regret for his entire life.

Dad paused and looked at me with a raised eyebrow. He wore a stern expression on his handsome face. A look that his suit, coat, cane, and bowler hat did well in complimenting. Though, this wasn't exactly the best outfit for our outdoor activity. I considered telling him, but I was sure he already knew.

"Some things are just nature taking its course," he said.

"Still...They're annoying. Territorial social creatures with a knack for theft. You should write that in that encyclopedia you're curating," I told him with a small laugh.

He tried to hide his laugh but failed. "You have your mother's laugh, Maggie," Dad suddenly said. "And her wits too."

"Oh, come on, Dad. Don't you dare get emotional on me. I swear, if you cry, I'll cry too," I warned.

Dad smiled and quickly turned around. I, however, managed to catch a glimpse of the tear in his eyes. It made me smile, for the most part, but also reminded me that Mom was gone.

Our walk continued through the foggy forest for a few more minutes. There were a few discussions where Dad would talk about a mythological creature, and I would tell him how they caused some of the many problems in society. In fairness, contrary to what my dad believed, I didn't blame the late President Abraham Lincoln for establishing the Mythological Organisms and Magical Creatures Hunters Association – MOMCTA. A mouthful, I know. Whoever advised the president on the name needed to be taught a thing or two about naming. Anyway, the president was right to fear the influx of magical creatures in the ever-growing United States of America. But then, of course, he was killed.

"Did you read the papers, Dad?" I suddenly asked.

Dad shrugged, an action he did when he knew what I was going to say and didn't approve, but still wouldn't stop me. "Yes, I did."

"Then you must have read how there's a werewolf infestation in London, Father. Barbaric werewolves," I told him. "They've killed many people, you know?"

A frown claimed Dad's face. He looked as if he was ready to give a long lecture on how I was wrong. The thought alone amused me. That was going to be an interesting talk. How on earth would he be able to defend the barbaric nature of werewolves?

But he never got a chance to say it.

Just then, the sound of hooves came from the fog around us. Neither of us got a chance to scream when a herd of horses came running toward us, galloping full speed and neighing loudly. The sounds of their hooves echoed round in a sickening rhythm.

I had but a moment to press myself against the closest tree. It was then I realized that I was wrong. They weren't horses; they were *unicorns.* Wild unicorns. And that was the least of my concerns. Where was Dad?

"Dad!" I yelled over the cacophony.

No answer.

My eyes scanned around desperately. I wanted to go and check on him. He was directly in the way of the unicorns. They could have crushed him. But I couldn't move. The herd was huge, and it would have been suicide to step into them.

When the last of the unicorns thundered past, I quickly peeled myself off the tree trunk. I was bruised from the handful of creatures that brushed against me during their run. But I didn't care. I didn't have to look far before I saw Dad. There he was, sitting on the forest floor, resting his back against a tree. He seemed to have managed to get into hiding too. I sagged in relief.

"Dad! Thank God. You had me worried there for a—" I began to say as I approached him.

But something was wrong. I stopped mid-sentence as I realized he wasn't moving. Not only that; his suit was stained with blood. I barely had a chance to gasp before I lunged my body at my father. I grabbed him and raised his head up. His eyes were empty and his mouth stained with blood. Tears began to stream down my eyes as

I saw the wound in his chest. He'd been staked by a unicorn's horn, killed by the very creatures he campaigned to save.

I instinctively pulled off his coat and began to shake him. No answer. I got up and began to scream for help. There had to be someone nearby. Anyone. But as my limbs carried me farther away from Dad's body, the truth laid itself in my heart.

My father was dead.

Two years later

Washington, D.C.

Each step I took was a seal on my fate. The building of Division III was now less than twenty feet before me. It's very existence seemed to mock my presence, as if it was looking down on me. A low hiss escaped my lips, and I shook off the doubt that clouded my mind. I was now a hunter certified by the state. I worked hard for this, and I deserved it. It was the least I could do to honor Dad. To avenge him. That thought alone strengthened my resolve, and I increased my pace to the white building.

I was wearing a dark red long-sleeved dress with a layered skirt that I had cut in the front from a long swanky Victorian dress to give my legs better mobility. It had layers of clothing underneath it, which were convenient to conceal my weapons. The dress had been styled to fit perfectly with a leather corset adorned with metal ornaments. I had a small bag in hand, and my black hair was packed into a tight bun. I walked in my leather strap boots with my hands covered in buckled gloves and a pair of very handy multi-lens goggles on my forehead.

The choice of styling was more out of a requirement for the job than my personal preference, though I did enjoy the modifications.

I was just a few feet in front of the white building when I noticed a figure in front. A young man, brown-haired and green-eyed, leaning against the door with a bored expression on his face. He was considerably handsome, with a fit body and a face deserving of kings. His kingly look extended to his dressing too. He wore a pinstriped three-piece suit which looked new, completing his look with a top hat. A stylish ascot tie, long coat, and golden watch chain completed his attire. His mustache reminded me of my Dad's.

His eyes slid off the wall and rested on me, lighting up with excitement. He gazed at me from head to toe, then back to my eyes. "Margaret Rose?" he said with a sly smile.

I nodded. "That's me."

"I'm Charles Edward. Welcome to Division III of the Mythological Organisms and Magical Creatures Hunters Association," he said, mouthing each word slowly, extending his hand and giving me a wink.

I shook his hand, resisting the urge to laugh out loud. I wasn't sure if I wanted to give a comment on the ridiculous length of the association's name or if I wanted to laugh at the fact that his name was made up of two first names.

He pushed the double doors open. "Come on in. I'll give you a tour of our base and introduce you to everyone in our team," he said. "They're all excited to meet you."

We walked into the building, stepping into what seemed like the foyer. It wasn't very fancy, but the furniture was fairly new and it was illuminated by numerous gas lamp throughout. There were steam-powered weapons on various parts of the wall, along with numerous other gear-tech devices. There were also plaques with inscriptions on them underneath some of the weapons. I was immediately fascinated. It felt more like some kind of hall of fame to me. I had the tiniest urge to stand there for a moment and observe it, but Charles clearly had a different idea as he darted through another set of doors without waiting to see if I was following.

The next room we walked into wasn't too different from the one we'd just exited. The major difference was the presence of about a dozen shelves, filled to the brim with books, a stuffed North American yeti at one corner, and a man reading a book.

"This is the library. It has everything you need to know about all mythological organisms and magical creatures," Charles explained. "Several of which were written by none other than your own late father, I've learned." He cleared his throat and kept walking. "Anyway, an assortment of books about automata technology and weapons is also there. It'd be good for you to familiarize with them. Though, I'm guessing you learnt plenty about that at the Association already."

"Yup."

Charles, the man with two first names, shrugged. "That's Wohali over there." He pointed at the Native American man. As Wohali was reading a book, I realized his right arm was fully robotic, like gears and all. Thank God for modern technology, I thought. "He's Cherokee and knows a lot about hunting. He's the second-in-command of this division," said Charles, keeping his voice low for the last sentence.

"I can still hear you," Wohali said in a thick North American accent.

I was ushered out of the library by Charles, who said, "He gets a little touchy when we mention the fact that he's second-in-command. You see, he was the son of a Chief back in his tribe, so… Well, it's kind of a sore subject."

"And who's the first-in-command of this division?" I asked, my curiosity getting the better of me.

A deep voice answered before Charles got the chance. "I am," it said. We were already out of the library and now in what looked like a brightly lit dining room. There on a chair, spreading jam over bread, was the biggest man I'd ever seen. He was shirtless and had only a pair of long, lime-colored pants on, which were cut off on the bottom, making them shorts. Orange suspenders held them in place. Military boots that could fit an elephant. This ginger was no man—he was a bear. "You must be the new recruit, Maggie." He looked me from head to toes, just as Charles had done. "You know, Maggie, you might need to work on your workout schedule. You could use a few muscles," he said.

"Okay, sir, " I answered softly, keeping my head down. As much as I hated to admit it, I was intimidated by his size, and it was clear that the beastly man knew it.

Charles didn't seem to carry the same sense of intimidation. He moved closer to him and tapped his muscles softly. "This is our ever-loving team leader, Edmund O'Sullivan," he said loudly.

"Don't tap me again," Edmund warned.

Charles heeded the warning immediately and muttered an apology as he took his hand off the huge man. "Don't mind the accent," he said to me as he moved closer. "He's Irish, via Boston." He leaned close to my ear and whispered, "But never tell him that he's Irish or he'll crush you. The fool swears he's American and wants to be referred to as one, but we all know better."

Charles didn't wait to see if I had a response before he made for the iron spiral staircase at the corner of the dining room. The staircase looked like it had been added recently. It made me wonder what had happened to the previous one, if there was one. I followed Charles upstairs, congratulating myself for my choice of footwear and cut dress. Who knew how I would have completed the climb successfully if I had worn something less comfortable and efficient.

I was led down a hall and into a room. Thick smoke instantly hit us as we opened the room's door. Charles coughed loudly and muttered some cusses, some of which made me cringe.

"Shen, what nonsense are you cooking up that's caused this?" he shouted.

There were blurry movements in the smoke and I heard the windows opening. I put on my golden goggles, which always came in handy. It took a few minutes for the smoke to clear and reveal the small form of an Asian woman, dressed up like the scientists back at the Association's headquarters in Virginia. A part of her face was stained black. She watched Charles and I through her own larger than life round goggles, definitely scrutinizing me.

"Good morning," she finally said.

"Margaret, this is Shen Zhu. Shen, this is Margaret. Your new roommate. Edmund's orders. Looks like you're gonna have to cut down your chemical experiments." Charles's words drawled out of his mouth carefully; he had a smile that made him look as if he'd just given Shen a burden.

I opened my mouth to say something to Shen when a pixie appeared out of nowhere. It looked like a deformed crossbreed between a humanoid reptile and some winged insect. It came directly for me with its teeth bared and a shrill roar escaping its lips.

Instinctively, I let go of the bag in my hand and shoved my clenched fist forward at the pixie. But, unlike it appeared, I wasn't trying to punch the pixie. On my command, the gears underneath the fabrics of my gown shifted in less than a second and a small arrow shot out of my sleeves, hitting the pixie in its head and pinning the dead pixie to the wall. The action caused the indigo blood of the pixie to splash over wall. Of course, it also earned surprised looks from both Charles and Shen.

"I hate pixies," I muttered, my hand still stretched forward and my eyes still on the dead pixie.

It was impossible to like those beasts, especially since they were the reason Dad was in that forest two years ago. It was impossible to like anything magical, when all they'd done to me was cause pain and destruction. My hate is what made me a hunter, and I very much planned on keeping it going.

"That was…awesome!" Charles all but squealed beside me. "You and I are going to get along just fine."

I finally got hold of myself and murmured a quick apology as I dropped my hand.

"No need to apologize, girl. You're fire. Wait until JJ sees you. By the way, where did you get that automata tech? I must get something like that for myself."

"Umm... I made it myself," I told him.

While Charles seemed even more amazed by that revelation, Shen Zhu kept frowning at the dead pixie on the wall. She was probably thinking of cleaning up the mess I'd made.

"Sorry. I'll clean up when I get back," I told her as I followed Charles out of the room and into the hallway. But the words didn't seem to rub off the look I deciphered as fear from the young woman's face.

This time around, we didn't go down the iron spiral. Charles led me to the uttermost end of the hallway, taking me to a balcony that had a flight of concrete stairs. I thought we were going to follow the staircase down, but Charles spun me around and led me up a similar staircase that led to the top of the building. There, I saw a boy, even younger than Shen; he didn't seem older than twenty, if even that. His skin was slightly tanned and he had a wave of dark hair on his head. He didn't seem to notice our presence, or if he did, he didn't seem concerned.

There was an intricate automata revolver in his hand, the kind that was always loaded with anti-magic cartridges. He also had his gaze on something, his eyes trained on the expanse of land behind the building.

"That's Juan Jose Rivera Amaya," Charles told me. "Everyone just calls him JJ, though. He's a Mexican runaway from Chihuahua, or some shit like that. He was in a *bandido* gang down in Texas, and at his young age, he caused a lot of ruckus. Some rangers finally caught him, and after making a deal with some higher-ups, this is how he's paying off his debt. Anyway, he's the best gunslinger in the division. He's also the youngest. Nineteen. The kid's a hoot. The only time he's not talking is when he's shooting something."

Bam!

JJ fired. A smile formed in his face.

I quickly scanned the expanse of land to try to figure out where he shot at, but I Charles nudged me away, down the stairs until we were at the bottom. We took a turn off some trees towards a large shed behind the building, where a black man worked intensively with a wild look in his face. There were numerous automata mechanisms and vehicle parts surrounding him.

"Here's Jesse," Charles said. "He isn't much of a people person and hardly speaks to newbies. But God, he makes the best weapons. You'll have to go to him for a weapon or anything you'd like when you need something. Jesse's the man! He might also be interested in that awesome gear of yours, by the way."

I cast my gaze on the man, who didn't even spare me a look. I kept staring at him, until he finally turned toward me. I smiled. It wasn't reciprocated. He simply turned to the side and spit. Not a very warm welcome.

"Okay..." I said.

"Oh, don't mind him. He doesn't mean ill. You know, he might not smile much, but when he does, it's beautiful. He's had a rough life, to say the least."

I looked around his work area; Charles was right. There were some awesome weapons in the workshop. The place was full of technology powered by steam and driven by mechanical gears and human ingenuity. But the only one that caught my attention was an automata crossbow. It seemed to have some complex system that allowed it to shoot multiple arrows, either simultaneously or in rapid sequence.

Unfortunately, I didn't have a long look at it before Charles left for the door and I had to follow.

"We have two more members in our division, the Alison siblings—a cowboy-cowgirl duo from Colorado Springs," he said as I caught up to him before returning to the main building. "But they're currently taking care of a herd of centaurs someplace. They should be back in a few days. I guess."

"Okay. Looking forward to meeting them. And thanks so much for the tour, Charles," I said.

Charles smirked. "It isn't a bother. Always happy to help a beautiful lady. You know what they say, it takes one to know one." He punctuated his statement with a wink.

"Narcissistic much?" I said flatly.

My words only made his smile widen. "So I've been told. Along the same line with 'handsome and sexy.' Anyway, if you need anything, my room is underneath yours."

"Oh, God," I said underneath my breath. Who had I gotten mixed up with? I quickly muttered an excuse before I went back up the stairs and down the hallway to my room.

Shen Zhu was still there, and she seemed to have already taken care of the pixie problem. "Sorry about earlier," I told her again.

She nodded gently.

There were two beds. I went to the bare one and dropped my bag beside it. The room, like everywhere in this house, wasn't fancy, adorned with gas lamps and candles. It was just the right amount of perfect. Though it was nothing like Dad's house back at the university campus in Philly, it was still fitting for my taste.

"By the way, what caused the smoke earlier?" I asked Shen.

The question seemed to have startled the girl as she jumped a little before turning to me. She then pointed at a table filled with test tubes and other scientific equipment. "I experiment a lot. I must have mixed the wrong chemicals."

I nodded and eyed the chemicals on the table. Mom was a scientist, too—a chemist of all things. And I'd spent a lot of time observing her, growing up. If there was one thing I'd learned, it was that none of those chemicals on the table could cause that amount of smoke we saw earlier. Shen was lying, that much was obvious. What piqued my interest, however, were Shen's blackened fingertips. I had a feeling I would be unraveling a few mysteries in the coming days.

"Listen up, team," Edmund said loudly. He didn't exactly have to put effort in his words, as his voice was loud naturally, but the Irish man still did. He'd walked in on us having breakfast. More specifically, he'd walked in on the rest of the team having breakfast, because someone—who went by the name Brenda Alison—forgot to make mine. Or so she claimed.

I'd expected a lot of things from joining Division III of the Association, but racism and xenophobia weren't one of them. I thought we had beaten all of that and had become greater as a nation after the war. I guess I was wrong. The prejudice was especially high from Brenda Alison and, surprisingly, Jesse Powell. I just couldn't understand it, since our team was so diverse—young and old, big and small, male and female, and every color of the rainbow. This was becoming the new face of our nation, and yet, we couldn't overcome the bigotry ourselves from within.

Shen had said it would take a while for them to get used to me, but the fact that it'd been four weeks already was annoying. Four weeks of training together, eating together, sleeping alongside each other, and living together wasn't enough for them to treat me as one of them. I ignored their actions mostly. At least, I had the two youngest—Shen, who had been really helpful in the past four weeks, and JJ, who never ceased to make me laugh. And Wohali, though he never really said much, shared the same love of books as I did.

Edmund continued. "We have a mission. The whole team will be working on this one," he said.

"Just tell us what it is already," Charles called out from where he sat in a clean brown suit. Shen had explained that Charles was some rich guy from New York City who was only here for the thrills and adventure. It explained a lot about his dressing and attitude.

"The east and the west will be united by building a railway from New York City to San Francisco," the Irish man said.

"Oh, yeah. I read that in the papers," Ronny said. He was the oldest and nicest of the siblings. A few days back, he gave me a crash course on how to use his automata sword—and yes, I told him a sword was odd for a cowboy. He didn't seem to care though.

Brenda slammed her mug on the table. Charles winced and reminded her that the table was mahogany, but she paid only the barest attention to it. "So, we're helping build train tracks now, huh? I know the Association treats our division like we're some kind of lapdogs, but this is a low blow. Even from them," she said, her fury clearly evident in her voice. "I signed up to be a hunter, not a—"

"Bloody hell! Can you all just shut up and let me finish?" yelled Edmund, slamming his huge arms on the table.

"Uh-oh!" Charles said quietly. He eyes still squinted when he saw the way Edmund hit the table.

"We aren't building tracks for the locomotive. As we all know, most of these magical creatures migrated west a few decades ago. Many of them have posed and will pose a lot of problems with the train tracks bring built. Our orders are to capture and contain," he explained.

A murmur of agreement passed through the dining room. Wohali remained quiet anyway, simply playing with his bronze mechanical arm.

"Quick question," Shen Zhu said, raising her hand.

Edmund nodded.

"When you say capture and contain, how exactly are we to do that? I mean, I've heard of some really fearsome creatures out that way. I mean creatures like the uktena, wendigos, and even unicorns."

"Pfff! I rode wild unicorns as a toddler for fun," Brenda said.

"I understand your concern," said Edmund, ignoring the blonde. "That's why Jesse is going to bring out the Mammoth."

Shen Zhu gasped. Charles whistled as if checking out a girl and every other person in the room made a sound or two. The Alison siblings looked at each other with wide eyes. Even Wohali appeared to take notice. All these things made me wonder.

"Hell yeah!" JJ exclaimed. "*A huevo!*"

"What…what *is* the Mammoth?" I finally asked.

***

"We're drawing near our first stop," Jesse announced. He looked from the captain's seat to the rest of us huddled up in our seats.

A knowing look passed between all of us. We'd been in the air for two weeks, and we were just reaching out first stop, and the most exciting thing to happen through the past two weeks was the revelation of the hyped Mammoth.

Shen Zhu had explained how the Mammoth came to be. Jesse Powell, our ever-efficient mechanic—who had revealed that his dislike of me was due to an unfortunate resemblance to his former master's sadistic daughter—was dared by the agency to build the biggest vehicle he could create. And that he did. Though, it'd taken him almost three years to do it.

The Mammoth was a two-piece steam-powered vehicle that could connect and travel as one massive device and could also split apart and run separately. The bottom part was an all-terrain tank-like vehicle, like a giant missile on a varying set of gear wheels. Its iron plates were painted black and its form was over four times the size of a regular buggy, though fully covered in metal. The interior was the most exciting part about it. It was entirely spacious and comfortable. The top part, where we were currently at, was a low-flying airship, fully equipped with a small kitchen, a weapons room, multiple beds, a bathroom with showers, and even a steam room to relax.

The two-story airship didn't look like any other I'd seen. With no open deck, it had two captain seats in the glassed front, which Jesse and Edmund occupied, then the back which was like a mini house for the remaining of us. Thankfully, Brenda wasn't here with us. She preferred to ride in the extra vehicle in the bottom. In the vehicle, which we called the tank, were Brenda and Wohali. The tank was brought along for one single purpose: containing the creatures we'd been sent to remove. This was the first time the entire team would be going on a mission since I joined, and it was my first mission. The first four weeks since I joined were mostly spent training, so I was excited, to say the least.

This was also the first time I would be wearing all my new tech, compliments of Jesse and sponsored by the federal government of the US of A. We were all given boots, gloves, and a weird mask. I also finally had a tailored automatic crossbow that I'd fallen in love with. But my favorite part was the gear-powered wings that Jesse had created for me at my request. I could open them on command and retrieve them as needed. Though I couldn't fly with them, it allowed me to glide through the air, as long as I jumped from a high point.

The Mammoth had a series of analog meters on the dashboard, and the hands of three of them were spinning wildly. Jesse was right, we were nearby. We all began to grab our weapons in preparation to meet our first challenge. I seriously hoped it could have been another time of the day. The sun was already setting and we were approaching a river. Nothing good was ever at the bottom of a river.

Charles winked at me as the vehicle came to a slow stop. I heard the unattached tank reach a stop too, beneath us. Charles's choice of weapons was surprising. I'd expected guns, because truthfully, he seemed like a gun guy. And guns would surely complement his handsome physique—not that I told him any of that, lest he spin off into hyper-narcissism. But instead, he had a pair of iron batons in his hand. I didn't need to be told their use. Electricity.

The side of the door opened, and Edmund revealed himself at the doorway. His stern gaze moved through all of us. "There have been rumors of a dragon-type creature in these waters. An uktena. We have strict orders to capture it alive and deliver it to the Association's branch in San Francisco. They want us to harvest it for scientific study of the beast. But you must know, the uktena isn't the only creature in these waters. So, be vigilant and careful," he said, as if rehearsed. When he left the doorway, we all came down in a single-file line, and Edmund added, "Now, one last thing. Though we were told to bring it alive, if circumstances dictate, kill the bloody beast." There was a kind of hate in his eyes as he said those words, a hate that possibly rivaled mine. Whatever could create such hatred in the eyes of someone had to be really bad.

One by one we jumped off the airship. First, Edmund landed firmly on his feet. JJ and Shen were agile tree climbers, going down in swift movements, like an Aztec warrior and an agile kung fu monk, synchronized in craftiness. I glided with my wings. Though very different in style, both Charles and Ronny used a rope gun to swing down to the ground. Jesse remained on the ship. We were joined by Brenda and Wohali on the ground. We all moved toward the river in stealth, our respective weapons of choice ready. Charles had a portable magical meter in hand, and it kept spinning wildly as we approached. He raised a clenched fist sharply, causing us all to stop in our tracks. We were already at the edge of the river. Charles moved on, stepping into the water and moving forward until he was knee-deep.

Silence. Only the sound of running water hitting the rocks.

He turned around slowly, observing every vibration in the water. His stealth and caution was very needed. Thanks to Dad, I had studied these creatures, and I knew plenty about them. The uktenas were giant ferocious horned serpents with an appetite for human flesh. They were commonly called Native American Dragons, because it was impossible to liken them to the dragons that plagued Europe centuries earlier. Their ferocity was still as wild as that of any dragon, and only a fool would approach one without caution. Charles was no fool; he had a dagger in his left hand, his pair of electric batons on his back, and he remained calm.

Just then, there was a ripple in the water, and out came the uktena in its infernal glory, splashing water around and diving straight for Charles.

"Engage," Edmund commanded, and we all followed into the river as fast as we could.

JJ was already on the offensive. The quick, young Mexican started firing at the uktena over and over again. His actions seemed to catch the attention of the water dragon, and the beast instantly dove for him, packing the full force of the water. Charles, Edmund, and Ronny followed immediately. Soon, there was a clash of men against dragon.

"We have to stand down," Wohali said. "Joining them will serve as a hindrance."

We all agreed.

I raised my crossbow at the uktena. I had a clear shot to its eye. I considered taking it, but I didn't get a chance. Before I could do so, I felt something grab hold of me in the water. And whatever grabbed me wasn't alone.

This was evident from Brenda's words. "There's something else in the water," she said, "and it just grabbed my leg."

A look passed between the four of us present; Charles, Shen, Brenda and me. A look that said, "It grabbed us all."

I instantly turned my crossbow into the water underneath me. I would have shot the arrow, but more hands grabbed hold of me. *Humanoid* hands, I realized. Then they jerked me under, dragging all of us into the deep.

Our attackers revealed their faces when we were under water. The sun had already fully set, but we didn't need light to know what we were up against.

Somewhere, someone announced, "Mermaids." It sounded like Shen, but I didn't bother to think about it.

The struggle had begun. It was me versus a splash of homicidal mermaids all intent on drowning us. Their faces and their scaled tails brushed through my vision as they dragged my body to a deeper part of the river. Somewhere, I'd lost hold of my crossbow. I reached for the pack of arrows slung around my body and grabbed a handful. Then, like a rabid dog, I attacked, stabbing anything and everything I could with my arrows. Before long, the mermaids abandoned their mission, and I struggled to push my body to the surface.

It didn't take long for me to reach the surface and suck in a handful of breaths. A little distance from me, there were splashes. I instantly dove for the location, and with my arrows still in hand, I stabbed the first mermaid I saw in the shoulder and dragged her off her intended victim. That action seemed to give whoever was underwater the opportunity to fight back against the other mermaids.

When the person kicked themself to the surface, I realized it was Brenda. She sucked in wind fiercely for a few seconds, her short blond hair sticking to her head. Then her eyes fell on me. "Thank you," Brenda managed to say, albeit grudgingly.

There was another set of splashing a little bit farther north of where we were, closer to the surface. Both of us launched our bodies toward the disturbance. By the time we got there, the splashing had already stopped. We both dove down. I saw a silhouette and grabbed hold of the person. Their body was ice-cold. When I reached the surface of the water, Brenda was also there, and she had someone in her hand too—Shen Zhu. I looked at the person in my arms and realized it wasn't a person, it was a mermaid. I quickly let go of her body. I'd been forcing myself to hold on to it, considering how the icy body burned.

Shen coughed up water and began to greedily suck in air.

"What did you do to that mermaid? She's frozen," I called out.

Brenda let go of the girl the three of us moved toward the shoreline.

"It's a chemical formula of sorts. Injected it into her bloodstream and froze her from the inside out," Shen explained, breathlessly.

I nodded and momentarily looked at my hands. When I touched the mermaid, there was something weird, and it certainly wasn't something chemical.

"Bollocks!" I whipped my head around in the direction the sound came from and saw Charles, soaking wet and stabbing his baton into the water continuously. The end of the baton, I noticed, was now sharp, like a nail or a knife. Guess his automata could do more than generate electricity. He stopped what he was doing and looked at us. "Oh, you guys are alive. Thought you were fish food already."

"I'll murder him," Brenda hissed.

***

My eyes looked behind me for what might have been the seventh time in the last ten minutes. When I looked back at the road, Ronny was looking at me with a raised eyebrow.

"What?" I said.

"You know, if the uktena was going to escape, it would have done that already in the last three weeks," he pointed out.

I couldn't believe we'd been on the road for five weeks. When we were done with the mermaid issue two weeks ago, we saw that Edmund and JJ had managed to bring down the uktena. It was loaded in a cage inside the tank and we hit the road again, clearing the path of the future train tracks of anything magical. The government had brought thousands of Chinese laborers to work on the railroad, which was how Shen ended up here.

So far, on our journey, we'd brought down a griffin and a group of gnomes. None of the experiences were fun. The griffin had seemed determined to cut off one of my arms. But that day Wohali and Edmund has shown us their true strengths. Edmund had clipped down the beast with his bare hand. God, that man was strong. He didn't even have an automata. While he restricted the movement of the griffin, Wohali punched it in the face with his robotic arm, leaving us with an unconscious griffin with a broken beak. It'd been a week and the griffin was still quiet in the cage it was placed in. Or it could probably be the fact that Wohali kept it fed that made it remain quiet. He seemed to respect these creatures, almost to the point of seeming regretful for hurting them. So he made amends by taking care of them while in captivity.

The gnomes, on the other hand, had been something else entirely. Jesse and Ronny had proven useful in bringing them down. The dark-skinned mechanic might have been cold and reserved on the outside, but he had a wild heart for hunting on the inside. He was more than just a mechanic, inventor, and captain. He proved this with the use of the gigantic guns he attached to his arms when battling the gnomes. Though, he and Ronny had succeeded in killing off quite a handful, a lot were still captured alive. Charles and JJ seemed to enjoy this hunting a little too much.

Other days in the past three weeks had been spent doing miscellaneous things while traveling. Like JJ teaching Shen Zhu and I how to shoot a gun. It didn't go very well. So I decided to stick to my arrows. There was also Brenda, who was tired of riding the tank. But she didn't even like the airship either. She'd claimed that cowgirls weren't built to ride vehicles, even if it was the Mammoth, and she preferred to ride unicorns or horses. She'd also been less unwelcoming to me, probably due to the fact that I'd saved her from a psychotic mermaid.

Now, Ronny and I were on the tank, and in all honesty, I missed the view from above. After all, I had quickly learned, the American Wild West was the land of the unknown; yes, a territory of savages and a place full of mythological creatures, but also so full of opportunities for adventures. And it was beautiful. From the forests to the deserts, from the plains to the mountains, from sunrise to sunset, the west was a magical place. Whenever detached from the airship, I graciously let Ronny do most of the driving, while I just kept glancing at the uktena in the back. Hence, his earlier statement about the uktena's inability to escape.

"Fair enough. But why is it so gentle and quiet? It's making me nervous," I told him.

Ronny laughed nervously. "Wohali sedated it earlier. Something about her suffering or so. He said that it should be out for a few days," he explained. Like his younger sister, Ronny had short blond hair and light brown eyes. Maybe late twenties, around my age. He had a fairly handsome face and his body wasn't in any way muscular. A feature that made Edmund pass unfriendly comments. I did wonder what the Irish man's deal with workouts and muscles was. Though I was afraid to ask.

"Oh! By the way, I wanted to run something I noticed by you," I told him.

He turned to me momentarily before turning back to the road. "Really? What is it?"

"The magic meters. They spin wildly when there's a magical creature around, right?" I asked. He nodded. "But if there was, let's say, a magic *user* around..."

"Like a witch?" asked Ronny.

I wanted to tell him that the professional term—or even the politically correct one— wasn't witch, but I dismissed the thought. "Yes. Like a witch. The meter wouldn't notice it, right? Only magical creatures and mythological lifeforms."

Ronny appeared to be in thought for a few seconds. "Hmm… I don't know. Maybe. No, you might be right, actually. I don't think the meter can sense magic users," he agreed, though not fully convinced.

I nodded.

That would fit into the theory I had about little Shen Zhu.

Suddenly, the Mammoth's airship came to a stop in front of us and the rest of the team exited it. We stopped the tank and Ronny and I followed suit, moving toward them. We were in some kind of savannah. Though, I wouldn't exactly term it savannah, as there was a thick forest not too far away.

"Looks like boss has been radioed," Ronny said as we approached the rest of the team. Before our departure, the agency had installed a brand new electromagnetic radio device. They said it would help in communicating with us. We'd all been fascinated by the new technology, especially Jesse.

"What's up?" I asked Edmund.

Edmund confirmed Ronny's statement. "I've been radioed from our base at San Francisco. A military airship from Denver will be coming to pick up the uktena; we're to leave it here with Wohali. We also have orders to rid that forest in front of us of magical creatures. Something about clearing way for the annexation of new territories in the northwest. Besides, we don't want anything coming from there to attack our locomotive train, do we?"

We chorused in agreement. Edmund then sent us into the forest in groups. I went in with Shen Zhu, who seemed excited to go with me. We'd grown rather used to each other over the past few weeks, becoming roommates in the airship as well. She was twenty-one, the second youngest after JJ. Charles had mentioned once that she was an orphan, though he had no idea how her parents died.

We walked to the forest together. I'd gotten a new crossbow. Jesse had made it for me from materials he had laying around. He also gave me a new set of arrows. But of course, I still had my handmade gear underneath my clothes—and my wings. We never could know when these would come in handy.

It wasn't long into our walk into the forest before we heard movement around us. Edmund had mention the presence of some rather ferocious creatures in the woods. He'd also said to capture as many as we could alive. By now, we all knew the reason—

scientific experiments to better understand them. But no one ever talked about it. It was an unspoken rule between us. When it came to the different government agencies, we as the hunters had our job, and scientists had theirs.

But whatever was within the shadows of this forest didn't seem like something we would like to bring in alive. The movements had stopped, and the only sounds Shen and I could hear was the sound of flies buzzing.

"Ugh! What's that horrible smell?" Shen said. "It's as if something died here."

My fear was that she was right.

The beast came out, revealing itself to be what I had feared—a wendigo.

"Oh, crap!" I yelled.

"What the hell is that?" Shen asked, rearing back.

"You don't want to know."

The beast had the skull of a deer on its head, with its antlers twisting into the sky. Its towering form was mostly bones with decaying skin stretched over them, hence the flies and the horrible smell. It wasted no time before it lunged at me, swiping its powerful claws at the most vulnerable parts of me.

I'd spent the better part of two years after my father's death studying all I needed to know about magical creatures and how to kill them. But not once did I come across anything on how to kill a wendigo. Not once. Because, from what I could find in literature, no one had ever killed one. So, I panicked.

I instinctively moved my crossbow before me and began to shoot at it.

Unsurprisingly, my arrows hit it fair and square, everywhere I targeted. But it just stuck into the body of the wendigo as though it was nothing more than a bag of bones. And for the most part, that was exactly what the wendigo was—bones.

"Um, Shen? This might be a good time for you to use your magic," I said, desperation creeping into my voice. Continuing trying to fight it off with arrows would be a waste of ammunition.

"What?" she said sharply.

At that same moment, I dodged the advancing claws of the wendigo and shot it in its hollow eyes. The attack didn't even as much as slow down the beast. This wasn't the time for Shen to play dumb.

"Now, Shen!" I commanded.

"How did…how did you know?"

"Can I explain later? I'm a little tied up at the moment," I snapped.

I snatched up a small boulder and slung it at the bony legs of the wendigo. This made the beast give out a sickening echoing roar.

Just then, I caught sight of Shen Zhu shoving her hands forward and muttering something under her breath. I dodged yet another advancing blow of wendigo and the beast erupted into bright blue flames, staggering back before collapsing to the ground in a clatter.

"Oh, wow!" I muttered as I looked between Shen and the burning pile of wendigo. She gave me a look similar to the one I was giving her. A look that said, "We need to talk."

Shen and I talked. The first thing we talked about was my promise not to tell anyone on the team about her abilities, about who she was. About *what* she was. We both knew well what would happen if Edmund found out. Not only would she be kicked out of the association, something much worse would most likely happen. We knew this because, though technological advances were changing the world at an alarmingly fast rate, magical creatures still roamed the earth. And most humans, especially in the US of A, believed that in order to advance as a civilization and face the incoming twentieth century, we should first eradicate the old practice of magic and everything superstitious, once and for all. And having a witch within the hunters would just be the worst.

I explained to her how sloppy she was at hiding her ability. I told her how I saw her smoky fingers on the first day and how her excuse about the chemicals didn't suffice. I mentioned how I knew it was magic used to freeze the mermaid and a lot of other telling signs back at home and throughout our journey.

Shen also had something to say, like how her parents were caught using magic while they laborers on the rail line and were killed. They had used it only to defend themselves. But no one would listen.

I responded by telling her that I knew what it felt like to watch a parent die and told her about Dad. It was tough, in all honesty, I wasn't sure why I did. I'd never told anyone about it since I left Philadelphia. But it somehow felt right to tell Shen. A bond had formed between us over the past two months, after all.

We weren't the only ones to encounter something undead in the forest. JJ had single-handedly brought down a dozen ghouls. He managed to bind them in chains after restricting their movements. Brenda and Ronny, on the other hand, had ridden unicorns they'd found in the forest. Brenda said something about feeling herself again. And Charles and Jesse had attacked a pixie hive.

Soon after, we hit the road again while Wohali waited for the dispatched airship to come for him and the uktena. The locomotive tracks were coming right behind us, and he would stay with them in the meantime.

Things weren't too bad for the next few weeks. We only encountered minor mythological creatures like fairies, which I didn't find as destructive or infernal as their pixie cousins. Charles even took a fairy as a pet and named her Handsome. He said he named her after him.

Before reaching the Golden State, Brenda and I managed to come to a tentative truce. She gave me a lesson or two on cooking, and I taught her some things about mechanical engineering. Brenda also had a shooting competition with JJ. He won, unsurprisingly. I helped Shen come up with better lies to cover up the fact that she had magic. I am also excited to share that Shen is teaching me some magic too. Of course, nobody else knows this.

Through this journey, I have grown. I came to realize that not all enchanted creatures were bad, just as Dad had believed and argued until his dying breath. I'd complain about xenophobia, racism, and bigotry, all while failing to recognize that I also felt this way toward all magical and mythological lifeforms. And of course, I'd been wrong; my intolerance had been unwarranted. You see, after this trip, I've come to see more than savagery in some magical creatures. In fact, I am even fascinated by some of these lifeforms. And I truly believe that we can learn much from each other.

Perhaps Dad was into something, after all. Maybe the fact that just like there were good people and bad people in the world, there were also good creatures and bad creatures. They were simply creatures trying to survive and adapt in an ever-changing, human-dominated world.

Lately, it almost feels as if I am becoming the very thing I feared. The very thing I hunt.

Dad would be proud of me.

CLAIRVOYANT LAW

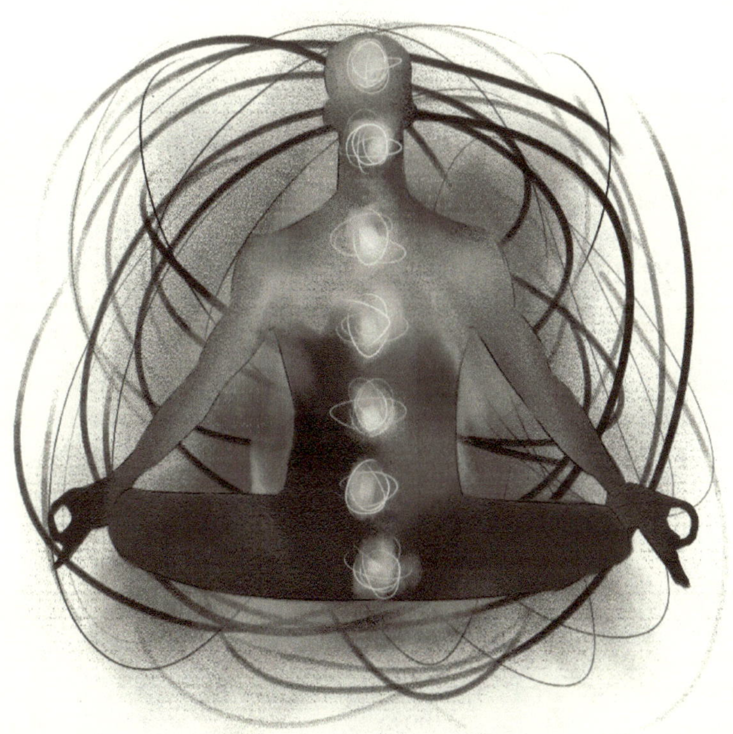

"I don't think I want to do this anymore, Norah." Violeta's voice was weak as she spoke, her eyes closed because opening them was a herculean task she didn't want to attempt.

The last performance had taken so much out of her that she was still recuperating after almost a week. Violeta hadn't admitted it to anyone, not her mom or her closest friend who doubled as her roommate, but she was afraid that if she continued this way, her entire body system would become irrevocably damaged because of the increasing seizures. Epilepsy sucked.

Norah had been brushing her hair, preparing for work. She had worked as Violeta's magician's assistant for a while, but when Violeta's health issues became more pronounced and she began to reduce the number of shows she did, Norah started working with a few others on Telepath TV, a show where magic and clairvoyant powers were displayed both on stage and on national television.

She came to sit beside her friend. "Do what? What don't you want to do anymore, Vi?"

"All of it. I'm just so tired of everything. My life..." She finally opened her eyes, the lovely, deep purple eyes that had earned her the name Violeta when she was born.

"Vi, you are scaring me right now."

At the wary look in Norah's honey-colored eyes, Violeta had to laugh a little. Even that sapped most of her energy. "Not that. I don't want to harm myself. I'm talking about my work. You know, all the performing. Going from Los Angeles to Las Vegas and back again every week is exhausting. And then the seizures after every show. I hate that I can't go out and have fun or, you know, do something cool anymore. I perform, and then I spend the week off recovering my strength, and then I have to do another show. It's a grueling cycle, you know? And, honestly, I'm just so tired."

Norah leaned over to brush the back of Violeta's palm. "I completely understand. So, have you thought of what you want to do instead?"

"I mean, not really. I don't know. I'm just…" She shrugged, her painfully frail shoulders winking out beneath the sheets. "I'm just thinking about it. I'll keep working until I've decided on that, I guess."

Norah nodded, leaping of the bed to go back to where she left the hairbrush. When she was done dressing up, she headed back to the couch and leaned down to press a kiss to Violeta's head. "I know you will be fine. I'll try to come up with something too, and I'm sure that between the both of us, we'll figure something out."

"Thanks, Norah."

"Don't mention it. I'm off to work. Make sure you take it easy for the rest of the day, okay? There is pizza in the fridge."

"Sure, I will. And thanks again."

"See you later!"

Violeta watched her friend sail out the door and imagined having that same enthusiasm for her own work. She used to, she remembered. Back when she'd just begun to discover the extent of her clairvoyant power and how to use it for her shows. There had been this excitement of being different, being part of the small population in the world with special powers.

The applause, the respect, and yes, even the apprehension and slight fear others showed in her presence had added to all the glory of it. Now, however, she wondered if the gift hadn't taken more from her than she had received through the use of it.

Like Jordan.

She didn't want to think about it, about him, but as always, when she was so weak and her defenses were down, the memories came flooding in.

Jordan had clairvoyant powers too, but different from hers because he could create illusions, making people see things that weren't real. He wasn't as powerful as Violeta was, though. Probably because he never really practiced. They had met at Sixth Sense, the yearly event organized by the Mystic Society of Southern California to celebrate people with clairvoyant powers.

It had been love at first sight, for her at least. And Jordan told her later that it had been the same for him. They started dating, moved in together, and naturally, she introduced him to Cyrus, one of the producers who televised her show. He started his own magic show. They had even done a few shows together.

One of Jordan's unshakeable rules in their relationship had been that she'd keep her powers under wraps when they were together. She did what he asked because she understood, had always known that her ability to read minds and feel emotions was pretty invasive.

Then one evening, she had been pretty relaxed after dinner, with a nice buzz going from the two glasses of wine she'd had. For one unguarded instant, she'd lost control of herself. Just one moment. And she heard his thoughts about the previous night. About... about Annie Lem, one of his young assistants on his own show. And her heart had shattered into tiny little pieces that she still hadn't been able to put back together.

Drawing her blanket up, she wiped her eyes and let out a deep breath. Forcing the memories out of her mind, Violeta drew herself up from the bed and staggered her way into the bathroom, where she splashed some water on her face.

She brushed her teeth and took a quick hot shower before walking to the kitchen with more energy than she previously had. By the time she'd microwaved and gobbled up two slices of the pizza and started on the third, she felt a lot stronger.

The calendar above the oven said it was Wednesday. Last week of September. Norah's birthday. Violeta was stronger now, and she wanted to do something to thank Norah for taking care of her over the past week. And she knew that if one wanted to thank Norah, there was really only one way to go about it.

A few hours later, Violeta was pleasantly exhausted. But as she finished up the decorations, she knew it was worth it. The clock dinged on the hour just as the front door flew open and her friend stepped in.

"Man, winter's in early this year, Vi. Any hopes we can get your friend with the pyrotechnic powers to come stay with us till March?"

"You really think Kenny's wife would allow him come stay with us for six months?" Violeta asked, bursting into laughter as she stepped out of the kitchen. "Sure, why don't *you* call and ask?"

"We'll tell her we only want his powers, and nothing— Wait, what's that I smell? Chocolate?"

"Maybe… perhaps…" Violeta shrugged, then leaped aside when her friend barreled towards the kitchen, laughing when Norah screamed. "Happy birthday, you fool."

"You remembered! And chocolate cake! Wow, Vi; you're my best friend in the whole universe, you know?"

"I know."

***

Two months later, Violeta's contract with the show ended. Though she was offered, she didn't renew. Instead, she packed up all of the things she had accumulated in the four years of working there. In spite of several requests, both from the show's producers and from some of her loyal viewers, she knew she couldn't do it all anymore. Her physical and mental health were at stake.

She needed to find a new career path. She was scared, of course. Who wouldn't be? After all, she was leaving the only world she'd known for years.

Placing the last of her personal items, a glass sculpture of a ballet dancer, in her box, she closed the flap and taped it. Then she carried it out, only to run into Jordan talking to—because why not increase her agony?—Annie. Striding past them with her gaze fixed resolutely on the box, she walked out of the network building and got into her car to make the drive from Vegas to LA.

She knew this would likely be the last time to do this journey in a very long time. And for that, she felt relieved.

***

"Come on, Vi. At least think about it. I mean, it's not like you're doing anything other than mope around the house all day."

"I don't have any training in law enforcement, Norah. There's no point trying to do something I won't be a good fit for." Violeta tugged on her oven mitts and slid the homemade bread out of the oven. "Did you look at that article that was released two weeks ago? The one about the mystic guy who wanted to work with the cops in New York?"

"Yes, I saw it. But that's different. The guy was a quack, Vi! He had no real powers like you do. Everyone knows the Violet Queen has more powers in her little finger than most clairvoyants have in their entire bodies."

Violeta thought about her stage title—the Violet Queen. She'd never be referred to as such again. "Clairvoyant powers are more centered in the brain than in the body, Norah." She laid the fresh bread on the counter and removed the mitts.

"Well then, everyone knows you have more powers in one of your brain cells than... Wait, you're trying to distract me, aren't you?"

Shrugging sheepishly, Violeta took the knife Norah handed her and cut some slices from the bread. She knew what Norah said about her moping around the house was true. It was January now, almost eight weeks since she'd stopped doing her show, stopped being the Violet Queen. And she had spent most of those weeks doing nothing but hanging out at home, binge-watching shows. Perhaps she was a little depressed and work could be good for her.

But work for the LAPD? That was quite a stretch.

She had wanted to be a police officer when she was younger. She wanted to be like her father, with a gun, a badge, and a whole lot of confidence in the law. But then he'd died in the line of duty, and her mother never even allowed her to dream about following in his footsteps.

Early that morning, Norah told her that her uncle wanted to meet her, and that he had a job offer. After weeks of wondering what she was going to do with her life, she had been excited. The meeting was still fresh in her mind.

"Miss Reyna. I'm really pleased to meet you." Captain Emilio Reséndiz of the LAPD was rather huge, about six feet tall with bulk that wasn't all muscle anymore, if the small jutting above his belt told a true tale.

"Captain Reséndiz." Violeta shook the hand he held out and gave him a brief smile. Norah hadn't told her what the meeting was for, only that there might be a job in the works. "Same here."

"I caught your show back in Vegas. You know, the one you did in October. My wife heard you would not be the Violet Queen much longer, so we finally decided to see one live before you...resigned."

"Oh. That's lovely to hear. I hope you both enjoyed it."

"Yes, yes, it was great." He waved a hand and, pleasantries exchanged, his gaze turned serious. "Miss Reyna, I'm sure Norah must have told you that

this isn't just a social meeting. I actually have a proposition for you." Violeta nodded for him to continue. "The LAPD would like to offer you employment."

Okay, that was so not what she thought she would hear. "The LAPD? You mean like, the Los Angeles Police Department?"

"Yes. You see, powers such as yours could be very useful in apprehending criminals. For example, your ability to read people's thoughts and emotions could serve the department well in determining the veracity of testimonies and interviews. And your ability to determine likely future events could also help in apprehending criminals."

Violeta felt a leap in her heart at being considered to work as an officer, a dream she had long ago abandoned. But still... "Uh, Captain Reséndiz, I appreciate you coming to me with this offer. I just don't think that working with the police is the career path I want to follow. I don't have the training or..."

"We could use a few weeks to do some basic training. It's not like we are all of a sudden going to put you in the field. In fact, quite a lot of your work would be done in the precinct– being an observer of interviews and things like that."

"Yeah...I just don't know if this is the right thing for me, Captain. No offense."

"Miss Reyna, I know this is a lot to think about right now. Why don't you just go over the offer and get back to me in... Will a week be enough?"

"Sir, I don't want to get your hopes up or anything."

"Well, police departments across the country have muddled for a while without clairvoyance, Miss Reyna. If you decide this isn't what you want, then no problem. Just take a while to think over it first before you refuse, that's all I ask."

When Norah came back from work and Violeta told her the details of the conversation, she was all for it. She'd been trying to persuade her to go for the job. "Why don't you just try it out? Maybe a month or two, see if it works for you?"

"The other thing is I'd have to tell my mom about it. And believe me, she wouldn't support the idea at all."

"You don't have to tell her," Norah said, picking up the remote and turning on the TV. "At least not at first. She's five hundred miles away, anyway. Wait until you're through with the trial period, and then, if you want to continue with the job, you can tell her. I mean, it's not like you're a kid anymore. You're old enough to make your own decisions."

Violeta didn't say anything, not for a while. "I just need to think about it for a bit." She tried the bread. It was delicious.

"Sure, okay. But don't just think of the cons, consider the good parts of it too."

***

When Violeta stepped into the precinct the Monday following her meeting with Captain Reséndiz, her heart was thudding. A lot of people had either watched her shows, or at least seen her pictures on billboards and magazines—she always wore bold, dramatic colors.

Today though, she'd chosen a soft gray jacket and black pants that were comfortable, yet professional, paired with studs in her ears and no other jewelry. Her dark hair which was usually curled by the make-up artists on the show was untouched now, simply pulled back into a ponytail. Without the makeup and clothes and overstated jewelry that she often donned when she was the Violet Queen, she looked normal. No one even gave her a second glance.

She stepped into the building, pulling out her phone. The captain picked up on the first ring. "I'm here," she said.

"I'll be with you in a minute."

As she waited, Violeta thought back to Friday evening, when she had called him and told him she'd thought about it and was willing to take the job on a trial basis. He had sounded relieved on the phone, telling her he would send her an email with the job requirements.

"Miss Reyna?"

"Captain." She saw him and nodded with a slight smile. "Good morning." She stood up to shake his hand.

"Good morning. Come with me, please. I'll introduce you to the rest of the squad, show you where you'll be working, and we'll discuss any issues you might have. Is that okay?"

"Yeah. Sure."

"After that we'll figure out things with HR. Follow me."

When they stepped into the bullpen, Violeta felt like she'd stepped into a lion's den. She could literally feel the waves of animosity flowing from everyone in there.

"Well," the captain started, shaking his head at the sight of his detectives and officers. "This is Miss Violeta Reyna. As I enlightened you all this morning, she will now be working with the

LAPD, joining us in this precinct. I expect you all to treat her with respect, help her find her way around, and ease her into the workings of the department. Is that okay?"

"As long as you told her that her job doesn't include passing out autographs, Captain."

Chuckles sounded from all around the room.

"Redding!" The captain snapped as Violeta's head turned to the direction where the voice came from. The man was certainly taller than Violeta, but by no means the tallest of the cops. He had dark gray eyes and dirty blond hair. He was staring at her with obvious distaste. "That's not the respect I asked for."

"Sorry, Cap. I was just making a comment. Just a jo–"

"Comment respectfully then," the captain cut him off.

"Right then," Redding continued. "I respectfully submit that the Violet Queen should be informed that her job description does not require the giving of signed autographs. Or interviews, or magic displays, or—"

"That's enough, Redding. Now," Captain Reséndiz said in an ice cold tone, his eyes sweeping the entirety of his subordinate officers, "if I hear one derogatory comment about Miss Reyna from anyone of you, you'll be put in for disciplinary action. Have I made myself clear?"

Mutters of agreement were overheard.

Shaking his head, the captain motioned for Violeta to follow him to one of the desks in the bullpen, the one at the back corner of the room. To her dismay, Violeta noticed that her desk was beside Officer Redding's space, of course.

"This will be your space, Reyna. Now let's go have that conversation."

***

The first thing Violeta was assigned to do was to unobtrusively observe a man who was called in to name his accomplices in a vehicle robbery. Apparently, they had all scattered when the police came, leaving him to take the fall.

She carefully watched him from the side of the room where she ostensibly served as a scribe, opening her mind to feel his emotions, to peek into his thoughts. A few minutes later, Officer Elisha Redding—also known as Officer Jackass—left the room and motioned for her to follow him.

"So? Did you get any impressions?" His tone was contemptuous and condescending, but she wasn't surprised. She already knew how he felt about her. She'd overheard him talking to another officer earlier, not that he hid what he felt, of course.

"I wonder what's going on in the captain's head right now. I mean, bringing one of those freaks of nature to work as a cop? Honestly."

Yes, she knew how he felt about her. How all the other officers felt about her. None of them had approached her with a friendly word yesterday, and the only reason why the jackass even spoke to her right now was because the captain had given him a direct order to work with her.

A part of Violeta wanted to go running to the captain, but any kid who had passed through the school system knew that snitching wasn't the way you made friends. Not that she wanted to make friends with any of them, but still.

She drew herself up and squared her shoulders so that it wouldn't feel like he was looking down at her, though she was at least three inches shorter than he was.

"All three people he named were his accomplices, yes. But he did leave a few names out. I was only able to get a few names clearly from his mind, and I think the most important one was Marlon. I think that was his boss, the person that sent them."

"And does this Marlon have a last name, by any chance? Or are your...powers so limited?"

"I see thoughts, Officer J— Officer Redding." Her eyes flashed in anger. "I read people's minds. What they are thinking about at a particular time. I'm sure you don't go around thinking of your acquaintances with their full names, right?"

Tearing the sheet of paper on which she had written her impressions out of her notepad, she stuffed it into the jackass's hand and walked away.

***

Redding did catch up with Marlon, as well as a couple of others on the wanted list. He did not exactly admit that he wouldn't have found them, or at least found them that soon, without Violeta, but he became a bit warmer to her after that. And in the following few weeks, as she assisted in solving more cases and preventing several others from even happening at all, the other officers in the precinct seemed to drop their animosity as well.

Her trial period ended, and she decided to stay on in the job. She hadn't told her mother about finding a new job yet, or much less what the new job was. She kept putting it off, even if she knew that she couldn't do that forever.

It was spring now, though the bite of winter still remained in the air. Violeta walked the few miles home from the subway station and thought about the criminal she'd helped apprehend that day. There was something still bothering her about him, something weird.

"Hey, Vi."

Her head snapped up as she heard the voice, her entire body stiffening. Her voice, when she spoke, was ice cold. "Jordan. What are you doing here?"

He stood right in front of her condo's entrance with his hands in his pockets and his feet shuffling. "I, um… I wanted to talk to you."

Violeta looked past him to the door and the windows next to it. It was supposed to be Norah's day off, and Norah hadn't told her of any plans to go out tonight. And if the light rays she could see through the curtains told the truth, Norah was in. "Why didn't you wait inside?" Not that she wanted the cheating scumbag in her house. She simply wondered why he hadn't tried to go in.

"I knocked. But your loyal bulldog took one look at me and slammed the door in my face."

"I've told you not to call Norah that. Though, yes, she is loyal. More than I can say for others." He winced. "Anyway, what do you want, J? I've had a stressful day, and I'd really like to rest."

"Yes, of course. Oh, and, uh, what do you do now, anyway? I mean since you left the show."

"Why are you here, Jordan?" She put her hands on her hips. He was still blocking her entrance to home.

He nodded. "Look I know you have the right to be pissed off about everything that happened. I was a bastard, and you didn't deserve to be hurt by my actions. I messed up, badly. And, well, I came because I wanted to apologize. I quit the network, and I'm back in LA too. I figured I would drop by and—"

"Okay," she interrupted. Violeta saw the curtains shift a little. She then gazed at him for a moment, as the fading sunlight made his eyes flash a variety of colors.

"Vi, I'm sorry. I'm so very sorry. You're one of the best things that ever happened to me, and I messed things up because I didn't know I had something so great until I'd lost it. That's why I wanted to apologize, and to let you know that...well, that I want you back, more than anything. I need you in my life, even if it's not like before. And I promise that if you give me a second chance, if you'd take me back, even as a friend, I won't take you for granted anymore. I realized my mistakes, and I promise I won't repeat them."

Violeta could feel his sincerity and longing, but the remembered pain made her hesitant. "Jordan, look…"

"No, no. Don't give me an answer just yet. Let's take it slow, okay? Think about everything I said. I'll see you around, Vi." With that he jogged away, and Violeta stared after him for a long moment, bemused. She shook her head.

When she finally stepped into her place, Norah excitedly pulled her to sit on one of the living room couches. "So, what did he want?"

"Like you weren't eavesdropping," Violeta replied with a stern look.

"Well, duh! Of course I was. But the window muffled most of the sound, so, unfortunately, I didn't catch it all. I heard something like an apology, though."

"Yeah, he came to apologize." Violeta toed off her shoes and unbuttoned her blouse. "And to ask me to take him back."

"What!" It was more exclamation than question. "Take him back? The nerve of that cheat. Of course, you said 'no,' though. Right?"

Violeta laughed. "One would think you were the one Jordan cheated on and not me, Norah."

"Yeah, well, you're too sweet to give him what he truly deserves." There was a long pause, filled with the sound of LA at night. "So, wait. Are you actually taking him back then?"

"I told him I'd have to think about it."

"What's there to think about, though, Vi? Just tell him no and to leave you alone."

"He was sincere, Norah. I...uh...I might've sneaked a peak at his thoughts to know he was telling the truth."

"Good. I am glad you did. But still, though, that doesn't negate what he did."

"True. But I believe in second chances. I don't know if I'm going to give him one," she said when Norah shot her a knowing look. "But I guess we'll see. I still love him, you know, in spite of everything. You must think I'm dumb."

"No, never. You're not dumb, Vi. But like I said before, you're just too sweet."

She did take him back, much to Norah's annoyance.

***

Violeta was just beginning her shift one morning when squad cars with blaring sirens pulled into the parking lot. "What happened?" she asked Officer Doyle.

"Did you see the ads about that special magic jewelry collection?"

"The one that's going to be shown at LACMA? Yeah, I saw them. What about it?"

"Well, some people decided to do a heist, make away with the jewelry. Only, there was some kind of new security alarm system in the museum freshly installed last week, so when they tried to take off with the stuff they took, they got trapped in there." Doyle nodded in satisfaction.

"Whoa. Crazy."

"Yup," he replied. "Word is, they got about twelve of them."

Before he could continue, Officer Jackass—it was more fondly used now—rushed in. "Hey, Reyna, we need you down in the interrogation room one."

"I'll be right there."

They were eleven, not twelve, and one was female. She looked frail, and though she seemed to try to hold in her tears, they still ran down her face.

"We'll leave her for last," Captain Reséndiz said. Redding nodded.

They were all to be interviewed separately, with Violeta observing each of them. It didn't take her long to work out that there was something deeper than they knew. After the third suspect, Captain Reséndiz called for a break. Violeta took the opportunity to talk to him.

"Sir, I think these men are just foot soldiers."

"What do you mean?"

"I think there's a bigger fish to catch. Someone more powerful behind them, pulling the strings. I don't know who or what. I can just sense it. It may be a cartel or maybe even some politician or something, someone with influence."

"Are you sure about that?"

"Yes. I think while questioning them, you may try to focus on their boss. Even if they are afraid and won't say who it is, I can still pick it from their heads, as long as they think of that individual."

The captain nodded at that. "Good plan."

When they started with the fourth interview, the captain took her advice and started to poke into where they got their orders from.

"So?" he asked after the interview.

"I got nothing. It's like there's something blocking me from seeing who it is. It's like..." Violeta froze. "Oh, this is going to be harder than I thought."

"What do you mean?" Redding asked anxiously.

"It's a powerful person all right. And something tells me the person isn't ordinary. I think they were working for a clairvoyant, one with extraordinary power."

"Another one of you?" Redding asked, annoyance coloring his tone. "Great."

"Hey, at least I'm working with the good guys here," Violeta said with an eye roll.

They had interviewed all of the men without getting anything about the criminal mastermind. Redding and the captain were obviously exhausted when the captain suddenly smiled.

"You know, I think you should have some experience with interviews, Officer Reyna. There is one last person we haven't interviewed yet. Why don't you try your hand at it?"

All through the captain's monologue, Violeta had been opening and closing her mouth. Now she spoke in a shaky voice. "Uh... Captain, I don't want to... I don't think I'm..."

"You have been observing interviews for months now. You have to actually start doing them. You know what to do when you are before a suspect. You'll be all right. And we'll be watching you behind the glass anyway."

Shaking, Violeta walked into the interview room. The woman with the sad eyes sat there, looking pale and fatigued. Violeta didn't want to use her powers just yet. She was already exhausted, and she knew that if she used it for too long now the seizures would start. Besides, the woman seemed innocent, without a prior record.

"Miss Jones?"

"Officer. I'm ready to cooperate. I promise I've never done this before. It was my boyfriend. He didn't tell me what he and his friends were up to. Oh God," the woman cried, bending her head and sobbing. "I wanted to go back, but I was so afraid. They didn't allow me, they said if I did anything to spoil things, they would kill me."

"Miss Jones, you mentioned a boyfriend." None of the guys had mentioned or thought about her being their girlfriend. In fact, not one of the man had even thought about her at all. Violeta was suddenly suspicious when the woman's eyes shifted and she saw something calculating in them. "Tell me about your boyfriend."

"Yes. He... He was the electronics guy. He had a gun too. I had never been so scared in my life."

Suddenly, Violeta felt the urge to leave the room. There weren't any more questions to ask Olivia Jones after all. The woman was completely innocent, a victim of circumstances.

Absently packing up her things, Violeta stood. "It's fine, Miss Jones. I'll get you cleared and going home in—"

Violeta's thoughts ground to a halt, her eyes flying up to meet the woman's. Then, her mind stopped. Images, thoughts, they all passed through her mind in a brief moment. But she did not have the time to scream before she was on the ground.

Everything went dark.

***

"Vi? Babe, how are you feeling?"

"Norah?"

Norah's image became more focused as Violeta squinted her eyes. She could hear the relief in her friend's voice when she answered.

"Yes, girl. It's me. How are you feeling right now? You had us all so worried."

"I'm sorry." Violeta closed her eyes momentarily and then opened them slowly, other faces coming into focus. "Jordan. Captain. What are you all doing here? Wait…where am I?"

Jordan pressed his lips to her forehead and smiled. "We came to drink hospital coffee. You know that lovely stuff that probably is gotten from the mud in plantations, instead of the actual plants. We heard it's delicious here, so we just had to come."

"If you're going to talk about our coffee that way, sir, maybe you should do it where none of the staff can hear you." Everyone turned. "Good day, ladies and gentlemen."

"Doctor Adrian," Vi said with a shaky smile. She hadn't felt so weak in a long time. "What happened?"

The others left the room while the doctor approached her bed.

"Vi. It's been a while since I saw you. When I spoke to you that last time you told me your new job was easier on you and that the episodes were happening less frequently and with less intensity. So, you tell me. What on earth happened?"

"I..." She was blank for a moment. "I don't exactly remember. I was at the precinct though. My guess is…maybe I overtasked myself?"

"Well, you need to take better care of your health and well-being. I'll tell Norah to keep an eye on you," he added with mock severity. "As I know it, the girl's as tough as a Navy Seal."

The thought of Violeta having to keep watch on her definitely made shivers run down her spine. "Please don't. I promise I'll take care of myself." She chuckled.

Doctor Adrian checked her eyes with a penlight. After he was done, he gave her a few stern warnings before he finally left. This time, only Captain Reséndiz stepped into the room. She understood why when he started talking about police business.

"Officer Reyna, the doctor told me that you can't remember what happened before the seizure started."

"Yes. I don't know why..."

"Well, let me refresh your memory a bit. Eleven people were arrested in their attempt to steal some magical jewelry from the museum. Among them, was a woman who you were interviewing before—"

"Oh, I remember. Olivia Jones." Suddenly, the flashes of thoughts and memories she had seen just before she had the episode came back. She opened her eyes wide. "She's the clairvoyant!"

"What?"

"*She* was the mastermind of the entire operation. Olivia Jones, yes. She is smart and calculative, and her clairvoyant power is her ability to manipulate the minds of other people so that they do whatever she wants. I realized that when I suddenly started to leave the interview room before I'd exhausted all the questions I wanted to ask her. But I read her. Though quickly, I read her, Captain. She has a lot of people to do her bidding, and she has been running a criminal organization for years. She was behind the murder of that congressman from Arizona, as well as some other high-profile murders that she was paid to do. Stealing, blackmailing. She does it all."

"And she's escaped," Captain stated. He pulled out his phone and started to tap.

"What?" It was Violeta's turn to be stupefied. "What do you mean? How?"

"We were all so concerned with trying to ger you some treatment, and by the time we thought about her, she was already gone. We figured she was harmless, so we didn't bother to do a thorough search for her. Redding!" he snapped into his phone.

Violeta listened to him give the concise facts of the case and instructions to begin a statewide search. When he was done, Violeta sat up. "I'd like to join in on the search."

"No can do, Reyna. We need you strong on your feet and at peak condition. And for that, you need rest."

"But I'm stronger than—" she stopped when he walked out of the room speedily. "Seriously?"

Norah and Jordan rushed back in.

"What's this about you attempting to leave this room before you're completely recovered?" Jordan asked, his finger sliding across her collar bone.

"Look, I'm perfectly fine, and if—"

"Violeta Reyna!" The voice was sharp as whip and just as effective. Nurse Madeline was a tough old lady who took no nonsense from anybody. Violeta had known her since forever, having spent countless days and nights in the Glendale Hospital growing up, and wouldn't dare cross her. "You stay in that bed until tomorrow, or else…"

It was the 'or else' that did it. Violeta did not want to face any of the horrors the woman no doubt hid behind the 'or else.'

"Yes, ma'am."

***

"I know where she is! Or at least the general area, that is." Violeta burst out excitedly as she stepped out of the interview room. They had just interviewed one of the criminals that Olivia had previously worked with, or used, as Violeta thought of it.

That's right; Olivia Jones didn't work with people, she used them. And for close to six weeks now, she had successfully eluded the LAPD.

"You do?" the captain replied.

"Well, like I said, sir, I can't be a hundred percent sure of it, but I got an impression out of the man's mind of a place he had very recently met her in it. And I saw that they'd met there many times before. That's gotta be something."

"That is something. A lot more than anything we have. Well, where is it?"

"Again, sir, I can't give you the exact location, but from the buildings that I saw in his mind, coupled with a street sign, I believe it's in or near downtown Orange, California. I know it, because I recognize the area," she added.

They looked online through the satellite images, trying to pinpoint a possible structure. They worked on it for a few minutes, until finally narrowing down the location to the exact building. She bumped fists with the other officers, then they turned to the captain for their orders.

"I've already called the Orange County Sheriff's office, since it's out of our jurisdiction. However, we will be taking part in the arrests," he added before they could get peeved.

There was a lot of preparation, as they would be leaving only a skeleton crew behind, not knowing what they were going to meet.

They were right to be prepared for any eventuality, because when they got to the building, chaos ensued. The captain ordered Violeta to stay back in the car, remain low, out of sight, until they captured Olivia. She didn't like it, but understood his reasoning.

As pandemonium ensued inside the building, Violeta got out and stood by one of the squad cars. Suddenly, she watched in disbelief as Olivia came running out of the red brick building.

From a distance, Violeta saw how several police officers who wanted to arrest her suddenly turned away and ran into the building. Violeta had known the woman was powerful, but not to this level. This was something she had never seen from any clairvoyant in her life.

But she also knew something else about Olivia. And she would use this to take her down, in its due time.

The captain's words echoed in Violeta's mind, to remain hidden, low, and in the car, no matter what happened. However, there was no way she was going to let Olivia go free. She couldn't. The woman was a danger to society. And, no matter what it could cost her, she was going to go after Olivia. So, without a weapon or protective shield, alone, except her powerful mind, Violeta went after Oliva, from a distance. She didn't want to spook her either. The knowledge that she had regarding her nemesis clairvoyant would coming in handy. Violeta hadn't told anyone about this information yet, not even the captain.

She pursued Olivia, making sure to stay out of sight so that the other woman wouldn't know she was being followed. Olivia continued to use her mind tricks, so that people who saw her coming looked the other way, as if she was a stray cat or something.

Oliva turned into an alley behind an old theater. Violeta followed after her, this time closing the distance. It didn't matter at this point if Olivia saw her. Finally, Violeta saw what she had been waiting for. Olivia stumbled, barely able to grab hold of the wall and stay upright. Violeta closed the distance.

"Hello, Olivia," she muttered, her voice soft yet clear. The criminal woman jerked and turned, her eyes widening in recognition. "You're tired, aren't you? You need to rest a while."

She could feel Olivia's intrusion in her head, trying to make her turn and go away. But Olivia was weak. Oliva's nose began to bleed.

"I'll kill you, Violet Queen…" It was barely a whisper.

Violeta had quickly read it in the woman's head that day at the precinct. The only reason Olivia had been captured with the other criminals and brought to the station that day of the magic jewel heist was because she had used up most of her energy in manipulating the men from her gang as well as the museum guards.

"I highly doubt that," Violeta replied.

Just as Violeta suffered seizures when she'd overdo it with her powers, Olivia became weaker the more power she used. It was like a battery running out of juice. Violeta knew that back in her hideout and on her way to this alley Olivia had used quite a lot of juice. She was quickly running out. And while Olivia would have been normally stronger, Violeta had barely expended any energy, saving herself until this moment.

Now, it was safe to approach Olivia, who was already weak mentally and physically. Olivia tried to battle, tried to push, but Violeta pushed back. Then Olivia's nosebleed became a cascade, and she stumbled and fell, her eyes filled with the horror of knowing that she wasn't the strongest one now.

Violeta approached her slowly, carefully. Her smile was bright, as she recited from memory the Miranda Rights while handcuffing her.

***

"And so today, we introduce a new department in the precinct," Captain Reséndiz said with a smile. "The Bureau of Mystical Enforcement." The entirety of the officers in the station stood up to applaud. "As head of the department, I want to introduce Officer Violeta Reyna."

The applause was even louder this time. As it died down, a voice could be heard very clearly. "You know Captain, I've been working here for a while. Why does Officer Reyna get to lead a whole department and I don't?"

Violeta laughed. "You're already head of the department of Jackassary, Redding. Don't know why you need another department to head."

More laughter ensued.

But then Violeta heard another voice. This one was in her head. And she recognized it clearly. "You think you won, but this isn't the end." Violeta's smile faded as she turned away from the cheerful crowd. "I'm coming for you, Violet Queen. Get ready, bitch. I'm coming for you," Olivia's voice warned.

METAMORPHOSIS OF AN ANGEL

"WHEN ONCE YOU HAVE TASTED FLIGHT, YOU WILL FOREVER WALK THE EARTH WITH YOUR EYES TURNED SKYWARD, FOR THERE YOU HAVE BEEN, AND THERE YOU WILL ALWAYS LONG TO RETURN."

— LEONARDO DA VINCI

My nose itches as I feel the insect's miniature legs dance on the tip of my nose. I hold my breath and tilt my head upward, trying not to sneeze. Diana and Josie giggle as the butterfly's wings cover them from my sight.

As I bring my finger up to my nose to brush it away, the butterfly flutters its shimmering blue wings and darts away before I can touch its body. My friends' laughter dwindles as our eyes remain glued to the creature gliding away, melting into the infinite colors of the city surrounding us.

"Well, that was a rare sight," Diana says, setting her cup of coffee in front of her. Even at a hundred and one, her youth hasn't vanished. Wrinkles haven't fully touched the bloom of her skin, with the exception of around her eyes.

Once again, I covet her undying beauty.

But she is right; I haven't seen any butterflies in the city for quite a long time. Or anywhere. In fact, if my memory serves right, the last time I saw one was when I was in my seventies, when my husband and I went to a butterfly sanctuary in Florida. I remember seeing them all resting on the branches and trunks. It certainly was much more beautiful than seeing all the colors on the screen that my grandson and great-grandson love.

I smile, savoring the old memory before sighing.

"Yes, it was," Josie answers after taking a sip from her cup. "Honestly, I thought butterflies were extinct."

"Well, the city's been cleaned from the very bottom to top to accommodate all these new technologies around us. So, it's no wonder there are no perky little things flying anymore," I finally chime in.

Diana shifts in her seat and leans on the backrest. "True. Speaking of technologies and all, it's getting harder and harder to catch up with all of it. My grandson wants me to buy him this...what did he call it...? Time-lock interface chip thing. Apparently, all of his friends in college have one, and that's where they all hang out now. I don't even understand it at all."

"I know what you mean," Josie responds. "Things are so different today. Back in our day, we would just post videos and memes online. I mean, who would've thought memes would die?"

I nod in agreement before taking a sip of my warm, heavily caffeinated drink.

When we were teens, we spent our time following dance crazes and doing different challenges to get attention. But we were young and beautiful then. Now, we're just old ladies bundled in layers of clothing that reminisce about the past and talk about grandchildren and great grandchildren.

But some things never change.

The kids today still want whatever is cool in the latest fashion and tech. The problem is that everything online now is far more complicated than simply posting, liking, and sharing, like it was back in our day. Young people today have a time-lock, which is a device where they can play games for what feels like ten days in their world, but it's only an hour in the real world. I know of these things only because my great-grandson, Lucas Jr., begged me to buy him one as well, some time ago. But after reading about side effects, I thought otherwise.

Chattering and reminiscing about our past over coffee by the beach has been our tradition for some time now. Diana, Josie, and I meet once a week in this less-dense part of the city by the sea to take our minds off our age.

As Josie continues to talk about her first great-grandchild, a white feather drifts down my cup. Immediately, its snowy underside is tainted with the brown beverage it floats on. I pinch it between my thumb and pointer and lift it close to my face to examine it.

Even if it is small, its prismatic hue tells me everything.

"This is an angel feather," I say as I look up to see a few angels above us through the open ceiling of the café patio. They're all flying around, going about their day using the wings they were given.

"You're right; it is," Diana confirms.

One of the majestic beings hovers slowly down toward us and lands softly on her feet without a sound, just a couple of feet from our table. She tucks her wings behind her and bows down, her almond-shaped eyes on the feather on my hand. She is wearing a tiny bathing suit, evidently either coming from or going to the beach. She is gorgeous.

"I'm so sorry, madam! That's my feather. I should take better care of my wings so they won't shed. I'm still getting used to these things."

What a nice young girl.

But then it hits me. This lovely, young-looking angel could be the same age as me, or even older. It's difficult to tell, since, once transformed, angels look eternally young. Still, though, to apologize for losing a feather, when she could've just kept flying like anyone else most likely would? I mean, at least she has manners, and I appreciate that.

"It's not a big deal, sweety," I tell her.

"But…I wouldn't drink that anymore, if I was you," she replies timidly.

Ah, that's right. The chemicals she uses to maintain her beautiful wings must have soiled my drink.

Still, I shake my head. "It's fine, my dear. Look. My coffee's gone cold anyway."

She waves her palms at me, taking a step forward, her voice more embarrassed now. "I'll buy you a new one, madam! Here, please let me pay for whatever you want."

"No, I mean it. It's all right." I smile, hopefully to ease her obvious nerves.

Oh, angels…

Diana and Josie back me up, assuring the angel that we're close to wrapping up our weekly visit. It takes some time for her to finally give in, still apologizing even as she flies off. I watch her fly into the blue sky towards the pier, admiring her beautiful form even as she melts into a speck in the far distance.

I envy them. I really do.

To live for another century, but this time eternally young and being able to fly, to experience old sensations anew and enjoy them without guilt, and to be more beautiful than Diana, or even my young self…now, that's nice.

That's what I've wanted for some time now. And it is all I've been thinking about for the last couple of years. I even have a plan already—to use my husband's pension on the transfiguration procedure.

"Sophia? Are you all right?" Josie asks me.

Her question brings me back to reality. I hadn't realized that I was reaching my hand upward, trying to catch the angel that had just visited us moments ago. Ashamed, I lower my arm and look back at the girls.

"Yes," I whisper, "I'm fine. I was just imagining what life as an angel would be. That's all."

Josie hums at the idea. She tightens her grip on her cane. "I think of it too, sometimes. But, transfiguration is just too expensive. Not to mention all the products to maintain your appearance."

"Yup. It's much pricier than gender reassignment, I hear." Diana whistles while she sighs. "But better than it too, I suppose. I mean, resetting your age, guaranteed living for another century or so, and experiencing the world from another angle. Shoot, count me in, girl!" She snaps her fingers.

We all laugh.

After a few moments of silence, Josie speaks again. "I don't know, though."

"You don't know what about what?" I ask her.

"The whole process. It's just that something feels...wrong about it. I mean, of course I'd be happy with all the things and upgrades, and I'd also want to stay in the world little bit longer. God knows I want to see my grandkids and great-grandkids grow older and enjoy them longer. But, don't you think there is something wrong and unnatural with the whole metamorphosis thing?"

I look at Diana, but she simply shrugs. I take a deep breath before replying. "Yeah, a little, I guess. I do understand what you mean and that we're supposed to die one way or another. That's life, after all. And I've heard it all. But...at the same time, though, when I think of Lucas and Lucas Jr., and then of his own eventual offspring...I sure would like to be around longer. You know what I mean? I just think death is cruel."

"Yeah, you've definitely have gone through a lot, Sophia." Josie caressed my shoulder.

"Yeah, I have. But for Lucas it's worse. I might've lost a husband and a daughter, and that was difficult. But my grandson lost everything: first when my daughter and husband died, and then when his wife had the accident just a year after, making him a widow with a young son. So, that's what I mean about living longer. You understand what I mean."

"Honestly, I don't, Sophia. I mean, I do understand why you want to do it and all. It's just that I'm personally not fully convinced about the whole transfiguration thing. Sorry. I know you have your reasons. But I feel like there are some things that are just better left alone as they are."

"Sophia," Diana intervenes, "I honestly think that Josie is more worried about the cost than anything."

Josie laughs. "Yeah, maybe. I mean, it *is* freaking expensive, after all."

I nod. "But I'm serious, though," I continue. "Think about it. If we were to become angels, we could catch up with all the new technology and interact better with our loved ones. I don't think they would be upset about it either, especially when we play with them. If anything, they'd be happier! Thankful to enjoy us for another lifetime."

"Or maybe they would hate having us around any minute longer!" Diana jokes.

Josie almost chokes on her drink as she laughs.

I chuckle.

"But, you're right," Diana says thoughtfully as she folds her arms. "Little Cody cries whenever I have to stop playing with him, and my granddaughter stays up all night trying to calm him down. I sure would love to see him become a young man too."

Josie sighs, her shoulders sinking low. "Okay, since we are all talking for reals now…I gotta be honest with you all. The truth is that I've been fantasizing about it for some time too. I never said anything because I didn't know how you two would react. But, yeah, it would be nice for sure. If only I had the money."

"What about you, Sophia?" Diana turns to me. "Do you actually want to be an angel, like, for reals?"

"Oh, that smile says it all!" Josie hollers before I can even respond.

"Yeah, I've been doing a lot of research on it lately." My big smile quickly turns to a frown. "But, unfortunately, I think we're past the age allowed for transfiguration. I looked into it."

"What do you mean?" they ask in unison.

"Well, as you know, the process of metamorphosis from a human into an angel is a relatively new trend, and because of this, doctors are still fixing up some issues. And like with any other similar procedure, this process comes with risks. From the studies that I've read, the maximum age to go through the process is sixty-five years. And we all know that I am…*we* all are almost double that age. People can do it later in life, but there are unusual consequences."

"Like what, Sophia?" Josie queries with eyes wide.

"Yeah, what kind of consequences are you talking about? And also, don't exaggerate. We are not almost double that age; we're barely centenarians."

"True." I laugh. "But, well, let's see. Many older citizens like ourselves have tried metamorphosis, but in the majority of the cases, I read that the results were unsatisfactory. Apparently, if done later in life, memories don't transfer at all for some reason. So, if we did it, we would essentially become new people. Yeah, we would live another century as young-looking, winged-human beings, but it wouldn't be *us* anymore. We wouldn't remember who we were before the transfiguration."

"Oh, wow. That's crazy!" Josie says.

"Yeah, I know," I continue. "They say that some of the personality traits transfer, but not all. And that's not even the worst part. In a few cases, some never even saw the end of the process. Now, I don't know about you, but the thought of never coming back worries me," I say as I shudder.

"Yeah, and all that money gone on a surgery gone wrong too!" Josie adds as she cracks her knuckles. "No, thank you."

"Wow, I didn't know that. I mean, that really sucks!" Diana states.

"Yup." I play with my contaminated drink. "If that happened to me, the truth is that I don't know what would happen to Lucas and his kid. Since his wife passed away, I am all that he has left. I wish I could do more for him. The poor boy lives paycheck to paycheck, and I believe that my great-grandson should smile more. But it is what it is, I guess."

A few moments of silence go by, that, even though short, feel eternal. I know that the girls just don't know what to say.

So, I finally break the awkwardness. "My grandson and his son are my only surviving family. And life hasn't been kind to them. And, honestly, I'd give up everything to see them have a better life. And *that* is why I still think that metamorphosis might be worth it."

Time in the teahouse passes quickly as the three of us talk about other much sweeter memories. After another hour or so, Diana, Josie, and I wave goodbye to each other before parting at the hoverbus station just outside the café.

My twenty-minute trip back home is calm. The hoverbus hums silently as it magnetically sails through the air just above the rails, making routine stops at marked stations. Peering through the window outside, I see other hoverbuses making rounds and transporting people like myself who aren't angels yet. Those few who sport wings, however, fly above us. Some alone, some in pairs, and a few others, in groups. They cast their shadows on the vehicles, yet their shiny wings glow a healthy white, unlike my withering gray hairs foreboding the end of my time.

As I continue to stare, I imagine myself floating in the clouds like an angel, free to do as I please. I close my eyes as I see myself diving great heights from the sky without worrying about a faulty parachute. I dream of visiting countless places without the need to ride the hoverbus with rowdy teenagers and lurking thieves. I envision being strong enough to work again. I fantasize about being young and beautiful, living a new life, but with my personality, all my knowledge, and memories intact.

But then a sad reality hits me, jolting me back from oblivion—living another century or so also means that I would see my entire family perish before me. Lucas is already in his thirties, meaning that I will see him slowly wither away. I would possibly see Lucas Jr. follow the same fate too. Since angels are not capable of reproducing, this would be the end. And seeing my family die all over again would be horrendous.

Unless, of course, they also became angels some time in their lives. Surely I can convince them to transfigure as well. Perhaps I could even pay for theirs, given that I'll be able to work again. Besides, by that time, scientist most likely will have figured out and solved all the kinks and issues of the procedure.

Approaching Harbor Boulevard. Repeat, approaching Harbor Boulevard, next stop.

The robotic voice reminds me that I am home. The bus's magnetic brakes quietly hiss, perfectly stopping with the exit doors parallel to the bus stop. I get up from the faux leather seat and step out, breathing in the Southern California warm air. The hoverbus rises back into the air and continues to transport the remainder of its passengers to their destinations.

This intersection area of Harbor Boulevard and Chapman Avenue has been my home ever since I was a young girl. I witnessed firsthand how it was transformed through the decades into the modern monstrosity that it is now. The smaller streets are connected by a translucent pavement that ripples neon circles with every footstep. I continue to walk and turn into my street, making my way home.

Unlike the new houses of glass and asymmetry, my home is a relic of centuries ago. Past the chain link fence is a porch where my grandparents and their grandparents sat to watch the stars twinkle when they were young. Those stars eventually faded and were replaced by the nightly glowing fireworks of the theme park a few blocks away. I can still remember those. But now, even those are gone. However, there are so many lights on the ground today that they outshine the ones in the sky.

The hardwood groans as it feels my weight on the steps, and the red-painted front door clicks as it unlocks itself when it recognizes my presence. From the small crack of the door I can hear the voice of my great grandson playing in the living room. As he hears the lock disengage, he swings the door wide and wraps his short arms around my legs.

I love this child. And I would do anything to stay longer with him.

After Lucas Jr. greets me, he ushers me into the peach-colored halls of the house. Navigating here is far simpler than the endless corners of modern-day offices. White smoke permeates from the kitchen to the right, while my grandchild disappears while scamping upstairs.

He is talking about the new game his friends are playing, but I can't fully make what he is saying. "Maybe I can join them in the time-lock in a little bit, okay, Nana?"

I smile.

I go straight to the living room and sit on the couch facing the holovision. There is an ad about the latest trending sportswear, designed for angels who love to fly at breakneck paces. Their lustrous wings reflect light in vibrant colors and shine a soft blue or orange in the nighttime shots of the video.

"Angels again… It's like they've forgotten about us natural people," my grandson Lucas says while making his way next to me.

I simply nod.

He lands with a soft thud and whispers something under his breath that makes the television shut itself off. His deep brown eyes gaze into mine before fluttering shut and shaking his head. "Sorry, Nana. I just don't like them angels."

"Why not, though? They're so pretty. Just today I met a—"

He lets out a boisterous sigh, interrupting my thoughts. He laughs at my expression.

"What?" I ask him.

"I can't argue with that, Nana. I'm not saying they're ugly, really. I mean, let's be honest...they're gorgeous. Too perfect, I would say. But that's just it; I don't like them because they're self-centered."

Self-centered? In what sense, I wonder? "Please elaborate, my child."

My grandson takes his time to think of his words. His gaze is less on me and more into the depths of his mind. When he is ready, he clears his throat. "I think they're only after the bursts of happiness they get online. I know we've been through that phase too, when we were kids, but they're on another scale. Like...you know how much we wanted attention online ages ago?"

"Oh, I remember. I remember how you often posted videos of your gameplay and asked me to share it on my feed." I smile.

His face flushes red and his brows furl when the memory rushes in his mind. "Nana... That was fifteen years ago. But, yeah. I guess... I mean, that's the point. Well, sort of. Now, imagine that's the only thing I wanted in life. Imagine that this attention was the only thing I ever want throughout my life, all the way until now."

I picture the scenario in my head. A thirty-something-year old man sitting in front of his computer, talking to a screen for hours on end, trying to get the world's attention nonstop. His efforts are viewed by a handful on one day, encouraging him to do more.

But the next day he gets no views at all, so he looks at what went viral the previous day and imitates it, just to get a share of the fame…only to find out that he was a day too late. He tries again the next day. Then again on the next, still believing he will be recognized for something online and the world will love him.

The effort is admirable, but there's a loneliness attached to it. It's something I experienced when I was very young, when I desired a thousand views and countless followers on my social media. Although Diana, Josie, and I skyrocketed to fame temporarily, a very long time ago, our viral status was swept away after a few months, replaced by someone else. Thankfully, by that time, we were mature enough to shrug it off. But I'd seen others turn toxic after they lost their online status to someone else.

"I see your point," I simply respond after gathering my thoughts. "That would be bad, agreed."

"I think it's depressing. Look, Nana, I know I've relied on you to make ends meet sometimes, but not unless I had no other choice, nor do I expect your attention all the time. I work, I take care of son, and I do my best at it. But thanks to these angels, the jobs are limited. You know this. And I try my best to live my life in a way that doesn't call for attention all the time, like these winged humans. I try to buy only what I consume, and dispose of the rest appropriately. I try to do my part in this world, where climate change is ever increasing, mostly due to the overpopulation. All it's all thanks to those… things that refuse to let go of this life. At least I accept what is natural and what is not.

And angels are a deviation of nature. And there's so many of them panhandling online and…I don't know."

I move closer to him and place my hand on his shoulder. "Lucas, what did angels ever do to you?"

"Nana, you don't get it. It's not what they do to *me*; it's beyond that. It's what they do to the world."

"And what exactly do they do to the world then? Tell me."

"Well, by having so many angels all around, it decreases the chances for natural humans to survive, as the population keeps increasing and the natural resources keep decreasing. Additionally, due to the abundance of these angels, global warming, overpopulation, and low availability of jobs are also an issue. Not to mention the possibility of romantic partners so quickly decreasing, thanks to all these flawless-looking beings, which is all young people prefer now. I think it's disgusting, just thinking one of them could be their grandparent. Ugh."

"Okay, I understand that." And I finally really do start to understand where he is coming from and why he feels the way he does.

But he's not done. "I just don't like how everything is so artificial now. Remember when we went to Switzerland when I was like seven or eight, I think? Maybe younger."

I can't forget that. It was on a winter at least two decades ago; my husband and I had decided to take his time for us all to bond. "I remember clearly, dear. It was a wonderful time." I smile.

"The feel of the snow in my hands was… It was cold, but it was real." He cups his hand in the air, remembering the cool feel of the snow on his palm. "I'd never seen so much snow; not like the ones here in Southern California. Then we went to the forest and saw so many trees. I was mesmerized. I might have been very young when we went, but the feel and the smell is unforgettable. It's nothing compared to the trees outside. They look the part, but that's it. No smell of dew at all."

I slowly blink at the last sentence. "I lost my sense of smell long ago, Lucas."

"Oh... What I meant is that it's the same with the angels. It's all artificial with them too."

"I don't follow."

"Hmm... How do I put it?" He stares at the ceiling, pensive. "Ah, okay. So, you know how most experiences today are fake? They're mostly virtual or whatnot. That's why I was talking about the trip. The visit we had felt so real and vivid compared to the virtual experiences today. Their consumption of fake memories and fake experiences is something I'll never wrap my head around on. Did you ever use the old virtual reality gadgets from before? Like the lenses and body suits, and all that stuff."

I nod. "When I was around Lucas's age, yes."

"Do you remember anything else apart from the things you saw?"

There is only one thing I can recall from that. "I felt light-headed. The sights were pretty, no doubt; but after fifteen minutes I felt very dizzy."

"Right. And as cool as you thought it was at first, it just didn't compare to the real thing, right? Now, let's imagine that dull and dizzy feeling repeated over and over for a hundred years, which is the average lifespan of angels after transfiguration."

He waited for me, but I had nothing, so he continued. "I would rather see the real world and feel real things, Nana. I want the true experience of life, as it was meant to be. The natural way. And once we're gone, we are gone. I've lost so much, just like you. But nothing I do will bring my lost loved ones back. Why would I want another century without them? That would be torture."

Again, I can see where his distaste stems from. Lucas doesn't just think that angels are all about the pomp, and I have to agree that some of them do live for that; but he actually despises the idea of a longer life without loved ones and the idea of continuing to lose so many people throughout a second chance at life. It is true that many—if not perhaps most—angels are models, like the ones we just saw on the ads, or influencers who sway people's opinions with their way of words. It is also true that many angels live life erratically, unafraid of the consequences, since they maintain eternal youth and beauty throughout their lifespan. However, it doesn't have to be this way. Plenty of angels work, live, and love, just like any natural.

I take a long breath to think of a response. "I see your point, Lucas. And I understand where you're coming from and why you feel the way you do. However, have you considered that maybe some people go through the arduous procedure of metamorphosis simply because they want to stay with their family and loved ones longer? Is it possible that for many of them, it's not that they're afraid to die, but rather, that they want to enjoy their loved ones even longer? I, in fact, imagine some, many even, that wouldn't mind working ordinary jobs and living life in a...normal way, I guess. Whatever normal means, anyway."

Lucas makes a look on his face, and then he breaks eye contact. I know he is struggling to picture an angel that is on the same level as he currently is. One who works from the ground up to earn a place in the world. One who's wrestled with the same struggles he has. One who's lost loved ones, but is simply trying this whole thing called life again.

One who could possibly be his grandmother.

"Okay, true," he says. "I guess it's possible that this might be a thing for some angels out there. Sure. But, still though, I think that's still selfish."

My eyes widen at his answer. "What do you mean, selfish?"

"Well, I mean, it's a nice thought at first. These people want to accompany their family longer, and sure, I can respect that. The idea is admirable, even. I can even imagine some of them taking on blue-collar jobs, even with their large, beautiful wings." He drew out a long sigh and lowered his head. "But they'll outlive their families again. Unless their respective loved ones also become angels. And then the problem starts all over again! And the cycle of the main issues that overpopulation bring about never desist. And if those loved ones don't, then it sucks again."

Lucas stood up and went to the kitchen. He came back with two glasses of lemonade and offered me one, which I gratefully took. He sat down again next to me.

"Let me put it this way, Nana. If I become an angel and my son didn't, I would see him live his life and pass away. And that would crush me, because that's unnatural. What am I supposed to do after everyone I love passes away? Do I keep making new relationships? I mean, I know I wouldn't be able to reproduce anymore, but those I'd love would eventually die. All of them. What will my mental state be? The grief would stick with me…I mean, you've lived long, Nana. Don't you feel the same way? Not only have you seen your grandparents and parents die, you've also seen your husband and your daughter pass. How do you feel about that?"

I turn away and shake my head.

He puts a hand on my shoulder now. "My bad, Nana. I'm sorry. I shouldn't have worded it that way. It wasn't my intention to be insensitive about—"

I raise my hand towards him to stop him. I know he means well. He really does. I have no doubt of that. I turn to him again. "Lucas… I've been widowed, and I've stayed by both your parents' side as they breathed their last. Yes, it was painful. I didn't want them to go. But when it's their time to go, it's time to go."

"Well, that's what I mean, Nana. That's what I've been trying to say. Going into a cocoon in some lab and coming out as a winged being, like a better, stronger, and younger version of yourself, is simply refusing that fact. It means not accepting nature's call into the afterlife." He isn't as enthusiastic in his words or as animated anymore.

There is a discomfort in my chest that I can't describe. It's not pain, I'm sure. It is more of a heavy weight, like the gravity of his wording hitting my chest. Lucas shifts in his seat and touches both my shoulders now, his face filled with worry. I bat his hands away to reassure him.

"Of course I feel sad. But sadness isn't the only emotion I have. I still have you to accompany me. I am blessed to still have my close friends. I miss your parents and grandfather so, very much, as I am sure you do too. But I still have you and baby Lucas. And that is more than enough. And I sure wouldn't want anything to take that away from me."

My grandson interrupts our conversation when he runs to us and climbs into my lap, wrapping his arms around me. "I love you, Nana." He then slides down and heads for the kitchen, tossing a "I'm hungry, dad," over his shoulder

The next few minutes are spent in awkward silence at the dinner table. We speak nothing of the conversation we'd had just moments earlier. Little Lucas livens up the table, talking about his day and all the games he played. His dad and I simply smile as we listen, though we have no idea what he is talking about.

Later that evening, after finishing my rituals, I lay in bed, thinking of what Lucas told me earlier. The entire conversation flashes through my mind. He seemed convinced that angels are truly selfish beings and that there is no going back from that. I imagine our conversation would have turned worse if I was upfront with him about transfiguring myself.

In spite of the fact that he's suffered so much loss, Lucas has a heart of gold. And I love him dearly. But he's also very stubborn. It's almost impossible to convince him to change his mind once he's formed his opinion about something. But he is still my grandson. And I don't want us to have a falling out. That would be far more painful than losing him to the hands of death.

Death. The thought of its imminent reality lingers in my head. And soon, for me, it's either that, or transfiguration.

As I close my eyes, my thoughts wander back to the angels I saw during my ride home earlier in the day. Especially those flying in groups. They were too far and fast for me to see if they were talking or not, but the way they flew in formation gives me the feeling that they must be a group of friends. Even the cute angel who apologized for shedding a feather on my drink didn't seem too bad.

I'm starting to have second thoughts about my plans to transfigure. If I chose not to go through the procedure, Lucas and Junior could certainly use all that money that I would leave them. It would undoubtedly come in handy, given their circumstances. Besides, at my age, there is also the possibility, and almost certainty, that I wouldn't remember them anyway after transforming. So, would it be worth it, if I wouldn't even be myself?

But then again, it might actually be worth the risk, after all. I mean, what if? What if the procedure does work properly and I'm still me?

Ugh! The uncertainty is killing me.

If I came back home one day as an angel, how would Lucas react? Would he accept me? Would he think of me as selfish? Or would he still think of me as his family, his loving Nana?

Lucas himself has scolded me time and time again for putting others above myself. He's always told me to be more selfish with the money I got from my husband's death and to spend it on myself. But Lucas needs the money and this house more than I do.

I've been going out with Diana and Josie, and our trips to high-end restaurants and glamorous spas are quite the experience. But even then, it hasn't even dented the savings that I've accumulated all these years, either.

My thoughts blur into a haze the more I think about this situation.

Wings…

Oh, to fly freely across the blue skies. To be young and beautiful. To have another chance at life. A life with my grandson and son. And who knows, maybe even another chance at love.

It's the things that humans dreamed of. Only, now it can be a reality. My reality. My dream come true. And those thoughts bring a smile to my face.

And with that smile, I fall asleep.

***

During the past few weeks, the idea of transfiguring hasn't left my mind. Even the times I've actually tried to push the thought away, it always comes back to me. Wherever I go, I am bombarded with advertising for wing-care products or commercials selling the dream of angelhood. I try to ignore them, but to no avail.

I pop out my phone to distract myself. But even there, I cannot escape it. An ad fills my screen. Taking up most of the ad space is an immaculate angel holding her hands high up, showing off her new figure and wings.

Live long and be happy. Become a new you, a better you! – Zimmerman's Charm Gambit.

I find it difficult to take my eyes off the advertisement.

Zimmerman's Charm Gambit…interesting.

I click on the image, and it immediately takes me to the site of the clinic. There are more angels on the banner, showing off their new looks. Some parts of their body seem to have a distinct sheen to them. One of the model's faces has a colorful reflection like the feather in my cup.

Just gorgeous.

I take a virtual tour of the Laguna Beach-based facility and see images of their latest-model cocoons. I read about their services, and then I look around a bit more, reading the testimonies from other people who've had their procedure done by this doctor, Lester Zimmerman. I click on his name, curious. He's a handsome figure with a steely look on his face. A winged human—an angel, himself. His profile boasts a detailed list of his skills, knowledge, clientele, and experience in human metamorphosis.

It undeniably piques my interest. And then, something in the ad shouts out at me.

Dr. Zimmerman is one of the pioneers in baptisma cell research. Most of the older senior citizens who want a transfiguration are referred to him to ensure the highest chance of success anywhere in the human metamorphosis market.

That is a claim I haven't seen anywhere else. I immediately double-check this on other sites just to make sure they aren't exaggerating. And, sure enough, search results confirm his involvement in baptisma cells, including his research on the specific formulation and count to make absorption effective. Of course I don't understand much of it, and the numbers and graphs make me as dizzy as virtual reality. But the important part I gather is that, indeed, this man is an authority in the field.

I smile and return to his clinic's website. Zimmerman elaborates about his procedure on a video. He requires his patients to submit a complete medical history and medical tests taken less than six months before the transfiguration operation. He lists other requirements before the procedure, all of which I have on hand, should I choose to proceed as planned.

This doctor is a very convincing man. He's unlike any of the other specialists I've researched. The others have a bland vision and mission for their clinics and always let the previous clients do all the talking in writing. But this one is different; it feels as if I am speaking to the man himself while I browse his site.

The very last tab asks if I'd like a personal consultation with him, only for serious inquiries, of course. It shows a range of questions such as name, age, health issues, financial status, and a calendar with available dates to choose from for a meeting. From the look on the availability, it appears that he must be a busy man, as only a couple of spots are open in the next three months. One of them is coming up soon. Beneath the calendar is a box asking potential clients to upload the necessary documents so the office can review them beforehand.

Excited, I submit all the requirements. However, I stop myself from pressing the submit button. I need to think this through first.

But I soon realize that it's only for a consultation, and that it wouldn't hurt. If anything, they could tell me if I'm past the age for a transfiguration procedure once and for all. This way, I can carry on with the rest of my life without the 'what if' feeling bugging me all the time. I mean, I keep seeing the recommended age range to undergo the process of metamorphosis, and I might be out of the running already anyway.

However, on the other hand, what if they tell me that I can still go through with it, with guaranteed success? It's worth the try. That's the point of a consultation, after all.

The consultation fee is not high, but it states that the prices for the operation will be determined upon different factors and after signing a waiver. I don't know if that is good or bad.

I guess I will cross that bridge once I get there. But for now, I would simply like to hear what Zimmerman and his team have to say. So, I finally press the submit button to secure the closest available date. Immediately, I choose to have an in-person appointment when given the choice.

The consultation appointment is secured. It's official; I will talk to them about my options this coming Thursday morning, and I can't squelch my excitement. And if Lucas asks when the day of the appointment comes, I can always tell him it's simply another check-up with my doctor.

I look up directions to the clinic and plan my hoverbus route in advance so that I don't have to worry about that the day comes.

The trip to the clinic goes as planned. It is located on a cliff, overlooking the beach. The clinic is a low-rise building, three floors tall. But it makes up for its height with its beautiful design, with sleek wing motifs embedded throughout.

The lobby follows the same modern theme from the outside. Walls imitating shimmering feathers and metal line the halls, lit up brightly by white tubes and natural light. Leather seats and glass tables dot the floor. Two other people are lounging here, minding their business while busying themselves with their phones.

"Good morning, beautiful," the receptionist welcomes me. "How can I help you today?" Though a natural, she is still impeccable herself.

"Good morning, young lady. I have an appointment with Dr. Zimmerman. My name is Sophia Brea."

She smiles and busies herself with her device. "Yes, madam. Okay, you're a bit early. Please just wait a bit in the lobby, and I'll call you when he's ready to see you."

I nervously sit in the lobby area, shaking my legs. I being to wonder why the other two naturals are here for. One male and one female. They seem too young for metamorphosis. Though I keep hearing that more and more young naturals are choosing to go through the process earlier on in life.

It doesn't take long before the lovely woman calls me. They're ready for me.

Doctor Lester Zimmerman is one of the most beautiful angels I've ever seen. He is tan and tall—I would say around seven feet in height. Okay, fine. This is probably an exaggeration. But the truth is that everyone feels like a giant to the fragile five-foot me. The point is that he towers over me as he welcomes me into his office.

His face is long and his chin sharp. From a closer distance I notice that his skin is smooth, with almost a plastic-like sheen to it. His long fingers are perfectly manicured, the shiny nails reflecting the lights overhead. I wouldn't be surprised if he modified his body himself further to accentuate his beauty.

"Thank you for choosing me, Ms. Brea. Please have a seat." His arm gestures at a velvet couch with a tall backrest in front of his desk. As for him, he slides quietly into his backless office chair, his wings folded and shrunk until they are hidden behind his back. "Would you like some water? Coffee, perhaps?"

"I'm okay. Thank you for your kindness."

"Ms. Brea, may I ask, how old are you again?" He goes straight to the point. I know his office must've reviewed the documents prior to my visit, so the question surprises me.

"I am one-hundred-and-two years young," I reply.

He smiles. "Indeed, you are."

The doctor then hums and pens something down on one of his paper notes on the table. His hands shuffle around, clearing his desk of other paperwork to reveal a chart with letters too small for me to read. His eyes and pen scan the chart, before noting something down again.

I put my arms on top of my purse, which is resting on my lap. I don't know what to say, so I simply look around his large, corner office. The view to the sea behind him is spectacular.

Thankfully, he breaks the silence. "I went over your medical reports. They are very impressive for someone your age. One-o-two, huh?"

I smile and nod.

"I'll go straight to the point, Ms. Brea. The good news is that, yes, your body can take the process. However, the bad news is that, unlike the normal procedure for my, um, *younger* customers, your metamorphosis process will take longer."

I tilt my head. "Why is that? And how much longer?"

"Baptisma cells find it difficult to settle in cells with slow absorption rates. Its short life span means you need to be exposed to higher levels to ensure they are fused with every cell in your body to trigger your transfiguration." He eyes the small sheet on his hand again. "Your body needs to be submerged in baptisma cells for at least three days. This is more than twice as long as our normal procedure of metamorphosis, and it also would require twice the dose than usual."

"I see." I didn't know what else to say. Three days compared to two centuries isn't anything, after all. For some reason I was preparing myself for something much worse. But I try to hide my enthusiasm. And then I realize what he is implying. "Are there any risks?"

The doctor shifts in his seat and clears his throat. "Well, as you know, with more dosage come greater risks." He lets the comment linger. "But here is the thing…" He raises his arms, and his wing shine a little, as if on cue for effect. "While I have been successful in most transfiguration procedures for the elderly, I have to admit that there is still a price to pay. The rate of failure might have dropped significantly, but that does not mean you will not lose something in the process. I cannot predict what you would lose. Common complaints include loss of the primary senses, excessive wing shedding, personality shifts, and as I'm sure you know, even loss of memory." His eyes mask any emotion he has while speaking of the dangers of the process.

"Yes, I've read plenty about that," I say. "To be frank with you, doctor, I do fear becoming someone I am not. I've heard about extreme cases where people have zero recollection of who they were in their previous life. What are the chances of that happening to me?"

"It's difficult to say. I don't have an exact percentage, to be honest with you. Is it possible? Yes. Anything is possible with human metamorphosis, after all. But, for the sake of being fully transparent, memory loss can range from short-term amnesia to complete loss *and* dementia."

There's a chance that I won't remember Lucas and Junior? There's a chance I will lose my marbles?

"But, again, I cannot predict what will happen. I'm simply sharing what *could* happen in your case, given your advance age. At this point, I guess, all we can do is try to be optimistic."

"Okay," I reply. "So, worst case scenario is I don't know who I am. Best case scenario is nothing bad happens, and I get to live as an angel for another century or so. And, the most likely scenario is something in between?"

"Something like that." He puts the pen down.

"Well, if it's something in between, then I sure would hope that it's only loss of some memories, rather than complete loss." I chuckle.

Doctor Zimmermann crosses his fingers on top of his desk. "Ms. Sophia, do you still want to go through the process with knowledge of these potential risks?"

I take a deep breath as I turn my gaze towards the horizon above the sea once again.

If I do this, my grandson will hate me. I might even forget that he is my grandson. And if that happens, all of this would be for nothing. Though I still get to live another life, having time to relearn things and to get to know him and his son again, and my friends...who won't last long. Though, I can make new ones. And, on the other hand, if I don't forget anything, I can always just leave the house to them if they no longer accept me. I can live alone and meet new people and start all over again. True, after this I will barely have any money left, but finding work as an angel would be much easier.

There are so many things I don't know about living as one. Even so, that's the thrill of it. Even if my grandson shuns me, I can still live. It's going to be like living through childhood once again, but with all my functions intact.

"...Yes, I do," I finally respond.

The doctor and I go through other things, such as my desired appearance and preferred features. As long as they exist within my genes, they can retrieve them and redesign my physique. While I want to look the same as my young self, I can't bring myself to concentrate. The options are almost limitless. The idea that I'm about to leave this body for a new one is thrilling, and yet, nerve-wracking.

I feel something in my chest. I remember this feeling. I never thought I'd feel this excited again in my life. At my age, there's almost nothing new to experience. How many times will I feel this in my new one? How many emotions will I relive?

"Nana?"

Lucas's voice snaps me back to reality. My mind wanders into recalling all the forgotten sensations that I did not notice I had made my way back home from the clinic.

He flashes a sweet smile toward me as he is preparing some food. "You look so happy today. Did you enjoy talking to your friends again?"

"Oh, um, yes," I lie. "And by the way, Lucas, my friends and I will be going on a three-day cruise next weekend to the Mexican Riviera."

"Again?" He keeps cutting vegetables.

"You know we love it." I smile.

"True. Well, that sounds fun. I'm sure it will be fun. Do you need me to pick you up after?"

I shake my head. "I'll find my way back home. Don't worry about me."

"Sure?"

"Yup. You know me. You know how much I love my hoverbus trips. Gives me time to think and stuff."

"True. All right. Well, if you change your mind, just give me a holler."

My great-grandson approaches me and embraces me before I can say anything. He gives me a kiss on my cheek. "When are you going to take me on one of your trips, Nana?" he asks.

Oh, my Junior. How I love this child.

"Soon. I promise. I'm going to miss you." I hug him back and kiss him in return before retreating to my room.

When the day comes, I feel even more nervous. After going through a few more tests and countless blood samples, the doctor leads me to another part of the complex. Compared to the bright white walls of the lobby and his office, this hall is earthy, lined up with wood and plants.

I gasp at the sight of large vats of grayish green liquid lining up at the walls. They radiate a steady hiss as bubbles form and float to the top. These are connected to several large cocoons. Even if the liquid is thick and viscous, I knew that there were people in them.

A female nurse, a natural, stays beside me the entire time as she guides me to an empty cocoon. The large device sighs when it's opened. The nurse waves her hand, wordlessly telling me to completely remove my gown and step inside.

Once naked, I clench my fists, steeling myself. I take a step, and then another. The nurse connects me to the dozens of tentacles hanging from the cocoon. "Don't worry, Ms. Brea. Everything is going to be okay. Dr. Zimmermann is the best in the business, and we've done this countless times," she says, as if to ease my nerves.

It works, if only for a little.

"You'll fall asleep quickly and won't feel a thing. And when you wake up, you will be an angel! Literally speaking." She smiles. "There is an odor, but it will only last for a little bit," she states as she seals the shell shut, bringing me complete darkness.

I guess it's a good thing that I can't smell a thing. "It's okay," I say to her with a smile.

It feels comfortable. Warm. It is somewhat gooey, but yet still pleasing. Even though my body starts to warm up quickly, I feel a blast of cold air on my face. The more I breathe it, the heavier my body feels. Faintly, I hear Zimmermann's voice outside, talking to the nurse. I can't tell what they're saying.

I'm getting sleepy… so… sleepy.

***

The first thing I notice through my closed eyes is a very strong, tangy scent. I know that smell… What is it again? Whatever it is, it's certainly powerful. It's bothering my nostrils, making me gag.

I open my eyes, and everything is bright. Almost blinding.

Where am I?

CONFESSIONS OF A LIFE WELL LIVED

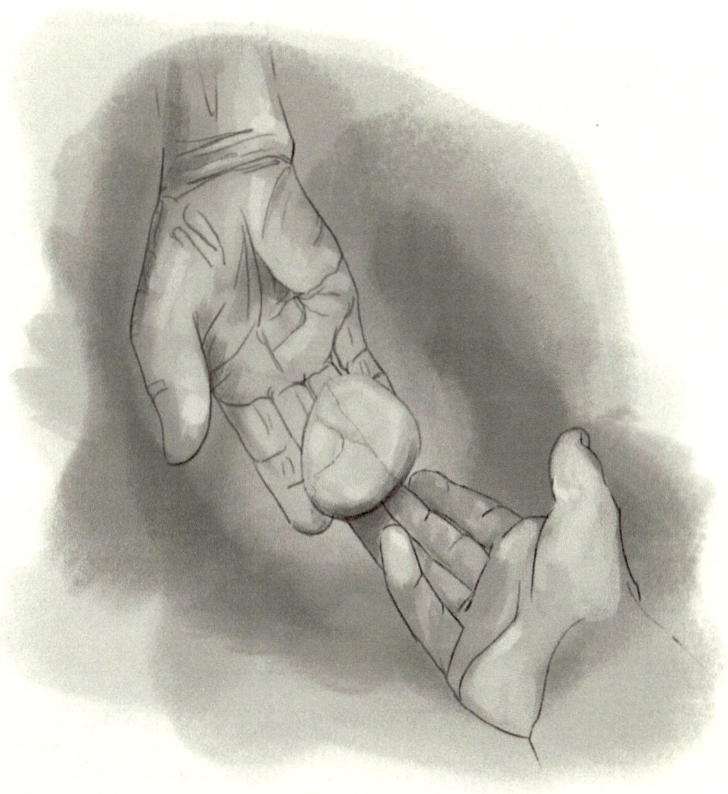

Steven del Real got out of the old car, slamming the creaking door behind him. The large, magnificent gate he'd driver through was closing. The Hacienda de la Joya blazed in front of him, and in the brilliant Southern California sun, the whitewashed walls were blinding.

He was willing to bet that on a clear day like today, Lorie Muller had an incomparable view of the Hollywood Hills and the Pacific Ocean from the faux watchtower that rose from the colorful, neatly manicured gardens.

Or she had, in earlier, happier days.

Steven shouldered his bag and headed up the drive, walking past the gently flowing fountain to ring the doorbell beside the carved wood door. Even though they were expecting him, it seemed to take a long time for the door to open. When it did, the elderly housekeeper frowned at him in confusion and mild alarm, as though she had no idea who he was.

"Hi." Steven gave her his widest smile. "Like I said to the guard, I'm Steven del Real. I have an appointment with Ms. Muller at one." He looked at his watch; he was a few minutes early.

"Oh!" The older woman nodded in enlightenment as she remembered. "Yes. Yes, please, come in, Mr. del Real," she said with a thick Hispanic accent.

She shuffled aside, and he entered the front hall. It was gracious in there, high-ceilinged and decorated with Mexican tiles, with another elegant fountain playing in the center. Two flights of stairs swept grandly to meet in a landing high above, with an aqua-tinted window glowing above. It was a beautiful entryway, but, looking at it, Steven felt a stab of melancholy. It was an entryway designed for parties, for elegant guests to hand their jackets to waiting servants and greet all the Hollywood stars, directors, and celebrities already mingling in a large, laughing crowd. Now, a deep hush reigned. Even the tinkling of the fountain wasn't enough to break this particular breed of silence—the silence of a house that contained a dying person.

Steven turned to the housekeeper. "Is Ms. Muller ready?"

"I believe so." She nodded readily enough, but there was a suspicious brilliance in her eyes.

"I'm sorry," Steven said gently. "This must be very hard for you."

She nodded again, wiping her eyes. "I've worked for Ms. Muller for forty-five years," she said quietly, voice only slightly choked. "I don't know what I'll do without her."

"I understand. From everything I've heard, she's a remarkable woman."

"That she is." The housekeeper seemed to pull herself together, straightening her skirt and firmly wiping away her tears. She cleared her throat. "If you'll follow me…"

"What's your name, if you don't mind my asking?" Steven said as she led him up one of the staircases, pausing at intervals for her arthritic knees.

"Not at all. My name is Bianca Miranda." She flashed him a surprisingly friendly smile.

He had to smile back. "Well, Ms. Miranda, perhaps you could answer a few questions for me later? If you're up for it, of course."

"Thank you, Mr. del Real. We'll see."

At the landing, they turned and soon stepped out onto an outdoor gallery, running high around the perimeter of a wide courtyard. Below them, deck chairs lounged around a crystal-clear swimming pool and oleanders bloomed freely. Steven felt the same sorrow he'd experienced in the entryway—this was a courtyard for friends and laughter and entertainment, and there would be none of that now, not for a long time.

Bianca led him halfway around the gallery, past blooming wisteria and bougainvillea climbing up the gallery posts, and halting before a pair of carved latticed doors. She rapped on them gently. "Ms. Muller?" she called.

Steven could hear the sound of birds chirping and squeaking within.

"Bianca?" The voice was thin and frail.

"The biographer has arrived."

"Oh, yes! Please, let him in."

Bianca opened the doors for Steven. "Thanks," he said as he stepped in.

"Good luck," she murmured back, and closed the doors before he could answer. He heard her shuffling footsteps walk away.

Steven looked around. He was in a dimly lit, but large and luxurious bedroom, shoes ringing on the tile floor. Tiny songbirds chirped and flitted in an elaborate cage. Handwoven rugs lay scattered across the floor and paintings and Navajo blankets hung on the walls. The shelves were crammed with books and various odd objects: a giant seashell, musical instruments from around the world, a Native American ceramic pot, a carved wooden box. Juxtaposed against these natural and historical items, a flatscreen TV hung on the wall opposite the bed.

The bed was large and curtained with airy blue gauze, currently drawn back and tied to the wooden bedposts. Underneath the fabulous blue-green bedspread, a wrinkled face peered at Steven with surprisingly bright eyes. "Are you Steven *del Real*?" she said in perfect cadence and pronunciation.

"That I am." He smiled. "Thank you for having me, Ms. Muller. I hope you're feeling well enough for our interview…?"

"Oh, well enough." She twitched one ancient, spotted hand in a minimal gesture of dismissal, and Steven noticed the cords attached to her flesh, leading to a tall white plastic framework hung with medical arcana. A crowd of medicinal-looked bottles and boxes had colonized the elegant bedside table as well, unsightly in this lovely room. "Please, Mr. del Real. Sit down."

He sat in the basketwork chair on the side of the bed opposite to the medical equipment. "Thank you again for agreeing to this interview, Ms. Muller. The publisher is grateful that–"

"Please," she interrupted. Her ancient, papery lips twitched in a smile. "Call me Lorie. And may I call you Steven?"

"Absolutely. Whatever you feel comfortable with, Ms.— Lorie." Steven began digging through his bag. "With your permission, I'm going to record our interview."

"Sure, of course. Just as long as there's no photographs." She gave a faint chuckle that turned into a cough. "I don't want your readers—or the gossip columnists—seeing me like I am now. Let them remember me in my heyday!"

She indicated a framed picture on her bedside table of an exquisitely beautiful woman in a long, elegant turquoise dress, her hair a pure golden color, indistinguishable from the true metal, her wide eyes an amazing blue-green that complimented the dress. She smiled from the photograph, holding up her newly won Oscar award.

"One of the first photographs in color, anywhere in the country. They gave me that award for my part in *The Endless Sea*," said Lorie. Her eyes, still that astonishing blue-green, crinkled in a secret smile. "Or so they thought."

"I'm sorry?" Steven asked, still setting up his equipment.

"I will enlighten you momentarily, young man."

She fell silent then, letting him finish setting up. He finally got the audio equipment up, and folded back his notebook on his knee.

"You still use a paper notebook?" Lorie said in soft surprise.

"I find it helps me remember better, and organize my thoughts." He smoothed the paper. "I use shorthand, though, so feel free to proceed at your own pace."

She gave a faint chuckle that turned into a cough. "No need to worry about that, young man. I can't talk so quickly anymore." She lay back, adjusting the bed with a remote control. "May I ask you a personal question, Steven?"

"Go ahead."

"Where are you from?"

Steven adjusted his glasses. "Um, Pasadena. Sorry, I'm not sure what you mean."

"I see," Lorie said. "I'm sorry, let me ask it this way. What is your background? As is in, where are your parents from. You have an interesting look and name, so, I am just wondering."

Steven didn't know how to react. He'd been asked this questions before; he just didn't expect it now. "Well, I'm an interesting mix, I guess. My father is from a city called Guanajuato, Guanajuato in Mexico. And my mom is from Kusadasi, Turkey."

"Ah, yes. Beautiful cities. Both of them."

"You've been to them?" Steven was pleasantly surprised.

"Yes, of course. Plenty of times. They're both gorgeous places. Haven't you been?"

"No. I wish." Steven chuckled. "I haven't traveled much outside of the US, to be honest."

"Oh, I have a feeling that you will, someday. Probably soon." She played with her hair. "May I ask you another personal question, Steven?"

"Sure, go ahead."

"Are you a man of faith?"

"Faith?" He drew back, blinking at this unexpected question. "Well… I… I guess not. I mean, I don't really think about those things too much." He gave her an apologetic smile. "I don't really go in for those things. Superstition or religion or anything like that, you know? But that's just me, personally. Why do you ask, Lorie?"

She nodded as though this was exactly what she had expected. "I'm sorry if I am intrusive, young man," she said, "but you see, faith is essential if you want to truly understand my story."

Steven's ears pricked. "Would you say your faith is important to you, Lorie?" His pen poised at the ready.

"Yes, but not in the sense you mean." She drew herself further upright on the embroidered pillows. The top half of the bed was almost vertical now. For a moment, as her straight white hair fell in soft curtains around her wrinkled face, Steven could see the ancient shadow of her fabulous beauty. "This was long ago, young Steven. It was a different world then, and I was a different person. So listen hard."

The ruined queen among her pillows cleared her throat before beginning…

This was back a long way, just after the war. The country was both still reeling from its wounds and wild with elation at having won. Everyone was so happy that the war was over, that our servicemen had returned. But at the same time, the pain was still fresh.

My own daddy returned with the other soldiers. He'd been gone so long, he was almost a stranger to my mother and me. It was hard to get to know him again, and I think the war damaged him. He drank a lot, and found it hard to let go of his war memories. He used to wake up at night, screaming. You see, having a German last name did not go well with the other soldiers. So, my poor daddy had to endure not only the trauma of war, but also the harassment of those he fought alongside.

That wasn't my family's only problem. We were poor, and I mean really poor. Our family owned a small farm, so we got some government assistance during the war; but after the war's end, that pretty much dried up. I think the assistance evaporated more quickly in our town than in other places because so many Latinos lived in our area. Imperial County. Our town was called Calexico, right on the border. I could see Mexico from my house. Half the houses were made of adobe, and I was the only blondie in town. Everyone spoke Spanish, even my family, who were Anglos. We had no choice but to learn.

I was an only child, as my older brother had died of polio when I was only two. I don't even remember him. There wasn't much to do for fun in Calexico for a teenage girl. You had to catch the bus to the town of Yuma, Arizona, if you even wanted to see a movie. Or go to Mexicali, on the other side of the border, to hang out with all the handsome Mexican young men.

When one of my friends—Maria Josefa Rosales, her name was—invited me to go visit her family down deep in central Mexico, my parents agreed. It was the summer, and I would be gone for several weeks, as the bus ride itself would take half a week. In all honesty, I think my parents were just glad for some time alone. And, of course, I was excited for new adventure and to get out of the scorching desert for a change.

Maria and I packed our bags and caught the bus across the border. It was easier to cross the border into Mexico back then. We rode the bus down to Maria's family's town, Pozos Buenos. It was a minuscule but very picturesque town just outside the bigger town of Tepoztlan, in the state of Morelos. And, unlike what we were used to in Calexico, everything was green here.

Now, the name of the town, as you might know, means "the good wells," and it was situated near a string of beautiful springs, all welling up with the purest blue water. People drew water from these springs, kids went swimming in them, and they were said to cure any illness or sorrow. I was told that they had been considered sacred to the Aztec gods, and even then people still left offerings on the shores and in the caves around the springs. Flowers, food, icons of the Virgin Mary, jewelry, that sort of thing.

But… I was a teenage girl, which means, of course, that I was also pretty dumb. Though we were used to the heat, we were not used to the humidity. And on one hot, humid day, I decided to set off, on my own, without telling anyone, to find the farthest of the springs.

Naturally, I got lost. The humidity was killing me, and I had no water. No one knew where I was, least of all me. There were no cell phones back then, of course—actually, Pozos Buenos probably didn't even have any telephones at all at that point either—so there was no way for me to get help.

I wandered through the hills, the air wavering with heat, into the shadows of a canyon. I had long lost the springs, and I was literally dying of thirst. The canyon narrowed. Weak and delirious, I crawled into a cave.

I thought I was hallucinating when I saw the old woman. She was an Indian woman, dressed in a colorful rebozo. But she was pretty damn scary-looking for a girl in my condition: she looked like a wicked Aztec witch, about to eat me up.

I might have started screaming, but she said something in her own language and held out a rock. A rock that was pumping out water, spilling over her hand, dripping onto the cave floor. It seemed weird to me, even in the state I was in, but I wasn't about to argue. I put that rock to my mouth, and I drank and I drank and I drank.

When I finally finished, I lowered the rock, half expecting the old woman to have vanished. She hadn't; she was grinning at me with toothless gums.

"Gracias," I said to her, and asked her, in Spanish, where she was from and where I was.

She didn't seem to understand me, to my surprise. She just rattled off something in her own language—Nahuatl, probably, but I can't be sure. She took the water-rock back, still impossibly pumping out water.

I asked her, again in Spanish, if she knew how to get back to Pozos Buenos. But, once again, she didn't seem to understand me. Instead, she took out another stone, much smaller than the water-rock. An emerald-looking green. An Aztec imperial jade.

As soon as she held the jade stone in her hand, I could understand her. Not what she was saying, since she wasn't saying anything—at least, not out loud. I felt her mind against my own. An old, old mind, full of long, deep thoughts. I felt her life wash against mine—a long, eventful life as a bruja *and* curandera, *working magic, performing pre-Hispanic rituals, and healing the people of the region.*

The key to her success, her thoughts whispered into my head, lay within the jade rock. It was old, this rock, from the time of the Aztec empire, and had once been part of a statue of the goddess Coatlicue, the earth mother. It gave its possessor magical powers: the power to speak into the minds of others, to control their minds. The old woman had used these powers for good, to soothe the thoughts of her patients when she had to, to force malefactors and violent people to go away and leave the community in peace. For many years, this stone, this piece of Coatlicue's blessing, had aided her and her community, and saved the lives of many, while ending the lives of the wicked.

But the bruja was old now, her thoughts whispered to me. Old and dying. It was time to pass on the jade to someone else. Someone young, full of vigor, with their whole life ahead of them. The goddess required life and youth for her magic to work. And so she was giving the rock to me.

There were certain rules that I must follow, her knowledge told me, if I wished to wield the stone's powers over human minds. First, that I must respect the stone by keeping it with me always. I need not worry that it would ever be lost or stolen, its powers protected against that, but I must never let another person touch it. The moment another person touched the stone, it became theirs. I would never be able to use the stone's powers again, once I passed it on to another human being. And pass it on again I would, eventually, for I would grow old and weak, as all mortals must, and the stone and its goddess required the hand of youth and vigor. If I died before passing the stone on, its powers would die too.

The old woman's knowledge seeped into my mind, exact instructions on how to get back to Pozos Buenos. Then, she gave me the stone, pressing it, still warm from her flesh, into my hand. And then she settled back, closed her eyes, and sighed out her last breath before my very eyes.

I left the cave, carrying the Aztec jade and the water-rock both. I sucked on the water-rock as I hiked along, following the path the old woman had impressed upon my mind, and so I was soon back in Pozos Buenos. There, I was met with fury. Maria's family had been out of their minds with worry about me. One of her young aunts even tried to hit me, raising her palm up high.

I stopped her. I stopped her hitting me. That was the first time I used the jade rock's powers. I reached out into her mind, and I prevented her slapping me. She just let her hand drop, seemed to forget about the whole thing.

No one noticed.

I told them about the old woman's body, back in the cave in the canyon, and some of the men drove a truck out to find her and bring her back. But, though they found the cave, they found no trace of any dead body. It was as if Coatlicue had swallowed her priestess whole.

I left the water-rock with Maria's family, as a thank-you gift, before Maria and I caught the bus back home.

Steven couldn't keep the faint smirk off his face as he finished the final sentence, pen scratching out the shorthand symbol.

"So this Aztec rock… lets you control minds?" he said. He could hear the skepticism in his own voice.

"Control them. Speak into them. Share my knowledge with them." Lorie half-lay perfectly calm and composed among her pillows, seeming not at all discomfited with his skepticism. "You don't believe me, young man?"

Steven shifted uncomfortably. "Well, I'm sure you, ah, need to keep an open mind—"

"No, you don't believe me. Well, why should you?" There came a faint movement under the bedclothes, as though her ancient fingers inched to grasp something.

Steven realized that he needed the bathroom. Without saying a word, he stood up, walked to the inner bedroom door, and stepped out into a gracious, carpeted hallway. He headed confidently down to a pink-and-gold tiled bathroom with gold fixtures and an oval, gold-brushed mirror. After using the facilities, he washed his hands with the rose-scented soap, dried them on the fluffy pink towel, and headed briskly back to Lorie's bedroom.

It was only when he'd sat down again, notebook again on his knee, that he realized what had happened.

"I… what?" He blinked. "What did I just do?"

"Went to use the toilet, young man," said Lorie serenely. "Funny, isn't it, how you knew exactly where the bathroom was without asking."

Steven's mouth opened. He closed it again. A long moment's silence passed, broken only by the birds twittering in their cage.

Steven tried to shake off the eerie moment. There was some rational explanation, he was sure of it. Almost sure.

But for now, it was best to get on with the interview.

"So, this Aztec rock became important to you," he said, straightening, pen at the ready. "Did it become your good-luck charm, would you say?"

"Oh, luck had nothing to do with it, young man," Lorie said with a chuckle.

She readjusted herself on the bed before continuing with her story…

Right from the very start, the Aztec gem served me well. I kept it in my pocket at all times, and it proved its use straightaway. When I got home from the trip, my dad was raging around the house. He'd broken a bottle, and the shattering noise brought out some horrible war memories for him, I think. He was stamping around, eyes all afire, raging about the Nazis, knocking all our furniture over, while my poor mother hung back, cowering before this madness.

I made him stop. Putting my hand in my pocket, closing my fingers around the Aztec jade, I made my father stop. My mind soothed his, washing away his war madness, his delusions, until he stood still, all his anger gone.

I was astonished, fearful of what I'd just done. But neither of my parents seemed to have realized what had happened. My father eventually moved again, to clean up the broken bottle, and my mother simply moved on. Neither of them remembered what had happened, or realized that anything was amiss.

Things got easier for our family after that. I tested the power of the stone on my father, and soon found out that I could make any of his rages halt. I could even make him stop drinking. Neither he nor my mother ever seemed to realize what I was doing. There would be that moment of strangeness, followed by amnesia. My father stayed sober, my mother stopped creeping around in fear, and so we were able to run the farm in a more rational fashion. Our emotional state improved, and so did our financial situation, as we worked together to turn a profit.

There were limits to the stone's powers, though. I could only use the Aztec jade when I was actually touching it directly with skin, and had the other person in my eyesight. I also had to concentrate hard, and I was always left a bit weak and tired afterward. There were things the stone couldn't do, too. For example, I could let my mind wash into another person's, but I couldn't read their thoughts. What others were thinking remained a mystery to me, no matter how hard I concentrated. I could only affect one person at a time, and, like I said, I had to be facing that person, maintaining eye contact. I could also only make them do one thing at a time. And, lastly, I couldn't force anyone to do something that was too much out of character. For example, I could make my father stop drinking, but I couldn't make him tear all his clothes off in public and run down the main street in his birthday suit.

Lorie paused. "Not that I tried to do such a thing to my own father, of course," she said carefully. "Forget I said that."

"Of course," said Steven, completely mesmerized. "Please go on. What happened next?"

What happened next, young Steven, was that I discovered that the stone's powers were quite ample as they were, even with their limitations. Using them, I was able to get a job in Calexico's general store, earning enough to help out my family and save up some for myself. I was able to go out with my friends to the cinema more often, and so I quickly fell ever more deeply in love with movies. I entertained Maria and my other friends with impressions of actresses, and we talked constantly of how we wished to go to Hollywood, to see the movie stars for ourselves.

When I was seventeen, we did just that. I used the stone to make Maria's older brother Jose drive us all the way here. We stood in the crowd to watch the winners of the Academy Awards process in, resplendent in their finery, the cameras flashing and dazzling like lightning.

That's when I saw him. Brian O'Neal, studio manager and director. I knew, the moment I saw him, that here was my opportunity. In all that crowd of actors and directors and judges, he stood out. He was looking right at me. Maybe it was my short white dress that did it. But whatever it was, I knew I had only one chance.

I closed my fingers around my Aztec jade and smiled into his eyes. 'You want to give me an audition,' my mind told his. 'You want to give me a chance.'

Moments later, someone who turned out to be a Hollywood assistant appeared at my side. "Miss?" He handed me a small paper card. "Please. Call this number."

And that was how I got started.

Steven grinned as he wrote down on his notepad.

"You still don't believe me, Steven?" Lorie asked, ancient blue eyes twinkling, though it was more of a statement than a question.

"Oh, no," Steven said, quickly and unconvincingly. "Of course I do. This stone gave you the power to make Brian O'Neal give you your first big break."

"That it did," she stated serenely. "Back home, I called the number using our brand new telephone, and scheduled an audition with Brian O'Neal. My mother drove me down to Hollywood; she was just as excited as I was. And I went to the audition with my stone safely in my pocket. I made sure to wear that same dress from the day he saw me."

Lorie paused, as if to create suspense. It worked.

"So? What happened next?" Steven asked.

The audition was terrifying. As I said, I couldn't use the stone to force someone to do something too much out of character, so I knew I had to impress Mr. O'Neal in real life. He would never pass anyone who actually did badly at the audition. So, I gave it my all, and I passed.

I got the part in the movie: one of the kidnapped maidens in Macaw Island, *a rather hokey pirate movie. It was a foolish part in a foolish movie, but I loved it. I couldn't have been happier playing the part of a damsel in distress, even though I only had one line. It was an astonishing experience, working on a real* Hollywood *set! Such euphoria, to act in a movie, to stretch my wings, and at such a young age. This, I knew, was where I was meant to be. I wanted more—much more.*

So, I used the stone again on Mr. O'Neal, to have him pay for acting lessons. I didn't have to do much to convince him, really – he was pleased with my performance and genuinely believed I was capable of more.

After my daddy died, my mom sold the farm back home and she and I moved to Burbank so that I could pursue this career path. We rented a tiny apartment. And, for the next few years, I worked on small parts and in television shows around acting school. I was insanely busy, earning next to nothing, and loved every minute of it. I worked hard, but always had my Aztec jade safe in my pocket, ready for use.

My first significant role was as the leading lady's best friend in the television show 10 AM on Main Street. *I admit I did use the stone to get the part, but I didn't have to nudge the director's mind too much. I greatly enjoyed the part and the show, and that role won me my first award, as the year's best supporting role.*

That was my first real recognition. Also, at the awards ceremony, I met my first real love.

"Marco Antonello, right?" Steven said. "The artist?"

"I see you've done your research." Lorie dimpled like a much younger woman. "My true first love, indeed. I'd had many men before, you see. I had started young, after all. But this was different. Marco worked as an artist on the sets, but he did a lot of his own painting, too. Look, there's his first portrait of me."

Steven looked at the wall – a large watercolor of a nude blonde woman hung, looking over her shoulder with a luminous smile. "I hope you didn't use the stone on him," he said, though it was hard to imagine that radiant young woman needing mind control to seduce anyone.

"I didn't use the stone for *everything*," Lorie said with a sniff. "Trust me when I say that I had ways on my own. You see, young man, Marco and I truly loved one another." She smiled, a soft, nostalgic smile. "We were so happy," she said softly. "Marco was such a kind, beautiful person. Being with him was like being bathed in sunlight— just pure warmth and cheer. We wanted to travel the world together, but of course, neither of us had much money at the time, and we both had commitments. We did get down to Chiapas, though, for about a month. It was a magnificent experience. We even had the chance to cross the border to Guatemala."

"Would you say that was the start of your interest in Latin America?" Steven asked.

"I've always had strong ties to Latin America, young man," Lorie said somewhat haughtily. "Mexico especially. I grew up on the border, after all, and all my friends growing up were Mexican. Also, I was given the stone in Mexico. I kept in touch with all my childhood friends through the years. But yes, I'd say this trip certainly deepened my feelings for the region. I was struck by both its beauty and its injustice." Her face darkened. "Such natural wonder, with such human brutality and inequity."

"Too true. That's probably why I never visited, to be honest," Steven said softly. "Did you ever think, back then, that you would become a major advocate for the rights of indigenous Central Americans and undocumented immigrants here in the States?"

"Well, no," said Lorie. "Though I did use the stone to get myself an interview on the news about the situation when we got home. Someone had to speak up." She laughed a little. "Though, I admit, I didn't realize that I would spend my whole life speaking up about it."

Steven chuckled slightly. Lorie Muller had been a major advocate for indigenous rights for decades, and had spoken up, loudly and consistently, for the rights and welfare of undocumented immigrants to the United States as well as for the rights of Native Americans. She had also worked to improve relations between the United States and Mexico, paying trips to Mexico as a sort of ambassador, and hosting Mexican diplomats in her home. Through the decades, she'd become a celebrity in Mexico, just as big, if not bigger, than she was here. "Would you say that your Aztec stone helped your cause at all?"

He blinked. *What am I saying?*

"Oh, it certainly did," said Lorie, not seeming to notice his moment of discomfiture. "Much easier to bend corrupt politicians to my will with a mind-controlling stone." She paused. "I had to learn to be careful, though," she said delicately. "Every action has consequences, especially at such a high level. And good intentions don't always lead to good outcomes."

"With great power comes great responsibility?" said Steven, quoting Spiderman.

"Exactly." Lorie nodded. "Mind you remember that, Steven, in your future career."

He shifted in his chair. "I'm sorry?"

"Never mind." She gave a small, mysterious smile.

"Okay, go on with your story, Lorie." Steven exchanged pens.

As I said, Marco and I were happy together, while our love lasted. But it didn't last too long. After a few years, we started falling out of love. We started arguing and fighting all the time. Huge rages, and broken glass.

Even though I told myself I wouldn't do this, I ended up using the stone on him during one of our quarrels. I'm ashamed to admit it, but I did. While we were shouting, I closed my hand around the Aztec jade and, for the very first time, used it to force him into something. I forced him to stop fighting me.

One might have thought my love would have protected him, but it didn't. He fell silent immediately, eyes glazing over like a drunk cow's. My beautiful Marco, turned into a mindless doll.

And I immediately realized what I'd done—forcing my will upon my lover, taking away his agency when he trusted me. It was horrible. A violation of his mind and spirit. I felt awful.

I withdrew from his mind immediately, and never tried to use the stone on him again, even when he packed his bags and left me for good. And I never used the stone on any of my subsequent lovers. Not once. It is a horrible, evil thing to force your own mind onto someone you love. I promised myself that I would not taint any of my following relationships with such thoughtlessness, such selfishness. And I've kept my promise to this day.

"Still," said Steven, "you managed to have a lot of fun, even without the stone, right?"

"Oh, indeed I did," Lorie said, eyes twinkling. "Well, it's not very difficult for a semi-famous, adventurous, and beautiful woman to make young men fall in love with her, especially when she's a rising movie star."

"True." Steven chuckled as he finished up his notes. "You say you didn't use the stone in your love life," he said, "but did you use it in your acting career?"

"Naturally, I did," said Lorie with a sly grin. "I may be opposed to enslaving my lovers' minds, but I never said I was a saint. I used the rock for many things, young man. It took me to trips around the world, I used it to meet countless famous people, and even to learn so many things. I, of course, also used the stone's powers to land myself a few... okay, many good roles. Though, as I mentioned before, the stone can't force people to act too much out of character. But I was easily good enough for those roles; I just had to nudge the directors' minds in my direction. Soon, my reputation and credentials spoke for themselves, and I didn't need to use the jade to persuade others into making the career I made."

"No one can doubt that you're a great actress, Lorie," Steven said sincerely. "I still love your take on Juliet in the 1972 remake."

"Oh, are you a Shakespeare fan?" Lorie said eagerly. "I am too. I loved playing Juliet as a dark, disturbed girl. I agree. That really was one of my best roles, if I do say so myself..."

Outside, the afternoon wore on, the sunlight slanting and mellowing to a rich gold before fading away, letting the shadows slide across the walkways and gardens. Eventually a warm dusk settled over the villa and grounds, blue twilight flooding the sky and filling the courtyard, while Steven and Lorie talked. They were interrupted only a few times, by Bianca coming in to check on her employer, to give her medicines and help her to the bathroom.

"Bianca really is incredibly nice to me," Lorie said as her housekeeper helped back, shuffling in to lie in bed once more. "I don't know what I'd do without her."

"Now, Ms. Lorie, it's the least I can do," said Bianca, smoothing down the silk throw cover and, to Steven's surprise, planting a kiss on Lorie's head. "We've been together so long," the housekeeper said, voice hitching a little.

"Indeed." Lorie twinkled at Steven. "Bianca would have quite a few interesting stories to tell you too, Steven!"

"Oh!" Steven, engrossed in Lorie's stories, hastily recollected his promise to interview Bianca. He checked his watch and looked outside—it was almost totally dark by now. "I'm sorry, Ms. Miranda, but it looks like it's too late for us to talk today. I'd love to speak to you as well, for sure. But, would you mind rescheduling?"

After some back-and-forth negotiation, Steven and Bianca settled on the coming Saturday as a good day for their interview.

Lorie listened with a benign expression. "Tell him the worst of me, Bianca," she said mischievously as Bianca prepared to leave. "Give him the goods! Don't hold back, girl." She smiled.

"Oh, that I will, Ms. Lorie." Bianca chuckled, but her eyes shone with unshed tears. "That I will!"

Steven watched her go, closing the bedroom door behind her, and turned back to Lorie. "I'm really happy that you don't mind my interviewing her."

"What? Not at all. Why would I? Like I said, she's got some great stories." Lorie waved a dismissive hand, but the movement was slow and stiff. Her face, crumpled back in the pillows, seemed half-collapsed in the warm gold lamplight.

"Do you feel you can continue, Lorie?" Steven asked in anxiety. "If you want, we can keep going another time—"

"No." Lorie shook her head. "I'm only going to be able to do this once."

"Well, you've certainly given me some great material!" Steven flipped through his notebook, stuffed with Lorie's life story. "What a life you've lived!" He paused. "Is it, ah, true that you slept with Chairman Mao once?"

Lorie chuckled throatily. "I've got better taste than that, young Steven! I never even met the man. I might've slept around with presidents and dignitaries, and I might've have numerous powerful men under the spell of my finger, but many of those stories roaming out there about me and my escapades are pure fantasy. Nothing but gossip." Her smile faded thoughtfully. "I daresay history might have been different if I had, though." Under the covers, her hand moved, picking fretfully at the small object she had hidden.

"Ah. Right. Your mind-controlling, magical Aztec stone." Steven wasn't sure how good a job he did at concealing his skepticism.

"Indeed. My mind-controlling imperial jade stone." Lorie pulled herself straighter, and her hand moved under the bedclothes. "Would you like to see it?"

"The rock?" Steven blinked. "What, like right now?"

"No time like the present." Lorie's hand was already snaking up from under the covers. "Eighty-four years I've had it," she said, closed fist emerging shakily into the light, "and I always obeyed the *bruja* who gave it to me. I never once let another person touch it. I didn't even show it to many people." Her fingers opened. "You're one of the very few, Steven."

In her open, veiny palm lay a pebble of murky green jade, gleaming dully in the lamplight. It was smaller than Steven had expected, somehow, and irregularly shaped, though smooth and polished from many years of handling. There was nothing special about it to Steven's eyes—it looked much like any other piece of old Mesoamerican jade he'd seen on museums and books.

"Thank you for showing me," he said sincerely. Whatever reservations he might have over the stone's supposed powers, he knew this piece of jade meant a lot to the world famous Lorie Muller, and his being allowed to see it was a great privilege. "It's beautiful."

"It is, isn't it?" Lorie admired the stone, turning it over in her fingers. On her face was an expression of sorrowful affection, as though she was saying a final goodbye to an old, dear friend, one whom she never expected to see again. “Hold out your hand, Steven del Real.”

Steven, startled, held out his open palm without thinking. Lorie turned the Aztec jade over in her fingers once more before abruptly dropping it into his hand, still warm from her own flesh.

“I pass the stone on to you, Steven del Real,” she said, voice suddenly clear and formal. “That the chain might not be broken and its powers not be lost, I pass the stone of Coatlicue on, to hands young, strong, and vigorous. Use its powers wisely, bearer of the stone.”

Steven, clutching the piece of antique Aztec jade, had no idea what to say to this. Lorie Muller lay back, settling deeper into her pillows. She looked sad, but also satisfied, and very, very tired.

“I think that’s enough, Steven,” she said, voice fading into thin wisps. “We had a great interview, and I wish you the best of luck with your book. But tomorrow is my hundredth birthday, and I want to celebrate it with Bianca.”

“Of course.” Steven quickly slid the stone into his pocket and started packing up, switching off the recording equipment and putting away his notebook and pens. “Thank you so much for agreeing to this interview, Ms. Muller.”

“It was my pleasure.” Lorie smiled weakly. Giving the stone to him seemed to have taken away a vital part of her strength, and she was fading rapidly now. “Like I said, best of luck with the book.” She paused. “And use the stone wisely, Steven. I mean it. Its powers are not light. It will open the world for you, in ways you cannot imagine.”

"I will," said Steven, with as much sincerity as he could muster. It was just a piece of jade, hanging heavy in his pocket. But he would not say so to the elderly, dying woman, especially not when she had given it to him as such a rare and magnificent gift.

"Good." Lorie's papery eyelids fluttered shut. "Now, don't go telling anyone about it, though. And please, leave the whole magic rock part out of my story. Would you?"

Steven though about it. So much of it had been about this. "I promise," he finally said.

"Thank you, young man. I trust you. That part of the story is just for you to know. Bianca will see you out," she murmured, voice drifting off. "Live your life to the fullest, Steven del Real. Goodbye."

"Goodbye and good night, Lorie," Steven said quietly, but Lorie Muller had already fallen asleep, and he spoke to no one. After a moment, he let himself silently out.

***

Six Months Later

Brilliant Southern California sunlight spilled across Steven's desk, casting his laptop keyboard into shadow. He paused to give a long, celebratory stretch. He'd written at breakneck speed, but at last, he was about to type in the final paragraph of his biography of Lorie Muller.

Steven smiled sadly, thinking of Lorie. He was one of the last people ever to speak to her. She'd lived long enough to celebrate her hundredth birthday with Bianca, and then died that very night, passing quietly away in her sleep. Steven had watched her funeral as one of the writers and reporters, from a distance—the great cortege passing by, the limousine decked with flowers, the windows respectfully shaded. The thousands of people filing past her coffin, laden with white lilies and marigolds. Calla lilies—the flowers of death, crowning an extraordinary life—and Marigolds, the bright orange blossoms signifying guidance for the deceased.

Steven had had the Aztec jade with him at the funeral. Indeed, he'd never been without it since Lorie gave it to him. A part of him felt foolish, but he felt he owed it to Lorie. After all, the stone, whether it had powers or not, had meant so much to her, and she had given it to him, a man she didn't even know. She'd told him to keep it with him always, and so he would.

It was in his pocket even now.

Steven took it out and held it in his palm, warm from his flesh. It was smooth and rounded and solid, a delight to touch, to hold. A piece of ancient history, and a priceless gift.

But did it actually have powers? Steven did not know.

To tell truth, he had not even tried to use the stone for such purposes. A part of him did not believe, another part did not want to try and fail, but mostly he just didn't want to. It was not power over others that enabled one to live a good life, after all. It was not any power of mind control that had animated Lorie Muller.

Steven placed the stone back in his pocket. Perhaps Lorie's lucky stone did not have the powers the *bruja* claimed, but that hardly mattered. Then, shaking out his wrists, he typed:

If we are to learn one lesson from the long and extraordinary life of Lorie Muller, let it be this: that we should live our lives to the fullest, in whatever form that might take. Life for Lorie was one long adventure, and so it should be for all of us. Lorie approached her life with zest and enthusiasm and confidence. Always, she pursued her dreams.

And so should we all.

Steven saved his work securely. He switched tabs on his computer and clicked to purchase his ticket to Guanajuato, Mexico. Then, stretching once more, he stood to go get a celebratory beer, making sure the Aztec stone was still in his pocket.

Just in case.

PERPETUITIONOMY: A CASE STUDY ON THE CONTROVERSIAL LONGEVITY PROCEDURE

Abstract:

Perpetuitionomy, the procedure through which human life can be extended, represents one of, if not the most, groundbreaking discovery in the history of humanity. The positive potential of such an innovation cannot be overstated. However, like all new technology, it also necessitates a considerable degree of skepticism and trepidation as humanity explores this strange and unknown path. Recent research reveals the potential positive and negative side effects of such a procedure. As such, a formal scientific analysis of this technology and its effects is long overdue.

Introduction:

According to legend, Cleopatra, Queen of Egypt, would indulge in daily baths of sour donkey milk, a task requiring over 700 donkeys to be milked daily. Mary, Queen of Scots, would have white wine poured in her bathes regularly. Today, models and mothers alike apply everything from urine to breast milk, bee venom, and even blood onto their faces and bodies, all in the pursuit of looking younger. Since time immemorial, humanity has desired an elixir for aging, a cure for aches and wrinkles, a fountain of youth. Until recently, science has largely come up short.

At the dawn of the twenty-first century, a few scientists began proposing a new form of medicine, experimental in form and scientific in nature. They toiled away, developing it in relative obscurity, unknown to the public. They called this *medicryne.* For decades, *medicryne* has been nothing short of a joke, a fool's quest, a mirage. Scientists who dared to even refer to it, let alone practice it, were mocked and risked their careers.

However, toward the middle of the twenty-first century, *medicryne* began advancing in leaps and bounds. The catalytic event happened when Harry the Hamster, as he became popularly known, had his lifespan nearly doubled, an addition of three years. The public began tuning in to watch Harry; the entire world was entranced by this hamster running around in his cage. He represented hope, possibility, potential.

Nonetheless, *medicryne* faced serious challenges as scientists tried to utilize what they'd learned, but this time on human subjects. For years, the science languished as experiments produced negligible results, and the fact that test subjects developed conditions or issues didn't help. It began to appear that *medicryne* would go the way of the many "miracle" technologies: full of so much promise, but in the end, just smoke and mirrors.

It wasn't until the breakthrough discovery of *Perpetuitionomy* that *medicryne* was thrust back into the public consciousness. By combining arcane forms of magic with *medicryne* in this remarkable procedure, scientists were able to see unprecedented results. Elderly test subjects, just months away from death, began living for many more years, and soon, even decades.

As the world watched test subjects gain back new life, money flowed into *medicryne.* Entire schools opened up and began training the modern generation of witch doctors: *Shamees.* Through a rigorous and incredibly competitive process, candidates can go through one of these postgraduate school programs to earn their *Medicryne Shamee (MS),* granting them the legal right to perform

Perpetuitionomy on any and all willing subjects, as long as they have the money and the desire to extend their life.

Now, the industry of longevity seems to have overtaken the medical world. Young and old, everybody wants to undergo *Perpetuitionomy*. Many scientists believe that this may constitute a breakthrough unlike anything humanity has ever seen.

Yet, recent findings point to the fact that *medicryne* and *Perpetuitionomy* may not be the silver bullets that we like to think they are. Years down the line from surgery, subjects are beginning to report strange and sometimes disturbing symptoms ranging from the relatively benign to the heretofore unheard of. These are not to be taken lightly, and serious scientific investigation ought to be undergone to further understand the full effects of *Perpetuitionomy*.

Medicryne, Perpetuitionomy, and the *Shamees* that perform it represent an incredibly exciting, groundbreaking step forward in humanity's quest for eternal life. However, as with all new technologies all possible sources of skepticism ought to be investigated. As the public rushes forward to extend their lives, scientists, starting with *Shamees* themselves, have a very real responsibility to explore and make known all aspects of this procedure – the good and the bad. Science can't let the profound potential of this technology blind it to the scientific process.

Yes, indeed, the siren song of eternal life is sweet, but that doesn't mean that we should rush headlong into the arms of the sirens.

Body:

Nearly one hundred-and-fifty years ago, at the turn of the millennium, Nick Bostrom published his now-famous *Fable of the Dragon-Tyrant.* In comparing aging and death to the cruel jaws of a dragon, he proposed that death, and humanity's acceptance of it, was foolish and misguided. That humanity merely had a form of Stockholm Syndrome, with many viewing death as beautiful, a part of life, and something to accept, not fear, simply because it was inevitable.

As the people in Bostrom's mythical kingdom debate whether to try to kill their dragon-tyrant aka cure death, the king's chief advisor of morality steps forward, proclaiming:

> *"the finitude of human life is a blessing for every individual, whether he knows it or not. Getting rid of the dragon, which might seem like such a convenient thing to do, would undermine our human dignity. The preoccupation with killing the dragon will deflect us from realizing more fully the aspirations to which our lives naturally point, from living well rather than merely staying alive."*

While a young boy, stepping forward from the crowd, states simply:

> *"The dragon is bad… I want my granny back."*

As *Perpetuitionomy* only continues to improve, day after day it seems that more would agree with the little boy over the advisor of morality; that the pain, the misery, the suffering that aging and death bring to us is too great, and that every opportunity to forgo it must be taken.

However, there still exists a small but vocal group who oppose the industry of longevity, who claim that it is anything from mere folly to highly dangerous and destructive to humanity. Generally, these groups invoke arguments that are highly spiritual, religious, and emotional. As such, a serious scientific investigation into the benefits and drawbacks of *Perpetuitionomy* is long overdue.

Perpetuitionomy consists of a procedure, conducted by a *Shamee*, who utilizes a unique blend of magic and *medicryne* to, in a general sense, alter the rates of senescence of cells in the body. This process alters several important protein production processes as well as the DNA governing the workings of the cells and, consequently, our bodies. While highly targeted, the procedure is by no means exact or infallible. While the success rate is very high (>99%), there are instances of failure and death as a result of *Perpetuitionomy*. Results, as we know of them now, are regular and predictable to within a margin of error of two to five years.

When undergoing *Perpetuitionomy,* patients inform their *Shamees* of how many years of life they would like to gain. The more years of life gained, the longer and more difficult the procedure, and thus the higher the cost. As such, when asked to extend life for twenty years, a *Shamee* can reliably extend a life for anywhere from fifteen to twenty-five years.

Consequently, with the current price of *Perpetuitionomy,* all but the most impoverished in the modern world can afford to extend their lives a modest amount, while the upper-class and super-rich have the possibility of doubling the length of their lives and beyond.

However, given that use of *Perpetuitionomy* has only come into widespread practice in the last thirty years, the upper limits of life are still a glaring unknown in the field. Many *Shamees* believe that *Perpetuitionomy* is not a limitless procedure; that one cannot continue to receive it ad infinitum, at least not without serious side effects.

Take the case of Ricardo Oldman. Billionaire, philanthropist, and household name for most of his long–and getting longer–life. He made his fortune off of e-commerce giant *EasyShop* in the first half of the twenty-first century. Always a lover of science and a first adopter of new technologies, Oldman was an eager and willing funder and guinea pig when *Perpetuitionomy* was first being tested, just over fifty years ago.

Given that he was in his nineties then, Oldman, living up to his namesake, is now in his 140s. The oldest man on Earth and in recent human history, Oldman remains an incredible resource for the study of how *Perpetuitionomy* affects its subjects.

At the age of 143, he is still fairly mobile, able to walk and move with relative ease. His physical condition seems to have deteriorated little, if at all, since he began receiving *Perpetuitionomy* just over fifty years ago.

However, as reported in *Harper's* two years ago, at the golden jubilee anniversary of his *Perpetuitionomy* procedure, the same cannot be said for his mental condition. Oldman's family claims that he frequently spaces out and daydreams for hours at a time, that there are spans in which nothing they can do will "bring him back." While having periods of extreme lucidity and attentiveness in which he displays remarkable cognitive abilities and memory, there are other times when he appears to have an extreme form of dementia, forgetting all but the very basic functions of life; language, recognition of his surroundings, even some basic motor functions appear to just "turn off" in his brain, and he, for all intents and purposes, enters a sort of waking coma. While he has always returned from these catatonic states, his family worries for the day when he no longer will.

Mr. Oldman has publicly claimed that he wishes to continue to receive *Perpetuitionomy* for as long as *Shamees* will administer it to him. No matter the side effects or consequences, he wishes to remain the guinea pig in a potentially endless experiment. He famously signed a legal document when he began, signing away his future right to withdraw from the agreement. Essentially, he and his *Shamees* are legally bound to continue to extend his life indefinitely.

The case of Oldman is extreme, but only because he is the first. While the reports of his complications and effects are merely anecdotal and don't constitute a serious scientific study, they will serve as important resources as time goes on and, as *Perpetuitionomy* continues to get cheaper and more accessible, more and more will desire to, like him, live into perpetuity.

Nevertheless, there is much ongoing study being undertaken regarding these side effects. A study was recently published in *Nature* highlighting the potential effects, both positive and negative, of long-term *Perpetuitionomy* use.

Started nearly three decades ago, this study began administering *Perpetuitionomy* to the residents of a nursing home in North Carolina. While half were chosen to undergo a life extension of thirty years, the other half, as a control group, did not. Unsurprisingly, many in the control group died, while nearly all (96%) of the residents who received *Perpetuitionomy* are still alive, at an average age of 105 years, 7 months. The researchers report that these residents are largely in the same physical condition that they were when the experiment started. Just over 90% those who could initially walk still maintain that ability, and 87% report no significant difference in pain over the almost thirty-year period.

However, 24%, a small but significant percentage, report an actual increase in mobility. They report feeling, as the researchers put it, “livelier and more vivacious” compared to before, almost as if their bodies are getting younger (Jones-Perez, et al.). They also report increasing strength and endurance. The residents underwent frequent physical testing, including light exercise like bike riding, walking, and the lifting of small weights. The 24%, or “reversers” as the researchers call them, only reported higher and higher numbers as time went on, while the rest of the group who received *Perpetuitionomy* were in a state of very slow but constant decline in strength and endurance.

In terms of mental effects, the results were starker and more alarming. Subjects went through regular cognitive testing and mental evaluations. Every six months they took a test that measured a whole host of cognitive abilities and took part in a series of psychiatric sessions to evaluate emotional intelligence, mindset, and outlook of life in general.

A large portion of the subjects (63%) experienced a slow but constant mental decline in nearly every area. While this decline happened at a lesser rate than those who had not undergone *Perpetuitionomy,* it was still pronounced and, by the end of the twenty-nine years, was significant and perceptible to friends and loved ones.

A smaller portion (18%) experienced some rather severe symptoms. Many quickly began to experience a high degree of dementia, confusing loved ones with strangers and even with inanimate objects. One man reportedly "was convinced his wife was a coat rack and found ways to rationalize how she would constantly move whenever he would hang his coat on her." (Jones-Perez, et al.)

Some in this group also reportedly began having hallucinations and frequent visions, ranging from the bizarre to the horrifying. Others became convinced they knew how to speak foreign languages they had never learned, proceeding to speak in complete gibberish. Still others developed unexplainable fears of random foods and liquids, screaming and crying if they were even in the same room as them.

As time went on, these disparate but alarming symptoms only worsened, with some by the end of the study existing practically in their own imaginary worlds, completely detached and removed from reality.

However, 19% of the group who received *Perpetuitionomy*–nearly all of them included in the group of physical 'reversers'–experienced a form of mental reversal as well. As time went on, their cognitive tests continued to improve, albeit slowly. By the end of the twenty-nine-year study, those in this group had become sharper and more attentive, and some had actually picked up and improved at new skills, from piano to chess.

While these are the preliminary results of the first study of its kind, the world has become entranced by these "reversers," wondering if *Perpetuitionomy* may unlock the secret not just to slowing or halting aging, but actually reversing it.

The possibility of "reversers" is not the only positive press *Perpetuitionomy* has received within the scientific and magical community. In fact, for all the fear and doubt that has been cast over the longevity industry by Ricardo Oldman and the nursing home study, far more tales of the wonderful benefits of *Perpetuitionomy* abound, both published in peer-reviewed literature and in the online community.

A story in *The New York Times* recently received national attention. It told of a family in Texas who, as a result of the use of

Perpetuitionomy, has been able to gather five generations together into the same household.

Wendy Dominguez, along with her husband Fred and their two young children, had moved back from Houston to McAllen to be close to her mother and grandmother when *Perpetuitionomy* first started gaining prominence. Once settled, she encouraged her mother and grandmother to undergo the procedure, as she desired more years with them.

Now, her children have grown up and had children of their own, and the family has all decided to move into a house together. Wendy Dominguez is now living to see her grandmother meet her own great-grandchildren, and she reports being the happiest she has ever been as she is so close to so much family.

This is hardly an isolated event, but rather indicative of a growing trend in America, and consequently the world; as the elderly gain the ability to extend their healthy years beyond what was possible pre-*Perpetuitionomy,* more generations are living together. This is a strong reversal of a longtime trend in the United States, namely that the average household size was growing smaller, as people had fewer children and spent less time with family in general. While the average household size was three and decreasing every year just thirty years ago, it has now grown back to five, as healthy parents and grandparents are living with their children.

Lauded as a "return of the family ethos" by *The New Yorker,* many point to this as one of the many wonderful effects of the extension of the human life span.

While the negative side effects being reported can be scary, the positive effects *Perpetuitionomy* has had on families and individuals everywhere are profound and moving.

Conclusion:

The industry of longevity has been the subject of much scrutiny and debate. With recent studies and negative media attention, many more are turning their gaze to the potential downsides of this revolutionary technology.

From a slowed, but still constant rate of physical and mental decline, to the possibility of dangerous and even horrific mental effects, the dark side of *Perpetuitionomy* has gained prominence in the media and scientific circles. Many are posing a question that the world seemed to remain willfully ignorant to in the early years of this technology: How much harm and damage can this technology inflict?

However, while the potential negatives garner attention, there are many effects that are viewed as positive and beneficial to society. From the strengthening of the family unit to the obvious prolonging of time with loved ones, many are extremely excited by *Perpetuitionomy* and the potential it holds going forward.

And, while *Perpetuitionomy* was originally lauded as a simple way to halt or significantly slow the aging process, the appearance of "reversers" in a recent three-decades-long academic study has generated a significant amount of excitement over the possibility that the procedure could contain some possibility of reversing aging altogether. The consequences of confirmation of this hypothesis almost don't need to be stated: from true eternal youth, to death, and the pain that comes with it, being vanquished forever, the possibilities are truly staggering and simply wonderful, to say the least.

While *The Fable of the Dragon-Tyrant* was written nearly a hundred-and-fifty years ago, it seems far more relevant today than it ever has been. As we contend with the imminent accessibility of *Perpetuitionomy* to everyone, regardless of wealth or status, we must contend with the questions, both scientific and ethical, philosophical and moral, that arise.

While *Perpetuitionomy* represents a potential change to human life of a magnitude never-before-seen, it also necessitates a caution and adherence to science, whether natural or mystical, of a similar magnitude, in order to ensure that humanity does not go down a dark path from which it cannot return.

THE PAPER CRANE

"Keep up, children! Heaven knows Principal Perez will have my head if any of you get lost downtown…"

I didn't have a hard time keeping up with Mrs. Kim, even as her voice trailed away. I had always been good at following directions, despite the fact that I wasn't the best example of a star student. At least, not since my mom had recently died from cancer.

I flipped through one of my favorite wizard stories as I walked, which featured magic, dragons, and elves.

"Hello? Earth to Raquel," whispered my best friend, Karla Naranjo. She slipped her sleek, dark hair over her shoulder. "You're going to get us in trouble if you don't put that away!"

"Us?" I said, and slammed the book closed. "Don't you mean *me?*" Everyone knew that Mrs. Kim blamed me for everything—even when it wasn't my fault. I figured that was just the way it was for fifth graders who had lost their moms to cancer. I hardly interacted in class anymore, so she must have understood that as a sign for trouble.

Karla rolled her deep, brown eyes. "Don't be so dramatic! Don't you want to look around? This school trip is basically for us."

She did have a point. Out of everyone in Mrs. Kim's class, we were definitely the biggest book nerds. Even still, I shrugged. "I've been here before, Karla. It's just the public library."

"So? Maybe we can find some new stories to read and exchange," Karla said, determined beyond belief. At times, I forgot she was only ten. Like me.

The downtown Portland library was known for its impressive architecture, even though it wasn't that old. It had glossy, silver shelves and a spiral staircase that led up to the second and third floors. Books of all kinds layered the walls around us, packed into the shelves in a meticulously organized fashion.

I clutched the book to my chest. "Speaking about that, you never returned that one book I lent you. The one about wizards and Merlin."

"Oh, drats! I keep forgetting. I'm sorry! I promise I'll give it back you soon. I know it's important to you," she said as her cheeks flooded red.

She didn't have to say why. I had recently become obsessed with wizards and magic fantasy. But also, most of my favorite fantasy books once belonged to my mother.

I swallowed against the lump in my throat and glanced away from my friend. I would practically die if Karla saw me cry. She'd already seen me depressed and alone. I didn't need to embarrass myself more. Lucky for me, I'd known her most of my life, so she wasn't about to abandon me over some silly emotions.

"Hey!" Karla said, and bopped me with her hip. "I know something that will cheer you up. It has to do with castle-bearing and dragon-murdering magic adventures…"

"What is it?" I asked, distracted. A group of boys from our class hung back against one of the bookshelves. They sniggered as we passed, causing my cheeks to burn. I hastily swept my curly, brown hair over my face and hitched my unicorn backpack higher up on my shoulder.

"Okay…Get ready. You're going to lose your breakfast over this news, I'm telling you."

"Karla, what is it?" I asked, laughing now.

She cleared her throat. "Drumroll, please."

I drummed my knuckles against the back of my book. Karla held her head high and grinned, accentuating her sharp, golden-brown cheekbones. "It's a new theme park! Fantasyland. And it's opening up right here in Portland!"

I stopped drumming as my mouth fell open. "No way! What kind of park?"

"Only the biggest, *bestest* park in the whole world!" Karla shouted. She tossed her arms out to the side, which I dodged just in time. "I'm not exaggerating. My dad told me—you know how he always finds out about these things in advance."

"I believe you," I said, though a part of me thought it was too good to be true. "So it's going to have rides, characters, the whole shebang?"

"It'll have all your favorite creatures: wizards, dragons, gnomes, and elves. The whole *shebang!* I heard the creatures are going to have this cool new AI technology or something like that to make them all feel more alive."

Excitement blossomed inside me. "That sounds awesome! What exactly is *AI technology*?"

"I don't know, but it sounds cool. It's supposed to make them feel realistic."

"I see," I replied. "And when does it open?"

"This weekend," Karla said. "I'm sure your dad heard about it, too! Ask him to take you. Better yet, ask him to take *us*."

I should've been excited it was opening up so soon, but all I felt was dread and anxiety. "Oh...I don't know if my dad will have time."

"Maybe your grandma?"

"Maybe. I don't think she approves of all that witchy stuff, though," I said, more as an excuse. Grandma Martha was often supportive of me—especially since my mom was her daughter. But I didn't want to burden either of them with something so...trivial. Even if it would make me the happiest girl in the world.

"You girls chatting about another one of those dumb story books?" came a boy's voice. My heart sank into my toes. I spun, just in time to see the boys from before. Nathan and Isaiah. The class-A tormentors of Mrs. Kim's unsuspecting fifth graders.

"What do you want, Nathan?" I snapped. He was the ringleader.

He shrugged his skinny shoulders and tossed back his fluffy, blond hair. "Nothing. I just heard you talking about that new park. You know it's for children, right?"

"Yeah, and that means it's for people without a life," Isaiah added, laughing. He leered at us with his bright, blue eyes and the stupid cowboy hat he always wore.

Karla curled her hands into fists. "Shut up! Maybe you just don't have any imagination."

Isaiah glared at her, but Nathan strode right for me. "What's that you got there?" he asked, his eyes on my book.

I hugged it tighter to my chest. "Nothing, it's just—"

He knocked the book out of my hands. It dropped loudly to the floor, opening to a page at random and spilling my collection of pink origami. A frog, a penguin, a flower, a couple of paper cranes, and some others were now littered on the floor—another fantastical hobby my mother had taught me. I bent down to pick them up, but Nathan beat me to it. He grabbed a paper crane off the ground and cupped it in his hand.

"You know that all your fantasy stuff isn't real, right? And it never was," he said as he wrapped his fingers around the bird and crushed it.

I gasped. Before I could stop them, tears welled in the corners of my eyes.

"Nathan! What's wrong with you? Give it a rest!" Karla said. She fished a metal water bottle out of her backpack and chucked it at Nathan's head. It bounced off with a sickening *thud*—Isaiah both laughing and groaning in sympathy.

But I didn't have time to feel grateful for my friend's intervention.

I scooped up my book and the rest of the cranes before running away. My ears roared with the sound of my own heartbeat, drowning out my friend who was for me. I let the tears flow freely.

I needed a place to be alone. *No one understands. Not even Karla. Because no one else lost their mother…*

I found a creaky door, opened it, and ran down the winding stairs. I couldn't remember ever entering this section before, but I figured it was probably just the librarian's exit. At the bottom of the stairs, I turned right, then left, and then stopped.

It had suddenly grown colder—and darker.

The hallway I stood in appeared murky, almost like it was half-submerged in water. But that couldn't be right. I could still breathe.

Walking forward, my steps echoed loudly back at me, as if the whole hall were empty, despite the shelves of books that lined either side. The architecture of this part of the library seemed older, somehow. It almost looked—and felt—like the interior of an ancient stone castle. My heart pounded in my head. I tried to turn back, but I couldn't seem to find the right hallway. I walked ahead, panting, then I ran. Somehow, it felt like I wasn't getting anywhere. The more I stepped forward, the more it seemed like I didn't move at all. Now panicking, I tried to make my way down the hall, expecting to hit some kind of dead end. I ran and ran, and the hall only led me past an endless array of shelves, rotting stone, and cold drafts.

I skittered to a halt, thinking. "Okay, Raquel. This has to be some kind of dream. Maybe you rested against a bookshelf and fell asleep?" But after pinching myself until I looked black and blue, I knew I had to be awake.

The problem was—I was lost in a library I had known my whole life.

First, I decided to regroup. I put my beloved wizard's book back in my backpack, as well as my cranes, which I packed carefully into the front pouch so they didn't crinkle.

Then, I glanced around. I peered at the books lining the shelves and noticed that years of dust speckled their spines and top pages. It looked like no one had been down this way in decades—not even a librarian.

I trailed my fingers along the books, looking for something—anything—to help me out. Then, I felt a sudden pull behind me, as if someone were watching. I formed my hands into fists and spun, ready for a fight. But no one was there.

Instead, I saw an ancient-looking book sitting all alone in the middle of a shelf, with a glossy, dusty-free spine.

I reached for it without thinking. *"Mystical Magic and Enchanting Spells,"* I read aloud, just as the book popped open in my hands.

"Oh!" I exclaimed, almost dropping it from my hands. But there was something about this book…My fingers tingled just holding it. It was as if it wanted me to hold it, too.

The book had fallen open to a random page in the middle. I peered closer, studying the strange words adorned there. It appeared to be written in a foreign language, though by the chapter title, **Starter Spells and Other Enchantments,** I knew it had to be some kind of magic.

I was no longer scared. I was excited. *Have I really just stumbled into a hidden hallway full of all things fantasy?* I couldn't wait to prove Nathan wrong. Of course magic was real…You just had to know where to look.

I pulled my finger down the list of spells, reading each of them in my head. Most of them were unpronounceable. I stumbled on one at the end, though, that didn't seem so hard to say. "*Inveniam…viam…meam?*"

The hallway rumbled around me. Dust fell from the ceiling and books toppled off the shelves. Screaming, I raced out of the hallway, turned a corner, and…

Found myself immediately back in the main library hall. I blinked. *What in the world? How did that happen? And so fast!*

Had the spell brought me back?

I saw that the entire class gathered around Mrs. Kim. They stood by the door, about to leave. Karla glanced around nervously at the back of the group looking for me. Ducking my head, I hurried to the librarian who sat at the front desk typing on a computer.

"Excuse me? I'd like to check this out," I asked, and handed her the book.

She pulled her half-moon glasses further down her nose. "That? I've never seen that before in my life. It must be one of the free ones. Take it! We won't miss it."

"Oh. You're sure?"

The woman waved a hand, nodding, her attention back on her computer. Quickly, I stowed the book in my backpack.

Karla gave me a look fit to kill once I rejoined the group, but I hissed at her not to ask. She would have to wait for an explanation—not that I would give her the truth.

"And so, children, that is why—ah, Miss Raquel Lucas. So glad you could join us once more," Mrs. Kim said, and shot me a simpering smile. "And where exactly did you run off to?"

"I, uh, had to go to the bathroom."

"Right. Well, everyone, pack yourselves onto the bus!"

Karla and I had hardly taken our seats when she rounded on me. "Alright, spill. There's no way you went to the bathroom! I followed you halfway there and I swear you disappeared. What happened? Are you okay?"

"Yeah, I'm fine, I just…took a wrong turn into the mystery aisle," I said, and bit my lip. That was half a truth.

"Fine. Don't tell me," Karla said, and smashed back against her seat. She crossed her arms and glared at me. "But you still better take me to Fantasyland!"

Looks like I'm already in Fantasyland, I thought, and grinned.

***

I sat in the cop car with my partner, Officer Ryan Michaels. Together, we listened to the dashboard radio in silence, grimacing whenever the static roared too loud for our ears. Other officers of the Portland, Oregon PD reported cases of bank theft, home burglary, and assault happening all across the city. Worse yet, Ryan and I had just been on a case the other day that screamed of murder—something we hadn't seen in this part of Portland for years.

Finally, the radio shut off. Ryan grunted. "Crime's getting worse, don't you think, Frank?"

I ruffled a hand through my curly, brown hair. "I can't stand the sound of it."

Ryan smoothed a hand over his copper goatee, with his long, red hair pulled back into a ponytail. "It's devastating to say the least. Keeps us on the job, though."

"I suppose," I said. Though ever since I lost my wife to cancer, I hadn't been liking much of what the job had to offer.

My personal phone rang. I straightened up, expecting my daughter, Raquel. She usually called when she got home from school, but only on her better days.

This was not one of those days.

I breathed into the phone. "Hi, Martha. No, not yet...Uh-huh, uh-huh, yeah, I know. Once Raquel gets home, make sure to give her that book for me, alright? You know why I can't give it to her myself. Well, I don't much like it, either, Grandma M, but you know how it is. Thanks for coming over again. Uh-huh, uh-huh, yeah, you take care, too. Love you, bye."

Ryan gave me a simpering look as I hung up the phone. "Your mother-in-law giving you grief again?"

"She just wishes I was home more," I said. "For Raquel."

My partner scoffed. "Don't we all wish that?" We sat in silence for another moment. It felt better than the last few days when all we heard was emergency sirens and calls for aid. Ryan fiddled with his police badge, staring out the dark, tinted window. With summer right around the corner, the sun hadn't yet set, and it cast a dim light on my partner.

"Hey, you hear about that new park opening?" Ryan asked.

"Yeah, it seems to be all the rage. They're putting in all that robotic simulating stuff, right?"

"Yessir. It's supposed to be pretty cool. My son and I are gonna go sometime next week. You should go with Raquel. I'm sure she'd love it."

"Actually," I said, grinning for the first time in a while. "I planned to take her this weekend. I already got tickets. It's a surprise."

Ryan leaned back in his seat, as if to assess me from a new angle. "Well, all-be. Look at you, Officer Lucas. Always providing the best for your daughter."

"All I can do is try," I said, my smile fading. "Come on, let's get home before they announce anymore crimes tonight."

***

At home, I slipped through the front door as inconspicuously as I dared. Grandma Martha noticed me anyway. She noticed everything. She had been a lot more vigilante since her daughter had died. She had also been staying with us more, coming over to make dinners, and keeping me company until Dad came home. It was lucky she lived in the area.

"Raquel!" she said, stopping me in my tracks. "How was your day, dear?"

"Fine," I said stiffly. "Can I go to my room now?"

"One moment," she said, slipped a full baking tray into the oven, and then crept around the island counter. She wore a long, red dress that flattered her plump frame and had her graying hair twisted into an elaborate braid.

Grandma Martha picked up a book with the title *Origami and Other Creations* on the cover. I frowned, recognizing it. "Grandma, did you take that from my room? I told you not to go through my things."

She paused. "What? Of course not! Your father picked this up for you while he was out. He told me to give it to you. He just called—he doesn't think he'll be home until late."

She handed me the pink book. I didn't have the heart to tell her that I already owned this book—it was one of the first ones Mom gave me before she died.

But even still, I was grateful to Dad for trying. I smiled. "Thanks, Grandma. I'll tell Dad I appreciate it, too."

She nodded and shooed me out of the kitchen with two hands. My heart skittered excitedly. Finally, I would get the chance to read more of that spell book.

I raced into my small bedroom and shut the door. We lived in a one story, so I'd have to be as quiet as possible so Grandma didn't hear me from down the hall.

Heart drumming, I pulled the new book out of my backpack and flipped it open. But as I scanned through a list of spells, I thought about my paper cranes and how Nathan had crushed one of them in his hands.

I opened the front pouch of my bag to assess the damage. Most of the cranes were still in good condition—apart from the one Nathan destroyed to torment me. Sighing, I placed them in the wicker basket on top of my dresser where I kept the first paper crane Mom had helped me make. This one was made with thick, red paper. I picked it up gently in my palm, and as I did, I swore I could still hear her laugh as we sat at the table, creasing the paper together.

Tears welled in my eyes, but I sniffed them back. Instead, I sat back down with the red paper crane in my lap. I flipped through the book, studying the various spells. It was *fascinating.* I felt like a real witch. In fact…

I bounced up, grabbed the backyard stick I had once tried to fashion into a wand, and held it in my right hand. I pretended that I had just been deemed the first real witch of Portland. To commemorate my new title, and position of power, I could do any spell I liked.

I flipped through the book, passing the spell I'd used in the library hallway. It meant "*to find a way.*"

"That explains how I got out of the library," I said aloud, and flipped the page in amazement.

There was a new spell that caught my attention. It pulled at my core and whispered to me.

The spell wanted me to try it out. Just as the book wanted me to hold it.

The meaning of the spell was *"to enliven"*. I knew that just meant *"to inspire"*.

I shrugged. "Okay," I said. "Sure. Why not?" I'd already performed one magic spell without fault. But what to practice *on?*

My eyes fell on the neatly folded red paper crane. The object already inspired me so much, being the first successful origami piece I did with mom—why not make it even more so? Perhaps it could inspire others, too, like stupid Nathan.

As my frustration boiled over into determination, I pointed the stick at the paper crane and said clearly, "*Inflamment acumina!*"

There was a burst of bright light, and I shrank into myself, holding back a scream. The white light surged out of the stick and zapped the paper crane. The object shivered, as if shaking off water droplets. Then, it spread its wings and flew into the air.

My mouth gaped open in a silent scream. I couldn't produce sound even if I tried. Shaking from fear, I dropped the stick, scurried into my bed, and hid under the covers. I peeked my head out, the covers still wrapped around my head and body like a babushka's cloak.

I stared in awe as the paper crane soared gracefully around the room. Its little, paper wings supported its movements. It looked fluid and real. Natural. I blinked rapidly and pinched my skin once more, waiting to wake up from a dream. But nothing changed. I was wide awake and everything was real.

"Whoa," I muttered, as I emerged from my makeshift cloak. "I'm a *witch*!"

I clapped my hands to my mouth, eyes wide. But all I heard from the kitchen was Grandma Martha banging dishes and cutlery.

Grinning, I slid off my bed and onto the floor. Sitting cross-legged, I examined the stick anew. How could it channel magic so easily? I had tried to shave off pieces of the bark with a sharp knife, but Grandma Martha had caught me and practically had a heart attack, so it looked knobbier than a real wand. Even still—I had performed magic. Was I just that powerful?

My skin prickled with excitement. Maybe there was a reason I loved fantasy stories. I was drawn to them…Because I was part of one.

The paper crane soared right over my head, slow and steady, then circled back to bop me lightly on the nose. *"Oh!"* I said and giggled. "Hello there. Sorry, I hid right after I created you."

The crane landed on my finger like a perch, and hopped around, turning its little head from side-to-side and flapping its paper wings.

"You're cute," I said and stood up. It jumped off my finger and flew around my head. I walked in circles around my room, giggling as the tiny, paper bird followed me wherever I went.

The front door opened, and I paused. Was Dad home so soon? I heard soft mumbles coming from the kitchen, then, "Raquel, dinner!"

That certainly was his voice. In a sudden panic, I clapped both hands around the paper crane. Its fragile body jostled against my palms, like a butterfly seeking escape from a jar.

"I'm sorry," I whispered to it. Then, louder, I called, "Coming!"

I looked around for a place to hide my new creation. My bed hung low to the ground and underneath it was dark and quiet. I gently released the enchanted crane there, where it fluttered against the bedframe's underside.

"Stay there," I whispered. "I'm going to leave the wand here, too, but I can't have my dad discovering you. Understand?"

The crane bobbed up and down on its wings, as if mimicking an agreeing nod.

"Great. See you soon, little bird!"

Still embodying a sense of disbelief, I threw the bed covers over the end, trapping the crane there, just in case.

***

"Raquel's taking a long time to come out of her room, isn't she?" I asked and glanced down the hall. "Maybe I should go check on her."

"Leave her be, Frank," Grandma Martha said, just as she placed a steaming casserole onto the table. "She'll come out when she's ready."

I tapped my knuckles on the table, eager to see my daughter again. Once Raquel entered the room, I beamed. She looked up and smiled, though her eyes glistened with worry. I must've been right to think she'd had another bad day.

"Hi, Raqie," I said.

"Hey, Dad," she responded, running her hands through her brown, curly hair. She took a seat across from me, reached for the casserole, and loaded her plate with food. I thought she might have been hungry—as she hadn't been eating much lately—until she started arranging it around her plate to look more like a castle.

I cleared my throat. "Raquel, did Grandma give you that book?"

"Oh, *Origami and Other Creations?* Yeah, I got it. Thanks, Dad. Really," she said, and glanced up once. "I, uhm, I already have it, though. Mom got it for me a while back."

Ugh! I shouldn't have said anything. Why did I? I swallowed hard.

"Ah, I see. Well…Maybe Karla would like to learn some folding techniques? You can lend it to her."

Raquel nodded eagerly. She tapped her foot against the hardwood floor and kept glancing back toward her room, as if expecting something.

Grandma Martha took off her apron and sat down at the table, where I shot her a look.

As we ate, Martha kept glancing from me, to Raquel, and back again. I really didn't want to spoil the surprise about Fantasyland, but there was so much distress—and sadness—in Raquel's eyes. At least, that's what I saw when she bothered to look at me. *It definitely was one of her bad days.*

"So! Raqie, I assume you heard about that new park opening in the forests of Portland? Fantasyland, I think it's called?"

She hesitated, her fork pausing in midair. "Yeah…I heard about it."

"Well…You want to go?"

"Yes," Raquel said quickly, then blushed. She recovered with a shrug. "Whenever, I guess. I think it's just opening this weekend."

"That's right. And guess who got us tickets to go?"

Raquel dropped her fork, where it clattered onto the table. "No! You got us tickets already?"

Martha beamed. "He did. It was going to be a surprise, but…"

I nodded. "It's true! I couldn't keep the secret. I even got an extra ticket in case you wanted to take Karla. I already cleared it up with her parents."

Raquel's face completely transformed from a drooping flower into a blossoming bud. "Oh my goodness, Dad, thank you thank you!"

She jumped out of her seat, raced over to me, and wrapped her arms around my head. I laughed and patted her shoulder, feeling happiness soar within me, too. I certainly didn't regret telling her now.

"Dad, you're honestly the best! I can't wait to tell Karla," Raquel said. "May I be excused?"

"Sure," Martha said, and inclined her head.

"This is gonna be so cool!"

Raquel raced away and slammed her bedroom door, though this time, I knew it was a happy slam. I glanced down at her half-eaten plate, more than satisfied.

***

Karla couldn't contain her excitement when I told her the good news. She screamed and practically cried all week—which was the only thing that distracted me from how long it took for the weekend to arrive.

Nathan and Isaiah didn't bother us much during the week, either, which was good. I was ready to cast a spell on them if they tried. At school, I carried my wand in my back pocket and hid the spell book inside one of my school binders. I wished I could take the flying bird with me, too, but I knew I couldn't afford to attract any more attention to myself. Besides, it was content in the little haven it found under my bed. Regardless, nothing could spoil this excitement. I was going to Fantasyland!

The drive to the park took *forever.* We passed a lot of cars heading in the same direction. We rode in Grandma's car. Dad drove, with Grandma Martha in the front seat, while Karla and I sat in the back, whispering frantically about everything we were bound to see.

"I hear it's supposed to be bigger than *Disneyworld!"* Karla hissed.

I touched the wand hidden in my back pocket, grinning. "It's going to be the greatest park experience in the whole world!"

"Girls, we're almost there," Dad said. "Look out the window so you don't miss anything."

Dad drove us down a winding path, with nothing but trees and other cars in our peripheral. As the car pulled around, a shadow stretched over us from above. Karla and I glanced up, just in time to see a thirty-foot, gleaming dragon pass right over us. Karla and I screamed happily at the same time. It looked just like a real dragon! Its scales were decorated in beautiful blues, glimmering greens, and rich reds. It stood out clearly against the backdrop of gray sky—an Oregon constant.

It soared in a circle, moving upside down and backwards as seamlessly as a rollercoaster ride and as flexibly as a living creature. Then, just like a coiling snake, it slithered back toward the forest.

"Whoa! Take us to *that!*" Karla said, causing me to burst into laughter.

"Right-o," Dad said, and pulled into the park's entryway.

Fantasyland appeared suddenly and out of nowhere—its entrance massive and welcoming. The parking lot stretched as wide as twelve roads put together, though it wasn't paved. They had replaced the typical trees with fake, AI images of them, with just enough space for cars to park between. Right behind the parking lot stood the tall, iron gates of the park, with a sign reading, **"Here be Fantasyland: Where Adventure Awaits."** On the sign were two axes crossing each other, and two grinning gnomes with long beards. The longer I looked, the more I was certain they winked at me.

I scrambled out of the car before Dad even had time to fully shut it off. Karla, too. He grumbled incoherent protests, but we didn't care. "This is *so* neat!" I shouted.

I grabbed Karla's hand and dragged her forward, the two of us laughing as we ran. "Hold up, you two, we have the tickets!" Dad called behind me, but I didn't dare slow down—not when my heart beat a mile a minute.

Karla and I danced on the spot at the gate, waiting for Dad to come with the tickets. A couple of workers stood there, smiling at our excitement that was so clearly spilling over. They wore jester's hats and robes. "Welcome to Fantasyland!" they parroted, as Dad and Grandma Martha finally arrived. The workers stamped our tickets with purple crowns and let us pass.

I was immediately in awe—everything looked amazing! Before us wound a golden road that passed through cottage houses with thatched roofs and medieval-looking taverns. At the end of the road was a giant, gray-stone castle, fit with dripping ivy and iron bars. There were roaring rollercoasters, spinning rides, and outdoor theaters.

But best of all, the only humans in the park were us, the other customers, and the workers at the front. Everything else was a creature of fantasy.

Elves and orcs walked past us, grunting and nodding. For once, they didn't seem to be fighting each other. At every stall, vendor, and store, a squat-faced dwarf with a pointed hat and long beard, or a long-faced and elegant-looking elf, greeted us. Fairies flew over our heads on real wings that glimmered like a clear rainbow. They giggled and laughed as they pulled at our hair and grabbed at our bags. I grinned back at them.

And that wasn't all. The more we explored, the more it was clear thousands of different creatures walked among us. Ogres stomped by, carrying clubs and looking menacing, just as goblins raced under our feet, cackling loudly. The dwarf vendors all sold hunks of dripping meat, as well as the finest swords, daggers, and axes, all dulled at the tips. The elves offered an admirable selection of wines, liquors, and ales, as well as fancy jewelry. They also sold fabulous-looking clothes. Dad bought some red wine in a fancy goblet, and I begged him to try some. After a shrug from Grandma

Martha, he handed it down to me. I took a sip and gagged as it went down like cough medicine. Everyone laughed.

We waited in line for all the rides, many of which were wooden cars in the shape of hippogriffs, dragons, and a Pegasus. There was also a ride called 'Avoid the Troll', where you spun around and around in a little cauldron. A troll stomped after you, shouting as you screamed for dear life. That one was beyond fun.

In between rides, Dad bought us stuffed toys, candies, and weirdly flavored ice cream. We stood at the stage to watch armor-clad dwarves fight with swords or perform long, swooning ballads. At the back, tall elves rode elegant horses in a performance joust that had us all screaming and hooting for the winner. Wizards adorned in heavy robes offered crystal ball readings and displays of magic. As the wind whipped past my face and I screamed happily on the rollercoasters, I knew this had to be the best day of my life. I didn't even care that the creatures were all made from robotic creations—they looked real enough to me. They even acted real, and that was all that mattered.

Karla recited facts about the park to us as we waited in line after line, engaged with ogres, dwarves, and elves, eating hunks of meat and potatoes at the tavern. She said that most of the creatures were tied to an invisible, holographic string that kept them chained to the park. She also said that their robotic brains were programmed to register and respond to all kinds of customer scenarios. At this, I only beamed wider. *Sounds real enough to me.*

We walked under twisting dragon rides, where human riders screamed. Wind rushed past my head, and I hugged my new stuffed gnome tighter to my chest. I was a witch, and I came to Fantasyland on the first day of its opening. What could be better?

At that point, we had perused most of the park. The day had passed us by in the blink of an eye, and as twilight arrived, my heart saddened. I didn't want it to end.

"Let's ride this giant one!" Karla said, pointing to the twisting, screeching rollercoaster.

We idled at the back, waiting. A shadow swooped over us from above. I glanced up and gasped. The dragon was back! It looked even more magnificent inside the park. It flew so low, its talons scraped the cobbled ground, and many patrons jumped out of the way. As it plunged past, its great, orange eye latched onto me. It blew smoke out of its nostrils, as if laughing. For a second, I saw my entire body reflected in its eye. Then, it winked. The thirty-foot dragon flapped its great wings and soared into the sky once more, where it released a belly full of fire.

"Now *that's* some great robotic technology!" Dad said.

"Come with me a second, Frank," Grandma Martha said. "Let's get the girls some medieval pretzels and cheese."

Karla nodded. "Sounds great, Grandma M. Thanks!"

Dad and Grandma Martha walked out of line and headed toward a kiosk run by a gnome in a crimson-red hat.

As they left, a wizard walked by with a couple of elves. They nodded at me and Karla, grinning wide, and I smiled back. *Their eyes are glittering and full of life.*

"These creatures can't be robotic," I said aloud. "They seem so *real.*"

"Oh, here we go again—Raquel can't see reality for what it truly is," came a loud, obnoxious voice. It was Nathan and Isaiah, waiting in line for the same ride as us.

Karla put her hands on her hips. "What are *you two* doing here? I thought you didn't like fantasy things."

Nathan waved a hand. "Everyone knows this park is supposed to be the best—it's the only reason we came."

"Yeah, we wanted to see for ourselves," Isaiah added, his eyes roaming around.

"And? What do you think?"

"*Lame*," Nathan said, and blew a raspberry. "The news was wrong. Disneyworld is way better—and bigger. Though I bet Raquel here is in heaven."

Karla glanced at me nervously. I shrugged. "So what if I am? You're clearly wrong. This park is amazing and way better than Disneyworld."

Nathan faltered. "Yeah, well, you probably never want to leave here. You're a fantasy obsessed witch."

My breath left me in a rush. "What did you say?"

"You heard what I said—you're just a fantasy obsessed *witch*—"

Without thinking, I yanked the stick out of my back pocket and pointed it right in his face. "You think I'm a witch, huh? Maybe I am! I'll show you that magic is real—*inflamment acumina!*"

I said the last spell I could remember, not realizing what it meant. As soon as I said it, a burst of white light bounced against Nathan's chest and flared out into the park. The spell hit everywhere and everything—the dwarves, the elves, and the gnomes. It hit the dragon as it curled past, causing it to pause and quiver.

The whole park shivered—rumbling as if alive, or about to have an earthquake. As the dragon began to roar, and the elves and dwarves blinked as if just waking up, I realized what the spell had done. It meant *enliven*…Meaning to *make alive.*

"Oh no," I said, even as excitement blossomed inside me. *Now, everything will truly be real.*

***

We had just paid the AI gnome when something strange happened. A blast of white light appeared out of nowhere and smacked the gnome in the face. He shivered and blinked, his eyes appearing much more alive. He took off his hat and tossed it to the ground. "What is this? I don't like the color *red,*" he grumbled, and then glanced at us. "And who are you?"

"Uh…" I said and glanced at Martha. "We just bought pretzels from you."

"*Pretzels?*"

A *boom* shook the sky, just as the dragon soared over the kiosk. This time, its tail slammed right into the top of the shop and collapsed it. The gnome screamed and jumped away just in time. The dragon roared, shaking the whole park, and flapped its great wings. When it opened its mouth to breathe fire, it lit up one of the taverns. Patrons ran out, screaming. I looked up and noticed that an elf rode on top of the flaming beast. The elf shouted and hollered, raising its free hand as if a call to war.

"What's going on, Frank?" Martha asked. "None of this seems right."

A sour feeling entered my stomach. "That's because it's not. Come on, we've got to—"

A parade of dwarves holding daggers, swords, and shields raced past, screaming something about battle.

Martha dropped the pretzels in surprise, but it didn't matter. We had to get back to the girls—and fast.

I waited for the dwarves to pass before racing forward with Martha in tow. "What's happening? Why are they all acting like this?" she asked.

I had no answer for her. A theory formed in my brain, but I didn't want to believe it.

By the time we got back to the ride, it was out of service. The long line from before was gone, with only a few kid stragglers holding toys to their chests and crying. But our girls were missing. My daughter was gone.

"Where could they be?" I shouted.

I glanced around, noticing how the fairies ripped off their invisible ropes and flew in all directions; how the gnomes kept pulling off their colored hats and smashing them to the ground; and how the wizards ran around, casting spells at trash cans and turning them into giant, roaring toads. There were elves the size of toddlers throwing tantrums, pixies tossing glitter onto people's heads, and ogres smashing their clubs into buildings, acidic spit flying from their mouths.

Spit. "Martha, these creatures are *alive.*"

"How?" she barked.

We ducked just as a wizard released a spell right above our heads. It hit the rollercoaster, causing it to start again and spin backwards down the tracks.

"I don't know, but first, we have to find Raquel and Karla. Come on!"

We ran through the crowd of orcs and dwarves, watching as they attacked each other with continued screams of war. The dragon plummeted through the sky, the elf still on top of it, and snapped a couple dwarves into its mouth.

We found Raquel and Karla cowering behind a bush. Raquel waved around a long, thin stick and kept muttering under her breath.

"Girls!" Grandma Martha said, and quickly hugged them. "What happened?"

"It was amazing! Raquel here, well, she…" But Karla stopped, looking cautious.

"I did it," Raquel said as she stepped forward. "I…found this magic book on spells in the library." She shot a darting look at Karla. Her friend nodded. "I got lost there while on our school trip. When I found the book in a weird hallway, it helped me out. I…said a spell and it brought me back to the main library. And then at home, I did another spell, and it actually worked! It's so cool, Dad. But, I think I accidentally did the same spell here, the only one I could remember. And, well…"

A troll stomped past, creating crater-sized holes in the golden street with its feet.

"I made them alive," Raquel finished, frantically searching our faces for a response.

"You think?!" Karla said, just as another troll came to engage the first. They battled in the middle of the road with their clubs raised high.

Of course I questioned my daughter's magical properties. "What do you *mean* you made them alive, Raquel Lucas?" I asked hesitantly. "None of this makes any sense. I am sorry, but I having a very hard time believing…understanding any of this."

"Dad…I know this must be very hard. Trust me, I, myself, am not sure of how any of this works, to be honest. But I promise you, I am telling you the truth."

"Look around, Mr. Lucas. It's all real!" Karla told me.

I looked around once more; I couldn't negate what my eyes were witnessing, that's for sure. I swallowed hard. "Well, can you change them back?" I asked Raquel reluctantly. It was strange enough to think that magic existed, and it was even more difficult to acknowledge that my daughter had magical powers.

Raquel shook her head. "I'm trying, but…" She flicked her stick again, but nothing happened. Tears welled in her eyes.

"Okay. Well, I guess it doesn't matter now, then. Let's just get to the parking lot," I said as I grabbed my daughter and her friend in one hand, and Grandma Martha in the other.

We raced through the crowded street, following the other humans that scurried to safety. Almost everyone fled in the direction of the parking lot. It was difficult with all the creatures flying overhead, cackling and yanking on our hair. The smaller ones weaved in and out of our legs, grabbing our ankles and nearly tripping us.

Fantasyland was no longer fun. Even Raquel looked scared. The other human visitors seemed to be having an even more difficult time than us, obvious confusion and panic in their faces due to the fantastic chaos surrounding us.

We finally made it to the parking lot with all the creatures gamboling after us. I veered right to throw them off and stumbled as we reached the grassy, forested part of the lot. Then, there was silence. I glanced behind me, panting, only to see that the creatures couldn't follow us. There was an invisible barrier preventing them from leaving. That meant none of them could leave the park. They all stood there, watching, and chills crawled up my back.

"Come on, girls. Let's get out of here before—"

"Wait!" someone called. I turned to see a wizard with a long, graying beard and a tall purple hat, waving a staff at us. He stood behind the invisible barrier, too, unable to enter the parking lot. Beside him stood two elves—one tall and skinny, the other short and small.

I shook my head firmly. "No! No more fantasy creatures today." I turned Raquel away toward the car, but she placed a gentle hand on my arm.

"Dad, it's okay. I—I think I know them."

"*Know* them?"

"Well, they smiled at me earlier. Before they were alive."

I squinted back at them suspiciously. The wizard kept waving his staff and standing on his tiptoes so that his matching, purple robe rose above his ankles.

"This better be good," I mumbled, and dragged Raquel back to them. "What? What do you want?"

"We need the girl," the wizard said in his dignified and ancient voice. "If she performed magic before to enliven us, then only she can perform magic to undo it."

"You want the magic undone?" I asked, mystified. I suspected they would all want to be alive forever. That certainly made me trust them a little more.

"Well? Did you perform magic before?" the tiny elf asked in a squeaky voice.

Raquel nodded. She pulled out her stick and tapped it against her palm. The creatures gasped. "A true magic wand! All natural," the taller elf said, her voice slow and certain.

"Only you can undo the spell, my lady," the wizard said.

"I—I don't know how. I only remember a few spells from the book, and I don't have it with me," Raquel said, and bowed her head.

"Nonsense! Of course you can do it!" the tiny elf squeaked.

"Yes, Finfair is right," the old wizard said. "You can do it. And we can help you perform the spell."

"Alas, we do not want to be trapped in these strange, robotic bodies forever," the taller elf said.

Raquel glanced around, considering. "Okay. If I was the cause, then certainly I can be the solution."

My heart swelled with pride at her words. *She's sure growing up fast.*

"Neat, Raqie!" Karla said, who had previously been staring at the creatures with her mouth agape. "Can I come, too?"

The wizard shook his head. "Only the one who performed the spell may join us now."

Raquel gazed at me nervously, but with one nod, I agreed. "Don't take her far."

"We will perform the spell right here, by the barrier," the tall elf said, and nodded. She had a motherly way about her—something that I trusted.

And with that, I watched Raquel head back into the park and disappear behind the invisible barrier. I had never felt so tired, or so drained. *This has been the longest day of my life.*

***

As I waved my wand, I figured any more magic would be impossible. I'd already defied the general laws of modern society, but as the wizard crouched beside me, he whispered a spell: *Resolvo magicae.* It didn't sound very complicated. The more I waved my stick-wand, the more frustrated I became. Nothing happened!

"You must believe in yourself, Raquel," the tall elf said. She placed a hand on my shoulder. "We cannot undo the spell you invoked. Only you can."

"I'm trying!" I snapped and waved my wand. Still no magic came. "What should I do?"

"Elronda is right. You must believe in yourself. Believe you can stop all this mayhem, and it will happen. But you must also want it to end," the wizard said. "It is up to you. For what it is worth, I believe you can." He smiled.

"So do I," said Elronda, the high elf.

"And me!" said Finfair, the small elf.

I took a deep breath. "Okay. Believe in myself. I can do that…"

And as the fantasy creatures galloped, flew, and stomped around me, I tried to picture a world where they were simply robots once more. Figments of my imagination. A part of me was saddened by the image. But I shook the sadness away. I had magic. Living fantasy would always exist in my world, and that's all that mattered. Besides, Fantasyland was more fun without them wrecking up the place. Half the buildings were on fire and all the rides were broken already.

Remembering how cool Fantasyland had been before, I closed my eyes and whispered, "*Resolvo magicae.*"

With a single flick of my wand, a shimmering film fell over the park. Everything stilled and silenced—frozen in time as the spell washed over them like a wave. The trolls stopped stomping, the ogres ceased chomping, and the fairies' wings forewent their flicking. Even the dragon landed back onto the ground with a loud rumble, sighing with wariness. The tall elf hopped off its back and slicked back its hair, looking around once before freezing in place, too.

"You did it," the wizard whispered, just before he disappeared entirely. I blinked, and the two elves froze along with everyone else.

"Yeah…I guess I did," I said, and grinned.

I rushed out to the parking lot, relaying the news, and hurried into the car. As we drove away, I peered out the back window and watched the human workers gather back together, looking both confused and tired. I yawned, realizing just how tired I was, too. Dad had barely driven a few miles before I dozed off on Karla's shoulder.

Over the next few days, Dad watched me like a hawk. He eyed me warily as I tossed the spell book and my wand into the trash, promising to never do magic again. Evidently, it was far too dangerous. Although, perhaps, it just wasn't the right time now. I had schoolwork to focus on, and I needed to be good for my dad.

The news described Fantasyland as a "dangerous adventure that everyone should try". They didn't mention much about the wild escapade I had caused—they simply reported the park would be closed for the next week due to sudden renovations. I was just glad it hadn't shut down completely.

Back in my room, I remembered my living red paper crane. I pulled back the sheets and peered in. "Hey there, little one. Sorry about all this…"

It wiggled feebly, clearly on the brink of losing its magic. I must have kept it in the dark too long.

Perhaps Dad won't notice—not if I tell the living origami bird to be secretive, I thought. *Perhaps the wand had nothing to do with it, and I can just recite the words I memorized. Besides, the paper crane did stay under here this whole time. So, why not?*

Smiling mischievously, I whispered the words one last time. "*Inflamment acumina.*"

The origami crane rose into the air with sudden energy and strength. It twirled around me, flapping its tiny wings, and I laughed. It bopped my nose again and landed in my palm.

"You know—you remind me of someone," I said, just as it dipped its small beak against my finger. *My mother,* I thought, and smiled. She would be so proud to see me like this—owning up to my mistakes and fixing things—but also, she would be amazed that I could use magic.

Grinning, I tucked the red paper crane into my pocket, knowing it would follow me around for the rest of my days. Fantasy wasn't dead, it was alive, and it was a part of my life. The thought brought me a moment of peace and I knew everything would be alright.

DREAM FRIGHT

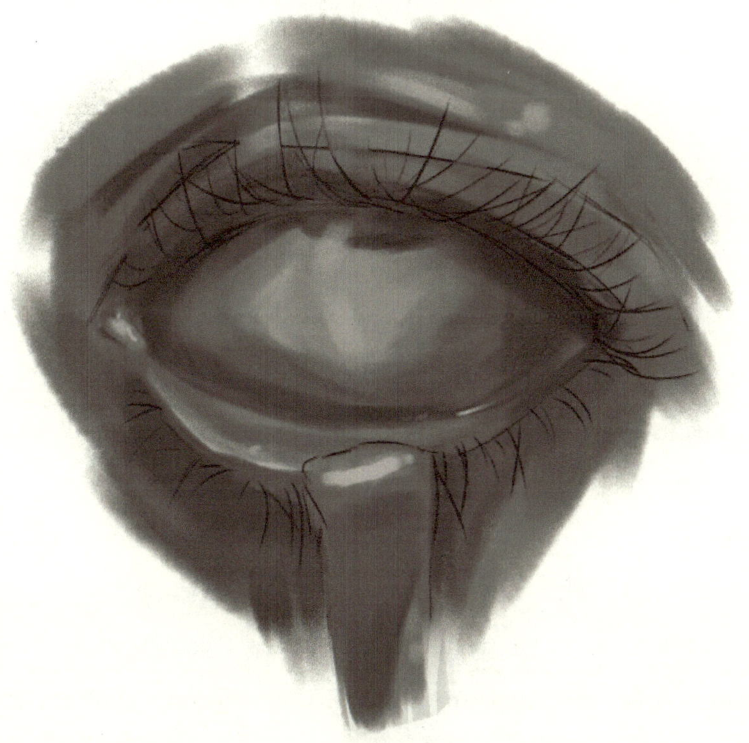

Sammy placed his hands on the sides of his head and concentrated. The migraine tormented him. He shut his eyes and imagined his hand going through the layers of his skin and bone, the tips of his fingers caressing his brain to soothe it.

The gesture generated friction between his hands and hair and Sammy shifted his thoughts to that. Heat swelled, and the more it grew, the more Sammy willed it to be hotter. The faster he scraped his head, the more vivid the image became.

"Ah!" he screamed as he concentrated with his eyes closed.

The heat turned into a searing flame and sharpened into a blast of soundless lightning. The shock sent his nerves screaming and his body crashed down on the bed. Blood and adrenaline coursed through him while he writhed around, messing and tangling the bed sheets around him.

It worked. The pain achieved what he wanted.

Sammy gasped for air as his migraine subsided, replaced with a numbness that came after every bolt of electricity. The ache in his head was gone, at least for now. Yet his arm still trembled.

Once the ringing in his head passed, he sat up and eyed the mess of his bedroom. Apart from his unkempt bed, the floor was also a disaster. The ghost of the once cream carpet peeked through the layers of paper strewn all over the place. Even the walls were a victim to his scribbling from months ago. Sammy shut his eyes again and willed himself not to read anything.

It took him a full minute of sitting still and breathing deeply to calm his right arm. When the shaking subsided, he got off the bed, crumpling the yellowing papers underneath his feet with each step.

Sammy kept his gaze off the walls and watched as his feet guided him through the dark hallways of his house. He passed by the bathroom mirror, now painted black, and took a quick shower before tossing on a white shirt and wool pants. Sammy then settled himself in the kitchen and prepared himself breakfast and lunch.

The window to his right revealed the rows of bright porch lights on his street. Fellow residents were parking their cars and shutting their doors behind them after long hours of work.

He, on the other hand, had yet to begin his evening shift.

After his dry meal, Sammy took off on his motorbike, channeling his energy on the handlebars to fuel the machine. Its quiet engine whisked him past the organized, dim streets of San Diego. While not as busy as Midway District, where he lived, life brimmed by the sidewalks and from the bars and diners that dotted the streets.

Sammy pulled over by the rollup entrance of his department. Workers filed out of the parking lot one by one, leaving behind delivery trucks and bikes to rest for the day. Others went on foot and hailed Sammy while he propped his bike up. Sammy slipped into the surveillance office and nodded at the last guard before taking his seat in front of the wall of screens he had to watch.

He placed both hands on the glass platforms on the table and concentrated once again. The skin of his palms were sucked in the device and siphoned energy from him. One by one, the sets of screens lit up and displayed the view from cameras scattered throughout the entire building. His dark blue eyes looked over each display for a few seconds before moving to the next, watching for any conspicuous signs of bandits or mischief makers.

Even though magic was siphoned out of him every second, Sammy focused on his work. Whenever someone went too close to the building or looked into the cameras, he drained more energy into the controls to memorize the finer details of their eyes, and if those were covered, the taste of their aura. The putrid bitter taste of alcohol trailed after the lurkers in varying degrees, with others reeking of cigarettes and dirt. The combined odors hit like a punch to the gut, but at least all of it was recorded.

Once again, nothing happened during his eternal eight-hour period.

His shift ended when the sun rose from its earthen grave. Couriers working in his office began to line up, one by one, by the staff entrance. Their palms and eyes were scanned before loading their trucks and bikes with various electronic goods and supplies. Sammy laid his hands off the grid, causing the screens to immediately go black.

His eyes begged to do the same. His eyelids were heavy and his legs were limp after sitting in the same position for hours, with barely a few blinks during the night. Exhaustion crept into every muscle and every part of his brain. It invaded his thoughts and begged him to rest for a moment.

He brought his hands up his head and shocked himself again. The pain made him arch his back and foam bubbled in his mouth. Sammy's knees gave in and crashed to the ground, and he landed on his elbows. His breathing was quick and uneven while the shock ran through his flesh and bones. The exhaustion waned away, leaving behind a painful numbness.

"Are you okay, Sam?"

Sammy felt arms on his shoulders, but he heaved, shrugging them off. He clutched the edges of the table and crawled back to his feet. Whenever the other guard tried to help, he swatted his hands away and locked his gaze on the floor.

"I'm fine," he responded through gritted teeth.

"What do you mean you're fine? Dude, you were on the floor and you're clenching right now. You're out of it again, bro. Come on, let me–"

Sammy batted his partner's hand away and forced himself out of the surveillance room. "I said I'm fine!" He hurried to his motorbike, ignoring everyone else who showed concern, and went on his way.

The drive home was far more difficult with the aching in his head, but Sammy had done this far more times than he could recall. One more sleepless day wouldn't hurt.

He parked his motorbike by the driveway and rushed into the sanctuary of his home. Sunlight poured from the windows in his living room, illuminating the dark interior he'd traversed many times before. Incomprehensible scribbles were etched on the walls, ranging from microscopic pencil marks to letters spanning from the roof to the floor. The entire floor was carpeted with scraps of paper that bore the same handwriting.

His handwriting.

A migraine came again, bringing with it a dizziness that shook him. The words on the walls and floors screamed and shifted in place, drawing his eyes to them. Sammy wanted to shut his eyes, but closing them meant entering his headspace and seeing those images he tried so hard to evade. If he even blinked, sleep could strangle him. On the other hand, if he kept them open, the words would haunt him. Still, this was better than the alternative.

Sleep was not an option.

He could hear the words yelling, the walls crying, the floor screeching, the entire house reverberating every wordless syllable he had written. To any other person, pure nonsense; to him, intricate details. And while some struggled with mental health issues, his curse was somniphobia. Though the real demon wasn't the fear of sleeping, but rather, what he saw in his dreams.

The mysterious woman. The words, conveying a prophecy of doom.

Sammy knew that if he shut his eyes, more words would come when he woke up. And he wanted no more words. No more details. It was too much. He did not need more words.

To some this would be a gift; to him, it was a burden.

Sammy looked around. He saw the writings on the wall. On the floor. On the ceiling.

Murder. National City. Fifteen-year old Asian girl victim. Caucasian man in a black tank top and balaclava. Tattoo of a black cross on his entire left arm. 10:14 pm. Tuesday.

Burglary with arson. Fairmount Village. Two families dead. Two men, one fair with blonde cornrows, another with left index finger missing. Monday, 2:13 am.

Jaywalking. Washington Street. No deaths. Man wearing a rock band t-shirt and ripped jeans. Blue phone case and white wireless headphones.

Car accident. His driveway. One pigeon. Sammy was the suspect.

Rape. Clairvoyant man. History of assault and battery.

And many, many more of these words. Crimes, death, crimes with death, crimes with magic. He knew how it would happen, when it would happen, who would be involved, and how it would all unfold. It always, always came true. Whether it was reported on the news or not. And all Sammy needed to do was close his eyes and sleep. His dreams would show it all. Details of future crimes.

A gift to some. A curse to him.

And he didn't want it anymore. He did not want to know. Having seen it all unfold with intricate detail derailed his sanity. Seeing the certain tragedy that tomorrow would bring was pure misfortune. Besides the hemicrania and nightmares, there was the fact that people dismissed his warnings of their soon-coming demise as simple foolishness. Lunacy.

Sammy had learned that no matter how hard he tried to warn others or tell them to stop whatever they were doing hours before their downfall or death, what was written in his nightmares could not be prevented or altered.

So, the words needed to stop. The words *should* stop. He feared seeing the mysterious woman again. And now he knew how to stop them. He had been doing it for weeks, and it had been effective until now. Don't fall asleep. Strike himself with electrical energy.

His brain itched and he needed to scratch that itch again. He clawed his head with both hands and focused on casting the spell again. Sammy pictured lightning forming from the sky and striking the top of his head, clearing his brain of all those thoughts and words.

He rode another wave of hurt. His nerves burned and the thoughts of closing his eyes left his head, replaced with a blanket of blissful pain. Its white noise healed him of the ceaseless anxiety in him and robbed his sight of the words he vaguely saw forming in his mind.

He shook his head violently. But he was so tired. He yawned. His eyelids felt heavy.

Oh, so very tired…

***

Sammy was lounging in the open sea with a clear sky above him. The briny scent tickled his nose and the warm water enveloping him ebbed as the waves carried him away from his mindscape.

A black speck disturbed the blue of the sky. Sammy squinted and tried to make sense of the shape. He reckoned it was bigger than a bird given its height and speed. Perhaps it was a plane or blimp, or even a hot-air balloon. It sailed past his vision and off to the endless horizon.

He twisted himself around and dove deep into the sea. Its clarity granted him a view of its depths, revealing the corals and fish it hid. Sammy never paid attention to the fish growing up, but he knew of the blue tangs and clown fish from that one old, animated movie. They all swam in their own groups. One group of fish swarmed all over him before diving deeper to the depths. Their colorful fins enticed him to follow.

The sea depths turned from blue to green the deeper he went. The fish were still within his sight, but the ones leading the group were now as blurred and distant as the speck he saw in the sky before. Sammy squinted again and his eyes picked up a familiar shade of brown on the seafloor. Curiosity took over, and he broke away from the fish to pick up a board of dark hardwood. He looked around and saw a trail of the same wood scattered around.

Following the trail led him to a large sunken ship. Its side was punctured by holes, but otherwise it was intact. He entered from one of the holes and explored the cramped hallway leading him to a staircase that went downward. The single door there swung open when he approached, leading him to its confined space.

A stray piece of parchment floated in front of his face. He grabbed it with both hands and made out the letters written on it.

I, Agamemnon, have taken Cassandra as–

The rest of the words blurred into the nothingness. The waters grew darker as the sun dipped back into the earth.

The last thing he saw was a portrait of a woman behind the captain's desk.

Sammy's lungs cried for air and his eyes snapped open. He had been underwater for so long; he did not notice how much time passed.

His eyes adjusted to the blinding glow of white above and all around him. Its glare eased whenever he blinked, revealing the lines and marbled patterns of the ceiling and the few pieces of furniture in the room. His ears picked up the sounds of unfamiliar devices blinking and beeping beside him.

"Sammy! I am so glad you're alright."

He felt something envelop his right hand at the same time those words were uttered. He turned his head and met contact with soft green eyes. Sammy blinked again, realizing who this woman was. The seawater he plunged himself into burned his throat dry and made any attempt to utter words a struggle. The rest of his body was unresponsive, exhausted from the long dive.

He stretched his tired limbs and rubbed his glassy eyes.

Sammy watched as Ellie sighed and leaned on the backrest of her seat. "I found you passed out on the living room floor, babe. I had to call 911."

Passed out? What was she talking about?

"You had your hands on your head. The doc detected burn residues on your scalp," his girlfriend continued.

Doctor?

Sammy scanned the room again. There were no writings on the walls and no sheets of paper on the floor. None of the furniture was his, and the bed was uncomfortably softer than the bed he had gotten used to laying in. It was a room much brighter than his own back home. The screens beside him were monitoring his current condition.

A hospital room.

His eyes were drawn back to his girlfriend and the look in hers demanded an explanation of what happened. But also worry; a worry she had learned to live with in the past year. He gestured for a glass of water and struggled to sit himself up.

"I was by the beach and drowned," he answered.

"Babe, the beach is twenty minutes away from home. I found you by eight in the morning, which is minutes after your shift. Completely dry and–"

"No," he shook his head. "Trust me. My clothes were wet."

Ellie let out a deep sigh, turned away, and waved her hand. "Again, babe?"

Even if she hid her face from him, Sammy knew she was pouting. She always did whenever he tried to explain himself to her. It was as if she did not believe him anymore, even though he was telling her the truth. He knew he went to the beach after work to stop the itch in his head and to stop the dreams from coming back and eating his sanity alive.

Painful silence passed between them before Ellie faced him again and spoke. Even if she was smiling, he felt her eyes glaring at him. "Were you shocking yourself to keep awake?"

"Yes." He looked at his fingertips. There was a faint black residue in them.

Her head shook again. "You do realize that this could actually make you pass out instead, right? Which would, of course, create the opposite effect of which you were trying to avoid in the first place…?"

"Whatever. I know what I'm doing, Ellie."

Ellie took a deep breath. "Look, I didn't tell the doc. Just… don't do that again. The doc is giving you some medication to help with your situation. But, please, babe, I mean it; don't hurt yourself anymore. That's not healthy. And you need to sleep! This insomnia is going to kill you."

Sammy nodded, silently. If he spoke, she would be angry again. "Okay," he whispered. He just wanted to dismiss the whole thing. He didn't feel like explaining himself or even want to talk about it. She didn't understand, after all.

Sammy saw that Ellie knew *of* his situation, but she did not understand the full scope of his curse. He was not hurting himself; he was helping himself much better than any medication the doctors prescribed him could. And so far, nothing had worked. If the medicine was supposed to relieve him of his prophetic nightmares, how come it did not work after taking it for months? These were supposed to have sent him into dreamless nights the moment he took them, but they only spiraled him into worsening visions.

Before they could say anything else to each other, the doctor knocked on the door and came in to check up on him. His words were far emptier and distant than Ellie's. He rambled on about his weakened state and taking time off work to recover. He talked about MRI and CT results and how he was in danger. After watching Ellie do all the talking for him, the doctor left them alone with the news that he was free to go the next day.

***

Sammy struggled to climb into his girlfriend's car. Most of his muscles ached, and whenever he stood up and walked, his vision was a tipsy haze. He was glad she was driving him home.

"Sammy…" He looked back at her through her reflection in the rear-view mirror. "Be honest with me, babe. How many days have you stayed awake this time? I know I haven't been around because of my family, but I can't stop thinking about you..."

Sammy tried to recall, but every time he tried remembering dates or sunsets his mind clouded. "I… I honestly can't remember. I know I slept when you were around."

"So, almost three weeks, more or less. Wow, babe." Ellie's tongue clicked while she shifted around her seat to buckle her seatbelt. She turned to face him and asked him to look in her eyes. "You can die, Sammy! I think it's time for us to try something new."

How many times had she said that? The last time she mentioned another person who might help him he was put into a deep magic-induced sleep that had far more unsettling and nightmarish imagery than his precognitive dreams. He shuddered when he remembered the slick warmth of flesh walls and the stench of blood at every corridor in that nightmare. He'd dreamt about the serial killer in north county.

"We've already tried everything, Ellie. The neurologist charlatan only helped us lose more money than we earn. And I even consulted that psychic lady that–" Sammy stopped as he noticed his girlfriend's brow curl. "What?"

"Doctor Clarke is a renowned neurologist, Sammy. He's not a charlatan. If anything, that psychic lady is the charlatan. And besides, Dr. Clarke said that he'd never encountered your condition before. But at least he prescribed tried and tested medicine to help you ease up. He can't perform miracles on you, and he can't just prescribe the strongest dose without knowing how the current dose affects you. But you also have to do your part. Medicine doesn't work if you don't take it."

Sammy grunted. But before he could reply, Ellie cut the air with her hand as she placed her hands on the ignition to start the car. "Let's just talk more about this at home. For now, let's keep quiet and give you some mental rest. You need it, babe."

Sammy knew his girlfriend was trying her best to be supportive. But she was also irritated. She was tired and done, not knowing what to do about this plague of nightmares haunting him. He didn't know what to do either.

When they reached home, Ellie helped him out his side of the car and into the house. She eased him down on the living room sofa and sat beside him. Sammy noticed when she spotted the bottle of untouched medicine lying on the coffee table.

Sammy shrugged and looked at the floor.

"We still have to paint all those off, huh?" she looked around the walls.

Sammy nodded weakly. He felt her scoot closer to him and take both his hands in hers. He could see how she hid her annoyance with a look of concern.

"Sam, listen to me. Look in my eyes."

Sammy took a deep breath and turned towards his girlfriend. "What's up?"

"I know you're trying hard to fight your nightmares. I know how scared you must be of falling asleep. I know you've seen… well, bad things. And–"

"You don't even know, babe. That's the thing. You wouldn't understand," Sammy interrupted.

"But I am trying! I've seen you try so hard just to stay away from… from seeing whatever will happen the following day. And I wish I could do more for you. But I don't know what else to try, babe. I need you to help me help you. I know it's hard for you to trust anyone to help you, but you can trust *me*. I don't just want to hire any hypnotist or alchemist or psychic wizard or whatever mystical thing you think might help. I want real science. But I can't also send you to every medical specialist out there. I understand why you turned down the meds and even why you stopped going with the therapist. But… what I don't understand is why you're not at least doing what she recommended. At least trying. At this point, I feel like you gotta try harder, babe. I am really worried about you. You are so pale, skinny, and you look so weak."

"I did try, Ellie. I tried to write positive things, good memories, and happy thoughts, just as the therapist suggested. But it didn't work. All that happened was that I remembered all the other stuff

I'd written down the previous days. All the evil waiting to happen. So much… pain and death. And that's why I stopped. I feel like if I begin writing again, even if it's good things, I'll eventually start seeing those things again. Reliving them, as I did in my dreams."

Ellie caressed his cheek. "Okay. And what about the medicine then?"

"It's not working," Sammy whispered, looking down. "It's not working at all. I don't know why. I tried, I really did. They only knock me out. But every time that I go to sleep, I still have nightmares… things that will happen tomorrow. Always bad things."

Ellie nodded. "I'm sorry, babe." She put her arm around him and put her head on his shoulder. "So, you said you went to the beach. What did you do there?"

"I swam with the fish. There was a ruined ship on the sea floor."

Ellie raised her head and looked in his eyes. She opened her mouth, but stopped and shook her head. "Umm… and what did you see in the ship?" she finally asked.

"I saw a letter. The captain's name is Orpheus something, and the ship was called Tempest. There was a picture of a woman in his room."

"Is it the same tall woman from the rest of your nightmares?"

Sammy racked his brain and tried to remember how the woman looked like. He did not see much in the dark of the sea, but glancing at it made him think it was a woman. He remembered the long hair and the soft, warm gaze in her eyes. He remembered seeing the same figure present in almost every single one of his dreams. She would always be a bystander in most of the crimes he saw. Whenever he tried to approach her, she would disappear and he would wake from his sleep.

"Yeah... I think so. Probably the same one, though I'm not sure."

Ellie hummed and stood up. "I'm gonna make us some dinner. And then, I tell you what. We'll both take the sleeping pills so we can both pass out. And hopefully, you finally get some real rest."

Sammy nodded in agreement. "Okay."

Once dinner was finished, they both took the sleeping pills. Then Ellie gave Sammy the additional two medication pills that would supposedly help.

Sammy took the meds from her hand, and thought about it for a moment. Then, for the first time in weeks, he put them in his mouth, despite his wishes. He steeled himself to swallow the two bitter pills just to keep his girlfriend content.

He blinked once slowly and then twice rapidly. And on the third blink, he didn't open his eyes. Instead, Sammy saw the world shift around him again.

A powerful gust of wind blasted behind and almost threw him off balance. His legs fought to find balance, taking him a few feet forward before falling on his elbows and knees. His fingers clawed to find something to hold on to, caking his nails with grime the more he struggled. The gust softened to a lull just as he grabbed a slab of concrete in front of him.

When he turned, he noticed a jacketed female figure. Small, middle aged, blond hair, and a forgettable face. A soft shimmer glowed all over her body. He recognized it as a spell. Next to them was a wall of fire sprouting from a grill. The woman yelled at some people on the other side of the fire, telling them something about staying put and remaining calm. He couldn't really make out her words exactly, but he assumed that's what she meant.

His ears picked up the cries of young children, with the wind carrying the faded sound. He could sense the sparkly residue from the fire landing on the grass, catching the blades on fire and spreading all over the lawn. The intense heat made Sammy want to flee the scene. Instinct led his eyes to the first street sign he could find.

He saw the intersecting corner. Elm Street and Granada Avenue.

He turned again, only to find that the blonde lady had her hands on the grass. She was extinguish the flames. Or trying. Except she was only making it worse in her panic. The flames latched on her jacket and very quickly devoured the house, as if it was a large magical monster.

Sammy blinked again. He was now a few minutes into the future. The house was barely a house and now resembled a large campfire that was just extinguished. Several neighbors stood by the street witnessing the atrocity. The jacketed young woman sat by the firefighters with her hands covering her face. She was crying. Two pairs of paramedics carried two body bags in stretchers to an ambulance.

They were small body bags.

Sammy got closer, but no one seemed to notice him there, as if he was only a ghost. One of the paramedics passed by him while she cleared her sweat with her arm. Sammy gasped, remembering the wavy brown hair and indigo eyes. She then turned to him, making eye contact, and showed a subtle smile before disappearing behind his back and rousing him to the waking world.

Sammy choked on his own saliva and jolted from his bed, fully waking up. He coughed a few times. He saw Ellie sleeping next to him, so he tried to breathe and not cough again to evade waking her up.

It'd happened again. He'd dreamed of something that would happen today, and he could not stop it from happening, even if he tried to warn the residents on the house by Elm Street and Granada Avenue. Even if he wrote this dream down to remember it on a piece of paper or a blank space on the wall, nothing would happen. Even if he posted about it on social media or called the news or the cops, it would still happen. Because it always did, no matter what he did. And the last time he had said something he was ridiculed by the same people he'd try to save.

Once again, the prophetic nightmare was unavoidable. Inescapable.

And this was exactly why he didn't want to take the meds. This is why he'd evaded sleep for over two weeks now, even if it was killing him. Literally. But Ellie had convinced him that taking the meds and sleeping was for the best.

And now, the migraines were back. The dark walls around the bed were shifting, the words written on them shaking in place, some of them spiraling all around him, threatening to crash into him.

His brain needed electric soothing. Quickly.

While hyperventilating, Sammy closed his eyes, clenched his teeth, and placed his hands on his temples, focusing on shocking himself. He needed the pain. He required the electric agony to soothe his brain. To mitigate the migraine. He needed the magic lightning to jolt him and wake him up. To keep him sane.

He wanted to forget the dream and everything he'd witnessed in his mindscape moments ago. All before waking up Ellie once again.

But no jolt came.

He needed to concentrate better. He took a few quick breaths shook his hands. He needed to just one shock. One quick shock was all he needed to be fine. His unstable hands snaked to the sides of his head once again and his nails dug into his scalp, scratching the surface. Heat less intense than the flames that destroyed the house radiated from those spots he was itching. He willed it to burst through his skin and muscles, targeting the entirety of his brain.

"Don't do it, Sammy." This wasn't Ellie's voice.

He opened his eyes and glanced at his sleeping girlfriend lying next to him.

"What the hell?"

He closed his eyes again and concentrated on his fingertips. Jolts. Magical energy. Lighting.

Nothing.

"Ugh! Come on." He shook his hands rapidly and tried once more.

"Don't overdo it, Samuel," the voice said again. "I need you sharp."

Sammy opened his eyes. He felt cold. The sheets slipped through his hands and disappeared into the clear, shallow water. The rest of the room disappeared into a hazy cloud of indiscernible shapes. Darkness became light. Blacks turned a blueish hue.

He wasn't in his room anymore. And sitting beside him was the same tall woman who appeared in his dreams. She was about the same size as him, only wearing a long cloth around her, kept in place by a cord. The woman leaned in, their faces only inches apart. Sammy wanted to crawl away, but the woman's gaze entranced him. Her lips curled into the same subtle smile she showed him earlier in his prophetic dream.

"Who… what are you?" he asked.

The woman chuckled and shrugged her shoulders. "The only thing you need to know for now is that I know what you're going through."

Sammy tried to study the look in her indigo eyes and sensed the knowledge inside them. Her eyes were indiscriminate and calm as she spoke. Her voice was soft, as if he was her child.

"You've seen these dreams too?"

She nodded slowly and scooted closer. "In a manner of speaking."

How could this woman carry such an aura, even if she had the same problem? His eyes failed to turn away from her, awestruck by her flawless skin, warmth, and lithe figure. He wanted to reach his hand out and touch her, but he decided against it and clenched his fists. Maybe if he did, she would get angry and she would turn away from him. He wanted someone to talk to, someone who could understand him for once.

"I've seen you in all my dreams. In my nightmares."

The woman simply nodded, but didn't say a word.

"Did you try to stop them from happening? All the bad things?"

The mysterious woman gazed into the cloudy nothingness of the dreamscape, breaking eye contact with him. But even if she turned away, he felt her grip on him. Or rather, he felt her embrace him with the air she breathed. She had an invisible leash on him, as if to protect him from falling into his nightmares and keeping him grounded in the real world.

A chuckle escaped from her soft lips. She turned her head and faced him again, only for her eyes to wander past him. He followed her gaze to find Ellie lying with her back towards him, now on his other side. She was gripping the blanket with both hands.

"What do you think of her?"

His eyes shut when he felt fear and anger well up in his chest. Even if she was asleep, Sammy could feel her disappointment in him. But she also loved him and simply wanted the best for him.

She'd been patient in spite of all his shortcomings. And dealing with this curse couldn't have been easy on her. And for a second, he had a moment of clarity.

"She loves me. But she hates this curse. Maybe even more than I do. She doesn't understand me even if I explain everything to her."

"Is that so…?"

The woman stood from the air she was sitting on and circled the couple. She leaned close to Ellie, studying her face while she slept. Her hand brushed against his girlfriend's cheek. His girlfriend stirred from her sleep and tried to nod her soft hand off. She murmured something, but he was too distracted looking at the woman. He wished to feel her touch instead of her caressing someone else.

"Ellie seems like a nice person. She loves you, indeed."

"Yeah. Wait, how do you know her name? What is this?" Sammy stood up, suddenly realizing the ethereal atmosphere and the eeriness of the encounter. "Again, please tell me who you are."

The mysterious woman smiled and sat back down, peacefully coaxing him to sit next to her. Ellie and the bed disappeared once more, returning the two of them to the inch-high pool of water that stretched into the nonexistent horizon.

"Are you real?" Sammy sat down next to her, though cautiously. "I mean, I only see you in my dreams. What exactly are you?"

There was a sudden bright light that blinded him momentarily. Sammy blinked again. When he opened his eyes, he saw that they were back in his bedroom. They were sitting on the edge of his bed. The mysterious woman tugged on the blanket and to his surprise, it moved. He noticed her shadow on the wall and floor.

She was real?

"Flesh and bone," she said as she stood in front of him.

"Good morning," the familiar voice came from behind him, almost scaring him.

Sammy felt warm arms inching up his back and shoulders. He peeked behind his shoulder and saw Ellie wrap her arms around him. She planted a kiss on his shoulder, then rested her head on him. "Did you sleep well? I felt you moving around a lot."

"Yeah," he replied. The answer sapped the energy he had built from his sleep and from his conversation with the mysterious woman. And yet, the woman did not react or said anything.

"Did the medicine work? It did, right?" Ellie asked again. "I mean, it's already 8 a.m. We haven't slept in this well in a long time."

Sammy half nodded, half shook his head. "I don't know. I guess. I mean, I passed out. I don't even remember coming to bed last night. In fact, I don't remember anything about last night at all."

"Well, I guess that's great news, babe. Let's keep it up, okay? Let's make sure to take the meds every evening and–"

"No," Sammy said.

The answer made Ellie gasp. "What? No, what?"

Sammy balled his fists and breathed in, collecting himself. "I don't want to take them."

"But Sam–"

"I already told you, I don't want to."

"But didn't you just say that they worked?"

"They didn't work. I mean, yeah, they made me sleep. But I still had a nightmare. A horrible one. I saw a house that burned to the ground. Two kids died in front of me, Ellie. And I couldn't do anything. It's happening today. And I know I can't do anything about it."

The tall, mysterious woman from his dreams came closer and placed a hand on his shoulder. Only now did he realize that she was there, flesh and bone.

"You!" Sam said looking up at her as the woman smiled.

"Me what?" said Ellie.

"No, not you. Her." He pointed towards the woman.

Ellie rubbed her face with both hands and sat on the bed next to him, where the mysterious woman once sat.

"What are you talking about, Sammy? You're scaring me." She put a hand on his shoulder.

"I'm not scaring you." Sammy shook his upper body to make her hand fall.

"Babe, calm down. What's going on? Let's talk about this dream of yours."

"The woman in my dreams talked to me," he said, still looking at her eyes.

Ellie slowly tilted her head. "Really? What did she say?"

"She also had the same dreams." Sammy then turned his head, facing the mysterious woman. "Right?"

"Of course, Sam," the lady in the long, silver cloth gown replied.

"Who are you talking to?" Ellie asked, following his gaze.

Sammy blinked slowly. He looked to Ellie, then the woman, then to his girlfriend again. He could feel her weight on him, and her warm breaths tickled the back of his neck. His hand ran through the woman's cloth. "The woman. She's right here listening to us. Look at her."

A bewildered look on Ellie's face appeared while she turned her head sideways.

"Nice to meet you, Ellie. I am Samantha, the woman in his dreams."

Ellie rubbed her eyes with one hand and blinked several times at his direction. There was a mix of anger, confusion, and exhaustion in her eyes. "There's… there is no one here, Sammy. It's just the two of us. What is going on?"

Sammy felt his body temperature rise with anger. His muscles tensed. Did she really not want to believe him? She was right there in front of him! She was real. What did she mean there was no one there? Why was Ellie blind to her?

Or was she just pretending she didn't see the other woman?

"Are you saying I'm crazy?" Sammy snapped. He stood up, clinching his fist.

"She doesn't seem to want my presence," the woman whispered in his ear.

"She even greeted you. She is *right here*!" He pulled at the woman's cloth dress.

"I *am* right here," the woman echoed.

"Babe," Ellie stood up, eyes glassy. "There is no one else here but you and me. I don't see anyone beside you, or behind you. And I didn't hear anyone else apart from you talk to me. You are scaring me, Sammy." Ellie was embracing herself and evidently holding tears back.

Sammy grunted. "This is ridiculous. First, you wouldn't believe me about my nightmares and their predictions. And now this?"

"Samuel," Ellie called him using his first name, something she never did. "Enough! I've done nothing but support you. I believed you about your nightmares and your sleep phobia. I have. I even took you to get help. However, like I already told you, not all of the crimes that your dreams predicted came true. Only some of them happened. But… now you are imagining things. This… woman from your dreams… she is not real, and she is certainly not here. There is no magic, babe. No mysterious woman that gives you prophecies. You're simply losing it."

Sammy could not believe his ears. How dare she accuse him of falsifying information? How dare she say he was crazy, especially when this gift had come at such a toll on his physical and emotional being?

"Screw you, Ellie. I see it now. You just want to sedate me and control me. You're not trying to help me at all."

"Babe. Don't…"

"Don't 'babe' me. Get out. Take your shit and get out of my house. Now!"

Ellie looked at him, not able to withhold her tears anymore. She ran to the bathroom and grabbed some stuff, rapidly throwing it into her purse. She put on her pants and shoes as fast as she could. "Screw this!" she yelled as she left.

Sammy and Samantha simply watched her without saying a word.

Ellie walked to the apartment entrance door and turned around. "You've finally lost it, Sam. You really have. I've been so patient, but this is too much now. I'm done. Not sleeping for weeks has truly made you crazy. But I'm done. Find someone else to take care of you now." She slammed the door behind her.

"She doesn't deserve you, Sammy. You are special and she couldn't see it." The mysterious woman went for a drink of water in the kitchen. "I thought she could be useful, but I see clearly now that we'll be better off without her. I need you for this mission and she would've only gotten in the way. I know you don't want to dream anymore, but I need you to be my messenger. I need you to finally succumb into my grasp and surrender to your gift… it's time to use it for good."

She came back and gave Sammy a glass of water. He drank it all in record time, not taking a single break to breathe. Some of it dripped onto his shirt.

"I think I am ready," he said. "I was scared, but now I see it. I can make a difference. I think I know why I've been given this gift. It's not a curse, and I have a responsibility to the world to stop these crimes before they ever happen."

"Now you're getting it," the woman was saying as there was a knock on the door.

Sammy took a heavy sigh and walked to the door as the knock came again. He blasted it fully open, "What do you want now, Ellie?" he was asking.

Except, it wasn't Ellie.

"Samuel Rivera?" one of the two uniformed men standing asked.

"Yes?"

"San Diego PD." Both men showed their badges. "May we come in?"

Sammy looked back at the woman who simply shrugged. "What is this about?" he asked the officers.

"We just have a few questions to ask you."

"We'd like to clear up a few things," added the shorter, younger one, trying to take a peek inside his apartment.

Sammy instinctively moved, blocking the view of the officers into his home. "Questions about what? I don't understand what this is concerning." He closed the door halfway.

"Mr. Rivera, there's been a series of events happening around the city, and we are wondering if you could clear up a few things for us."

"Ah, yes." Sammy opened his eyes wide open. "I was wondering when you were going to finally start taking me serious. I tried calling several times to warn you before. But you all thought I was crazy. I even tried to reach the victims, but–"

"Samuel…" the short one interrupted him. "May I call you Samuel?" He continued without giving Sammy a chance to respond. "There was a fire last night. There were multiple people who witnessed a… um… a drag queen. This person is wanted under suspicion of arson. What's interesting, however, is that this… drag queen got onto a bike. A bike just like yours, Samuel."

Sammy was confused.

"A fire? Yes, I dreamt about it. I was gonna call about it to see if we could prevent it. By the corner of Elm Street and–"

"Granada Avenue," the tall, darker officer finished for him. "Green house. The same. Two children died, Mr. Rivera. What do you know about that?"

"Like I said, I dreamt it. I have these nigthm… these visions. I can see the future. I usually write them all down. Come in." Sammy opened the door and allowed the officers to come in. Sammy raised his arm to show his art throughout his apartment. On the walls, on the floor. Even in the ceiling. Details. Crimes. Some major, some minor. "I've been having all these visions for some time now. I tried to suppress it. I haven't been sleeping very well. But I now see how this is a gift, and I am ready to help now. Samantha… she's been helping me." Sammy pointed towards the tall woman in the kitchen who waved at the officers.

The officers looked at each other, then walked around, carefully reading Sammy's chaotic scribbles throughout the place. They looked at each other again.

"How do you know of all these details, Mr. Rivera? Some of these things are things that only the police know about."

"Like I said, I dream them. And I write them down before I forget them. I was going to write down about the fire too, but I had an altercation with my girl… ex-girlfriend. Actually, funny story, I thought it was her who was knocking on the door. That's why I–"

"Samuel Rivera, you have the right to remain silent," the short, stocky officer suddenly placed handcuffs on him. "Anything you say can and will be used against you in a court of law. You have the right to an–"

"What the hell are you doing?" Sammy demanded. "I'm only trying to help!" He tried fighting them.

"It's okay, Sammy," the woman told him. "I'll get you out. They're foolish, just like Ellie, but soon they will see the truth."

"If you cannot afford an attorney…"

"What is going on?" Ellie yelled from the open the door.

"And who might you be?" the tall, dark skinned officer asked.

"I'm Ellie, Sammy's girl… ex-girlfriend. I forgot my phone charger, so I came back for it. What is going on?" She walked into the living room, tramping over the hundreds of papers scattered across.

"We are taking Sammy under suspicion of arson."

"And other stuff," the shorter one added.

"Babe, tell them! Tell them the truth, Ellie. Tell them about my gift." They were walking Sammy out.

"It's okay, Sam," Samantha said, "I'll take care of you wherever they take you. Nothing can stop us. You are special, remember that."

"I *am* special," Sammy said.

"Arson?" Ellie questioned. "When? He was in the hospital, and I've been with him for the past, I don't know, twenty hours or so."

The two officers looked at each other.

"There was a fire last night. And several witnesses–"

"Last night? I was with him all night!" Ellie told him. "You have the wrong man. Sammy needs help, but he is innocent."

"Sorry, miss. We can figure all that out at the station. We might need you to come along as well. We might have some questions for you."

"I'll follow you. Let me just get some stuff."

With that, the officers took Sammy away, leaving Ellie alone in the apartment.

"Woman!" Sammy screamed. "Woman, help me."

The woman appeared in front of Sammy, outside the apartments. "Go to sleep, Sammy. Just close your eyes, and I'll take it from here."

As he was dragged away, Sammy willed himself to sleep.

There was an ocean, and he was flying above it… Samantha, the tall, enigmatic woman flying next to him, holding his hand. He smiled.

It would be okay.

***

Ellie ran towards the room to get her charger plugged in by her side of the bed. She then remembered she had some of her clothes still in the closet. She figured she might as well take all her belongings already. She wasn't planning on coming back here, after all. Sammy and she were done. This time for good.

She walked around the bed and opened the closet door. She noticed something strange in the floor, but didn't pay much attention. She began to collect a couple of her dresses, blouses, and jackets hanging. She pulled them out and placed them on top of the bed. She looked at her clothes and took a deep breath.

This was really it. Three years of her life down the drain.

She turned and went back to the closet, but now, in plain sight, she saw it. There was a long gown, obviously homemade, with some sort of silver cloth, hanging on the end. Above it, by the corner, there was a woman's wig. Brunette curly hair. She grabbed it and turned towards the bed.

She noticed from that angle, in the bottom corner of the bed, almost hidden, that there was a car battery with cables. An electrocution device.

"What in the world?"

She put the gown and wig on the bed and pulled out the device. She ran her finger over the gown as it had some black dust on it. Was that… ash residue? It looked recent, though she had no way of knowing for sure.

"Oh, Sammy… what have you done?"

Her mind raced through the past weeks. To the past night. Had she been completely out? Was he out while she was asleep?

And the reality of it all shook her. Her hands trembled.

There was no magic, of course. She knew that all along. However, she now truly finally realized that there were no prophetic nightmares either. And there was no mysterious woman. Sammy *was* the "woman" in his dreams, and he'd probably caused all those atrocious crimes himself.

Sammy was no necromancer nor a gifted prophet, but simply a man with major psychological issues. She knew he needed help, she just didn't realize to what extent. But it all made sense now. Her hands shook as tears fell down.

Sammy needed help, and she'd help him.

Ellie quickly ran towards the kitchen for a plastic bag and came back. She took the wig and gown and threw them in. And then she walked out of the apartment.

TATA'S SECRET

Myrna stood in the bright California sunbeams slanting into her kitchen and smiled at the crowded counter. Tata's secret mole recipe included an ungodly number of ingredients—from plantains and chicken broth to cinnamon sticks—but that was part of the joy of making it. She cackled to herself as she cut bread for morning toast.

Heavy footsteps, and Myrna turned just in time to see Joseph stop dead in the door frame. "Oh, no," he said in horror, eyes playing over the packages, bowls, and cans. "You're not going to make that mole again, are you?"

Myrna swatted him with a dishtowel. "You have no faith," she scolded good-naturedly. "This time it will come out!"

"You say that *every* time," her husband sighed as he proceeded further into the kitchen. He picked up the Mexican chocolate and gave another deep, despairing sigh. "What a waste of good chocolate."

Myrna took the hexagonal yellow package from him and put it on the counter again. "This is verbal and psychological abuse, you know," she declared with a wink. "Domestic violence."

"*Domestic violence* is one of those crazy meals you insist on serving Joey and me at least three times a week. Come on, Myrna, the last time you cooked this mole Joey actually threw up!"

"Joey *just* turned three; his stomach is still developing. But he'll learn to love it, you'll see."

"And the time before that we had to throw it all away. Even *you* couldn't eat it. Admit it, babe…you're just…not good at cooking those recipes."

"My Tata Dan cooks those recipes," Myrna said defensively. "And he's a maestro celebrity chef! He has movie stars and world leaders eating in his restaurant! It's in my blood! I'm his only grandchild."

Joseph chuckled. "Yeah, honey, but that's your grandfather, not you. You couldn't make one of his recipes come off right to save your life!"

"I grew up in his kitchen. He fed this food to me every day. And I love making his food. It feels…" She cast around for the right description. "It feels *right* for me to make his food, Joseph. I love making it. Even if it doesn't come out right every time." Myrna's voice went small. "Even if doesn't come out right *any* time."

Joseph's eyes softened. "I get it, honey." He leaned down to kiss her cheek. "Keep cooking what you want. I know it makes you happy." His eyes danced. "Just as long as you don't mind me ordering pizza on mole night."

Myrna laughed and gave him another light swat. "You're such a punk!"

"Yeah, but you love delivery pizza too, don't lie." Joseph laughed as he slid the bread slices into the toaster.

As Joseph finished making breakfast, Myrna went upstairs to rouse Joey from his slumber. *Aren't three-year-olds supposed to be balls of energy in the morning?* she wondered as she hauled her son's semi-conscious body from his truck-shaped bed.

"Lemme lone," murmured Joey, blinking sleep-creased eyes.

"Come on, baby; you've got playgroup today!"

"Hate playgroup," grumbled Joey as Myrna tugged him over to the closet to be dressed. "Wanna sleep."

"Well, even if you didn't have playgroup, you'd still have to get up. Come on now, up and at 'em."

"Are you cooking again, Mom?" Joey asked, yawning.

Myrna beamed at her son. It seemed love of food really was genetic. "Yes, I am, Joey. Tonight."

Joey's eyes went wide, all trace of sleepiness gone. "Oh, *no*!"

Myrna sighed as the toddler began sobbing and crying and begging her not to cook him any dinner. What a horrible family she had, she thought. None of them had any faith in her cooking.

Myrna finally got Joey downstairs, where Joseph shoveled breakfast into him before sweeping him out the door. Joseph was generally the one to drop Joey off at playgroup, since his job started later than Myrna's, at least on Wednesdays, Thursdays, and Fridays; on Mondays and Tuesdays the nanny came in early as both Myrna and Joseph both whirled off to work by six.

It took advanced timekeeping skills just to keep up with their schedules, Myrna often reflected wryly. No wonder she never could master any of her grandfather's recipes—when did she have *time*?

Well, at least today was a work-from-home day. Myrna busied herself cleaning up from breakfast and setting up her at-home workstation as the day brightened outside and the neighborhood of Silver Lake in Los Angeles awoke in an outcry of traffic and the early-morning activity of countless human beings.

Myrna was just settling into her lovely, luxurious at-home workday, sipping coffee and opening her software, when her phone buzzed. Taking it out, she blinked in surprise at the caller ID before she put it to her ear. "Mom?"

"Myrna?" Brenda's voice came down the line, sounding strange and underwater. "Oh, thank goodness, *mija.* I thought maybe you wouldn't pick up."

Myrna felt a familiar stab of guilt: she hadn't gone to see her mother in so long, even though she lived right here in the Los Angeles metro area, just on the other side of the hills. It had been even longer since she'd last been to see Tata, and he lived even closer in Los Feliz. Of course, they were all very busy: Brenda still worked fulltime and Tata had his restaurants to run, not to mention numerous appearances on cooking shows. And ever since Joey had been born, it had been more difficult than ever for Myrna to set up a time to see everyone. It had been too easy just to let it slide.

"Why wouldn't I pick up, Mom?" she asked, trying for a teasing tone.

"Well, you never know. You could be making soup, or not powered up your phone, or be busy talking to one of your clients. You're a busy professional woman, I've always understood that, so if you didn't pick up, I was planning on leaving a message—"

"Mom." Myrna put off her mother's babbling, gently but firmly. "What is it you wanted to say to me?"

A long pause. "It's Tata, Myrna. It's your grandfather."

"What about him?" Myrna asked, though she suspected she already knew. Her heart sank down a long, dark pit.

Sure enough: "He's dead, Myrna. The nurse found him dead in his bed this morning."

It was another glaring, brilliantly sunny day when the white Honda Fit pulled up in front of the empty house. Myrna cut the engine and sat in the sudden silence, looking at her grandfather's hillside house.

Brenda had insisted that she go. *It's fine, sweetie,* she'd said. *It was good of you to come stay with me, and bring Joey with you. But you should go to your grandfather's place, see if there's anything you want. He'd like you to have some personal keepsakes, at least. I'll look after Joey for the afternoon, it'll be fine.*

You're sure? Myrna had said doubtfully.

Go on, girl, go to your grandfather's, said Brenda, waving a hand. *Let me have some time with my only grandson.*

And so, Myrna had gone, driving through LA's endless snarl of traffic to the bright white hacienda-style house that had belonged to Dan Molina, celebrity chef, and his beloved wife, rest in peace. It was in one of LA's more affluent neighborhoods, naturally, all sprinklers and velvet lawns and well-clipped oleanders. Tata's hacienda boasted its own neat square of green grass before it, just starting to go brown as it had stopped receiving its scheduled drinks.

She should take care of that, Myrna reflected as she exited the car, slamming the door shut behind her. Or perhaps not. Perhaps it was only appropriate that, after Tata died, his house should begin to die with him.

She took a heavy sigh and opened the front door, fumbling with her keys. She closed her eyes against the gust of cool air that greeted her. It was imbued with the past: she could still smell all the scents of her grandfather. Onions predominated, and also spices and chili, and a hint of the aftershave he always used. But it was starting to fade now, Tata's scent. Already it had died from her nose.

Myrna proceeded hesitantly into the house—the same house she'd grown up in. It was cool and dark inside, most of the blinds drawn, but she could still see clearly just how little had changed. Tata and Nana had gone for the comfortable rather than the stylish, with puffy sofas and shaggy rugs, which had been perfect for Myrna as a child. She remembered many happy hours spent playing in the white-painted hallways of Tata and Nana's house, leaping from sofas and sliding along the polished wooden floors, while Tata laughed and called advice from the kitchen, where he stood over his stove.

Myrna had to close her eyes again, breathing hard.

When she could move again, she headed further in. Her eyes played over the photographs mounted on the living room walls behind glass: photos from her grandparents' childhood in Mexico, where Tata had learned to cook from his own grandmother; their wedding pictures; numerous portraits of Brenda as a child and others when she was older; and portraits too of Myrna, Tata and Nana's only grandchild and the product of an unmarried teenage pregnancy. But there were awards and certificates too: large, important-looking pieces of paper proving that Daniel Molina had won many prizes in cooking Mexican food, cooking in the state of California, cooking in the American Southwest, and cooking generally. There were photographs of Tata standing before his stove in his restaurant kitchen, him posing with the restaurant staff, Tata catering all kinds of events for the rich and famous. There was even a picture of Tata catering an event at the White House, and another of him serving food to some former president of Mexico. Tata had gone everywhere, even as his restaurant chain back in California grew.

Myrna wondered what on Earth she and her mother Brenda were going to do with the restaurants. Her Nana was long gone, and they were now the sole inheritors of Tata's food empire. Myrna Garza and Brenda Molina now owned controlling shares, and Brenda and her husband were already very active in the chain's administration. But they needed to find a chef for the flagship restaurant here in Los Angeles. But where could they possibly find one to replace Tata? Not just his cooking, but his personality.

Myrna remembered the roars of laughter from the restaurant patrons and the standing ovations whenever Dan Molina came out give one of his quasi-speeches, quasi-performances. One of his best acts had been to roll out tortillas and toss them around the dining area like Frisbees, to much acclaim from the crowd. How could they ever replace that? And the restaurant here in LA was famous, with many important patrons. If the quality of food and service declined there, it would decline everywhere.

Myrna pushed away such mercenary thoughts. Now wasn't the time for them. She continued her tour of her grandparent's house, where she lived until she was eighteen.

Her footsteps rang hollow in the corridors as she peered into every room, all the while fighting the feeling that he was just about to appear around the next corner. She even caught herself poking her head out the sliding glass door to the backyard, expecting to see him snoring in his favorite deck chair, a paperback book draped over his face. The deck chair was still there, but it stood sad and empty, the absence of Tata like a shimmering ghost.

Myrna deliberately left the kitchen until the last. She knew it was going to be the hardest room to face. She hesitated a long moment before stepping in, crossing the threshold from wood to linoleum.

Sunlight dazzled blindingly off the steel faucet, and Myrna squinted her eyes shut. When she opened them again, tears filled them. For this was her Tata's kitchen: the room where he'd spent most of his time, his continent of wonders, his wizard's workshop, where he had conjured all his most famous recipes. Where his food became magical.

Myrna meandered around, touching things at random: the two refrigerators, the vast stove, the shiny oven door. She ran her fingertips over the mixers and blenders, the *tortillera*, the ancient stone *molcajete*, and smiled at the archaic crayon drawing she'd presented to Tata as a child. How amazing and how marvelous that Tata had kept it after all these years.

Myrna went to the window, overlooking the backyard. This deep, wooden windowsill had been something of a shrine for Tata—he'd kept all his most important awards pinned to the wall here, along with photographs and other *papeles importantes,* as he'd termed them. The sill itself, however, was dominated by a small wooden chest elaborately carved in Mayan designs. It stood on the sill now, squat and heavy on its wooden legs.

Myrna looked at it a long moment. Tata had always forbidden her to try and open this chest, or even touch it. *It's special, mija,* he'd said. *It contains some of my most important things.* Young Myrna had naturally been intrigued, but had never gotten the chance to explore—Tata had always seemed to know when she was getting too close, and appeared as if from nowhere to smack her hand back.

But there was no one to smack her hand this time. Nana had been gone for decades, and now Tata was gone too.

Fighting the wave of sorrow this caused, Myrna took hold of the chest's heavy lid and swung it open.

She wasn't sure what she expected to find inside, but it wasn't this. Slowly, Myrna reached in and took out the notebook.

It was a plain, spiral-bound notebook with a red cover, very ordinary in every respect. She turned it over in her hands, studying it in bemusement: such a mundane thing to be kept in Tata's special, secret chest. She checked the box's interior, but it was empty. This one notebook was all it contained. Why did Tata guard it with such zeal?

Myrna flipped the book over and opened it, flicking through the pages. They were all covered in Tata's untidy scrawl, in pencil and ballpoint pen. Recipes, Myrna realized: these were Tata's recipes.

But also something else.

At this, her heart began to pound, and her hand shook a little. Trembling all over with euphoric excitement, she hurried to sit down at the table and laid the notebook down with considerably more reverence. She opened the book carefully, and looked to see which page she had landed on.

The recipe for his special Mexican mole. A smile tugged Myrna's lips. How appropriate.

"Your mole, Tata," she said aloud as she laid a finger on the recipe, tracing her grandfather's handwriting. "How magical." She smiled.

It was only then that it happened.

***

When Joseph returned home from work that night, he was greeted by his son, hurtling up to throw his arms around his legs. "Daddy," Joey whispered in horror, "Mommy's *cooking* again!"

"Shh, Joey. We have to be kind to Mommy, okay, baby? Her Tata just died. So let's make sure we are super nice..." Lifting Joey into his arms, Joseph strode into the kitchen, where Myrna was indeed standing over a steaming pot of—Joseph groaned internally—Mexican mole. Restraining a sigh of resignation,

Joseph leaned in to kiss her on the cheek. "Hey, honey," he said gently. "How did it go today?"

The look she gave him was surprisingly bright-eyed and chirpy. "It went well, actually," she said cheerfully. She stirred her mole on the large pot, letting some of it drip down from the wooden spoon. "Better than I expected. I made the most amazing discovery."

"Really? What?" Joey was wriggling in Joseph's arms, so he let the toddler slide down. Joey tugged on his mother's apron.

"Mommy? Do we have to eat that food again?" he whined.

"How sharper than a serpent's tooth, is a son's ingratitude," Myrna misquoted tranquilly. She dipped her spoon into the mole again and held it out to Joseph. "Here, honey. Have a taste."

Despite his own resolution to be nice, Joseph backed up. "Uh, Myrna, I, ah—"

"Come on, Joseph. Please?" Myrna jabbed the spoon at him threateningly.

Joseph gave another internal sigh. There really was no way out of it, he supposed. Leaning in, he sipped a tiny amount of mole off the spoon.

Joseph's eyes flew open. "Myrna…"

Myrna waited, a smug smile on her lips.

"Myrna…this is *good*!" Joseph tasted more off the spoon. "Actually—wow! This is *amazing*! This is the best mole I've had! As in, ever."

Myrna had to snatch the spoon back, laughing. "As good as my grandfather's?"

"At least as good as Tata Dan's," Joseph said fervently. He stared at his wife. "Myrna, how…? What did you do differently?"

"I followed Tata's old recipe," said Myrna, returning serenely to her mole pot.

"But…you've followed his recipes before. Many times before. And, yet, they never come out so well," Joseph said. "Come on, Myrna, spill it. What's different about this recipe?" He took a whiff of the aroma.

Myrna gave the mole one last stir and turned off the heat. "I didn't just follow the recipe this time," she said in a quiet, reflective tone, staring down at her creation. "I *led* it." She heaved the pot off the heating element. "Come on. I made some chicken to go with it and Mexican rice. Let's get to eating it."

Myrna and Joseph carried all the steaming dishes into the dining room, where Myrna had already laid out the best china, with gleaming cutlery and colorful Mexican napkins. Joey hopped into his usual place, a high chair on Myrna's side, and, settling down, the family began to eat.

Joseph initially braced himself to take a bite—Myrna's chicken was always too dry and too tough—but the fowl melted in his mouth, the perfect texture and temperature, juices exploding in his mouth. He poured on a ladle of mole over his meat, and the results, at his next bite, were even better. "Oh, my! This is… lovely." He smiled.

Myrna smiled back at him. She looked more beautiful than ever.

Joseph couldn't put it together. What had she done? Was it the hairdo? That dress? Whatever it was, she was as lovely as her meal.

As he ate, a strange feeling came over Joseph. He looked at his wife, misty-eyed. "Myrna," he said softly, "do you remember our wedding?"

"Of course I do," she said, smiling at him. "We got married in that beautiful day at Descanso Gardens. The day I became Mrs. Garza." Her face glowed with her smile.

"That was a wonderful day," Joseph said. "Do you remember the weather? It was so perfect—so sunny, and not too hot or too dry. You were wearing this amazing Mexican dress that your great-aunt…"

"I've still got it, you know. Hanging in my closet." Myrna's voice was growing soft with nostalgia too. Around them, the soft, warm breezes of their wedding day puffed under a clear blue sky. "You were wearing a gray suit. You looked so handsome, waiting under the arch made of roses." The scent of roses wafted through the dining room, and a few stray petals blew across the table.

Myrna and Joseph, wrapped up in their memories and adding more and more details, did not notice the magic happening around them. Joey merely giggled and tried to catch the petals. He was too young and too innocent to realize that things like this did not usually happen, even when mole was made right.

***

"You know, Myrna," said Joseph a few days later as he and Myrna cleaned up the kitchen after yet another fantastic meal, "you should really think about taking over as chef at your grandpa's restaurant."

Myrna looked up from sweeping the floor. "Chef? Me?" She laughed aloud.

"Why not?" Joseph rinsed off another casserole dish. "Your cooking's gotten so great lately. And you've always loved the idea of following into your family's line of work." His face went soft with wonder. "Besides, every time I eat one of your dishes now, I feel…I don't know. Happy inside. Like there's only good memories, nothing bad. Every meal is magical." His eyes were dreamy.

"Yeah. Maybe," said Myrna, smiling mysteriously, "but that doesn't mean I know how to run a restaurant kitchen, you know. It's intense back there."

"Just think about it, though. You already know a lot about the restaurant business. And Dan Molina's granddaughter, carrying on the family tradition, would be fantastic PR!" His face lit with professional delight. "I could totally run your new publicity campaign."

"Thanks, my love." Myrna kissed his cheek. "I'll think about it."

Joseph put aside the dish to drain. "Well, you really should. I don't know what's happened to you, but all I know is that you sure need to share this new food with the world!"

"It's not *new* food, Joseph. It's just… food made right."

"Here's a thought." Joseph turned to face her fully, eyes alight. "Why don't you cook the banquet at your grandfather's funeral."

Myrna's smile faded. "Joseph… I couldn't…"

"You *could*," Joseph insisted. "Lots of important people will be coming, won't they? And they'll be expecting to eat your Tata's famous cooking."

"The restaurant staff already has it covered, Joseph. And Mom's getting it all organized."

"Can't you at least make the mole sauce?" Joseph pleaded. "Come on, your mole has turned, like, nuclear amazing!"

"You mean it gives people radiation poisoning?" Myrna laughed. But, despite herself, she was starting to catch Joseph's enthusiasm. He was right—her cooking *had* improved beyond all knowledge. And it *would* be wonderful if she could carry on her family's tradition.

What Joseph didn't know, of course, was that Myrna already *was* carrying on family tradition now, every time she turned on the heat on her stove, or stirred a soup, or baked a cake. Every time she cooked anything, in fact. She couldn't help it. She was carrying on tradition, but in a way nobody could possibly have imagined. Except, perhaps, Tata.

At the thought of her grandfather, something caught in her heart. Myrna bit her lip. "All right," she said at last. "I'll call Mom and see if I can't make the mole sauce at least. It's probably what Tata would have wanted."

***

The day of Chef Dan Molina's funeral dawned soft and warm.

Myrna Garza, dressed in somber black, greeted attendees in the vestibule of the events center with her mother, shaking hands and accepting condolences with total strangers: star chefs, famous food critics, important patrons who had eaten so many of Tata's wonderful meals.

"A fine, fine man," said a tall white man who Myrna recognized as a former U.S. senator, though she couldn't recall his name. "I remember once, we were all eating in the private dining room of his restaurant here in LA, and the conversation, well, got a little heated." He laughed self-consciously. "Just as we were all about to stab each other in the eyes with our forks, your grandfather walks in, juggling wineglasses! We couldn't believe our eyes! We totally forgot to fight, and he kept us entertained for over an hour. Amazing man." He shook his head wonderingly. "Do you have any plans to take over the restaurant, Mrs. Garza?"

"My mother and I now…we already own controlling shares," said Myrna. "As for the cooking part, though…well, I guess we'll see." Indeed they would. Myrna's stomach tightened with nerves, thinking of the banquet to come later.

Speaking of which… Myrna excused herself and snuck quietly away from the tide of well-wishers, to run down a corridor and dash into the huge industrial kitchen, swarming with activity with uniformed men and women.

"Sorry, coming through. Sorry!" Myrna ducked and dashed around the hurrying restaurant staff to the vast, bubbling cauldron of mole. Its scent washed over her, an almost perfect blend of spices, nuts, sugar, chiles, chocolate…but it needed a little extra. Myrna sprinkled a dash of something and stirred it in.

There.

"Relax, boss!" Alma Rodriguez, one of Tata's chief cooks, stepped in with a laugh, startling her. "You got it started, now I've got it covered."

"Thanks, Alma." Myrna smiled. "But you know I'm not actually your boss, right?"

"You're the old man's granddaughter, which is good enough for me." Alma waved her off. "Now, go on. You've got to kiss some more ass, for the good of the restaurant and the Molina name."

"Wow, you make it sound like so much fun," Myrna quipped, rolling her eyes and earning herself a swat with the dishtowel. Myrna escaped amid a gale of laughter, to return to, as Alma put so eloquently put it, more ass kissing.

The funeral itself, when it finally began, seemed to take forever. As the eulogies droned on, from a seemingly endless parade of celebrity chefs and critics, Myrna sat in a purgatory of grief, boredom, and tension. Her eyes kept darting to the side door of the small auditorium. How would everyone react when…? She wished so much that Joseph was here, but someone had to look after Joey. He and their son would appear after the surprise.

Finally, it came time for Myrna's own eulogy. She stood up in a sway of black skirt that matched her hair and heels. Clutching her notes, she walked to the podium.

The auditorium seemed much larger from here, full of unfamiliar, expectant faces. Tata's flower-draped coffin also seemed far harder to ignore. Myrna fumbled with her notes behind the microphone. If she couldn't pull this off… *Tata, please, help me.*

And then she saw him. Dan Molina, her Tata. Standing unobtrusively at the back of the crowd, wearing his old apron. Anyone, seeing him, might have thought he was one of the catering staff. He smiled at Myrna and gave a friendly, affectionate wave and eyeroll at the crowd. *Go on, mija. Give 'em a good show.* He tilted his hat.

Myrna knew she was imagining things. Though, with her recent discovery, she wasn't sure. She readjusted her notes on the podium and cleared her throat.

"Friends and family," said Myrna, amplified voice ringing across the auditorium through the speakers. "People who knew and loved Daniel Molina. I welcome you all here, just as he always welcomed everyone into his restaurant and into his life. My Tata was known and loved across the nation as a great chef and a colorful character—and a fine and generous man. He served presidents, dignitaries, and movie stars in his restaurant. And yet, every Wednesday evening, he gave free meals to anyone who came to the kitchen door. Tata believed that good food was for everyone, and that everyone deserved to be fed well."

Myrna paused. In the front row, her mother Brenda was wiping away tears, but she was smiling too.

"The fondest memories of my childhood are of playing in my Tata's kitchen. We'd lost my Nana very early on, but he was the only grandparent a growing girl ever needed. And I was lucky to have him in my life. It was always sunny and warm, in my memories, and my Tata was always cooking something delicious. I still remember the sombrero-shaped cake he made for my eighth birthday, with eight exploding candles. I thought my cake would blow up when he lit the candles!" Myrna paused for everyone to stop laughing. "That was Tata—he always had a surprise up his sleeve." She cleared her own tears. "And so, in the spirit of Dan Molina, I have a surprise for you."

Myrna sneakily pressed the alert app on her phone and, almost instantly—for they had been waiting—all the doors to the auditorium opened and the staff trundled in the cloth-draped carts. Behind them came a live Mariachi band, guitars at the ready.

The funeral attendees all gasped and cried out as, with a flourish, the staff lifted the silver lids and the scents of the food wafted out, to a fanfare from the musicians. All of Dan Molina's signature dishes lay ready for consumption—with many earthenware pots containing steaming mole sauce.

"As we celebrate Chef Molina's—my Tata's—life, let's all eat here, with him, together one last time," said Myrna. "It's what he would have wanted."

She descended the podium to cheers and applause as the Mariachi started playing in earnest and everyone got to their feet, eager to line up and start eating. Myrna and Alma got all the attendees organized, making sure they all got plates and bowls and cutlery, and a happy chatter arose as everyone got their food. Soon happy moans and expressions of joy lit up around the auditorium as the delightful tastes hit their tongues.

Myrna was just eating her own turkey mole when Joseph ducked in, Joey on his hip. "So how's it going, babe?" he asked, kissing her on the cheek.

"Fabulously." Myrna waved her hand. "Take a look around."

Joseph looked, and everywhere he saw delight, contentment, and joy. Every face seemed suffused with happiness. Funeral attendees laughed and chattered, or they just chewed, expressions full of near-ecstatic concentration. Sighs and moans rang out, and Myrna and Joseph could almost experience the memories all the diners were reliving—the memories of excellent meals, of great parties, of successful banquets, of laughter, of friendship, and of a wonderful man.

Not a single person, not even Brenda, was feeling sad as they ate Tata's food, slathered in Myrna's magic mole sauce. Only good memories came to anyone's mind. Only happiness. Only delight.

For that was the magic that had been in Tata's recipe book. All the skill and practice and knowledge of Dan Molina, of his own grandmother, of all the ancestors before them, right to the pre-Hispanic women who had knelt before adobe hearths, had poured into Myrna on that sunny day in Tata's empty kitchen. Their knowledge had flowed into her mind, their skill into her hands. For this was the magic: the magic of her ancestors, the tradition of her family. The love of food, family, and friendships. The magic to bring joy to the present, and happy memories from the past. To remind all who ate their food of the precious worth of their own lives.

Joseph shook his head as he watched the diners. "I don't know what you put into that food," he murmured to Myrna, "but, holy crap, I want some right now."

"Me too!" piped up Joey, wriggling to get down from his father's side.

Myrna laughed and kissed them both. "I didn't put anything in that food, except what Tata always did." Magic. "But you can both definitely have some. Come on, there's still some plates left, and you can have a lemonade, Joey."

Myrna led her husband and her son forward to partake of the magical food, to feel the joy of their lives in the midst of death. And none of them, not even Myrna, saw Dan Molina watching them, a gentle smile on his face, or noticed when he snatched a full wineglass from the side of an uproariously laughing food critic who had once written Dan a snarky review, and drained it down.

Ah, Baja wine. Lovely.

Dan put the glass back and cackled in delight at the critic's startled bewilderment when he reached for his glass and found it empty. Then he headed on his way, still snickering a little.

REPLICAS

I didn't grow up being scared of monsters under my bed or monsters in my closet. No, those fears weren't for kids like me. Instead, I was scared of the evil spirits my *Abuelita*, my grandma, told me about before bed.

Abuelita was a sweet old woman, but she sure was superstitious and filled to the brim with dark stories. My mom and dad weren't around a lot, always working, like any other immigrant parents, so I spent most of my time with Abuelita, curled up in bed while she fed me those stories. Abuelita had a poor memory, so sometimes the versions of the stories she told varied from time to time, changing specific details or missing them entirely. The one that terrified me the most was her story about the evil spirits. She told the story so many times, it was impossible to forget.

"They come at night," Abuelita would say after I was tucked in bed, "slipping through the cracks of your window when you're fast asleep, bringing the chill of night with them."

My eyes would travel to the window to make sure it was locked tight. Abuelita would catch me doing it and smirk. A very dark and old smirk; her wrinkled skin would stretch as that smirk took up her face.

"If it's a night terror, it will slip into your mind through your ears and give you a bad dream. But if the spirit is a body snatcher, it will steal your face first... then your body... your memories... and finally, your life." Abuelita would pause for emphasis between each phrase and trail her hand over every part of my body before circling back to my heart. "And don't even get me started about *el Cucuy*!"

My eyes would somehow find its way to the window again, watching the dark night and the fierce gusts of wind that took over the streets of San Francisco. I would imagine the wind transforming into evil spirits and slipping through the cracks of my window and making their way to me. Not exactly the best thing for a child to imagine.

"Once a body snatcher takes over your body and takes your place in society, you'll know. You'll feel it vibrating through your bones that you're in the wrong body. That though your consciousness and face and memories are the same, the body is not. You'd know, my sweet Ernie," Abuelita would say. "But don't worry. They can't come for you as long as I'm here. Not even *el Chupacabras* would dare come show its face when Abuelita is around."

After that, I would take my eyes off the window and calm down. It was as if Abuelita's words were all I needed. My safe haven. The shield that would protect me from all the horrors that laid out the window. Then, I would fall asleep. Mom used to say I loved Abuelita more than her. While that wasn't true, I did respect her a lot. In my eyes, she wasn't some wrinkled old lady who lived with us. She was a battle maiden who fought the evil spirits, keeping them from stealing my body and soul. It was because I knew—*thought*—Abuelita would always be there to protect me.

Not anymore.

It's been well over twenty years since Abuelita passed away, and contrary to her tales and superstitions, no evil spirit ever came to steal my body. Or at least, that's what I thought. Unless we were going to count Alice, my next-door neighbor, who comes in whenever she wishes. This Asian lady could pass as an evil spirit any day, with her wrinkly pale skin and lanky frame. But the only thing she ever came to steal—or help me consume, in her words—were the food items in my refrigerator. I wondered where all the food she eats goes to. Her bony structure managed to look perpetually unfed, even though she always ate more than I did. I wasn't bothered by her habits, though. Since I haven't stepped out of my apartment in over a year, she helps with my grocery shopping. So, I guess, it's only natural she also *helps* with consuming them.

However, if there were no evil spirits and if Alice didn't sneak into my room, how did my complete Harry Potter series go missing? I could bet my entire shelf on the fact that Alice had no hand in the theft. The poor woman couldn't read a book in English to save her life. A pity actually, since all the good stuff in life was buried within the pages of my books. Anyway, someone or something made it to my room and stole my Harry Potter series.

I mean, I could just place an order for another one. Thank God for online shopping. It gave me even fewer reasons to set foot outside my house. I was pretty sure there wasn't anything that exciting or new to see in San Francisco since the pandemic lockdown was called off. Though Alice claimed there was so much more to see, and being cooped up at home wouldn't get me anywhere. What did she know, anyway? The biggest concern in my life right then was that I may or may not have been harboring a thief. Placing an order for a new set of Harry Potter series, since I never knew when I might want to read it for the fourteenth time, seemed like the next step to take. But other things have also been missing.

Or rather, *misplaced*.

Before going to bed a week ago, I was a hundred percent sure my toothbrush was in the bathroom, where it belonged. But waking up the next day, I met it on the kitchen counter. Let's not begin to talk about the day I found a pot filled to the brim with lasagna in my kitchen. I mean, it was my pot, and my lasagna, but I swear, I didn't cook it. And I know that Alice didn't either, because that night, she was at her friend's place. I did eat the lasagna though, and it was delicious, which solidified my claim that Alice didn't make it because she was a terrible cook.

A lot of strange things have also happened over the past few weeks, and the possibility of it being the work of those evil spirits Abuelita used to talk about was suddenly beginning to dawn on me. Abuelita did say there were many types of evil spirits apart from the night terror—*el Cucuy*, the body snatcher, or *la Llorona*. Who knows, maybe I'd somehow allowed a roommate-spirit or sleep walker to slip in one night. Okay, I know it sounds absurd. I'm not as superstitious as my family, after all. But there had to be a reason behind all these happenings.

Considering it now, it could be that I was sleepwalking. That could explain the lasagna and the toothbrush, and the broken mirror in the bathroom. Though that still left out the missing stack of books. What could have happened to them?

There was the scary and totally unnecessary option of visiting one of those shrinks who could science everything away and banish the thoughts in my head about evil spirits. But that would require going outside to relate with people other than Alice and the cute pizza delivery girl who came every Friday. And in truth, I wasn't ready for that. Not stepping out the door for over a year had the tendency of doing that to anyone. It wasn't as if there was anything exciting outside. Just people, and people always tended to lead to bad things. Moreover, I had more than enough online friends and acquaintances already. And thanks to online shopping and my fifteen-hundred-square-foot apartment, I had everything I needed there. A gym, my books, and enough movies and videogames to last a lifetime. A doctor was most certainly not needed.

Okay, true... just as Alice insisted, a therapist could certainly help with my agoraphobia. But I just wasn't ready to be "helped."

I finally forced myself out of bed. I'd spent enough time thinking about the missing books and about Abuelita's stories about evil spirits. I had work, and a scheduled Zoom meeting. Missing it wasn't an option. Though my thoughts still lingered on the strange happenings. Evil spirit or not, something had to be done about it, and fast. For the briefest moment, the thought of me being a werewolf who transformed at night and did random stuff crossed my mind and I grinned. I found myself scanning my room for claw marks and turned away with a pout when I found nothing. Absurd thought, but for some reason, it sounded plausible in my head. Blame all the fiction I read.

"I'll get to the bottom of this," I said to the room, pointing a warning finger at the ceiling before walking into the bathroom. Maybe if I'd lingered a little longer, I would have noticed the low creak of my closet door.

***

"What the hell happened here, Ernie?" asked Alice with a concerned look on her face.

I looked between the intruder and my room. For a second, I thought it wasn't my room. But those were my books all over the floor, that was my vase broken and the cactus in it trampled, and that was my closet wide open with my clothes scattered about. Definitely my room, but it looked like I'd stepped into an alternate reality and I was faced with another version of the room.

"I... I d-don't... I don't... What are you doing here?" I stammered out, turning my attention to her. She could just as easily have been responsible for this mayhem that had befallen my room. And Alice of all people knew I hated people in my bedroom. So why was she here at seven in the morning? I regretted ever giving her access to my place.

The concerned look on her face twisted into a frown as she took a step back. She was clad in her brown work uniform, which hung over her tall, bony frame like a veil over a ghost, and she had a nose mask strapped around her ears, resting on her chin. She worked at the new coffee place down the street, helping in the kitchen. At least, that was what she told me.

"I was having breakfast in the kitchen before going to work, when I heard you scream and came here as fast as I—Stop looking at me that way. It's not like I'm some kind of criminal, Ernesto. You tell me, what happened here?" She was raising her voice now, and there was a bit of hurt in those dark eyes of hers.

I sniffed and rubbed my eyes with the back of my hand. I'd woken up to the mess in my room and screamed. That must have been what alerted Alice. I got out of my bed instantly. "Okay. Yeah. I'm sorry. I shouldn't have looked at you in such accusatory manner. But... I have no idea what happened here. I... I, umm... woke up like *this*. I honestly have no idea what happened."

The concerned look on Alice's face returned. Deeper this time. The feeling of her scrutinizing me made me feel uncomfortable. I could feel her gaze over every inch of my tan skin. "Are you alright, Ernesto? You've been talking about some strange feelings for some days now. And now this?" she said. After a moment, she added, "And there was also the lasagna issue the other day."

A bit of the tension I felt left me and I managed to produce a grin. "Of course you remember the lasagna," I told her and turned back to the mess in the room. I sighed as I took in the sight. Why was this happening? And what was causing it? Then I made my decision. "There's only one thing to do."

Alice nodded. "See a doctor," she said with a smile.

"What? No!" I grunted. "Never mind."

"What, then?" she asked.

"Get some surveillance cameras."

Alice facepalmed. "Definitely see a doctor, boy. What do you need surveillance cameras for?"

I smirked and looked away. "Getting surveillance cameras is the best thing to do at this point. I'm gonna install them all over the place to record what's happening and find out who's been doing all these... *committing* these wretched acts," I decided to explain to Alice since she didn't quite grasp the fact that for me, stepping out of the house was never an option.

"And this is better than seeing a doctor?" she asked, leaning against the doorframe and wearing a tight smile on her face.

I picked up one of my books. "Yes. It's definitely better. What's the worst that could happen?"

"Um, you could get hurt," Alice said firmly. "I mean... Look around! It looked like there was a struggle here. Like two people fought or something."

I frowned. "Really? There's no one else here, Alice. You know that."

Alice rolled her eyes. "Of course. Look around you. Shit, man! It's quite obvious to me. Why isn't it obvious to you? Look, over there," she said pointing at my bedside, where the cactus vase had broken, "seems to be where the fight started and all. Then the struggle continued to where your shelf is and finally the clothes room."

"You mean my closet?"

"Yes, that."

"Oh, my goodness, Alice. You've been watching too many crime dramas, Alice. Or worse, Mexican or Korean *novelas*. I'm pretty sure I'd know if there was a struggle in my room," I told her while picking up more books.

Of course, cleaning up this mess wasn't on my plan for today. Why couldn't anything go the way I wanted?

Alice's cheeks flushed. "Fine, Ernesto. Maybe it's just the fact that I've been watching a lot of TV; but when you get punched in the belly, you'll remember that I told you so." She hmphed and turned away.

I rolled my eyes behind her and cringed when I heard her return to my kitchen. Alice was something. I couldn't believe I tolerated her presence or her intruding this much.

"Can't I wish for a personal fairy godmother to help with my cleaning like the stupid cartoons? Is that too much to ask?" I muttered to myself as I picked up more books.

A moment later, I dumped the books on my bed and picked up my phone. "Now, how much are surveillance cameras?" I asked no one in particular.

I was determined that this was definitely the right thing to do. I'd be able to catch the culprit red-handed. And God knew if it was

Alice who turned out to be behind everything, I would come for her head. I really loved that cactus vase. It was Abuelita's. I would get hold of whoever was responsible for breaking it.

***

I still think about Abuelita's stories a lot. I think about what she said about the body snatchers. "*And once a body snatcher takes over your body and takes your place in the society, you'll know. You'll feel it vibrating through your bones that you're in the wrong body...*" I could swear on my entire book and movie collection that I could feel it. I could feel the vibration deep within my bones. This was not my body. It felt like a jacket. A jacket that didn't belong to me.

I know what you might be thinking; I'm overthinking it all. Maybe I was. Maybe I was simply still that same kid who believed in those folkish evil spirits. Maybe I was the same kid who was scared of spirits slipping through the cracks of the windows to attack me. But I could feel a wrongness in me. Like someone had taken something really important from me, although it felt like the thing that was taken was never mine to begin with.

I told Alice about it when she came over a few evenings ago. She still thought I needed to see a doctor. Of course, I did not. I did check the internet about the strange happenings in my room, but I ended up getting write-ups on the paranormal. Ghosts. Imps. And even some mentions about demons. Ridiculous.

My feelings aside, I eventually fixed the surveillance cameras all over my house. I figured that would clear all my doubts about harboring a thief. I was even starting to agree with Alice's theory about sleepwalking. However, for some reason, I forgot all about the surveillance cameras. I mean, there was the fact that I had a whole lot of things to do for work. It wasn't easy working for an IT company–other than being able to work from home, of course. The past few days, my boss bombarded me with a whole lot of work, and that might have contributed to the fact that I forgot about the surveillance cameras. There was also, surprisingly, no other incidents after the wrecked room issue. It was as if the culprit decided to take a break from tormenting my life. I would have appreciated it if they cooked lasagna for me again, though. But if wishes were horses...

However, I was once again reminded about the irregularities when I woke up one morning to find my bookshelf moved. The brown monstrosity of a bookshelf usually took the end of the wall opposite my bed, close to my door. It was quite exquisite. The deep color of the shelf was a nice contrast to the warm colors of my bedroom, and that was one of the reasons I picked it out. But, instead of its usual corner, I found my bookshelf moved to the other end of my room, beside my closet.

Of course, there were drag marks on my rug, which meant whoever dragged it must have made quite a lot of noise. But for some weird reason, I didn't wake up when that happened. It was then my brain cells sparked and I remembered I had surveillance cameras. Now, I would be able to catch the culprit red-handed. So, I got up and left my room.

For someone who's spent years working at an IT company and had been doing well so far, it was quite difficult for me to navigate my way around the footage. I figured I should have read the instructions for use before I discarded them. Thank God for the internet. Following the guidelines I saw online, I made my way to the first night I installed the surveillance cameras.

I figured there was a chance going through the footage would take a lot of time, so I decided to get some snacks from the kitchen. As soon as I was done, I made myself comfortable and began to watch the footage on my laptop. There were just two of the cameras in my bedroom at two corners. But they were enough to see the entire room.

Two hours in, there was nothing eventful taking place. It was a Saturday and I didn't have any work to deal with, but I couldn't quite spend the entirety of my day watching footage of me sleeping.

I decided to increase the speed to the highest. And that was when I saw something by my walking closet. A tensed breath escaped me as I slowed down the footage. Then I watched the process again. A shadowy head crept out of the closet slowly, and soon, a dark skinned figure fully stepped out.

My tensed breath got even more worked up as the figure made its way to my bed and climbed over me as I laid in bed. I awoke instantly—well, the me that laid on the bed awoke instantly—and tried to fight off the figure above me. I leaned closer. The footage before me wasn't just terrifying, it was impossible to believe. I had no memory of me fighting off any naked person who came out of my closet. But here it was before me. I watched attentively as the naked guy from the closet strangled me as I tried to fight him off. In time, I stopped struggling and went quiet. I was dead. The me in the footage was dead. The more the realization dawned on me, the more terrifying it got.

However, I was in for more surprises.

The dark-skinned figure began to undress the dead version of me. All the while, he'd skillfully avoided looking at the cameras, but now, while he undressed the dead version of me and began to wear my pajamas, he looked behind him, directly at the camera with a blank look on his face. My breath escaped me. The person who killed me was... me.

I watched the screen blankly as my murderer wore my pajamas and dragged my dead body into the closet he came from. He turned off the light of the closet, came back, and laid in my bed, returning to sleep like nothing had happened. And indeed, it looked like nothing had changed. There was the new me there sleeping calmly.

I managed to sum up some courage. Now wasn't the time to be terrified. I needed to understand what was happening. I increased the speed of the footage. It continued to the next morning, until the new version of myself in the footage awoke and continued his daily business. It was almost as if he had no idea what happened the previous night. I moved to the next night and the same thing happened. But this time, the new version suffocated the old-new version with a pillow before stripping him naked and dragging him back into the closet. He took his place in bed and it went on that way through the third night and the fourth night. My eyes scanned through the footage and the more I went through them, the more the tension in me increased.

Abuelita's story began to make its way to my mind again. But this wasn't an evil spirit that came in through the cracks of my window. It was not *el Cucuy* or *la Llorona*. It was a clone who took over me. Who took over my life. Then the biggest realization dawned on me... Was I a clone too? Had I also killed the ones who came before me and dragged them into that hellish closet which led to God-knows-where?

Abuelita said I'd feel it when I was a victim of a body snatcher, and I felt it. The song Abuelita used to sing to accompany her story echoed through my head over and over again as I watched the footage. Her old voice moved through my mind in a sickening tone, and I jumped from time to time, sure that another clone would come to end my life.

"Holy shit!" I grunted when I reached last night's footage. The closet light turned on again and another figure stepped out of the closet, devoid of any clothing as usual. He performed the same routine of walking towards the bed in an attempt to strangle me—or whatever was on my bed. But I woke up just as he attempted to strangle me, and we began to struggle and fight.

At a point, I pushed over my shelf and everything came crashing down before the clone. He was, however, quick to evade the shelf and he leaped on me, wrapping his hands around my neck. We were both on the ground for a few minutes before the clone got up and watched my dead body blankly. He then wore my pajamas, dragged my naked body into the closet and turned off the light. The clone rearranged the shelf, but seemed to struggle with the exact position to place it. So, he dragged it to the side and went to bed.

Increasing the speed of the footage, I realized that the clone was me. The present me who had no memory or recollection of all that had happened. I mean, if I killed a clone of myself and stuffed him into my closet, I'd know, wouldn't I?

I decided to do the next best thing. Call Alice. Or maybe that wasn't the next best thing to do. I tried my best to narrate the revelation to her over the phone, but she kept saying she was worried about me and thought I should see a doctor. She mentioned a shrink, not a therapist this time. I probably shouldn't have said all those things about the evil spirits to her, but there was just so much to tell her. So much I didn't make sense of. And in all fairness, I was confused about how everything worked myself. The realization that once night falls, another "me" would walk out of the closet to murder the previous "me" was insane. But what was more insane was the fact that I wasn't my real self.

Then, I did the second best thing. Since talking to Alice proved to not be worth it, the internet would surely have something for me. So, I punched in any keywords that might help with the search. It took a while before I came up with anything. Finally, I found a blog post by some Russian woman named Anya. She'd written about not feeling like herself lately, and feeling like she was living someone else's life. Some guy named Gustav said in the comment section that he felt like his skin was not his own either, and Ayesha07 wrote about some recurring nightmares about her killing herself, strangling herself in the middle of the night.

I gulped.

I soon found my phone slipping through my hands as I turned my focus back to the footage. I moved to the live footage of my room and the tension and fear I'd been feeling multiplied. As I stared at the closet through the screen, the feelings I felt turned into anger, and finally, into resolve. It was night already, and some naked clone of myself would be coming out to end my life and steal my life. Not if I got to him first.

My journey to the kitchen was quick. I grabbed a knife and carefully made my way to my room. Now, I was greatly considering stepping out the apartment. It felt like a better choice than being strangled to death by a replica of myself. But I had to take care of this first.

I was in my room in no time. I looked around carefully, and even found myself looking at the surveillance cameras. Abuelita had been wrong. The evil spirits didn't come in by riding the cold night wind or slipping through the windows. They came from the closet. A nice, large, walk-in closet in this case.

With a tight grip on my knife, I turned the closet light on and plunged the knife into my clone. Except there was no clone there.

Just clothes. There was no corpse or blood or literally any sign of life—or the absence of it. Nothing out of the ordinary, in fact.

Confused, I began to remove my clothes in the closet and threw them on the floor behind me. There was nothing there. No secret passage or portal to somewhere. There was just my cold sheetrock wall and a now half-empty closet. I staggered backwards. It made no sense whatsoever. Maybe Alice was right. Maybe I needed to see a doctor after all. I dropped the knife by the small shelf beside my bed and picked up a handful of my clothes. I could as least return them back to their rightful place.

I felt a tensed breath behind me and turned around instantly, only to be welcomed by a sharp pain on my body. The knife, I realized. The knife I planned to use on the clone was now buried in my belly, and standing right before me was... me. At that moment, as the life slowly slipped out of this me, all I remembered were Abuelita's words. She said they'd steal my face first, then my body, my memories, and finally my life.

Taking in the naked form of the person before me and looking into his dark eyes, *my* eyes, I could almost feel him absorbing my memory, because I began to lose grip of it. I tried desperately to remember Alice, my job, my house... Nothing. All I had were shadows of what I used to have, and slowly the darkness began to welcome me into its abode.

Abuelita wasn't here to protect me from the evil spirits anymore. But as I kept watching the clone before me, knowing he would soon slip on my pajamas and resume my life without any memory of this happening, one thought struck me, and I smiled.

He'd die tomorrow.

Then, there was darkness.

MIRAGE

The alarm went off, its shrilling sound permeating the room. Ozzy groaned, hitting the snooze button as he stretched languidly, rubbing his sleepy eyes in the process. Osvaldo "Ozzy" Pereira was a fifth grader who lived in South Las Vegas. A small kid with spiky brown hair and a lean frame, he, along with his best friend Johnny, had a dream of becoming famous magician one day.

Ozzy got up lazily from his bed, making his way to the bathroom in preparation for school. Soon, he was done and ready to leave.

"Ozzy, don't forget we're going for dinner with the Parkers," Mrs. Pereira said as she handed him his lunch.

"Yes, Mom. I know."

He kissed her goodbye and walked towards the door. Stepping out into the warm, crisp air, he breathed in, anticipating the adventures awaiting him.

Just then, Johnny stepped on his porch. "Let's go, bro!" he yelled. Johnny was the opposite of Ozzy, robust and tall. Larger than all the other fifth graders.

"Coming," Ozzy replied as he rushed down the steps, nearly tripping in his haste to meet the school bus waiting for them on a corner a few blocks away.

"What's up, dude?" Johnny said as they shook hands.

"Nothing, just chilling." Ozzy munched on some potato chips from his lunch.

Johnny snatched the packets of chips, emptying some into his hands before handing over the nearly empty packet back to Ozzy.

The two friends boarded the school bus, greeting their friends who hollered and yelled their names.

"Hey, Ozzy," the tormenting Bronson yelled, walking towards them.

Ozzy went pale, knowing that this encounter wouldn't turn out well. He sighed. "What do you want, Bronson?" he stammered.

"Just a buck or two. Maybe a bag of chips will do." Bronson sneered, slowly advancing towards him like a predator about to catch his prey.

"I don't have money, Bronson. Go bully someone else. Or just go back to your sixth grade crew," Ozzy said bravely.

For a moment, Bronson appeared to be dumbfounded. Ozzy had never spoken to him in this manner before. He turned to see the bus driver and then back at him. "We'll see about that later," he hissed before storming back to his seat.

"Whoa! Where did that come from?" Johnny asked.

"Honestly, I have no idea. But I'm feeling good about it," Ozzy replied, a light grin adorning his face.

"Yeah, let's just hope that 'we'll see later' doesn't mean something worse."

"True," Ozzy said pensively. "True that."

The school bus moved, as some students in the back rhymed to some beats playing from a small Bluetooth speaker.

"I've got to be back home early today; we have this dinner with a family from church," Ozzy said.

"That sucks. I thought we were going to practice spells. What time do you have to be back?" Johnny asked, blowing loud bubbles from his chewing gum.

"I don't know. Early, I guess. Like right after school."

"Lame," Johnny said.

The bus pulled up at the school gate as the students scrambled off. Ozzy and Johnny took their time, allowing the other students to get down first. They were in no rush to get to class.

The school bell rang, indicating that the first class had just begun. The two friends ran to the class, not wanting to experience the wrath of their teacher, Ms. Usher, who had a permanent scowl on her face.

"Good morning, class," Ms. Usher welcomed her students.

"Good morning," some of the students replied while others were simply not interested.

"I hope you have your assignments done," Her sunken eyes bored into the students like she could see their innermost sins.

"Yes, ma'am," Johnny said, passing his and Ozzy's forward while collecting the piles of those who had done the assignment.

***

A few hours later, the bell rang, signaling the start of lunch recess.

"Be back on time," Ms. Usher yelled as the kids made their way outside.

Ozzy and Johnny made their way to the cafeteria. It was half-filled with students, some already lining up to get their lunch. With his lunch bag, Ozzy looked for a table for him and Johnny, as the latter had already joined the queue waiting in line for his food. He saw an empty table at the far end of the hall. Johnny soon joined him, his tray filled with an assortment of packaged foods.

"What are you gonna do after school?" Ozzy asked, emptying his trash in a nearby trash can.

"Well, I don't know now. I'm probably just gonna play some video games at home or something."

Just then, the bell rang, signaling the end of the lunch period.

"Lucky."

"Well, I'd much rather practice our magic, to be honest. But you ruined my plans, so…" Johnny shrugged his shoulders.

"Whatever. I mean, you can practice on your own."

"Yeah, but you know I suck. Besides, it's not fun by myself."

"True," Ozzy said as they walked back to class. "Well, you could stay after school with the magic club. They meet today."

"Oh, yeah. Good idea. I'll probably do that. But that means that you'll go home by yourself. And Bronson will be there."

"Oh, crap. You're right. It's fine, though. I'll just go straight to the bus and sit next to the driver."

***

After school, students rushed out, eager to get home. Ozzy was the first, just in case. He made his way to the bus and sat right behind the driver. Luckily for him, Bronson and his sixth grade crew never made it to the bus.

Once he reached his stop, Ozzy made his way out to walk the couple of blocks towards his home. He walked lazily, dreading the dinner later. He kicked some stones and empty bottles on the street lined up with halfway constructed homes, wooden frames left intact, as the construction crew had gone home. His mind was so occupied that the sound of a dog barking scared him. But the dog wasn't barking at him. It was facing something inside the empty construction site. The dog barked fiercely until a bright light struck it, chasing the dog away. Ozzy's heart began to pound harder.

What was that?

As the dog ran away the opposite direction, Ozzy made his way towards the open fenced gate of the unfinished home. He peeked through it, seeing a purple radiance behind some wood planks. It was a small glowing creature. The little thing crouched upon seeing Ozzy. It seemed scared.

Ozzy moved closer, not wanting to scare whatever it was. Though he was scared himself. The life form was hiding. But from whom? From what? And what was this thing? Ozzy had never seen something so strange, yet beautiful before. Ozzy made his way around the materials on the floor, seeing it better. The life form trembled and started to glow more. Ozzy raised his hands, trying not to frighten it. He moved closer, as a bright light emitted from the creature's body.

"Stop!" Ozzy said, closing his eyes to the blinding light. "I'm not going to hurt you."

The light dimmed. The creature stopped trembling, as if it had understood him. As if it knew he was no threat.

"Hi," Ozzy said gently, crouching closer to the strange creature. He was in awe of the beautiful thing. He'd never seen anything like this. "What are you?" Ozzy whispered.

"I am Mirage. I am of Alan Stone, creature born from his immense powers," it said, a look of curiosity on the creature's face.

Ozzy stilled. "You speak!"

The creature nodded.

"Alan Stone… as in, The Mage?"

The creature nodded in silence again.

Ozzy's eyes grew wide open, as flashbacks flooded his mind. His whole short life he'd wanted to be like The Mage. To perform in front of tens of thousands of people, doing marvelous things. To be a renowned magician whose art was known far and wide. Though, in recent times Stone wasn't doing so well and rumors had it that his show was gradually fading because people were no longer interested in magic. Ozzy, of course, had no idea why people would think that. Magic in itself was very intriguing to him and his generation. However, creating a new life form, now *that* was unheard of. What kind of magic had he used?

Remembering that he wasn't alone, Ozzy faced this strange creature and noticed that the light was now fully dimmed. At this point, Ozzy had a good look at the creature for the first time. It was hairy with large round eyes that stared at him. In all, it was really cute.

"I… um… I am a boy, a human being. If that's what you mean," Ozzy said. "My name is Ozzy. Well, my name is Osvaldo. Osvaldo Figueroa. But everyone calls me Ozzy."

"Human being... In this world, are you all humans?" the creature asked.

"Well... no. We have animals, like dogs, and cats, and horses. Like the dog that was barking at you," Ozzy said.

"Yes," he creature said. "Mirage did not like the dog."

"Mirage? Is that your name?" Ozzy asked fully sitting in the floor. He put his backpack off and put it next to him.

"I am Mirage, of Alan Stone," the creature replied. Even his voice was cute. "My name is Mirage, for that is what I am. And everyone calls me…" the creature stopped. "Well, no one calls me anything. But I am Mirage, for that is what I heard them call me."

Ozzy smiled. "Well, nice to meet you, Mirage. And, what exactly are you? And what are you doing here?"

"I am Mirage, of Alan Stone," it repeated. "I am born of magic. I am magic myself. And I am here because I was birthed out of magic, by Alan Stone. That's why I am here."

Ozzy chuckled. He couldn't believe what he was seeing. "Okay, Mirage. But, tell me, what are you doing *here*, as in this… construction site?" He looked around. "How did you get here?"

"I escaped. I want to be free. No longer captive to Alan Stone. I made my way here, and I hid, for I was scared. Dog wanted to hurt me. I shone my light at him. Am I safe here?" Mirage asked.

Ozzy beamed, seeing this as an opportunity. "Yes! You will be safe with me. I can take care of you."

"And I can take care of *you*," Mirage replied as his eyes grew even larger and brighter.

The creature looked around as if waiting for danger to pop out at that minute. He began to shine faintly.

"What are you doing?" Ozzy asked.

"Mirage protect," it said. "I am ready."

Ozzy looked around. He laughed as he stood up. "Mirage, there's nothing here. Don't worry. We are not in danger."

Mirage stopped glowing and looked up. "Ozzy safe?"

"Yes, Mirage. We are both safe here. I live a block away. Would you like to come home with me?"

"Yes. Mirage home with Ozzy. Mirage stay in this world for a while," it said. "Mirage protect Ozzy. Ozzy protect Mirage."

Ozzy grinned, doing a fist pump in the air. He carefully lifted the creature, depositing it into his backpack. He continued his journey home, glad that he got a new friend. A magical friend.

***

Alan stone, popularly called the "The Mage," was a renowned magician. He was an idol in this art—or at least, he'd been one once. In his height, he'd been the very best of the best in the industry. Now, the Mage was getting older and his shows hadn't been doing great. Mr. Lorenzo, his manager, had threatened that if the rates didn't go up, the show would gone for good.

The Mage was depressed. Everything he'd worked for was crumbling right under his nose.

Mr. Lorenzo explained to Alan that the only condition for the show to go on was if he could create something that had never been seen before. Something fresh, that pushed the limits of magic itself. Something original, as people weren't easily impressed anymore.

Alan had a limited time to come up with this, or else his show was gone for good. Alan was at crossroads now, his mind racing haphazardly. He knew he had to take a drastic approach to his magic, or the famous Mage would only be a memory. A has been, like many other Vegas performers before him. After a long, sleepless night, Alan could only find one solution to his predicament–to master the science behind the life form spell. To bring his illusions to life was a very dangerous feat, and it would be difficult. But there was nothing the desperate old man wouldn't do at this point.

Alan began preparing. The only way to go about this was to acquire alchemy potions and spells from the dark web.

"I think it's time to employ a little dark magic," Alan grinned. "No matter what the cost may be."

Far into the early morning, the great magician studied lost ancient spells, whilst trying his hand at creating different life forms. Some managed to survive for longer than a few seconds, while the rest died off once they got into the world. Nevertheless, Alan persisted, practicing incessantly. As the sun rose at last, most of his life forms survived longer than the usual time he had previously timed them. The small monstrous creatures jumped about his lair, creating balls of light, which they used during play.

Alan looked down at his creations, satisfied. Never in his mind had he ever conceived the notion of creating something so strange yet beautiful with his magic. Up until now, it'd been illusions, slight spectacles, and simple spells. But this was something beyond what anyone from this generation had ever heard of.

"My little minions, listen up," the Mage commanded. The creatures all stopped what they were doing and stared eagerly at their master, listening with rapt attention. "We're going to make so much money together, and of course, have lots of fun," he grinned.

"Yay! Money and fun!" They cackled, not quite understanding the meaning of those words.

"Just do as I say and you will be rewarded," the Mage lied.

Alan knew that after each performance, he would destroy his creations because they would be a danger to him and the society at large. Though small and innocent, these mirage-looking creatures had great powers, and if not harnessed properly, they would be a curse.

"We begin tomorrow," he said, as the life forms continued to play and shine in different colors.

***

"I'm telling you, this isn't fake, Lorenzo. Just convince him to give me a chance, one last chance is all I ask," Alan said into the phone. "You'll both see what I mean about something so incredible."

"Okay, I'll try my best. But this is the last chance, Stone. If this doesn't work well, he already made it very clear that you're out by the end of the month," the manager said from the other end.

"I understand. But trust me, he won't want to get rid of me after he sees what I have to show him," the old man said before ending the call.

Soon, all was set for his small performance. Even after performing countless magic shows in front of tens of thousands, Alan was nervous because this one would determine whether he was in or out of the industry. A small stage was set in front of two chairs. Mr. Lorenzo sat next to Mr. Rufino, the boss, owner of the Gold Rush Hotel and Casino, where The Mage currently performed six nights a week. Rufino was also part owner of the NHN, a much larger and more famous casino resort, and Alan knew that if he did well, Rufino could open bigger doors for him in the Vegas entertainment industry.

Apprehensively, The Mage began his show. Almost immediately, Lorenzo and Rufino appeared to be wowed. This encouraged Alan to keep going, this time with more charisma. And the creation of his new creatures began. The life forms were brought forward to the astonishment of those present. Mr. Lorenzo stared in shock at what was before him. It was evident that never in all his years of managing clients had he ever seen something so strange, unique but beautiful. Mr. Rufino, on the other hand, remained unmoved. But there was a big smile on his face from the moment the creatures came about.

The Mage gave the creatures instructions, and one after the other, they began to emit light so bright, it covered the small stage room. The life forms performed all kinds of magic tricks that were never seen before on their own, as The Mage continued with theatrics of his own. At the end, The Mage got a standing ovation from the two-person crowd. Mr. Lorenzo shed tears of joy, clapping till his hands were quite red.

Mr. Rufino shook his head in disbelief. "Wow, Alan... that was spectacular. A truly magical experience. Now, tell me, where did you learn that trick from? And why had you been holding off all these years?" the casino owner said.

"Well, as you know, Mr. Rufino, magicians have our little secrets. In due time, you will get to know, I guess. But for now, it's my little secret," said the Mage, evading the question. He would never dream of revealing this secret that brought a new light into his somewhat dark life.

Mr. Rufino chuckled as he patted Alan's back. "Well, that's fine. I don't need to know how you do what you do. I just needed to know that you can do them. I tell you what, Alan. What would you say if I were to offer you a spot for a better show at a larger casino resort, right on the strip?" Rufino asked.

Alan was beyond elated; he had a hard time believing his good luck. "You mean, as in the NHN, sir?"

"Why not?" Rufino shrugged. "I mean, this kind of performance deserves a killer production in a top-of-the-line amphitheater. I'm just saying."

Alan cleared his throat. "Um, yes, sir. Yes, that would be fantastic. Would your partners agree to that?"

"Oh, don't you worry about that. That is for me to deal with. A little talk here and there might do the trick," he said confidently. "I might just need to set up another private performance, that's all."

"We can arrange that," Mr. Lorenzo hurriedly said, not wanting to be left out of the conversation. "That's not a problem."

***

In a matter of months, life changed for Alan Stone. Word soon spread around the world about The Mage's sensational new show coming up. Tickets were sold out in advance for the first year. But, unknown to him and anyone in his team, one of his life forms had escaped after a practice performance, before Alan had the chance to disappear it into oblivion. And this creature was now in the hands of a fifth grader south of the city.

***

Over the next few weeks, Mirage proved to be a good friend to Ozzy, who rarely went out without him, though always hidden. Ozzy informed his best friend, Johnny, about Mirage, but he made him swear that he wouldn't reveal it to a single soul. Ozzy's parents noticed that his behavior at home had changed slightly and confronted him about it. They wanted to know why Ozzy kept more to himself and why he spent all his time at home in his room, talking to himself more and more.

Mr. Pereira, Ozzy's father, called him in one day, evidently to inquire about this change of behavior.

"What's up, Dad?" Ozzy said as he munched on an apple.

"Hey, kiddo. How was school today?" Mr. Pereira asked, leaning on the kitchen island. He was a tall, burly man with muscles, a result of his constant visits to the gym. Looking at Ozzy and his father, one could see that there was a big contrast between the two of them. The only similarity was their spiky brown hair–"the Pereira trait," as his mother used to say.

"It was fine, I guess. Classes have been good, and I kinda learned a new magic trick. Wanna see?" Ozzy said, eager to show his dad this new trick where he could dim the lights of any place.

Mr. Pereira chuckled, being a pro at magic himself in a previous life, he knew how Ozzy felt having discovered a new trick. "Ozzy, you can show me another time. I actually wanted to talk to you about something. Your mother and I have noticed that you've been spending more time than usual in your room. You hardly ever go outside to play. Is everything okay?"

Ozzy was a bit surprised. He knew this question was coming, but he wasn't ready to divulge the answer yet. Mirage was a secret only he and Johnny knew about and he wanted to keep it that way.

"Everything's fine, Dad. I've just been occupied with homework. Johnny helps me out, that's why you've been seeing him more often. But nothing to worry about," he assured, though his heart was pounding.

"Alright, son. Well, you know you can talk to me any time about anything. I'll be in the garage if you need me," Mr. Pereira said before walking out of the kitchen.

Ozzy took a deep breath of relief. *That was close.*

He made his way into his room but upon getting there, he discovered that to his utmost horror, Mirage was missing.

"Mirage! Mirage, are you here?" Ozzy asked frantically while searching everywhere in his room.

There was nowhere he hadn't searched. He didn't want to draw the attention of his father, lest Mirage be discovered. Ozzy's heart was threatening to come out of his chest as different scenarios played through his mind. He tried a spell that could help him locate Mirage, but it didn't do anything.

"Hullo human," Mirage said, coming in through the window.

Ozzy heaved a huge sigh of relief. Seeing him how gave him the greatest joy ever. "Where have you been? You almost gave me a heart attack!" Ozzy demanded to know.

"An attack of the heart?" Mirage asked as he glowed. "Humans are interesting. I have no heart. I went to check out my new environment," Mirage simply said nonchalantly.

"Well, don't go out alone next time," Ozzy said. "You need to ask me first!"

Mirage's light turned a dim blue. His big eyes became droopy. "Mirage promises," the small creature said, crossing his tiny arms in a show of allegiance.

"It's okay, Mirage. It's just that… well, out there, not everyone will be as welcoming as I've been with you. People will probably hurt you. And there are a lot of dogs too."

"Oh, Mirage no like dogs."

"Yeah, I know. Stay with me, and I'll protect you, okay?"

"And Mirage protect Ozzy."

"Yes, exactly." Ozzy smiled. Mirage tried his best impression at a smile, which made Ozzy laugh. "Anyway, I need you to help me with a new magic spell. I tried, but it just isn't strong enough."

"Come, let us sit down and work it out and soon," Mirage said. "Ozzy, you will be the greatest magician. Even greater than my first master," Mirage said.

For the rest of the day, Ozzy and Mirage worked on different magic tricks. They worked hand in hand, creating different magic spells and potions. At a point, Ozzy's magic almost set the room on fire because his magic was still too young. Johnny called, but Ozzy waved him off, declaring that he was too busy at the moment. His mind and body were directed on the light creature who was now creating magic in his room. Mirage never knew he could do this, and he was in awe of his own powers.

They worked late into the night, ending only when Mirage complained that he was tired and needed to rest. By now, Ozzy was obsessed with the creature and solely depended on him for his magic.

***

The next day, Ozzy decided to take Mirage along with him to school. It was a decision he made on a whim. Though in reality, he feared that Mirage would escape his room again and wander off.

"You'll come with me to school today, Mirage," Ozzy announced excitedly.

The little creature was thrilled. Ever since he got to Ozzy's house, he wasn't allowed to go anywhere for fear of him being captured or worse. Ozzy's announcement was well received.

"But we have a problem. How can we hide you from people?" Ozzy said, a slight frown on his face.

The small light creature glowed, his small face transforming into a beautiful smile.

"Remember Ozzy, I am magic. I can camouflage and become invisible, one or two spells can do that," Mirage said.

Ozzy beamed, glad with this news. Mirage was proving every day to be more and more valuable. Ozzy never wanted him to go. He couldn't imagine what his life would be without Mirage. "Alright then, let's get you into my backpack just like when I first brought you home."

Mirage climbed in, making himself comfortable in the small bag. Ozzy set off, as usual grabbing his lunch before leaving.

***

Alan Stone's new show brought him more fame and recognition than ever. Armed with a new marketing team and with a new costume and set designers, The Mage was ready to take the world by storm. As usual, the venue was sold out, spectators from both far and wide booked tickets months ahead. The magnificent NHN Resort and Casino showcased a larger-than-life image of The Mage in front, facing the famous strip.

The Mage was glad that his new creations brought him fame and was able to revamp his already dying career.

"Ah, the man of the moment," Mr. Rufino announced as he walked in accompanied by a pair of young women, one on each side, all beaming with smiles. He was a happy man, as business was great, all thanks to Alan Stone.

"I am at your service," Alan said, creating a ball of light out of nothing, using only his hands. There was fatigue in his eyes, but he still gave a fake smile.

Lately, Alan Stone had been looking for a way to make his creatures stronger. He wanted them to last a little longer before destroying and creating new ones, as the spell required too much energy from him. He figured that, since he was performing nightly, seven times a week, he could use the same creatures two nights in a row, instead of creating new ones for each show.

Mr. Rufino laughed, in awe. "Now, that's a neat trick," the casino owner said. The two girls played with the floating ball of light, incredulous to what they were witnessing.

"My pleasure," Alan replied. "Now, Mr. Rufino, I recently learned that you tried your hand with magic in your younger years. Is that right?"

"Oh, that's nonsense. I mean, there's really nothing out there I didn't try, to be honest. But, the truth is that magic appears not to like me and so, I simply gave up. Now I stick to business. Business and women." Mr. Rufino winked at The Mage.

Alan smiled as he eyed the two blondes. "I see. Well, that's too bad. You see, Mr. Rufino, magic requires patience," he said, snuffing the light out of the girls' hands, as if sucking it in with his mouth.

The girls clapped in awe.

"Patience is not one of my virtues," Mr. Rufino said, making his way out of the room, pulling the young girls with him.

"Be ready for my performance tomorrow," Alan called out. "It will be… magical!"

***

School was boring, nothing out of the ordinary. Some bullies tried to use their magic to hurt other students, but the teachers in charge made sure that this was averted. Ozzy kept Mirage hidden in his backpack and only informed Johnny about it.

"Dude, you're crazy! What were you thinking, bringing him here? Don't you think it's dangerous?" Johnny asked.

"Don't sweat it man. No one's gonna know," Ozzy said, so confident. "Besides, I can't trust him enough to leave him alone at home anymore. What if he wonders off again and gets caught? Or worse, what if my mom finds him in my room? Then I'll be dead for sure."

"I guess," was all that Johnny managed to say.

Just then, the school bell rang, announcing the beginning of another class. The two friends rushed in. The class went by smoothly, and soon it was time for recess. Ozzy and Johnny made their way to the basketball court which was usually quiet. Ozzy brought his backpack with him. They had hopes that Mirage could teach them one or two tricks. Luckily for them, the courts were empty.

"Let's do this," Ozzy said, unzipping his bag to bring out Mirage.

Johnny looked around to make sure no one was watching them.

"The human's bag was hot," Mirage whined, shining red.

"Sorry, Mirage. We couldn't risk anyone seeing you," Ozzy said.

"Hi Mirage," Johnny saluted. "We were wondering if you could teach us new tricks with light or something."

"Oh, yes. Mirage has lots of light tricks," the little creature said, bouncing on its little feet on the asphalt.

"Oh, what do we have here?" Bronson cackled, coming in as if out of nowhere.

His sixth grade goons sneered, happy that their prey was now in their net. Bronson had evidently been waiting for an opportunity to get back at Ozzy for embarrassing him on the bus.

"Quick, into my backpack," Ozzy said, stuffing Mirage into his backpack.

"What do you want Bronson?" Johnny asked, clenching his fist.

"Payback, baby," Bronson said, pushing Ozzy on his chest.

"Hey, stop that," Johnny commanded, coming in between Bronson and Ozzy.

"What *you* gonna do about it?" one of the bullies asked, stepping in. He was taller than Johnny.

Bronson created a small fire ball, aiming it at Ozzy, but the latter quickly deflected by creating a light ball on his own.

"You're seriously going to use magic on us?" Ozzy said.

"I do what I want. Besides, you really think your measly powers can stop me?" Bronson laughed, cruelly. His friends echoed in laughter.

Johnny also formed a light ball on his own, but this was quickly destroyed by another bully pushing his arms down.

Ozzy and Johnny were surrounded now with no means of escape. All their efforts to escape proved fruitless. Bronson and his friends were bigger and stronger. Quickly, the outdoor basketball court was filled with students, coming to witness the fight between the sixth grade bullies and the two fifth grade friends.

Just as Bronson moved to strike the final blow, Mirage popped out of Ozzy's backpack, quickly creating a light wall that shielded the two friends and blinded the attackers. Mirage grew in size, as it created a large bright light that engulfed the basketball court. For the first time ever, Ozzy saw fear in Bronson's eyes.

"Leave my friends alone!" Mirage thundered, snuffing out the light before quickly going back into Ozzy's backpack.

"What was that?" one of the students yelled in horror.

The rest of the students, including all the bullies dispersed swiftly, screaming in fear as the bell rang.

Ms. Usher, the fifth grade teacher was informed about the incident. After recess, Ozzy and Johnny were summoned for a quick meeting with her before students entered her classroom.

"So, what is this I hear about a fight, a monster, and some light show during recess?" Ms. Usher scowled.

The boys remained silent in fear and also in awe at Mirage's power.

"I asked you both a question," she insisted.

"Nothing, ma'am. Nothing happened," Ozzy stammered.

"We don't know anything about any monsters or a light show, Ms. Usher," Johnny added. "All I know, is that we were playing peacefully, and some sixth graders came to bother us unprovoked."

"I see. Fine then, I'm calling your parents for a meeting after school. You're dismissed, head back to your class for your remaining lessons," Ms. Usher said.

The two boys ran back to their respective classes, breathing heavily from the recent activities. Ozzy dreaded the meeting; his parents were surely going to find out what he'd been hiding. He could only hope that he wouldn't be grounded for life.

***

"As I said on the phone, there has been reports of some unusual sightings associated with your son," Ms. Usher began, addressing Mr. and Mrs. Pereira.

"I just don't quite understand what you mean," Mrs. Pereira said. Mrs. Pereira was of medium height with long, dirty blond hair and a chiseled jaw.

"Your son has allegedly been found with a strange creature that supposedly emits light," Ms. Usher said. "Several witnesses reported the incident."

"How is that even possible?" Mr. Pereira asked. He turned to face Ozzy.

Ozzy simply looked down towards his backpack laying on the floor between his feet.

"So, in essence, you don't know if your son possesses such creature or anything about that?" Ms. Usher asked, scowling harder.

"Of course not! Ozzy, what do you have to say for yourself?" Mrs. Pereira queried.

"I... um… no, nothing. I don't have any possession of any light creature or anything else. Like I explained to Ms. Usher, Johnny and I were minding our business, then these bullies came," Ozzy said.

"Then you wouldn't mind me searching your bag then," Ms. Usher said.

"Wait. What bullies are you referring to, son?" Mr. Pereira asked. He then turned towards the teacher. "Has this been addressed, Ms. Usher?"

"Mr. Pereira, I assure you, we take bullying very seriously in this school. That will be dealt with accordingly. For now, we are dealing with what several students witnessed, and that is your son and his friends having some sort of… monster that blinded many students in the basketball court."

"Whatever," Ozzy said. He pulled up his bag and handed it over to Ms. Usher. The bag was opened but nothing unusual was found. Everything was in place. Ozzy sighed in relief, knowing that Mirage had most likely camouflaged himself. At the same time, however, he felt a pang of sadness because he couldn't let the world know that Mirage was only a harmless creature.

"And you, Johnny, are you going to cover up for your friend too?" Ms. Usher said.

"Ma'am, like I told you before. I know nothing about this. We're innocent. Those sixth graders were only jealous because we could perform more magic than them. Bronson and his friends have been picking on us and they found this as a perfect opportunity to get back at us," Johnny explained. "But you don't seem to care much about that anyway."

"Okay, I think we're done here," Mrs. Pereira said. "I expect the school to do something about this bullying."

Before Ms. Usher could say anything, Mr. Pereira stood up and motioned for the boys to follow as well. They all walked out of the door.

***

Ozzy's mother went to pulled the car and asked the boys to wait for her by the school entrance. This gave the boys a chance to speak freely.

"Dude. That was amazing! Your little friend is amazing! He became so huge…" Johnny's level of excitement seemed to be growing.

"Yeah. I sure wasn't expecting that. When he says in his cute little voice, 'Ozzy safe?' or 'Mirage protect Ozzy,' I never really saw it happening. At least, not like that," Ozzy replied.

The boys saw Bronson and his crew looking warily at them from a distance, waiting for the bus.

"Hey, Pereira! I know what I saw," Bronson yelled. "What kind of magic are you hiding?"

The boys ignored him, trying to evade all interactions with the bully, particularly in relation to Mirage.

At that moment, Johnny tapped Ozzy. "Bro, your mom's here."

Ozzy turned around. "Just in time," he said as his mother beckoned them over from inside the car.

***

Alan Stone was exhausted. However, he kept evading rest. It was only a small price to pay for greatness, after all. He was proud of his magical light creatures and the fact that he had finally managed to make them last more than twenty-four hours. He refused to acknowledge, however, that the difference in the energy he extended doing either–creating and destroying them after each performance or giving his life forms longer life spans–was not much. He was, in more ways than one, burning himself out.

Of course, he had no idea about the escape of Mirage. He had no time for any of this; he had a performance he had to prepare for. Alan looked over to where his creatures played amongst themselves. He felt the weariness creep up as he watched them. Though he had cast a spell to enclose them, he felt that he could not leave them unattended. He knew they were too dangerous if left free.

This batch should last one more night, he thought after sealing the room with another spell.

Alan laid his head down on the fancy hotel room table for a moment. Very soon, without his awareness, he slipped off into a deep sleep.

The room phone rang after what seemed to be a few seconds. It had really been hours. It was evening time, nearly time for Alan Stone to perform. It was on the third ring that Alan jerked awake. He was so disoriented that he did not pick up immediately. On a fourth ring, The Mage answered. Even he could hear the fatigue in his "Hello?"

"Stone! Your people are waiting for The Mage. Where the hell have you been?" Mr. Rufino didn't sound worried too often.

Alan looked at the clock. He had just a few minutes to clean up and make an appearance. The pre-show rehearsal had already started. Or should've by now.

"I'll be down in a minute, Mr. Rufino," Alan said before hanging up.

He saw the life forms before he noticed it. Some of them played with a light ball that emitted a red glow. *That's weird*, he thought, hurrying toward a nearby mirror. Bloodshot eyes greeted him along with a trickle of red down his left nostril. He wiped it off hurriedly. Turning back to his creatures, he saw that the color had dissipated. As he washed his face, he knew they would return to their bright selves.

He turned to the life forms, giving himself a sort of motivational speech. "And you, my cute little devils, will make sure that The Mage goes down in history as the greatest magician ever to take the stage."

The creatures looked up at him, eyes opening wide. They sure were cute.

Hurrying now, Alan hoped the spectacular performance he was surely going to bring the crowd would atone for a minute or two of tardiness.

***

Johnny stayed at the Pereira's for dinner. Before the food was ready, the boys went upstairs to Ozzy's room. When they opened the backpack, Mirage was nowhere in sight. The boys looked through Ozzy's backpack, trying to feel anything, making sure that Mirage was still camouflaged somewhere in there. They called out to him in whispers, but, they got no answer.

"Does he usually do this?" Johnny asked, in a low, somewhat worried tone.

"Sometimes…" Ozzy's answer was unsure. Then, he added after a pause, "But, never for this long."

"Well, to be fair, he's been in there for hours!"

"If he's even here," Ozzy replied, though it was merely a whisper.

As they were searching everywhere for Mirage, neither of the boys had noticed Mrs. Pereira standing by the door, staring at them.

"Mom! How long have you been there?" Ozzy asked, exasperated.

"Not long. But long enough. I came up to tell you that dinner was ready."

"Long enough for what?" Ozzy asked as he turned to his friend, who had a worried look in his face.

"What are you boys looking for?"

Ozzy and Johnny quickly got off their hands and knees, denying that they were looking for anything.

Mrs. Pereira replied, "Okay. Perhaps I should ask instead, *whom* are you looking for?"

The boys were agitated, but didn't answer.

"Well, come on downstairs, boys. You can tell me over dinner." With that, she turned around and went down the stairs.

Ozzy and Johnny exchanged looks and slowly made their way downstairs without either of them saying a single word.

Halfway through their meal, which was accompanied by small talk, Ozzy felt convinced that his mother was not going to make too big of a deal about Mirage. He figured at least letting her know wouldn't hurt.

"Mom?" he said, voice trembling.

"What's up, Ozzy?"

"Mom, there's… something I want to tell you. I want to come clean and tell you the truth about what happened today at recess."

Johnny kicked Ozzy under the table while shaking his head in disbelief.

"Ouch!" Ozzy exclaimed. But he ignored his friend as his mother noticed what had just occurred. "Mom, the truth is that…"

"We have a magic creature!" Johnny beat him to the punch line. "We are sorry, Ms. Pereira."

"What?" Mrs. Pereira asked as she sat back down in her seat.

Ozzy looked at him, then back at his mother. "Mom. So… here's the thing. I was walking home one day from school. And there was this light in the new homes they're making in the street behind. Anyway, I got close, and it was this… well, I don't know what exactly it is. This ugly-cute thing was shining. Long story short, his name is Mirage, and I've had him all this time. He lives in my room. And it was Mirage that saved us today in recess. These sixth graders were bullying us, and he came out of nowhere and defended us. He got big and he shone, and well, honestly, I don't know exactly what happened. But… yeah."

"It was super cool, Mrs. Pereira!" Johnny cut in.

"I see," Ms. Pereira said. She then shook her head.

"You see?! That's all you have to say, Mom? Seriously?"

"Well, this confirms my fears," she told them. "Your father and I had our suspicions, Osvaldo, that something weird was going on." She rarely called him by his first name.

"But, Mom, Mirage is sweet. He's…"

"Osvaldo," she stopped him raising her hand. "You know well that I've never been a fan of you or your father being so into magic to begin with. However, you must realize that using *this* kind of magic, whatever it is, breeds great consequences. Magic always has a price. And magical life forms… that's… that's something else entirely." Mrs. Pereira was speaking so quietly now that Ozzy and Johnny might have well not been in the dining room.

The boys shared another long look. Ozzy thought of what had happened in the basketball court, how huge and angry Mirage had gotten. Ozzy was going to start again about how harmless and cute Mirage really was, but he suddenly remembered what Mirage had told him.

"He said he wanted to be free," Ozzy said out loud, looking between his friend and his mother.

"Of course he did, dear. It's why we don't make our magic come alive," Mrs. Pereira said. There was still worry in her tone. She turned to Johnny, "You should get home. It's getting late and I promised your mother you'd be home early. Besides," she turned to Ozzy, "Ozzy and I have a lot more to talk about before his father gets home."

Johnny turned to Ozzy. "Okay. But what about Mirage?"

"I'll find him," he replied. He then turned to his mother. "*We'll* find him."

***

Something bizarre started happening in Las Vegas. Something that never happened before. Dubbed the brightest city on earth, the city of lights, this was a big deal. Though most people just figured it was power surges happening, perhaps due to overuse, it was something else. In the darkness bursts, chaos ensued throughout the city, especially inside the casinos. But these were not simple power outages. Though nobody knew, these were caused by The Mage's light forms. And the longer he kept them, the more outages occurred.

The day after Ozzy had come clean about Mirage, while driving around doing errands, Ms. Pereira noticed in the street a larger than life screen announcing The Mage's show at the NHN. She almost crashed when she saw the short clip. She stopped and called her husband.

"Lucas, you're not gonna believe this."

***

Lucas Pereira waited patiently by the hall that connected to the NHN's grand lobby. He'd learned that at any given moment, The Mage would come out through one of those secured doors and make his way down the hall. It didn't take long for the doors to finally open. Alan Stone, The Mage, accompanied by two security guards walked out.

Mr. Pereira noticed the blood dripping from Alan Stone's fingers. "Alan! Alan, I need to speak with you," Mr. Pereira said. The Mage looked exhausted and much older than his years now.

The two security guards turned to him and were about to engage him.

"Alan, it's me! Lucas Pereira's son."

Thankfully, the showman turned to face him; a bright smile formed in his face. "Lucas? Is it really you, little Lucas Pereira, Junior? It's been a while." He motioned for the guards to move out of the way as he came towards him and gave him a weak hug. "I was so sorry to hear about your father's passing. I was sad when it happened, you know. We were close, even though many years went by."

Mr. Pereira nodded. "Yes, it's been a couple of years now. But thank you."

"Indeed." The Mage cleared his throat and fixed his showy burgundy coat. "So, tell me, Junior, to what do I owe this surprise? Are you still in town? Because if you are, I can give you some tickets to my show. I promise, it's like nothing you've ever experienced before."

"So I've heard. But, that's not why I am here. Well, yes, in part."

Alan Stone made a frown. "I see. Well, come, sit down." He motioned for Lucas to follow him towards a nearby table in the lobby. The two guards a couple of steps behind them.

"Thank you. I won't take much of your time. I know you are a busy man."

"Well, yes, indeed. You are right. In fact, now more than ever. But, anything for my great friend's kid."

"I don't know how to say this. I… um… well, my wife and I saw the trailer commercial for your new show. And we noticed some light creatures of some sort."

"Ah, yes! My mirages," Stone replied. "They are the stars of my show. Fully created by magic. I no longer use illusions, my friend. This is the real deal now. I'm talking the kind of stuff that your dad could only dream of in our earlier days."

"Yes. Well, the reason why I am here is because my son–" Mr. Pereira was interrupted by a loud bang on the far side of the hall. The sound was quickly followed by countless screams. "What was that?" Mr. Pereira asked, almost rhetorically.

The Mage stood up. The lights started flickering in and out throughout the casino and lobby area. Chaos ensued as people started a commotion.

"It was… well, I don't know," The Mage answered. "But that came from the amphitheater."

"Yes. He is here with us," said one of the two guards on the radio. "I see. We'll let him know."

"What is it?" Alan asked.

"Sir, you need to come with us."

"What is it, damn it?" he asked again, this time more determined.

"Ms. Stone, it appears that one of your… one of your creations grew in size and is causing pandemonium with the performers. It's destroying some things, emitting some sort of light rays."

"Junior," Stone turned towards Pereira, "We'll continue this chat some other time. As you can see, I have some business to attend to." With that, The Mage walked away towards the end of the hall, making his way to the amphitheater.

***

Mirage came back to Ozzy, who was a bit more wary of the small creature now. That was until he was assured, "Mirage not hurt Ozzy. Not."

"Where were you? I've been looking for you for two days! I was so worried, Mirage."

Mirage shined blue, his eyes opened wide. "Mirage was free. Mirage explore city. Mirage friends in danger. Mirage not want Ozzy to worry."

"Ugh, Mirage! I was so worried."

"Mirage needed to feed."

"What do you mean? I thought you didn't eat."

"Mirage and friends feed electricity. Electricity go out in city. We light."

"So you caused all these things? A couple of hotels were destroyed, Mirage! Please tell me you didn't have anything to do with that. My father barely escaped! I heard about The Mage and all the madness in the strip."

"My kin destroy city," Mirage said, almost sadly. He had picked up a lot of things fast. Emotion was one of them. "Some friends escaped. Not all. I must stop them before too late."

"I see. And how do you plan on doing that?" Ozzy asked, quietly.

"Mirage not know yet, Ozzy."

"Will I see you again?"

Then the lights went out, bringing complete darkness around him. By the time the lights came back, Mirage was gone.

Part of Ozzy waited for Mirage to come back, but he felt he was gone for good. Las Vegas was shaken. Somehow, the crimes of Alan "The Mage" Stone had not broken any state boundaries. The main damage had been at his show, and about a dozen people lost their lives; hundreds, injured. The fame he was greedy for had cost him everything.

But in spite of it all, Ozzy would never forget the creature of light that stood up for him–Mirage.

***

"So, yeah. That, my dear friends, is why you don't dabble in dark magic. And remember that any magic, as long as it is done with selfish motives, is dark," Johnny told the younger kids.

"What happened to The Mage?" One of the children at the magic summer camp asked.

"He passed away in prison," Ozzy said.

"What happened to Mirage?" a young girl in ponytails asked.

Ozzy shrugged, hiding his emotions with a fake smile. "I have a cat named Mirage."

THE ORPHANAGE

Five years had passed since the wizard's curse that brought about the end of magic. However, some magic lingered.

Thanks to this spell, the world had been purged of most adults who wielded any sort of supernatural ability, whether hidden or public, leaving around a third of the world's children without parents. While the nations recovered, government facilities were established to gather the orphaned young ones and shield them. They kept a keen eye out for those children who had magic, as it was now evident that the magic protein sequence was embedded in the DNA and many times passed along genetically to progeny.

"If any of you here have been experiencing bizarre dreams or done something supernatural or out of the ordinary before, you must let us know. Your life might depend on it," Ms. Holly Weber announced through the microphone.

As Bruno looked around, the stench of sweat and urine from other kids standing in the hall attacked his nose. But it wasn't this that bothered him. Bruno's hands trembled as Ms. Weber's voice resonated through the speakers again.

A few hands rose, then more joined in.

Unsure, Bruno began to raise his hand as well, still trembling from fear. He had observed the way that the children out in the world with intact parents looked at him, with disgust and trepidation. At the age of nine, Bruno was no stranger to the cruelty of the world.

"Dude, keep your hand down," Diego whispered instantly.

Bruno did as he was told.

Itzel held his other hand and gave it a gentle squeeze. "We got your back," she uttered. "Don't say anything."

Bruno smiled, thankful that his childhood friends were also there with him. As Weber's commands continued, he kept his hands down, unmoved.

"Those of you who've raised your hand, follow the gentlemen to your left."

The few kids did as they were told and went into a different room.

"Those of you remaining," the loud, old, croaked voice came again, "will be sheltered, fed, and lectured until you are old enough to work."

"I have a bad feeling about this place," Diego said in a softly hushed voice.

"Hey, shut up, dumbass," the tall kid with the nametag that said Pablo said, kicking Diego's slender leg.

Diego winced. "Ah! What the heck?"

The three friends turned to look at Pablo, who gave them a quick move, as if he intended to punch them. They quickly ducked, as Pablo laughed at them.

Bruno glanced scornfully at Pablo, but he knew he was in no position to take him in a fight. Pablo was a beast of a boy. His vast physique would make one think he that was a teenager, but Bruno knew that this institute was only for elementary-aged kids.

Perhaps there'd be a different way at a different time.

"Now, in a single line, walk slowly, and follow Mrs. Paula Keller towards the room on your right," the woman ordered.

***

Bruno felt something strange in the air that night, as if an essence of demise was lingering within this gloomy place. While on his bunk bed, Bruno could hear the whistling of leaves and the calm voice of his mother beckoning on him. If it were the first time this was happening, he would have been forced to believe it, but it wasn't. This had been going on for some time now, ever since they'd arrived at this forsaken children's home.

He knew something was off about the place, but he just couldn't place his finger on it. At least, not yet.

The voice soon faded when he had failed to succumb to it, the light of the hall where all the bunks with the children resting on them flickered. First once, then twice, until the darkness eventually won. Bruno sat up, knowing well that all his roommates were fully asleep. He could not hear a sound.

Suddenly, he couldn't feel a thing–not even his own feet or the bed in which he laid.

And then the metallic sound started.

Oh, no! It's happening again. Someone is going to die.

"Itzel, Diego, can you hear me?" he called to his friends, trying to be loud enough for them to hear him, yet soft enough not to wake anyone else.

Diego lay on the bunk above his and Itzel who was below.

"Guys…?" he repeated, to no avail.

How is no one hearing this?

Bruno heard the sound of metal trailing the walls once again, followed by the screeching of an animal. The squeal of the animal sent a wave of paralysis, freezing him momentarily, followed by a sudden quiver of fear. The inability to see anything in the pitch black didn't help. His heart threatened to jump out of his chest. Bruno could not lift a finger or shake off the sweat on his forehead.

Bruno knew it was magic. But he didn't know who it could be. And what kind of power was this, that created some sort of monster? All Bruno knew is that it had to be another kid here. After the curse swept the land, only children had magic powers, though these powers faded once they became adults. But each gifted child could only do one magical ability. Society looked down upon magic and everything superstitious because people felt it was unnatural; an aberration to nature. And because of this, all children with abilities were prohibited to practice magic. Those who were caught practicing were disciplined harshly. Or worse. Bruno sure knew to keep his power a secret.

But all the children with magic had been taken away when they first arrived, not to be seen again. He would have been taken as well if he had raised his hand. So, who could it be?

Did someone else slip in, just as I did? But, why is he or she doing this?

A familiar, cute, yet menacing roar came from the empty room besides their sleeping chamber; Bruno recalled the roar because, unlike the other metallic monster, this was one of his animals.

Oh, no. That's Everett!

Everett was his secret companion–a blue, cotton-stuffed plushy dinosaur that his mom had given him when he was five.

Bruno was gifted with the magical power of bringing inanimate objects to life. On the surface, he was an ordinary child with an overactive imagination. At night, however, when everyone was asleep, he magically transformed his stuffed animals into living creatures. But being gifted also meant having recurring nightmares. Luckily, here in the orphanage, he found purpose in his gift. Some of the other children who knew about his gift played and interacted with the plushies happily as an escape from the sad reality of their lives. Bruno always made sure to change the stuffed toys back to inanimate objects before returning to bed, so that they wouldn't have any trouble.

Crap! Did I forget to turn Everett back tonight?

"If you're ever in trouble," the words of his mother surfaced on his memory as she gave him this toy years prior, "trust Everett here. He will always protect you, even when you don't expect it." Up until moving to the institution, Bruno always slept with Everett. But they weren't allowed to sleep with anything here, so they had to leave the toys in the toy room.

Bruno suddenly understood; Everett didn't have to be animated by him. He could come alive on his own. His mother had given Everett to him not just as a gift, but also as a protector. And somehow, he had sensed Bruno's fear and connected to his magic.

Everett roared again barging into the room. Then the screech came from the other side of the room again, followed by the large flapping of something wet. Bruno tried to see, willing his eyes to adjust to the darkness. But the harder he tried, the more he realized he could not move any part of his body.

Bruno heard the two creatures charge towards each other, and then just as the large angry roar came, stillness followed.

Oh, no! What is happening?

The silence was immediately followed by the loud cry of Everett.

The large hall had become a battlefield overnight, and yet, no kid but Bruno had been awakened by the commotion. How was this possible?

Then, he saw it. Though faintly, Bruno saw the creature. Except, this wasn't a cute creature, like his plushies; this was a monster. Even in the darkness he could see the beast. It was slightly larger than a human. It had what looked like a dragon tail with scales, claws no shorter than six inches, pointy ears, and sharp teeth.

Everett, being just a three-feet tall dinosaur, didn't stand a chance.

The creature pulled out its flaming tongue, while it coiled its tail around Everett, squeezing him tightly. Everett cried out, struggling to break the hold. But the more he struggled, the tighter it grew.

"Everett!" Bruno screamed.

The monster looked around, but Bruno quickly lay flat on his bed again, pretending to be asleep.

Bruno closed his eyes but could still hear the monster as he walked around, still keeping a tight hold around Everett.

How is no one else hearing this? What is happening?

Bruno was petrified. But he was worried about losing Everett too. While still pretending to be asleep, he heard the creature growl and saying something.

"You don't have a soul," the raspy feminine voice came out. "What *are* you?" it said, asking itself rather than Everett. "Oh, I sense so much powerful magic in you. Tasty." It squeezed Everett tighter, causing it to open its mouth, then the flaming tongue made its way into it, feeding on Everett's life source.

Bruno tried to remain as quiet as possible as tears left his eyes. He could feel a sharp pain at the back of his neck, like a hot iron searing through his skin. He would scream, but his own voice only echoed through his head. Something was wrong and he knew it. It was as though a part of him was being drained away; the connection he felt with Everett slowly whisking into thin air. Everett let out a final cry and then collapsed, turning back into its inanimate form.

"Hmm… Interesting," the beast said. Then the footsteps faded away.

Too afraid to move, Bruno remained in his bed, crying. He stayed there, not sure if the creature would come back. He lay still, until, without realizing it, he eventually fell asleep.

***

Bruno woke up hyperventilating, wet from his own sweat. He wasn't sure if he had another nightmare. The lights in the hall were on and several kids were awake already. The light in the high windows indicated it was already morning time.

But then he remembered. The noises, the darkness, the creature, and Everett.

Everett!

Whatever the creature had done to Everett had a direct impact on him. He immediately sat up on his bed, breathing heavily.

"Everett!" he said out loud as his eyes widened, adjusting to the brightness of the room.

He jumped off his bed, only to see Pablo holding the stuffed dinosaur toy. The force of landing from the second bunk brought about a pain he never knew was there in the first place. He winced, and then let out a cough.

"Everett!" Bruno muttered again in between coughs, as Pablo walked towards him.

"Seems like one of your kiddie toys found its way to my bedside."

"Give it to me," Bruno said out of breath.

"Or what?" Pablo retorted, pushing his forehead, which caused Bruno to fall against Itzel who was still sitting on her bed.

"Give him to me," Bruno said again, angrily.

He was out of breath and drained of all energy. He could barely bring himself to stand straight without falling.

"Are you okay?" Itzel asked him.

The bell went off, and Ms. Weber strode in, disrupting the gathering of the children. Pablo stood tall, hiding the dinosaur as best as he could behind him.

Everyone knew toys were not allowed in the sleeping chamber. And even Pablo was scared of the mean lady.

"What is in your hands, Pablo?" she asked in her usual harsh tone. "I will not ask again."

Pablo trembled at Ms. Weber's intense gaze. He gulped as the demeaning eyes gazed into his. He pulled the large toy from behind him, handing it to her. Her eyes widened for a bit then she concealed her disbelief.

Instead of grabbing the dinosaur, she turned swiftly, "Time for compound cleaning, children. Everyone out now. Time to go get ready for the day," she ordered, totally ignoring the plushie. "Leave that on your bed, Pablo."

Bruno saw Pablo gleaming as Ms. Weber let him keep Everett. It was not like her to show compassion, not even for the tiniest bit of things. He heard that she had once stripped a boy naked in her office and forced him to walk around the room for peeking at the girls while taking a shower. And though he wasn't sure if the story was true or not, he didn't doubt she was certainly capable of being cruel.

Bruno remained quiet the whole time, a trickle of sweat forming on the side of his forehead.

As Ms. Weber left, Pablo threw the toy on his bed, looked at Bruno, and smiled. He then walked away without saying anything.

Bruno walked towards Pablo's bed and picked up the toy, inspecting as best as he could. It appeared to be normal. Unharmed. But he couldn't risk trying to bring him alive right now, so he took it and placed him on his own bed.

"How did Pablo even get a hold of Everett?" Itzel asked. "What did he even mean that it had made its way to his bed?"

"We need to talk, guys," Bruno whispered back to Itzel and Diego. "There is something fishy going on here."

"What do you mean, fishy?" Diego responded.

"Someone is using magic; I don't know who. There was a spell last night. But somehow, I wasn't affected. In the middle of the night, everything went dark, and everyone was totally out. Everyone except me. And there was this… creature. A monster. Then Everett came and tried to protect me… I think. I'm not entirely sure what exactly was going on."

"You are not making any sense, Bruno. What are you talking about?" Itzel said as she fixed her bed.

Bruno took a deep breath. "Okay, sorry. I know… I am confused myself. But there's someone else here who can do magic. Except, this is different. It's not… I don't know, it's not cute! It's scary. And whoever, or whatever this beast monster thing is, I think it killed Everett."

Itzel and Diego looked at each other. Diego put a hand on Bruno's should, but remained quiet.

Itzel spoke. "Bruno, Everett cannot die. He is a toy. I thought it was you who brought him to life… whatever that means."

"Yes, I know. But… I didn't. Not this time. Everett came alive all on his own. And as this monster came in here, Everett came in riding, as if trying to rescue us or something. Like I said, I am confused myself. My head hurts."

"So, what happened after?" Diego asked.

"I don't know. It was as if I was paralyzed. I was awake, unlike everyone else here. But I couldn't move. I mean, I did move, because I sat up, and then I laid back down. But I couldn't command my limbs to move. It was weird. And I think my fear triggered Everett. Unfortunately, Everett didn't stand a chance against this thing. And I really think that..." Bruno stopped and stared at his toy laying on his bed.

"You think what?" Itzel asked.

"I think Everett is dead. I can't feel the connection anymore."

"You really think your plushies can die?" Diego responded. "I've seen you animate them time and time again."

"This is different, though. Everett is the strongest of them all, because he's been with me the longest." Bruno's eyes got moist. "The rest don't stand a chance against this thing."

"I'm sorry," Itzel said. "What do you think this creature wanted? What is it planning to do?"

"I don't know. But I must get Everett back. I need to figure out what happened to him. If I can establish even the smallest connection, then maybe I can figure it out."

"But didn't you just say that there's someone else with magic here?" Diego asked.

"Yes," Bruno responded. "There has to be. Last night was obviously a spell, and that creature was mythical. I think it fed on Everett's energy or something."

"Then, don't you think its best we leave Everett with Pablo? I mean, Ms. Weber told him to put it in his bed, and he did."

"What are you saying? Everett was given to Bruno by his mom," Itzel retorted. "Why would we let Pablo keep it?"

"Just hear me out. The whole orphanage just saw Pablo with Everett. If Ms. Weber and the rest of the staff think that it's his…"

"Then the person that killed him will think Pablo is the one that controls them," Itzel interrupted.

"Exactly." Diego smiled. "This way, we gain more time to find the real person, while the staff's eyes are on Pablo."

"But what if they try to kill him?" Bruno asked. "He's an idiot and a bully, but I can't let him die in my place."

"Then we better find the person before they attack again," Itzel said. "Unless, of course, it *was* Pablo."

Nobody said anything, they simply stared at each other, thinking about the possibility. Without saying a word, Bruno grabbed Everett and walked it back to Pablo's bed.

As the three friends were the only remaining in the room, Ms. Keller walked in.

"Shouldn't you guys be with the others?" she said, scaring them.

The three friends began to stutter. They turned towards each other seeking rescue, but when none came, they relied on a more subtle response. Inconspicuously, they began to make their way through the door.

"Nice hair, Mrs. Keller," Bruno said as he made his way past her.

"Nice dress, Mrs. Keller. Your husband must be very thoughtful," Itzel said, following behind.

Ms. Paula opened her mouth to protest, but she could not quite find the words.

Then Diego said the most preposterous of them all. "Nice shoes, Paula. They look good, for a change."

All three chuckled.

Mrs. Keller had always worn the same shoes to work every day, which they must have known. Her jaw remained dropped as the friends hastily moved towards where the rest were already cleaning up.

***

Bruno and his friends stood outside the complex, separated from the outside by only thin metal wires that ran around the compound.

"What are you three doing standing there? Get to work!" One of the staff called out from a distance.

All three quickly picked up the gears, fixing themselves in the suits. They put on their masks and fiddled with the chemical tanks. In unison, they began to spray the field.

"So, how are we going to go about this?" Diego asked.

"I don't know," responded Bruno.

"It could be any one of them," Itzel said, scanning the large number of children, all working in the field. She stared at a girl who laid on all fours, evidently exhausted. "Hey!" she called out to Bruno and Diego.

"What's up?" Bruno replied.

"You said Everett fought with the person, right?"

"Yes. Well, not person. With the… monster."

"Could it be that Everett might have landed a blow that would affect the person later?"

Bruno thought about it and simply shrugged.

"If it was something internal, they might not feel it until it grows worse," Diego responded.

"Well, I think we found our girl. Nina," she said as she pointed towards her.

"Nina!" the two said simultaneously with their jaws totally dropped. They raised their heads to see her struggling to rise to her feet.

"But Nina is tiny. She's only like seven, I think. And the monster was huge."

"Well, maybe that's her gift; maybe she transforms into a beast," Itzel retorted.

"Maybe…" Bruno said.

But while thinking about the monster, the fear of the previous night overrode him. Suddenly, he could no longer move his legs; it was as though he was repeating the night.

"Bruno!" Diego said trying to shake him off. "What's wrong?"

"Bruno, are you okay?" Itzel called him sharply.

But Bruno didn't move. He was there, frozen. He felt his body temperature rise rapidly. It was like a dream state taking over him, until he could no longer connect with his physical surrounding.

"Ouch!" Bruno screamed as a deft punch landed across his face.

"Ouch!" Diego shouted back, but being the punch deliverer, he held on to his wrist then flung his fist softly.

"What the hell, man?" Bruno complained.

"Hey, it worked, bro."

"Boys, stop it. What do we do, then? Look, they're taking her away," Itzel said in a hushed tone.

Bruno stared at the scene of Ms. Weber leading young Nina away. Nina turned, and for a few seconds, her tender eyes caught Bruno's. When they met, it was as if though he could see through her soul.

"Guys, I don't think she is the one," Bruno finally said.

"What? Everett most definitely landed a punch or more. And look at her; it's affecting her. That's probably why Ms. Holly is taking her, either to the doctor or to take her away too," Diego stated.

"I really don't think so. I just… feel it. We need to ask her," Bruno said, putting his spray pistol down.

"Great! And what exactly are we supposed to do?" Itzel dropped her tool on the floor as well and placed both her hands on her hips. "Are we supposed to waltz up to the super villain of the orphanage and tell her, 'Hey, Nina, if you don't mind, could you please tell us if you are the one that turns into a monster at night and who attacked our plushie friend? Oh, and by the way, if you don't tell us, we two regular human kids, who, by the way, cannot perform any magic whatsoever, plus this one boy with the super cute magical gift of making his toys come alive will beat you up if you don't tell us…?" Itzel laughed mockingly.

"Exactly! That's what we need to do. But we must figure out how to solve the problem of getting through the staff first."

"What?" Itzel was incredulous. "Are you serious? Diego, can you help me here?"

"I don't know. I'll stay out of this one," Diego replied.

"I'm telling you guys; I don't think she is the one. Just trust me on this one, please." Bruno looked at his friends, who simply nodded quietly. "She probably just has the flu like some of the other kids. I think whoever it is, got to her last night," Bruno said, the three of them staring at the direction where Nina was being hauled inside. "Or…"

"Or what?" Diego queried.

"Or, maybe… and hear me out here… Maybe, Nina also has a gift. I sensed something special when she started at me just right now. I don't think she is the monster, but she might also be gifted, and they found out."

"I guess that's possible," Itzel said picking up her tool from the ground.

"Yeah," echoed Diego. "Anything is possible now."

"Guys, we gotta do something, though." Bruno picked up his tool and began walking towards the direction of the clinic.

Diego and Itzel followed along.

Halfway through the field, they were halted by Yuridia, one of the other children.

"Wait," Yuridia said in her high-pitch voice while stretching her hand towards them. She became conscious of herself again, brought it down, and bowed her head as she moved towards them.

"What is it, Yuridia? We are on a mission here," Bruno said in a hasty manner while casting a glance at the clinic door closing behind the staff taking Nina inside.

"Yuri, what's going on?" Itzel said softly.

"I know you want to save Nina, but you can't."

"Huh?" The three friends questioned in unison, as their eyes widened in horror.

"What do you mean, Yuridia? And, what exactly do you know?" queried Bruno as he got closer to her.

"She's like us, Bruno… like you and me. And now Ms. Weber knows that. But you can't help her without them finding out about you too," Yuridia said.

"Wait, what? You're… you are gifted too?" Diego said. "No freaking way!"

Yuridia ignored the comment. "Bruno, I know who is gifted here and who isn't. I've known for a long time now. It's… it's part of my gift. But I can explain that later. For now, just know that Nina is in trouble, but if you try to help her, you'll end up getting yourself into trouble."

"What else do you know?" Itzel asked the shy girl.

"I know that…" She stopped and swallowed hard. "I also know that Ms. Weber is gifted."

"What?" all three asked.

"Weber!" Bruno said. "The monster at night." It had begun to make sense to him. The female voice, now that he thought of it, it did sound like Ms. Holly Weber, yet hoarser. The query about the toy and the feigning of forgetfulness over the topic. How had he missed it? It was her all along.

"Yes," Yuridia looked down, as if frightened.

"You've seen her too?" Diego asked.

"I see her every night," Yuridia whispered.

"Oh, wow!" Itzel added. "That evil bitch! And to think that she is supposed to be one of our caretakers. What the hell is wrong with her?"

"Seriously," Diego added.

"How do you know all of this, Yuridia?" Bruno asked. He was trying to comprehend it all.

"I… I can see things. Among other things."

"What does that even mean?" Itzel asked.

Yuridia looked around, making sure none of the other children or staff could hear her. "Look, guys, I know that I'm the newest girl here and all, but ever since I came here, I knew who was good and who wasn't. You have to trust me. I know I can trust you. Bruno, I knew you were gifted too, since the beginning, but I didn't know what your gift was. Until one night I sensed magic, and I woke up, only to find you three playing with some of the younger kids with your plushies. And then I realized that you could make them come alive. I thought it was cute, but I didn't want to barge into your thing, so I just went back to sleep. But then, one night, I felt something I'd never sensed before. Not even before the magical adults died. This was something evil, and it frightened me. It wasn't until the next morning, when Ms. Weber yelled at one of the kids that I sensed it again. And I knew she was evil."

"Wait, I thought only children had gifts now. How is that possible? As an adult, she would've… or should've dropped dead when the curse went out." Itzel raised a great question.

"That's what I was thinking too," Diego said.

"Yeah, that's what we were *all* thinking," Bruno added.

"I don't know." Yuridia wiped her face with her sleeve. "All I know is that she is not a good person. Like, at all."

"Wait, she's been the one taking all those who fall ill with the flu to the clinic. But none of those kids have returned. And remember when we three first came in with a large batch of kids, how she asked for those gifted to go somewhere else? And we never saw them again. And… I heard her say something to Everett. It's as if she took his essence. She said something about him having strong magic and being delicious. Tasty, is what she said!"

"What are you saying?" Itzel asked.

"Hear me out. What if she feeds on gifted children, and that is how she keeps going?" Bruno's eyes were wide open, fueled by an eureka moment of discovery.

"Oh, crap! That does make sense," Diego said. "So, what do we do?"

"That's not all," Yuridia said. "This whole flu thing, I think she is the one causing it all. That's why so many kids have died."

"Dang, this bitch is not just mean; she really is evil, after all!" Itzel shook her head in disbelief.

"Yuridia," Bruno said, "you said that seeing is your gift, among other things. What do you mean by that? I thought gifted children could only have one gift."

"Not all. There are a few of us that can do more than one. And I believe Ms. Weber is one of those."

"What else can you do?" Diego asked.

Yuridia moved her fingers while looking at the field in the distance and the field began to glow, except, it wasn't really glowing—it only looked that way to the trio of friends. It felt as if they were in a whole new world, or another dimension.

"Wow! This is way cooler than your plushies," remarked Diego.

Yuridia closed her fingers and the vision cleared out. She raised her head to meet Bruno's eyes. "It wasn't real. I can create illusions, but only those I want to see can see them. That's why no one else reacted the way you three did."

"Okay, that actually *is* pretty cool," Bruno said.

"Yeah, I guess. Check this out." Yuridia opened her hand and a flame of fire the size of a large apple appeared floating on top of it.

"Wow!" said Itzel. She put her hand close to it, quickly retreating. "Ouch! It burned me."

"It's just your imagination," Yuridia quickly said as she dissipated the fire. "Whatever your eyes see, your mind believes. The mind is a powerful thing."

"So, that means that your illusions can be… real?" Bruno asked.

"Kinda. I mean, real enough, I guess. Just as long as the person seeing the illusion believes it's real, then yeah."

"I see," Bruno stated as he nodded. "Cool, indeed."

"But listen, enough of that. I just need you all to trust me here. If you go after Nina, Ms. Weber will know that one of you is gifted. And then she will come for you and take your essence," Yuridia said. "Honestly, I don't think you'll survive. I don't even know what her other gift or gifts are."

"But we've got to try! We can't let her keep on taking children just like that. And if there's a chance, even a small one, of saving Nina, then we must go after her," Bruno replied.

The four remained quiet for a moment, not knowing what to say.

"I've got a plan," Diego suddenly said.

"What?" Bruno asked as the two girls looked at each other.

"We should go straight to Mr. Mason."

"And why would we go to the director?" Itzel asked.

"We go to him and tell him that we have something important to report. We can go together or separately. But we all report that we have witnessed multiple cases of magic in the orphanage. He'll probably have to contact the authorities. Of course, we can't tell him who is gifted, and we tell him that we have no idea who it is, but this means that he will have to catch the person doing it. That way, if freaking Holly comes barging again with her stupid tail, then she will be caught."

"Assuming Mr. Mason is not in on it too," Bruno stated.

"True," Diego said.

Itzel looked back at the clinic. "Exactly. Because otherwise, we'll be screwed."

"Well, let's hope for the best, then," Bruno said as he turned around going back to work on the field before they got in trouble again. "Mr. Mason it is."

***

After finishing their duties, the three friends made it to Director Mason's office to lay out their complaints. Unfortunately, he refused to believe any of it. They'd wasted their time, and now, they were all on their own. In fact, things had only gotten worse–to play it safe, Mr. Mason ordered the seizure and disposal of every toy the children had in their possession.

Defeated, the kids made their way back to the sleeping chamber. While walking in the long hallway, they noticed through the windows two of the staff leaving the clinic with what appeared to be a small body covered in a white cloth. They all knew who this was.

Bruno felt as if his heart broke into a million pieces. Grinding his teeth, he clenched his fist tightly as tears began to stream down his eyes. Nina was a sweet, friendly girl. One of the youngest ones in the orphanage. In the past several months, Bruno witnessed Nina offering her food to anyone if they hadn't been satisfied with theirs. And now, she was gone too.

But at least Bruno knew now who the culprit was behind all these vanishings and deaths–Ms. Holly Weber. The monster. He wondered how the other staff in the institute helped her or why they chose to turn a blind eye to all her mayhem.

Perhaps they were all in on it too.

Diego and Itzel stared in silence. Itzel cried softly.

Bruno thought back to the last time he'd felt such antagonizing pain and hatred for one person. He reminisced back to the night when his parents died.

Bruno remembered being in his room that night. He recalled the whizzing sound that came from above the house caused by the steady wind that coursed around it, threatening to blow the house away. He closed his eyes, as he was reminded of the branches falling off the large tree beside his room window and how they immediately became lifeless before hitting the ground.

Bruno had pulled the door open with an animated Everett beside him and ready to attack, when his mom rushed out of her room commanding him to go back inside and lock the door behind him. A few short moments later, Bruno heard his dad asking someone downstairs what he was doing. Bruno's parents were both gifted; however, unlike him, they were the conventional type. This meant that they couldn't use their gift simply from thinking or touching. No; instead, they had to recite words to create spells. Unfortunately for them, if ever attacked by gifted ones, this gave their enemies an edge over them.

Bruno heard his dad reciting something aloud.

In all the commotion, the only thing that Bruno could make out was the indistinctive voice of his favorite uncle. "Are you done, big brother? Is that really it? Well, now it's my turn."

At first, Bruno thought he'd heard wrong. And, for the first time, he directly disobeyed his mom. He opened the door and headed quietly to the stairs with his faithful dinosaur beside him. But he'd heard right. In the living room was his uncle conjuring the wind and branches from outside, while his dad lay on the ground, struggling to get up.

"Oh, I will wipe away everything that knows of your existence from the surface of the earth, big brother."

Bruno's eyes widened in horror, and he gasped loudly. Both his mom and uncle turned in his direction.

"Bruno, run!" him mom screamed.

But Bruno stood there, frozen. Somehow, he was unable to move, much less run away.

His uncle dashed a wave of energy orbs towards him, but his mom quickly got in the way. One of the orbs punched a hole through her.

The announcement bell went off, scaring Bruno back into the present. The children were being summoned for dinner at the cafeteria.

As they turned around to make their way toward the large dining hall, they noticed a group of uniformed men striding toward the sleeping halls, being directed by Ms. Weber. The men were dressed in blue suits, hauling bags and boxes with them. The kids looked at each other, but no one said a word.

As they gathered by the table to eat, Bruno quickly sat down and tapped his feet continually against the ground. His head resting on his folded arms. Instead of eating, he furiously bounced his teeth against his nails. Diego untied his scarf and rolled it around his arms, forming a ball with it. He began throwing it from one hand to the other. Itzel remained still, motionless, simply staring at her food.

"So… what do you think those men are doing in the hall?" Itzel asked while using her utensil to play with her food.

"I don't know. But whatever it is, I don't like it," Diego answered.

"Yeah, me neither," she replied. "Bruno, any thoughts?"

Bruno didn't answer.

"Bruno!" Diego repeated.

"Oh, sorry. I'm here." He sat up straight. "It's just… the whole thing, you know? Nina. What Yuridia said earlier today. And now these men being led by Ms. Weber. Yeah, I don't know who they are or what they're doing. But whatever it is, it can't be good."

Mrs. Keller came walking towards their table. She stood next to them. "Bruno, Diego, Itzel. What's wrong? You haven't taken a bite of your food."

"Huh!" They all looked startled at the mention of their names.

Diego quickly pounced on the food, as if suddenly realizing that he was actually starving, but had simply been too invested in his thoughts to notice. Itzel soon followed, though slowly.

"Mrs. Paula? I mean, Mrs. Keller," Bruno called out.

The old woman turned to him with a smile and full attention. "Yes, dear?"

"The men with blue shirts that went into the sleeping hall…"

"Yes. What about them?"

"What are they here for?"

Diego stopped his chewing and looked up at Mrs. Keller, quickly joined by Itzel.

"Oh! They're an AV company."

"A what?" Diego asked while spitting some food on his plate and scratching his curly hair.

Mrs. Keller chuckled. "The young men are from a company in the nearby town that Mr. Mason contacted. They are here to install cameras throughout the buildings so that we can keep an eye out for you guys and take care of you better. It's so sad that a lot of you have been falling ill quite so rapidly, and no matter how many tests our doctors do, there seems to be no cure," she said politely.

Though the news she'd just shared could be an impediment, Bruno always felt that Mrs. Keller was one of the few caretakers they could rely on. Unlike many of the other adults in the facility, she was always trustworthy and didn't lack a certain motherly love about her ways. And though usually naïve, her words were comforting. She also kept Pablo from bullying, which always helped.

"Also, we heard that there's suspicion that some, or at least, one of you kids might be gifted," she continued. "And you all know well how we feel about magic here."

This last declaration came as a blow to Bruno. He was immediately gripped by fear as Mrs. Keller's gaze met his. His heart started racing, pounding harder, as if he had just run a race.

Do they know it's me?

"I must warn you three, though. Please make sure to be wary of this person, or persons. Gifted people are very dangerous.

Rather than to use these powers for good, they usually use it to cause havoc. So, if you find out who it is, don't hesitate to tell one of us," she whispered leaning close to them. "If anything, just remember what happened to your parents, darlings." She smiled.

Ouch. Her words hurt. Very quickly, Bruno's fear turned into resentment.

How dare she? Just when I was liking her.

"Thank you, Ms. Paula," Itzel said. "We'll do that."

***

By the end of the day, the kids retired back to the sleeping hall, utterly exhausted from their daily routine. They noticed the cameras positioned at all corners, giving them a sense of safety. There was no way the monster would come back if the cameras were there. It might have a way of paralyzing people through a spell, but technology would outperform magic.

The children fell asleep almost as soon as they laid on their beds. Everyone, except Yuridia, and perhaps, Bruno.

Yuridia laid on her bed, restless. After staring at the dark ceiling from her top bunk for some time, she rose, analyzing the cameras as their shiny red lights indicated they were on. Using the dim lights from the outside that came through the high windows, she could see across the room and noticed that Bruno was not asleep either.

Quietly, she climbed down the bunk bed, trying not to wake up any of the children. Barefoot, she turned towards the door, as she began to sweat profusely.

Yuridia remembered how whenever Ms. Weber came in as a monster, she would always feel her body turn cold. However, she struggled to distinguish between what was illusion and what was real.

Just the previous night, she had witnessed how a purple stuffed dinosaur toy turned into a small T-Rex and fought the monster she'd seen coming by at night. But she wasn't sure if she had imagined it, as part of an uncontrolled illusion she constantly had, or if it was real. She'd struggled with illusions since she was younger, especially at night; however, when she heard the inseparable trio of Bruno, Itzel, and Diego secretly talking about it right after the encounter with Pablo in the morning, she knew she hadn't imagined it. Which meant that when Weber turned into a monster was real.

Though relieved that she hadn't imagined it, unlike so many other things she'd seen, at that very moment, she wished it had actually been an illusion. Because if it was real, then that meant that they were all in real danger.

Especially the gifted ones, like her.

She felt shivers throughout her body and goosebumps on her skin.

But she had to do something about it. She wasn't sure what to do yet, but she was determined to try anything to prevent any more children dying. All she knew was that as the night grew darker, it was only a matter of time before the door swung open and the terrifying essence-eating being came back.

Luckily, the shivers and goosebumps she felt were due to her nerves. Her body wasn't cold yet, and this was good news. For now.

Yuridia remained by the entrance. She heard steps from a distance, the edge of heels colliding with the wooden floor, the sharp sound penetrating the silence. But she couldn't tell if they were approaching or receding from her.

Suddenly, the entire room behind her started to become infested by an impenetrable darkness. She turned, fearing for the inevitable. The spell was starting again. Her whole body quivered, and it became instantly cold. Yuridia pressed her hands against her mouth, trying to prevent any sound from escaping. She rushed back to her bed as quickly as she could, as the sound from the heels in the hallway turned into something heavier.

She thought she had time and she had figured that the worse that could happen was one of the staff finding out she was awake. But it was too late now.

The door swung open as the creature stood by the entrance. But this time, it raised its head to look straight at the cameras. Yuridia noticed that the red lights were no longer visible. And her jaw dropped.

The monster then sniffed around. And then Yuridia saw it clearly; the monster was, indeed, Ms. Holly Weber, transformed. There was no doubt it about it anymore.

Yuridia was trying carefully not to use too much magic, as the Weber monster would be attracted to her. But she used enough to concentrate on Bruno. And she was able to visualize him, in spite of the pitch blackness. He was there, on his bed, awake, just like her and unlike all the other kids under the spell. But something was different today–Bruno could move freely, unlike the previous night. She saw as Bruno reached under his blanket, pulling out several toys that he had most likely secured before they were tossed. He extended his hands above his head while closing his eyes as if to concentrate, then he tossed them to the ground by his bed.

Immediately, they all sprung alive.

"Not today, boy. I am not in the mood to play," the monster said as she swirled around, entrapping some of them with her long tail.

Bruno's eyes opened wide in horror as she made her way towards him.

The remaining toys, who had transformed into living beings, continued to attack her, causing some damage. But it didn't stop her from trying to reach Bruno's bed.

If only he had more toys available.

"I know you can hear me, Bruno," the monster said. "And you've seen me too. So, it is you, my dear, the special one, after all. Who would've guessed?"

"Leave me alone!" Bruno screamed.

All the other kids remained unmoved, deep in their slumber.

"What do you want with me, evil lady?" Bruno demanded again from bed.

"You are the one who can resist my powers." She stood right in front of him, watching as he quivered in terror.

Bruno fully covered himself with his blanket.

"Oh, poor boy, it's taking such a strain on you." She brushed her long claws across his blanket. "You know, your pet put up a good fight last night. It's so sad he had to come to an end. On the bright side, though, his energy was of great benefit. And soon, I will be powerful enough to perform the ritual. I just need… how shall I say? …just a little more of that power source. More of… well, you, my dear."

Yuridia saw Bruno laying helplessly on his bed as the woman's tongue flicked through his covered body. His body quivered underneath the blankets.

She had to do something.

"Get away from him!" she screamed from the other end of the room. She quickly jumped down from her bunk, and put her arms up, ready for a fight.

Ms. Weber turned swiftly to face her.

Yuridia used her gifts to make herself look like a big, powerful warrior. Her face was covered in furs like that of a red fox, her eyes made of similar red—not blood red—but that of flames. Her voice changed as well. Big muscles. Her eyes glittering every time she spoke. And a large pointy weapon on her hand.

"Interesting," Ms. Weber said. "There's more than one, I see. And you, my dear, who are you beneath all that facade? Show your true self, girl!"

"I said, *get away from him*!" she screamed again, but this time her voice reverberated through the room, tearing cracks into the walls and breaking the windows.

A powerful illusion. But only an illusion, nonetheless.

The monster stopped, evidently surprised by Yuridia's power. She released Bruno's toys and made her way to Yuridia. Yuridia panicked, but kept her resolve intact. Thankfully, the animated toys would not budge, and as if full of courage once again, started to attack in harmony, injuring the hideous creature. Yuridia took advantage and threw her spear into the monster, who barely managed to dodge the strike. But she'd been struck lightly, making her bleed.

"Enough!" Ms. Weber yelled in her normal voice, as she abruptly transformed into her human form.

The dreadful darkness quickly vanished, making way for the dim moonlight coming in through the now broken windows. Some of the kids started to toss and turn, a couple of them threatening to wake up.

All of Bruno's toys became inanimate in an instant, dropping on the floor wherever they were at the moment.

Ms. Holly fell towards the wall and turned on the lights. She then threw herself on the floor as her arm bled.

Yuridia, still in illusion form, came closer, ready to strike the evil lady. But before she was able to, Ms. Weber raised her head to the cameras and smiled.

Yuridia stopped in her stance and looked up as well; the red lights on the cameras were suddenly on. She quickly realized the severity of the situation and took a deep breath.

"Oh, no!"

"Oh, yes, my dear," Ms. Weber said with a vile grin on her face.

At least half of the kids in the hall were awaken by the commotion and the bright lights. Yuridia could hear some of them muttering incomprehensible things.

In a panic, Yuridia quickly closed her eyes and began to dissipate the illusion. The windows began to rearrange themselves, all the small glass pieces flying from the floor to their respective spaces, making them intact. The cracks on the walls disappearing, as if they'd simply been pencil marks, now fully freshly painted on. The spear stuck on the door vanishing. And her form rapidly turning back to her true form–from a tall, strong warrior into Yuridia, a slender nine-year-old girl in pajamas with double ponytails.

Unexpectedly, several of the institution staff stormed into the room, almost tearing the door down. One of the guards shot a tranquilizer into Yuridia, hitting her twice in the thigh.

Almost instantly, Yuridia's world began to fade to black. She felt dizzy.

"Yuridia!" Bruno screamed from his bed as the men grabbed her to take her away.

Ms. Weber rose to her feet and turned to Bruno. "We will continue this some other time, boy. But, for now, I have something more interesting to deal with. Something… *someone* even more delicious," she said as she and the staff made their way out the room with Yuridia.

***

It had been four days since any of them last saw Yuridia. The whole place had gone stiff. No one at the orphanage spoke of it; not even anyone from the staff. And no one asked about her. There was no speech or news coming from Mr. Mason's office during the morning announcements.

It was as if though the incident never happened.

Bruno was thankful that Ms. Weber hadn't been around since that night. And no one seemed to know where she'd gone either.

"We need to get out of here," Bruno whispered. "Like… today! We need to leave."

"I know. But how do you plan on doing that?" Itzel asked.

"I don't know yet, but I've been thinking of a plan."

"And what is your plan?" Diego inquired.

"Use the statue."

"Huh?" Diego asked again.

"The statue."

"You mean, the big one by the entrance of the ranch compound?" Itzel asked. "The one with horses?"

Bruno nodded. "The same one."

"Okay, please elaborate. You're not making any sense, Bruno," Itzel said.

"I've been thinking about something that my mom told me when I was younger. She shared with me that my gift was to bring inanimate objects to life. She never said my power was to give life to toys. My whole life I've only animated plushies because that is all I ever owned. But I think my mom was simply trying to protect me. To shelter me. I know… I sense this feeling deep within me, and I am certain that I can bring life to those horses too."

"That would be awesome!" Diego said excitedly.

"Shh, keep it down, you fool." Itzel hit him lightly in the back of his head.

"Sorry."

"Listen, guys," Bruno continued, "I was thinking that maybe I could animate them and use them break through the fence, and then ride them away from here. However, there is one thing we must do first."

"What is that?" Itzel asked.

"Find Yuridia."

"What? She's probably dead by now. And you, more than anyone else, knows that," Diego said as he crossed his arms.

"No, I actually *don't* know that. And neither do you. So, I say, we have to see first. Losing Nina didn't settle right with me. And Yuridia saved me. You didn't see it, but she was a hero. I'm telling you!" Bruno took a deep breath. "I want to return the favor, and not leave her behind. Yuridia is gifted like me, and we are in the most danger. The other kids will be okay."

"Fine! I guess right now would be a good time to tell you both what I heard Pablo saying to his bully buddies yesterday during shower time."

"Oh, yeah? What is that?" Bruno wondered how that could help.

"He was telling them something about an underground tunnel that leads to a creepy room from the clinic. He found it one time before they put the cameras up throughout. So, if he is even telling the truth, maybe, and just maybe, they're holding Yuridia down there."

"It's worth investigating."

"Okay. So… not to sound redundant, but regarding that, what's the plan?" Itzel asked.

"I don't know. I don't even know if it's true. I'm just saying it could be." Diego raised his brows and shrugged.

"I got it," Bruno said. "We'll tell them that I have the flu."

***

Bruno reached the clinic. Weirdly, he found it empty.

"Hello? Anyone here?" he asked no one in particular.

There was no response. He walked in and saw the calendar on the wall; marked on this day it said in red, "Staff Meeting: 4 pm." It was 4:15 pm.

Hm, so it wasn't weird; it was luck.

Bruno knew that dinner was at 5:00. This gave him 45 minutes max. He made his way all the way in, and after a few minutes of scouting, he finally located the door to the underground passageway room. Hastily, he reached for it, rushing down through the dimly lit stairs.

The hallway was long. But it didn't lead to one room, as Pablo had mentioned. No, it led to multiple rooms. Several doors lined the hallway, which had much better light than the initial stairs.

Bruno went through each door, but they were all locked. He tried to listen through to the other side, but heard nothing from any of them. He continued, until the hallway made a turn to the right. As he turned the corner, Bruno saw one last door at the end. This one was fully open. He rushed to it, coming to what appeared to be an operation room. There, on the opposite side of the door, Yuridia was tied to a chair. She had on a hospital gown, and she was connected to an IV line and what appeared to be a urine drain bag.

Bruno run to her and quickly loosened the belts. "Yuridia," he whispered.

No response. She seemed weak. Skinnier than what he remembered.

"Yuridia!" he tried again, this time louder and while gently tapping her face. "Wake up."

Yuridia sluggishly opened her eyes.

"You… you're here?" She sounded exhausted. Her face was pale, as if drained completely of blood; her feet struggled to hold their place.

Bruno disconnected what he could and helped Yuridia stand up. He assisted her in walking through the long hallway and stairs, all the way back to the clinic. As they reached the clinic's ground level, he heard her voice.

"And where do you think you're going?" Ms. Weber asked from behind.

Bruno turned, surprised by her sudden intrusion, especially since she hadn't been around just seconds earlier. But he had come prepared. Bruno groaned like an animal, narrowing his eyes. He dipped his hand into his pocket and retrieved two animal crackers he'd saved from the cafeteria the day before. Dropping them to the ground, they immediately changed to live animals.

"Now, Yuridia!" he yelled, making sure his friend understood the sense of urgency.

Yuridia closed her eyes, and the small creatures grew to life size, making a mess of the medical offices.

The first was a rhinoceros, followed by a tiger. The large rhino dragged its feet backwards, brushing it against the ground, just before it ran right through Ms. Weber. The tiger remained behind, growling.

Ms. Weber didn't have enough time to react, as she was thrown back by the beasts.

Bruno saw the clock on the wall; it read 4:37 pm. They still had time. He heard Weber transform into the beast in the back, and chaos ensuing. But they had to leave now. He helped Yuridia out of the clinic as she said something to him. In all the commotion and rush, he didn't understand what she said.

"What was that?" Bruno asked as they walked towards the campus entrance.

"She's dying," she repeated.

"Who?"

"Weber. She is dying. She told me herself."

"What exactly did she tell you?"

"She talked a lot during these past couple of days that she's held me captive. She told me that she uses us, gifted children, to slowly reverse the wizard's curse that ended all gifted adults. That's how she's been able to stay alive. That's why she joined the staff here in the first place. And she has all the staff under some sort of spell. Including Mason. That's how she's been getting away with it. But she said that you and I have been the only ones capable of resisting her spells. So, she wanted to take her time with us."

"I see. So, if it wasn't for us, and those she's killed, she would've been dead already."

"Yes. But the more she fed on gifted children, the more unstable she got. That's why the monster is so unpredictable."

"Well, her luck has just run out."

"But, Bruno, she took a lot from me. Those illusions back there won't hold for long. And she would've killed me if you hadn't come for me."

"There is no way we were going to leave you here. You're one of us!"

"Thank you." Yuridia hugged Bruno as they reached the other side of the building, facing the statue, where Itzel and Diego waited for them.

"Let's go. Hurry," Diego screamed.

"What are we going to do?" Yuridia asked.

Itzel and Diego pointed at the fountain.

"Ask him," Itzel added.

Yuridia turned to Bruno, but he didn't reply. He was concentrated on the statue of full size horses in the middle of the large fountain.

Suddenly, the gray concrete started to glow, blinding the children momentarily. The noise of horses neighing ensued.

"Let's go!" Bruno commanded.

Four wet horses waited for them to ride.

"You can do that?" Yuridia asked.

"There's no saddles on them!" Diego disrupted.

"I've never ridden on one before," Itzel said nervously.

As if on command, the horses came to them, halted, and lowered themselves to be ridden. Immediately, the kids climbed on their respective animal as best as they could.

"We don't have much time," Bruno said.

As they rode fast towards the gate, the alarm went off. Several security guards began to chase after them.

"Yuridia, do something," Bruno yelled from his horse.

Yuridia closed her eyes; they had drained her with some kind of science, extracting the magic in her, but she still had enough juice.

But nothing happened.

"Yuridia!" Itzel screamed.

"Sorry. I don't know what's happening. I might not be strong enough."

"Oh, crap! Maybe this was a bad idea, you guys," Diego said while trembling on top of his fast ride.

"Try again, Yuridia. Concentrate. I believe… *we* believe in you!" Bruno was trying his best to encourage his friend. Although he wasn't fully convinced himself that she could still do it.

Yuridia closed her eyes once again, as tears began to stream down her eyes. She wiped them off, trying not to fall from the horse.

Still, nothing.

"Change of plan, guys. We go to the field. The fence there is low enough for the horses to jump," Bruno commanded.

As if his thoughts were command, the horses all shifted direction towards the produce field. Then straight towards the fence.

"Oh, shit!" Diego cursed. "Are you sure about this?"

But Bruno didn't answer. He was determined.

"Oh. My. Goodness!" Itzel screamed as she pointed in front. "There's a guard up there!"

"And they have guns!" Diego added.

But the horses weren't stopping.

"Let's do this," Yuridia said. She closed her eyes and raised her hand towards the front. The guards by the fence dropped their guns and started running in all directions, panicked. As if running for their lives.

Bruno smiled at her. He didn't know what Yuridia made them see, but whatever it was, it had worked. "Nice," he said.

Yuridia smiled. Slowly but sure, she was back.

Bruno's horse was the first one. It jumped high enough to clear the fence unscathed. The other three followed, leaving the mess behind.

Bruno, Itzel, Diego, and Yuridia had managed to escape the wrath of the monster. Though they weren't sure if Ms. Weber had survived, at least they had finally defeated her. Nonetheless, they knew they had left many other children behind. And because of this, they would return soon to rescue them as well. But this time, they'd be prepared.

For now, however, they rode towards the sunset. They rode towards freedom. They rode away, with no destination in mind, as long as it was far away from that evil place–the orphanage.

OTHERWORLDLY EXPERIENCE

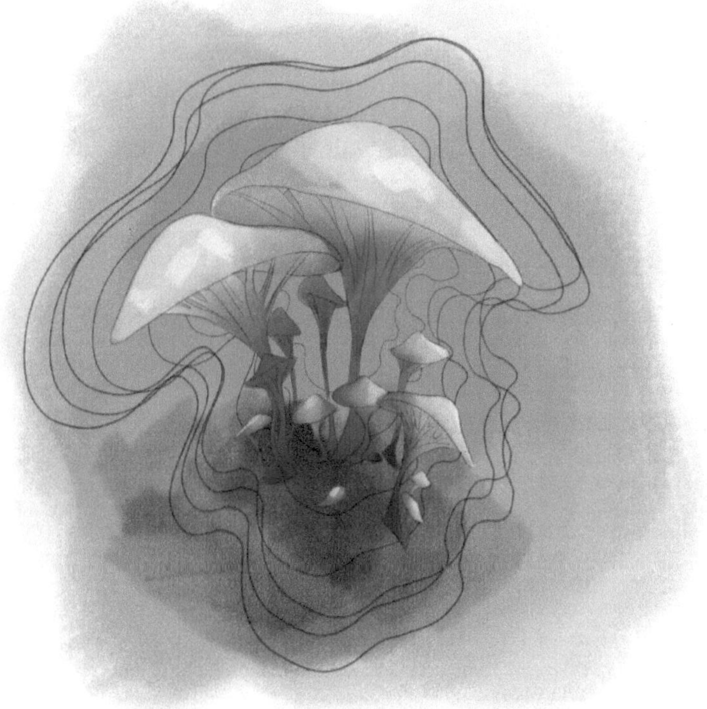

The windy city of Chicago blasted me with a fresh, springtime breeze. It was classic May weather, but I hardly noticed. I was high as a kite—in more ways than one—and I didn't even need to wear a jacket.

Natalie Sanchez had agreed to hang out with me this weekend. She was my college roommate's sister, but as he was also my best friend, it wasn't difficult for us to arrange a meeting. She was only one year younger, so it wasn't too weird. But first, I had to study for Organic Chemistry, which equated to the second reason why I was high as a kite. Lately, I couldn't study without taking a designer drug – *Drellium.* I stood outside now to pay my buddy for the new dope.

I popped two more of the colorful pills into my mouth and swallowed them without water. They were pills similar to Adderall, but coated with a special, new kick. I didn't know what it was exactly, and I honestly didn't care. As long as it worked, I didn't mind. Besides, I had never been against the dangers of experimentation.

"Whoa, take it easy there, Aaron," my friend said. He was also a pre-med student, but clearly, not as brave as me. "The effects of this one are substantial…"

"Good thing I'm looking for a substantial good time, then," I said, and grinned.

I swallowed again and felt the effects start to take hold. My concentration shifted, so I was focused solely on my friend's face. I saw the depth of his pores, peeking out from behind beige-colored freckles. His sandy blond hair hung in front of his sky-blue eyes, which darted about in veiny flecks of white and gold.

"Awesome," I whispered. "Thanks, Big Rick. This is definitely going to help me study."

Rick perked up. Most people did when I offered up nicknames for them. "Great! Well, glad to hear it. That'll be..."

I pulled out a hundred dollars, all in twenties, and thrust it into his hands. "Keep the change."

"Wicked! See you later, Aaron K."

"It's Kim! Aaron Kim. Come on, Big Rick. You know that," I said, winking, and spun away.

I gave the boy a peace sign behind my head. Even though the sun had already set, I reached for my Aviator shades and slipped them over my eyes. It didn't matter—I knew no one would stop me or notice.

I strolled through the still-crowded streets of Chicago, whistling a soft tune. People hoverboarded by, wearing their virtual reality glasses as they swerved and dived around invisible monsters. Others watched holograms of big-business know-it-alls screaming about the economy, displayed wide across an entire building. Cars rolled down the street on their own. In this era, every rider was a passenger.

I passed through electric car charging stations, walked by a farmer's market full of fresh, GMO-grown fruit and vegetables, and careened around the abandoned city hall where you could try to summon life from other dimensions. As if. Even I knew that it was just some crazy ritual crap—a.k.a., not real.

Another sharp breeze ruffled through my spiked, black hair. My ears caught the sound of hollering kids, followed by thumping music. My drugged-up mind focused on its pumping beats and I followed it without thinking. The sounds led me to the city square I loved and adored—it was where all my usual haunts sat, waiting for me.

I grinned up at the flashing lights, which brightened under the dim backdrop of night. There was no moon in sight—typical, since we had to place a dome over the larger cities to protect them from failed patches of ozone.

It was still pretty early, so I had time to explore before cramming for Chem and actually attending class. What was the rush?

My pupils dilated and my brain buzzed as I headed straight for the music. A burly bouncer stood at the door to the neon-colored building. The music thrummed and shook inside my bones.

"Hey, Little Mick. How's the weather inside?"

"Aaron Kim, it's good to see *you,*" he said jovially. "The weather's good in there. But be warned—it's dropping like ice and fire."

"Perfect," I said, and shimmied past him without paying. "You going to the next music festival?"

"Of course! And I expect to see you there," Little Mick added. "Let me know, and we can pitch in for a tent."

I nodded and gave him a peace-love-and-sex sign. As I strode through the red-tinted hall, the bouncer shouted back, "Hey! You better be studying hard, kid."

Kid was an understatement. This club was meant for twenty-one and over, but even at twenty, I got in without any questioning.

The electronic music pumped and broke inside me, blasting a cacophony of ear-splitting madness throughout the air. It echoed through the dim, misted room with a slow-burn buildup. Then, as soon as the neon lights spotted the room entirely in rainbow, the bass dropped. Everyone jumped, danced, and pumped their fists. I sidled over to the bar, where I spotted a couple of other people I knew. Without me having to ask, they bought me a few drinks. Alcohol, plus the pills, turned my body into a whole pack of pumping endorphins.

As the club popped on their lights, I considered heading to the school gym for my middle-of-the-night workout routine. But at the insistence of the bouncer, I decided to head home and study a few chapters. It's not like it was hard for me to grasp the material, but I wanted to see how well the drugs improved my focus, at least before the effects wore off.

The entire walk to my dorm, I buzzed with fresh energy, despite it being close to four in the morning. The holograms had shut off, so the buildings appeared eerily still, and no one dared zoom past on hoverboards. Not this late at night.

Back in my dorm, my best friend, Jareth, slept soundly in his bed. We shared a room and a small living area, so it was more like a suite. My eyes fell on the couch, where I pictured his sister, Natalie, asleep this weekend. Jareth snorted in his sleep and I shook the thought away. I could think about her later—when she was actually here.

Jareth didn't budge as I pulled out my Organic Chem and Biology books. I opened the books and tapped certain passages, which popped off the page as short, holographic videos and voice-overs. They explained the material much faster than any tablet, and certainly much faster than reading it would.

As the night waned into day, I blew through four chapters in each book. The drugs held out the whole time. My body sizzled like it was on fire, without the pain, and adrenaline forced me to focus on every individual detail. Come morning, I felt like the champion of Organic Chemistry.

Jareth's alarm went off and he snoozed it four times before he finally just tossed the hologram machine to the ground. He sat up, rubbed two hands down his golden-brown cheeks, and ruffled his sleek, raven-colored hair.

He fixed his black eyes on me. "Good morning, *hermano*. How long have you been sitting like that there?" He yawned.

I turned to him slowly, as the pills still held me hostage. He caught the ravenous look present in my almond-shaped eyes and burst into laughter.

"Bro! Your eyes are like… so red."

"I'm still doped up," I said, and shut my Chem book. "I've got a midterm today. Wish me luck."

"Dude, you're gonna need it. You look like the walking dead. Glam as all get-out, but still dead."

"Well, my friend… if you're going to be a zombie, you might as well do it in style," I said, unfolding my shades and slapping them on. I tapped their sides, where a holographic and reflective mirror bounced out. I combed through my hair and slapped my cheeks to brighten up my skin.

"Can't argue with ya there," Jareth said, and grinned. "Hey, by the way… I don't think I can go to that escape room with you guys this evening. Apparently, Natalie wants to do some mall shopping or something, and mom said I have to go with her." He rolled his eyes.

At the mention of her name, my heart skittered a step, though I doubted Jareth could tell. I focused on smoothing the sides of my hair with a comb. "It's cool, dude. Good thing there's at least three other people going. And I'm sure I can get more if I need; though I personally think it's better with less anyway."

"Makes people think harder."

"Precisely," I said, and shot my best friend a wink. "Still, see you guys afterwards?"

"Yeah. Natalie and I should be here when you're back from the escape room. We can order in and watch something or just hang out."

My heart definitely skittered a couple more beats. I took a small breath to calm it. "Cool, cool. Sounds good, my friend. Alrighty then, see you later."

When I shut the door of our dorm, there was a new skip to my step.

Jareth was awesome, and he was right about most things—but he was wrong about one. I wouldn't need any luck, today or otherwise. I never had trouble with luck.

***

The test flew by with almost no circumstance. I totally aced that midterm—it certainly helped I had taken those drugs during study time.

To celebrate, as already arranged, I met my friends out in the windy city's streets for our pre-planned escape room outing. I liked all the people that came, but I wished that Jareth had come and brought Natalie along with him. Maybe she hadn't wanted to come. Not a good sign for our soon-to-be relationship. Escape rooms were my main haunt—even better than techno clubs and electronic music festivals. Though the festivals came in an awfully close second.

The escape room stood just across from Jareth's haircutters and my favorite ice cream joint. I often went there after smoking a few *other* joints.

It started out easy. The employees led us into a single room with a bookshelf, a couple puzzles on the walls, and a safe on a table. As soon as they closed the door, I grinned around at my friends.

The two girls, Beatrice and Cynthia, worked on the puzzles, as the other guy present, Dan, sorted through the bookshelf. A quote sat on the wall: "To escape this puzzle, simply look for a nine, then make that double."

The girls couldn't seem to figure it out. They stared at the puzzle in front of them, which contained a maze of hidden pictures and numbers not visible to the naked eye. The colors were too red and compounding.

Beatrice made a frustrated sound. "I don't get it! I don't see a nine, or an eighteen, or…"

"I could look at every page nine and eighteen in these books?" Dan offered from behind.

"No, just move over," I said, and shoved the girls aside.

Below them, and hidden on a shelf, sat a pair of 3D glasses. I put those on and read the puzzle again. There, I saw the number nine, besides a word: Charles… and then an eighteen, with the words: Dickens.

"Did you by any chance find any Charles Dickens books over there, Dirty Dan?" I asked.

"Oh, yeah. They've got his whole collection over here."

Unhelpful, I thought, and glanced back at the puzzle. There was another line from the quote above, hidden in the 3D ink: "Once you've found your man, you'll need a title. Think of where it all began—with a double P and a plan."

Beatrice thought of this one. "Oh! I know! Charles Dickens' first novel was *The Pickwick Papers*. Published in 1836. Is that on the shelf?"

Dan shuffled through the bookshelf. "Got it!"

"Open it, open it," Cynthia squealed and raced over to him.

I stared at Beatrice. "Nice. How did you know that?"

"I'm a British Lit. major, remember?" she said, and shrugged.

I nodded with a smile.

Inside the book was a key, which opened one half of the safe, where there was another puzzle. That led us to another book, with another open cavity, and another key.

Safe to say we eventually found the right one.

Once we properly escaped, the employees congratulated us and gave us a coupon for the next time around. There were still a couple of rooms in this place we hadn't visited yet. I smiled, hoping that the next time would be with Natalie and Jareth.

Outside, the wind bristled against us with a hot, muggy attitude. We said goodbye to Cynthia, who had a tutoring session she had to attend, and watched her hop on her speed-bike. Her blonde hair flew behind her head as she skittered away—no helmet necessary.

"That escape room was easy peasy lemon squeezy," Beatrice said. She tossed her pretty, black curls behind her head. "Once Aaron found those glasses, it was smooth sailing."

I waved a hand. "I agree with you. It was far too simple for our combined intellect."

"Maybe they'll open up some harder ones in town," Dan said. "I'd like to see some new themes myself."

"Yeah—maybe," I said, though I had stopped thinking about escape rooms. My mind rested on Natalie. "So, you guys want to come back to my digs, or what? Jareth said we could hang out tonight."

"Yeah, sure," Beatrice said. "I'm down."

Dan nodded, swiping his ginger hair out of his green eyes. "Yeah, sounds cool. You live on campus, right?"

"Your parents must be loaded," Beatrice said, and raised her thick eyebrows.

I laughed. I didn't bother confirming it for them.

The brutal Saturday gale hammered against us as we walked. The whole way, my heart pounded with the expectation of seeing Natalie. I wondered what she decided to wear, if her hair hung loose and long over her chest, if she wore jeans or a tight sexy skirt like last time.

When we entered the flat, I didn't see Jareth or Natalie. I felt my heart sinking. They weren't back. But then, Jareth's hand rose from under a blanket on the couch and I spotted both their heads, resting just above it. I smiled.

"Comfortable much?" I gestured to the others around me. Everyone said hello as I introduced the group to Natalie. I cleared my throat. "This is Beatrice and Dan… and this Jareth's sister, Natalie."

"Hey," she said, and popped out of the blanket completely. It looked like she wore a tight, V-neck top that accentuated her torso. Her long, black hair shimmered, sleek and shiny as it rained down her chest. I swallowed. It was yoga pants, not jeans or a skirt. She looked as beautiful as ever. "Nice to meet you all, finally."

Her dark brown eyes latched to mine, and she smirked, as if she could tell what I was thinking. "Nice to see you again, *Señor Kim.*"

"Did you miss me, or what?'" I replied smoothly. Though when her heavy eyebrows disappeared into her hairline, I half-regretted it. *Cool it, Aaron,* I told myself, and rubbed the back of my neck to ease my nerves.

Until she replied, "Always," and winked.

"So—*this* is your guys' dig, huh?" Beatrice said, hands on her waist. "Nice. Not bad at all for a college dorm."

"Yup." Jareth stared at her with the kind of filmy, starry eyes that I recognized all too well. "So, how was the escape room?" he asked, his eyes on my friend. "I'm so sorry we couldn't make it."

Dan shrugged. "It was fine, I guess. Not too challenging, to be honest. It took us less than thirty minutes to solve it."

"Yeah, because I solved it," I said, causing both Dan and Beatrice to break into loud protests. I waved my hands. "Settle down settle down—you two definitely helped. We *all* contributed… this time."

Beatrice laughed.

Dan shrugged. "Eh, it doesn't matter—I'm sure we'll find another worthy escape room eventually."

"How many have you guys done?" Natalie asked.

"Who knows?" Jareth replied. "Too many."

"Maybe we could make our own escape room," I said. "We could open it up on Halloween and charge people extra if they can't solve it."

Everyone laughed, but I was only half-joking. Beatrice walked slowly around the living area, her hands behind her back. She glanced into our bedroom, smirking and nodding her head. Dan sat on the couch's armchair, staring around and tapping his knees like a drum.

Jareth kept staring at Beatrice. I tried to get Natalie's attention, so we could make fun of him together, but she was busy glaring at her freshly manicured nails.

I sighed and sat down beside my best friend. "Hey there. Whatcha doing?" I teased and elbowed him. He shrugged, blushing. "Did you guys have a good time shopping?"

"Oh, yeah—we found all kinds of *sweet* deals," Natalie said, and laughed.

Jareth rolled his eyes. "Actually, we mainly just went into candy stores. That's the joke."

"Speaking of candy…" Natalie nudged her brother, then winked at me. My heart fluttered inside my chest.

"You guys got candy?" Dan asked. He jumped off the arm and sat cross-legged before her. His face looked far too eager. I raised one eyebrow at him.

Natalie laughed loudly. She leaned forward and punched Dan lightly on the shoulder. He grinned back at her. I felt a spasm of jealousy erupt in my stomach.

"See? He gets it," she said.

"Gets what?" I asked, as casually as I could.

"Tell him, Jar!"

Jareth glanced at his sister once before leaning toward me, his eyes sly. "We got some *other* kind of candy—if you get my drift."

I knew what Jareth meant. Candy also referred to drugs. I couldn't help feeling excited at the prospect. "Was it from Big Rick? That guy doesn't have the highest confidence in his buyers."

Jareth shook his head. "Nah, man. Remember how last year during spring break my family took a trip to Mexico? Dude! I must've forgotten to tell you this—but, my cousins took us up to the forests in the Oaxaca mountains. Up there we met this crazy old hacker druid while we were backpacking. Some Europeans told us about him at a hostel, and we went looking for him."

"A hacker druid?" Beatrice asked from across the room.

Jareth spun toward her. "Yeah, he was like a hermit with all kinds of hacker technology. He showed us his drug hut in the middle of nowhere. I think he grows the drugs right there and sells them online for cheap. Anyway, he was a cool guy. And he practically gave them to *us* for free. His hair was in long, white dreads, and he wore this weaved frock. It was pretty psychedelic!"

"He also reeked rotten," Natalie added, making us all laugh.

"What are they?" I asked, beyond intrigued—even before Jareth pulled out the drugs from his pocket, wrapped in a brown paper bag covered in plastic wrapper.

He removed the plastic, flattened out the bag, and revealed shriveled up green mushrooms. They looked nastier than most shrooms I'd ever seen, but they were shrooms, nonetheless.

"Shrooms?" Beatrice said for me, her face scrunched up.

"Yeah, I don't know how delectable those are, homie," I said.

"No, listen—they're a new kind of drug. Supposedly, they were fresh off the market." Jareth waved his hand closer and whispered, "They're electro-psychedelic mushrooms. Bioengineered in their natural environment for an enhanced high."

Dan whistled. "Wait, what? Do tell."

"Well, fresh last year," Natalie said. "But who knows if they're still any good. I found them stashed at home, cuz we'd forgotten about them since we came back. I brought them to Jareth today."

Jareth's black eyes twinkled. "Anyway, yes, Dan. I guess they're meant to give the user an 'otherworldly experience' or something like that. Like regular psychedelic shrooms times ten. At least, that's what the hacker druid told us."

Beatrice snorted. "Nothing like the words of a hacker druid to get you loose and relaxed!"

As Jareth passed around the bag, I took a single shroom and dropped it into my palm. It sat there lightly, though I held it with a strange heaviness. It sounded powerful—all the more reason to try it. Recently, I had become a connoisseur of all sorts of wild, new drugs. Most of them ended up fine, with more than half-good trips. But most of them I had also bought myself from Big Rick or another well-known acquaintance. This was something entirely different.

"And you're sure it's safe?" I asked, surprising myself.

Natalie scoffed. "What? You don't trust old Mexican hacker druids, *Señor Kim*?"

Everyone laughed at that, settling me.

Natalie leaned over her brother and placed her hand on my knee. Even though I wore jeans, my skin sizzled under her touch. "Come on, A. Do it with me. It'll be fun."

From her position, I could see down her shirt, but I didn't dare look. Instead, I gazed deep into her dark, chocolate-colored eyes.

"Yeah, sure. Why not?" I said evenly. "It'll be fun. What's the worst that could happen?"

"Well, if Aaron Kim's in, then I'm in too," Beatrice said.

Dan seconded with a nervous, "Here, here!"

Everyone held a shroom in their hand now. Natalie gazed around at everyone with sly eyes, waiting for a challenge. But when no one dared, she said, "On three, then. *One… Two…*"

On *"three,"* an extra loud gust of wind hit the window, causing half the party to splutter and choke on their respective mushrooms. The wind pushed a tree branch against the window, which *rapped, rapped, rapped*, as if trying to get inside.

Feeling suddenly nervous, I took a deep breath and also quickly shoved the shroom into my mouth, swallowing it whole.

***

The living room twisted and spun. In a matter of seconds, my entire perception flipped upside down. When I blinked my eyes, I saw the couch, miles away, and me, suspended from the ceiling. But… I wasn't upside down. Only the living room was. My friends sat around me, their limbs elongated and their joyful groans echoing loudly through my ears.

My head felt weighted and heavy. I blinked again.

The room's color completely drained, so that everything appeared dark blue and gray and black. Thick, bold lines outlined the couch, the TV, the doors, and the windows. When I reached for them, my fingers went right through them and only touched the lines. At my touch, the outlines jumped away from me and traced another couch, another TV, another door, another window. Suddenly, we were in a room full of half-formed mirror images—like accidental clones. I glanced around and saw my face everywhere, reflecting like the facets of a black diamond.

My friends laughed and screamed; I wondered if they saw the same images as me. I tried to speak to them, but my mouth felt glued shut; my tongue stuck to the roof of my mouth.

Make it stop, I thought, as the room spun and whirled. *Make it stop… Please!*

My friends' laughter increased, rising in volume, until it pierced my ears and made me wince.

"Stop," I managed to mutter, just before I passed out cold.

***

My vision wavered as I blinked my eyes awake. Everything remained blurry for a second, and I heard my friends groaning and rising around me. *They must have passed out, too,* I thought, and straightened up.

I sat on the floor, along with everyone else. Dan and Beatrice lay on their backs across the couch, while Natalie hung off the armrest. Jareth clung to the back of the couch like his life depended on it. But none of us were upside down. Neither was the furniture.

However, the room had maintained his eerie, dark blue glow. I rubbed my eyes furiously, hoping to get rid of the image. But it was like the color had permanently changed. The room was warmer—much warmer than usual—and strangely still. Objects I couldn't place floated around my head. They appeared to be more like dust particles, or pieces of ripped up paper. When I reached for them, though, they slipped right through my hands as if I was a ghost.

"Where *are* we?" Beatrice asked, and rubbed the back of her head. "And what the hell happened?"

"We had a bad trip," I said, and stood up. "But… we're in the same room."

Jareth stared around, his hands reaching for the floating dust particles, too.

Natalie stared at them, her brows furrowed. "It sure doesn't *look* like the same room," she said.

I didn't answer, busy strolling around the room like Beatrice had before—when there was nothing strange about it.

As I neared the door, I reached my hand out, only to have an invisible force stop me. It pressed against me from the opposite side, and I realized it was a barrier of sorts. An invisible shield blocking us in. Heart pounding, I walked the perimeter of the room and pushed on areas of the wall where we should have been able to escape. I pressed against our shared room, the door, the window. But nothing gave. At every spot, an invisible barrier pressed back, immovable. I couldn't move past it, no matter how hard I pushed. It was making me dizzy, as panic started to seep in.

"Whatcha doing, *hermano*?" Jareth asked nervously.

I panted and stepped back. "There's a barrier around us. It's invisible, but it's blocking all our exits."

Natalie straightened up. "What? What do you mean?"

"We're stuck," I said. A zap of panic came over me, and I pounded a fist into the barrier. A thousand electric blue lines zigzagged up the wall and onto the ceiling, where they disappeared into a flurry of nonsensical numbers.

"What… the…" Dan was saying.

"I told you!" Natalie shouted. She spun at her brother, her face manic. "I told you not to trust that crazy old hacker druid!" She punched him repeatedly in the shoulder. "This is not good!"

"Hey, ow, ow—*ow!* Get off me, Nat." He shoved her off, where she crossed her arms and glared at him. "What are you talking about? You never once told me to leave those drugs. Admit it. You wanted to try them just as much as me, ever since the trip last year."

"Fine! Maybe I was curious. But I certainly wasn't prepared for *this.* You said they were safe."

"No, *you* said they were safe."

"Well, the hacker druid guy said they were safe!"

"Yeah, well, he was probably lying. He just wanted us to either buy the crap or get rid of it. Or get rid of us. And I guess it worked, didn't it?"

"Jareth, as soon as he mentioned the word 'e-shroom,' you were all over him, begging to taste it right there on the spot."

"Well, you're the one who brought them today. So…"

Natalie opened her mouth again, her eyes full of fury, but I cut in quick, "Guys! Come on, it doesn't matter who said what. We all agreed to take the drugs. And now we're stuck. We're all in this together."

The force of these words sat heavy on my shoulders, like a silent, tangible fear. I swallowed the lump in my throat.

Natalie nodded as she hugged my arm. I welcomed her.

"Listen, all," I said. "Maybe this is just some sort of puzzle. Like an escape room. A weird, virtual psychedelic one, but still an escape room. Surely we can find a way out if we work together."

"Hey, there's an idea. Good thinking, Aaron," Dan said. He strode to every corner, beating on the invisible edges and watching the electric trails zoom across the barrier.

As the electric trails met, they collided into a resounding *zap* and *whizz* that almost sounded like music—or a small child gasping. And at every collision, the nonsensical numbers reappeared.

Beatrice covered her ears and moaned, while Natalie spun her head at every new zip and gasp.

"Hey, Dan, maybe keep it down a little...?" Jareth asked him.

But he pounded the walls with no abandon.

I focused on the numbers. They blazed across the ceiling: *5 @ 6.3, 10 @ 12, & 4 @ 3.15.* Then, they disappeared. The room was silent and dark once more.

"Well, what the heck does that mean?" Natalie snapped. She ran her fingers through her hair. "It's just a bunch of numbers and decimals!"

"Yeah, and what about those 'at' signs?" Jareth supplied—rather unhelpfully.

"Everyone, calm down. Let's just focus. Remember—it's just like an escape room."

"Sure, except most escape rooms have employees that will still let you out, even if you can't complete it," Beatrice muttered.

"We will get out of this," I pressed. "We wanted one that was up to our intellect. Right? So, just… let me think."

I walked around the room, considering the numbers anew. Why were there decimals and "at" signs? What did that mean? It was like a nonsensical version of holographic text talk.

That's when I noticed the big, boxy clock on the wall. Jareth's mom had put it up soon after we had moved in. She had picked it out for him because supposedly it reminded her of an old game he had played, where the main character was a square-shaped clock that used its minute hands as swords.

"That's it," I suddenly realized. Everyone turned to me, their red eyes wide, and giddiness filled me up at the intelligence of my own brain. "That's it! Half the numbers are associated with time—or at least, the positions of the minute hand on a clock. They signify when both minute hands share the same space. Six-thirty, twelve, and three-fifteen." At each time, I jogged around the room and pointed to the door at the bottom, to our shared room at the top, and to the clock, which hung off the right-hand side of the room. The window sat on the opposite wall—almost like it was staring at the clock.

"*Okay*?" Natalie dragged the word out long. "And what are we supposed to with that?"

"We need to think about the other numbers… The ones proceeding those associated with time." I formed my hand into a fist, thinking, and then understood. "We have to pound the walls!"

"*What?*" Beatrice groaned. "Please, no…"

"Just cover your ears," I said, and began to pound the walls accordingly. Five times in the position of 6:30, ten in the position of midnight or noon, depending on your mood, and four times in the position of 3:15.

The creepy music soared once more, sounding like wailing or light gasping. Then, something fell from the ceiling. Dan, Natalie, and Beatrice screamed.

Jareth hurried over to collect the object. It looked just like a blank piece of heavy paper. I took it from him and turned it over. We all saw bright, neon colors, all placed into intricate patterns.

"It's like a 3D glasses puzzle," I said. "Too bad we didn't steal those ones from the actual escape room…"

"Try your sunglasses," Jareth said, to which everyone gave him a strange look. He shrugged, far too casual for the situation. "Yo, this is clearly an alternate reality simulation. Let's be honest now; things don't work the same way here."

"He's right," Natalie said. "That's got to be it…"

"Well, we have nothing to lose," Beatrice stated.

"Okay," I said. "Let's do it." Grinning mischievously, I slapped on my shades and pulled the paper close. But I couldn't see anything from just staring at the paper. I remembered the various applications contained inside my Aviators and clicked on the last thing I had used. The portable mirror.

It worked as a two-way mirror so you could view yourself from both sides if needed. And as I held the paper beneath it, it transformed into a magnifying glass. Words popped out of the page.

"Speak… And they will listen."

As soon as I'd finished reading it, the paper caught flame. I dropped it, wincing, just as it completely disappeared into thin air with a crackle and *pop*.

"What the *freak* is happening!" Natalie squealed. "I don't like this. I really don't like this at all."

But my heart thrummed with excitement. Everything we had used before, in the other escape room, had come back into play in this one—in one form or another.

"Don't worry, I'm confident we got this," I said, and grinned.

Everyone just gave me a dumbstruck look.

"But I'm not sure I understand… *Speak and they will listen?"* Dan asked. "What does that mean?"

"It's referring to the dust particles," Natalie said, with sudden confidence. "Quiet down, everyone. If you listen closely, it's like they're whispering something to us. It was them the whole time, making those sounds—not the electric lines colliding."

I felt a little unnerved by this fact but didn't dare contradict Natalie. Especially now that she'd stopped freaking out so suddenly.

So, we all listened to them as they passed, our hands out as if to try and catch one. But all they did was slip right through our fingers.

"No, don't try to catch them, they don't like that," she said. "Just... listen..."

Sure enough—as the dust particles whizzed past, they sounded like tiny babies, babbling and whispering and wailing. I shivered.

She was right.

"Okay, well, um... great dust particles, will you kindly let us out?" I tried, remembering we also had to speak to them.

Their whispering grew louder, until it sounded like ghosts were in the room with us. At this, Beatrice covered her ears and closed her eyes.

"Maybe you have to be more specific," Jareth said, who appeared to be way too calm.

"Alright. Dust particle creatures, uh, we need you to let us out of this room. Perhaps with a key? Please...?"

"And a door," Natalie added.

We locked eyes, where I felt the sizzling smolder of a connection. My goodness, even in this bad trip she looked so hot. Once we got out of here...

The dust particles began to bunch together. They zoomed over our heads and collided with each other in a *bang* and burst of electric blue color.

Natalie screamed and I ran to her instinctively, gripping her hand and not caring that everyone could see. Jareth didn't even fix me with a dark look, too busy staring at the apparently alive dust balls himself.

Dan ducked as they smoked and exploded, their whispering wails as loud as a cannon. When the dust settled, we all stared at the giant, key-shaped particle before us. It looked far too big for a normal keyhole. Besides, I didn't see any place it would fit.

"Holy shit. It actually worked," Beatrice said.

Dan glanced around nervously. "Do you think it'll let us grab it?"

"Only one way to find out," Jareth muttered, reached forward, and grasped it. This time, it didn't slip through his fingers. He shuddered. "Bro! It feels slimy and cold. Tell me where to put this thing so I can let go."

"Well… We haven't touched the left-side of the barrier's wall, where the window is. Maybe that's the spot with a door through the barrier?" Beatrice suggested.

"That's not a bad idea. That would be at the 9:45 spot, if we're still thinking about it like time," I said.

Just then, a loud *gong* rang out, like a dinging grandfather clock. It rang and rang, resounding inside our heads and causing almost everyone to cover their ears.

"Go to the left-side, Jareth!" I shouted.

He vaulted over the couch. The dust particles wriggled and writhed in his hand, making the key look like an oversized, furry rat.

Gong. Gong. Gong.

Jareth tried shoving the dust particle key into the barrier, but there didn't seem to be a place for it. "This isn't working, dudes!"

"Beatrice!" I suddenly shouted. "What is *The Pickwick Papers* about?"

"What?"

"*The Pickwick Papers!* That Charles Dickens' story that got us out of the other escape room. Remember—the one in Chicago's city center?"

"Oh! It's about this man who gets in a disagreement with his landlord, this old widow who he's also in love with. And they end up thrown in prison for some debt—"

But at the word "prison," the dust particle key suddenly slid into a slot along the wall. Jareth stood there for a moment, his mouth agape, until he grabbed the key with both hands.

"If we're discussing Charles Dickens, how about *Oliver Twist.*" He twisted the key, where a familiar click sounded. "Eh, eh—get it?"

But no one grinned along with him. I certainly wasn't feeling cheery anymore. Somewhere between the dust particles whispering and the loud gong, this psychedelic escape room had stopped being fun. As a door-shaped hole in the invisible barrier swung open, the gong sound abruptly stopped.

"It's leading us right to the window," I breathed. "Let me test it first. Everyone, stand back!"

My friends obeyed and stood back against the opposing barrier walls as I crept toward the open door. It didn't swing shut on me. And with slow, shaking limbs, I managed to step through.

The room felt different out here—colder, stiffer—and the color appeared less gray. I ran to the window and started to unlatch it. Only, my fingers slipped against the latch—it was sealed tight with frost. Frozen. I couldn't move it. I tried punching it and breathing on it, but it didn't seem to matter.

The cold persisted. Even outside the barrier, we remained stuck in another dimension. An alternate reality, where it looked as if we couldn't escape.

I glanced around, hoping we could slip through to the door, but I could tell the invisible barrier bordered me on all sides. I could see its outline in the cold.

"Hey, Trix," I said, as calmly as I dared, "how did the characters from that Dickens' book get out of prison?"

"Well… literally, he paid for her debts. But figuratively, the only way to end his love's suffering was to suffer himself. Or something like that."

"And their debts?"

"Frivolous stuff. Long travels, gambling, *drugs*…"

Everyone sucked in a breath, aware of the symbolism.

Self-suffering. Unwanted debts. Forced martyrdom. Were these the prices we had to pay for our own self-indulgence? For our ridiculous choices?

"Shit," I whispered. "SHIT!"

"Whoa, easy there, Aaron. We'll get out of this," Jareth said. "It's just a bad trip, *hermano*."

But I didn't say anything. Instead, I leaned against the forever-latched window, panting, and thought I saw a shadow on the outside. The outline of a tree. Its branch tapped against the window, *rap, rap, rap,* and this time, it sounded like laughter—more like *rapataprap*.

"So—the tables have turned," I muttered, and chuckled, my breath fogging against the window's glass. "We didn't let you in, so now you won't let us out, huh?"

"Are you okay, Aaron?" Natalie asked with a concerned look on her face.

"No," I replied. My chuckles rose in volume, until I was laughing hysterically. "No, because I can't figure it out. It's… it's too hard. We're stuck. We are *stuck*."

As soon as I said it, the gong sounded again, followed by the dust particles' whisperings. Everyone screamed. Beatrice and Dan started to cry, as the room warped and twisted and spun—just like it had when we'd first taken the shrooms.

Stupid shrooms!

It was a trip, alright—a very bad trip, indeed. One that we should have never messed with. I had walked through my reality like a god—impenetrable and unshakeable—exactly like this room. But in this room, I was no one. I couldn't move it or shake it my way.

Not this time.

These shrooms taught me one thing and one thing only: Perhaps there are just some things that should not be taken.

THE BOY WHO WOULD BE ROBOT

Aytor didn't mind being different. In fact, Aytor rather enjoyed it. While the other kids at school played with soccer balls, video games, and action figures, Aytor preferred the company of machines. Engines, circuits, wires—these were his friends. They didn't talk too much, they didn't ask confusing questions, and most importantly, they didn't judge.

Aytor had always been different, though growing up he wasn't quite sure what made him different from everyone else. When he was nine years old he learned about his diagnosis of autism; but words like "autism" and "diagnosed" didn't make much sense to him. What he did understand was that he didn't think the same way other kids did. He didn't like the loud noises in the cafeteria, didn't understand why people's faces showed so many different emotions, and didn't know why he had to make eye contact when it felt like his eyes might burn if he tried too hard.

But there was one thing Aytor did understand—machines. Especially robots. The way they moved, how their joints clicked and clanked in perfect synchronization, the calm, predictable tones of their voices. They made sense to him. Unlike people, robots followed rules. They weren't messy or chaotic. They did what they were supposed to do. They didn't shout or expect you to guess how they were feeling. Robots didn't have feelings. They just... were.

And now, at twelve years old, Aytor was already an expert at taking things apart from machines and robots and putting them back together. His room was filled with gadgets, most of which no longer worked as their manufacturers intended. But in Aytor's hands, they took on new life, becoming part of his elaborate imagination. He would mix the parts of an old toaster with a broken RC car to create something new—a tiny, clunky machine that hummed and whirred in the way that comforted him.

The world outside his room was often too loud, too fast, and too confusing. But inside, surrounded by his makeshift creations, Aytor found peace. Most of all, though, Aytor wished he could be a robot himself. A robot wouldn't have to deal with emotions he didn't understand, or people who looked at him like he was broken.

In the evenings, after school, Aytor would sit on the living room floor with his collection of robot action figures. There was R-12, his favorite, a sleek silver android with red LED eyes, and X-Treme Bot, a bulkier, clunkier model that came with a remote control to make it walk. He imagined what it would be like to live in a world where he was just like them, a perfect machine, unbothered by the confusion that came with being human.

One afternoon, after a particularly exhausting day at school, Aytor sat cross-legged on his bedroom floor, staring at a pile of dismantled electronics. His mind hummed as he thought about the kids in his class who didn't understand him—the way they whispered behind his back, the way their laughter seemed to sting. Why did people have to be so complicated? Why couldn't they be simple, like robots? And on that moment, Aytor decided that he didn't want to just play with robots—he wanted to *be* one.

In his lap sat the shell of an old tablet. It had stopped working months ago, but Aytor never threw anything away. He picked up a screwdriver and began to unscrew the back, his hands moving automatically. He liked the sound the screws made when they came loose, the quiet click of plastic separating. His focus was intense, the outside world melting away.

As he worked, an idea started to take better shape in his mind. What if he could build something that would make him more like a robot? Not just a machine he could control with a remote, but something that could help him become who he really wanted to be—someone without the confusing emotions and the difficulties that came with being human. A robot wouldn't get tired of socializing. A robot wouldn't have to figure out what someone meant when they said one thing but clearly meant something else.

His heart raced at the thought. He knew this was what he had to do.

***

Aytor's mother, Myrna, found him in his room that night, lying on his bed with a screwdriver, carefully unscrewing one of his creations. She sighed softly as she watched him. She was used to his obsession with robots and all kinds of electronics by now. Growing up, Aytor never really play with toys the way other kids did. Instead, he always took them apart, studied them, and then tried to put them back together. It had always been this way.

"Aytor," she said, sitting down on the edge of his bed. "What are you doing, sweetheart?"

"I'm trying to figure out how R-12 works," he replied without looking up. His voice was calm, robotic almost, the way it got when he was focused. "If I can figure out how he works, maybe I can make myself into a robot."

Myrna's heart skipped a beat. She smiled gently, even though a pang of worry settled in her chest. "What do you mean?"

Aytor hesitated, unsure if he should say what was on his mind. Finally, he blurted out, "I want to be a robot."

Myrna's eyes softened as she looked back at him. "Why do you say that, sweetie? Why would you want to be a robot?"

"Because robots don't feel things the way people do. They don't get confused, and they always know what they're supposed to do. I don't want to be confused anymore, Mom. I want to know what I'm supposed to do all the time. Like a robot." Aytor's his voice grew more frustrated as he tried to find the right words. "They don't get overwhelmed, and they don't have to guess what people are thinking all the time. I don't want to guess anymore."

There was a long pause, and Myrna felt her throat tighten. She felt something like this was coming. She had seen the signs in the way Aytor isolated himself more and more from the world, retreating into the comfort of mechanical things, where there were no surprises or emotions to figure out. But now that he had voiced it, it hit her in a way she wasn't prepared for.

"Aytor, being a robot wouldn't make you happy," she finally said softly.

"How do you know?" he asked, his brow furrowing as if trying to solve a puzzle.

"Because robots don't get to feel love, or happiness, or excitement," she explained. "Robots don't get to enjoy all the beautiful things about being human. Like when you solve a tricky math problem or when you hug me goodnight. Those are things only humans can do."

Aytor was quiet for a moment, processing her words. Then he shook his head. "But it's hard being a human, Mom. I don't know what people are thinking. I don't know what to say to them. Being a robot would be easier."

Myrna placed her hand on his, holding the screwdriver in his grasp. "I know it's hard sometimes; but I promise you, you don't have to be like everyone else to be wonderful. You don't have to be a robot to be special. You're already perfect as you are. And, sweetie, being human isn't just about the tough stuff. You also get to feel joy, excitement, and love. Robots can't feel any of that."

Aytor didn't respond. His face was blank, but Myrna could tell he was deep in thought. That was how it was with Aytor. His feelings didn't show on the outside, but inside, there was always a storm of thoughts whirring around. Like gears in a robot.

"But what if I don't want to feel anything?" Aytor asked, his voice quieter now, almost sad. "What if I just want everything to be simple?"

His mom took his hand, squeezing it gently. "I know it feels like being a robot would make things easier. But I love you because you're *you*. The way you think, the way you care about your robots, the way you see the world. If you were a robot, you wouldn't be Aytor anymore."

Aytor stared at his robot. Myrna knew he didn't know how to explain it to her, how heavy it felt sometimes to be himself, how hard it was to keep up with everything when the world was so different. But his hand felt warm in hers, and for a moment, he didn't pull away.

***

Over the next several weeks, Aytor worked tirelessly. After school, he would retreat to his room, armed with wires, metal parts, and various odds and ends he had scavenged. Every day, he came closer to realizing his dream. He drew up plans on crumpled sheets of paper, diagrams filled with lines and arrows that only made sense to him. He told no one what he was doing, not his parents, not his teachers. They wouldn't understand.

He called his project "The Integration." It wasn't just going to be a costume or a machine—it was going to make him more like the robot he wanted to be. He imagined it as an exoskeleton that would wrap around his body, a suit of armor that would help him navigate the world without fear or confusion. It would help him talk to people the right way, help him understand their feelings even when they were too complicated. It would make him strong and logical, just like the robots in his favorite shows.

As the pieces began to come together, Aytor felt a sense of control he rarely experienced. Each piece he soldered into place, each wire he connected, brought him closer to his goal. He didn't need to rely on anyone else. He was building something on his own terms, something that would finally make sense to him.

The Integration was taking shape, but it wasn't perfect yet. There were moments of frustration when things didn't work the way he expected. But unlike the confusion he felt in social situations, the problems with his machine were solvable. When a circuit malfunctioned, he could trace the error. When a motor refused to turn, he could replace it. There was always a solution, and Aytor liked that. He wished people were like that too.

His mother would come and check in on him daily. She would ask him about his project, but she would simply say he was busy. She wouldn't understand. She couldn't.

One evening, after weeks of painstaking work, Aytor put the finishing touches on his creation. The Integration was a mishmash of metal plates, wires, and small motors, but it was beautiful to him. He attached the last wire and stood back to admire it. His heart pounded with anticipation.

It was time.

He slipped into the suit, his fingers trembling with excitement. The cool metal pressed against his skin, and for a moment, Aytor hesitated. What if it didn't work? What if it wasn't enough? But then he shook the doubts from his mind. He had come too far to turn back now.

He pressed a button on the inside of the suit, and the Integration hummed to life. A soft blue light flickered on the chest plate, and Aytor felt a surge of excitement. He walked to the mirror, his reflection distorted by the wires and plates that covered him. But he didn't see himself as a boy anymore. He saw a robot—a logical, calm, and efficient machine.

For the first time, he felt powerful. He wasn't just Aytor, the weird kid who didn't know how to fit in. He was something more. Something better.

The next day, against his mother's wishes, Aytor wore the suit under his clothes to school. He could feel the metal against his skin, and it gave him confidence. When he walked down the hall, he imagined himself as a robot, moving with purpose. He didn't worry about the other kids staring at him. He didn't feel nervous when the teacher called on him in class. The Integration was working.

But as the day wore on, something strange started to happen. The suit began to feel heavier, the wires pressing into his skin uncomfortably, scratching him. He couldn't move freely either. During lunch, Aytor found himself sitting alone again, tired from carrying the extra, uncomfortable weight, and with the familiar sounds of laughter and conversation swirling around him. He had expected the Integration to make him feel different, to help him fit in. But the more he tried to act like a robot, the more he realized something was wrong.

The suit wasn't making things easier. It was making things harder.

By the end of the day, Aytor felt exhausted. His muscles ached from carrying the weight of the suit, and his mind was a jumble of confusion. When he got home, he tore off the Integration and threw it onto the floor, frustration boiling inside him.

He had wanted so badly to be a robot, to escape the feelings and confusion that came with being human. But now, looking at the pile of wires and metal at his feet, he realized something important. Being a robot wasn't the answer. It couldn't make the world easier to understand. It couldn't fix the things that made him feel different.

Aytor sat down on the floor, his shoulders slumping. Maybe he didn't need to change himself to fit in. Maybe being different wasn't something that needed to be fixed. The world was complicated, yes, but so was he. And maybe that was okay.

His eyes flicked to the discarded pieces of the Integration. They were just parts, just machines. They couldn't think, they couldn't feel. And as much as Aytor sometimes wished he could turn off his emotions, he realized in that moment that his feelings—however confusing—were what made him human.

He picked up the crumpled plans for the Integration, smoothed out the paper, and folded it carefully. It had been a good idea, but it wasn't what he needed anymore.

Aytor walked to his window and looked out at the world, the late afternoon sun casting long shadows across the street. Aytor stood at the window for a long time, watching the world outside. Cars passed by, people walked their dogs, and children rode their bikes along the sidewalk. It was the same chaotic world he had always known, the one he struggled to make sense of, but for the first time, he didn't feel the overwhelming need to change himself to match it.

He turned away from the window and looked back at the remnants of the Integration, the wires strewn across the floor like abandoned puzzle pieces. He knelt down and began to gather them up, slowly and methodically. He didn't feel angry at the suit anymore. It wasn't the suit's fault. It had been an idea, an attempt to make life easier, but now he understood that it couldn't fix everything. And that was okay.

As he collected the pieces, Aytor felt a sense of calm settle over him. Maybe it was time to build something else. Something new. But not to change himself—this time, he would build something just for the joy of creating it.

***

The next day at school, Aytor stood on the playground, watching the other kids run around and play. They were loud, so loud, and their laughter seemed to ring in his ears like a bell he couldn't shut off. He shifted uncomfortably, hugging his arms around himself as he stood by the chain-link fence, trying to focus on something else—anything else.

"Aytor!" a voice called, snapping him out of his trance.

It was Noah, a boy from two classes below him. Noah was always nice to Aytor, but he was also full of energy, always jumping around and talking a mile a minute. Aytor didn't always know how to talk back to him, but Noah didn't seem to mind.

"Hey, wanna come play tag?" Noah asked, bouncing on his heels. "We need one more player!"

Aytor shook his head quickly. "No, thank you."

Noah tilted his head, looking at Aytor curiously. "Why not? It'll be fun!"

"I don't like running," Aytor said, which was partly true. But more than that, he didn't like the unpredictability of tag. The way everyone chased each other, the random directions they would run. It made his brain hurt trying to follow it all.

"Okay," Noah said with a shrug. "You wanna come help me build a robot, then?"

Aytor's head snapped up, his eyes widening. "Build a robot?"

"Yeah!" Noah grinned. "We're making one out of boxes and stuff. It doesn't work, but it'll look like a robot when we're done!"

For the first time in a long while, Aytor felt a spark of excitement. "I'll help," he said quickly, following Noah to the edge of the playground where a small group of kids of different grades were gathered around a pile of cardboard boxes, tin foil, and empty soda cans.

They were taping boxes together to form the body, wrapping tinfoil around them for a shiny, metallic effect. Aytor immediately began to focus, his hands moving over the materials with precision. He found himself giving directions, telling the other kids how to make the robot look more real, how to shape the arms and legs properly.

As the minutes passed, he felt something strange—a feeling he hadn't felt in a while. It wasn't confusion or anxiety. It was something warm, something good.

He was… happy.

That night, Aytor lay in bed thinking about the robot they had built. It wasn't a real robot, of course. It couldn't move or talk, but it had felt good to build it with the others, to work together with them, even if just for a little while.

Maybe his mom had been right. Maybe being a robot wasn't the answer. Robots didn't have friends. They didn't get to feel the satisfaction of working on something with other people, of being part of something bigger than themselves.

When his mom came into his room to say good-night, Aytor looked up at her and said, "Mom, I think I don't want to be a robot anymore."

Myrna smiled, her eyes softening as she stroked his hair. "I'm glad to hear that, sweetheart."

"Can I still play with my robots, though?"

"Of course," she said with a laugh. "You can always play with your robots."

Aytor nodded, closing his eyes. As he drifted off to sleep, he realized something. Being human was hard sometimes, but it wasn't all bad. There were good things about it too, like building robots with friends and feeling your mom's hand in yours.

Maybe, just maybe, being a human wasn't so bad after all.

***

The next few days were different. After school, Aytor still spent time in his room, surrounded by his machines and gadgets, but he no longer felt the pressure to build something to fix himself. Instead, he worked on smaller projects—things that made him happy, things that sparked his curiosity. He built a tiny robot that could crawl across his desk, a light-up circuit board that flashed in patterns he programmed himself, and even a small mechanical hand that could wave back and forth. These creations didn't have to solve any problems. They were simply a part of who he was, an expression of his love for building and tinkering.

At school, things weren't perfect. The other kids still didn't always understand him, and Aytor didn't always understand them. But he found that it bothered him less now. He had friends in his machines at home, and at school some of the younger kids were now nicer to him after the whole robot-building experience. That was enough for him.

One afternoon the following week, as Aytor sat in his usual spot in the school cafeteria, tinkering with a small device he had brought from home, he noticed someone sitting down across from him. He looked up to see a new girl from his class, Jenny, watching him curiously.

"What are you working on?" she asked, her voice soft but filled with genuine interest.

Aytor hesitated, unsure of how to respond. He wasn't used to people asking about his projects. Most of the time, they either ignored him or gave him strange looks. He was more surprised that it was a girl from his own grade that was talking to him.

"It's a... motor," he finally said, holding up the small device. "I'm trying to make it spin faster without overheating."

Jenny nodded, her eyes brightening. "That is so cool! I don't know much about motors, but my dad fixes cars. I've heard him say something about how engines overheat if you push them too hard."

Aytor blinked, surprised by her response. He wasn't used to people making connections like that, especially not in a way that made sense to him.

"You want to help me with it?" Aytor asked cautiously, still unsure if she was just being polite or if she was genuinely interested.

Jenny smiled. "Sure! I can't promise I'll be much help, but I'd like to learn."

For the rest of lunch, Aytor showed her how the motor worked, explaining the basics of circuitry and heat dissipation. To his surprise, Jenny asked good questions, and even when she didn't fully understand, she seemed patient and eager to learn. It was a new experience for Aytor—talking to someone who wasn't just pretending to listen, but actually wanted to know more.

Over the next few weeks, Jenny started joining Aytor more often during lunch. Sometimes they talked about his projects, other times they just sat quietly, both of them working on their own things. Aytor found that he didn't mind the silence when he was with her. It wasn't the awkward, uncomfortable silence he often felt around other people. With Jenny, it felt like the kind of silence you share with someone who understands.

***

One day, Jenny was absent. This was hard for Aytor, as she had become his reason for coming to school. With her, he could talk about robots and other cool stuff. But with her gone, he felt lonely.

"Do you want to play tag?" Noah asked during lunch, his eyes bright with energy.

"No," Aytor said firmly sitting on the table. The idea of running around in random directions gave him a headache. He'd explained this before, but Noah didn't seem to get it.

"You never play," Noah said, sounding disappointed. "What are you going to do then?"

"I'm working on Axiom." Aytor pulled the newer small robot from his bag, holding it up proudly.

Noah squinted at it. "Axiom? That's a cool name. What does he do?"

"She," Aytor corrected him. "Axiom is a she." His fingers brushed over the smooth surface of the figure, admiring its perfectly symmetrical shape. "She's going to be a robot that can do anything—think faster, react faster, and never make mistakes."

Noah gave a low whistle, clearly impressed, even if he didn't fully understand. "Cool. But wouldn't it be more fun if she could shoot lasers or something?"

Aytor frowned. "That's not the point. The point is that she's better than a person. People are messy. Robots are perfect."

"Perfect? How?"

Aytor didn't have the words to explain it to Noah, not in a way that would make sense to someone who loved the chaos of tag. "Because they don't get confused. They don't have to figure out what someone is thinking or feeling, or guess when they're supposed to talk or be quiet. They just know. They're never wrong."

Noah shrugged, clearly not getting it, but not making fun of him either. "I guess. You ever wish you were a robot?"

Aytor paused, his eyes narrowing as he stared at Axiom. "Yeah. I wished that I were a robot for a long time. But now, I am not sure."

Noah looked at him in surprise. "Really?"

Aytor nodded. "If I were a robot, I wouldn't feel the way I do now. I wouldn't get scared when the fire alarm goes off, or when someone asks me a question and I don't know how to answer it. I wouldn't get mad when people don't understand what I'm saying. Robots don't get mad. They just do their job, and they do it right."

Noah seemed to think about that for a moment, shifting from foot to foot. "But if you were a robot, you wouldn't be able to have fun or eat ice cream or—"

"Yeah, but…" Aytor cut him off. "People only think about fun and feelings and emotions, but it doesn't help them. Being a robot would be easier in many ways. No confusion, no mistakes." His voice was rising now, a tinge of frustration creeping into it.

Noah took a step back, clearly unsure of how to respond. "I guess I never thought about it like that," he said carefully. "But…I don't know, man. I think being human is still kind of cool."

Aytor shrugged, not wanting to argue. Noah wouldn't understand. How could he? Noah was good at talking to people, good at running around and playing silly games. For him, being human probably wasn't so bad.

"But I tried it already. It didn't work. I think my mom was right. Being a robot is not the answer."

"You tried what?" Noah asked, evidently confused by his facial expression.

"Never mind," Aytor said.

"Okay," said Noah so nonchalantly. "I'm gonna go back to play tag. Come if you want."

But Aytor simply stayed where he was. Oh, how he wished Jenny were there.

***

The next day, Jenny was there. And this made his day. To make things better, after school, Jenny asked Aytor if he could show her more of his machines. He hesitated at first—his room was his sanctuary, the one place where he didn't have to worry about what others thought of him. But then he realized something. He didn't have to be afraid. Jenny had never judged him, never made him feel like he was strange for the things he loved. Maybe it was okay to let her into his world.

He called his mom to ask for permission, and it was surprisingly, even enthusiastically given. And Jenny's parents didn't seem to mind at all. When they arrived at his house, Aytor led her to his room. He opened the door slowly, unsure of what she would think. His room was cluttered with wires, half-built machines, and tools strewn across every surface. To Aytor, it was organized chaos. To anyone else, it probably looked like a mess.

But Jenny didn't seem fazed. She stepped inside, her eyes wide with curiosity. "Wow, this is amazing," she said, turning in a slow circle to take it all in. "You've built all of this?"

Aytor nodded, his heart swelling with pride. "Yeah. It's... it's where I feel most like myself."

Jenny walked over to one of his projects—a small robot that could follow a line drawn on the floor. She crouched down to look at it more closely, then glanced back at Aytor with a grin. "Can you show me how this one works?"

For the rest of the afternoon, Aytor and Jenny worked together on the different robots and parts, testing them, making adjustments, and laughing when they went off course. And for the first time in a long while, Aytor felt like he didn't need to hide who he was. He didn't need to be a robot to feel strong or understood. He just needed someone who was willing to see him for who he really was.

***

Later that evening, after Jenny had gone home, Aytor sat on the floor of his room, surrounded by his creations. He thought about the Integration, the suit he had once believed would make his life better. But now, he realized, it wasn't about changing himself to fit in. It was about finding people who appreciated him for who he already was. There were people like Noah, Jenny, and his mom, who might not fully understand him, but seemed to accept him as he was.

His mom had been right all along. He thought about what his mom had said days earlier, about being himself. The idea of not being Aytor anymore was strange. Maybe there were some good things about being human, like the feeling of his mom's hand in his, the excitement he felt when he figured out how to fix a broken robot, and the joy he felt when Jenny asked about his projects. Maybe being human wasn't always bad. Sure, it was still hard, and he didn't know if it would ever stop being hard not being neurotypical. He wasn't sure if he'd ever truly stop wishing he could be a robot, just for a day, just to see what it felt like to not be confused, not be scared, to always know exactly what to do. Or maybe, at the very least, robot-like.

Still, he smiled to himself, feeling lighter than he had in a long time. Maybe being a robot wasn't the answer, but building robots? Now, that was a part of him! And that part didn't need to be fixed or hidden. It was something to be proud of. And he was great at it.

Aytor stood up and crossed the room to his workbench. There was still so much more to create, so much more to discover. But now, he knew that he didn't have to do it alone. He could build, he could tinker, and he could share his world with others, one piece at a time.

And for the first time, that felt more than enough.

STORY NOTES

THE COSTUME CONTEST

I had this plot in my mind for quite some time before finally writing the story. The idea of magically turning into whatever you dressed up on a Halloween party sounds equally fun and dangerous. I guess in the end it all depends on what you choose to dress up as. For this story, I knew I wanted the main character to be an excellent sleuth. And even though I am an enthusiastic fan of Bruce Wayne (Batman) and Sherlock Holmes, I also have an affinity towards Agatha Christie's mysteries. For this reason, I chose to go with my third favorite detective from literature – Hercule Poirot. I also felt it would add an interesting element to the whole investigation process, particularly when being paired with a sexy vampire as a contrast. Though magical in nature, I wanted *The Costume Contest* to feel as homey as possible. It was for this reason that I chose to host the party in the famous Queen Mary boat, a place where I've personally attended multiple parties such as the one depicted in the story.

Question: If you knew for certain that you would turn into your costume at a party, what character would you go dressed as?

HUNTERS

I've always loved steampunk culture. I enjoy the stories, the cool artwork, the fun outfits, the awesome videogames, and the intricate designs. I also love the blending of genres. *Hunters* is my attempt at doing a steampunk fairytale. Nonetheless, I didn't want to host the story in Victorian England. Instead, I wanted it to feel at home; therefore, the American West made sense. For this reason, I wanted to include in the mystical creatures pantheon the most famous Native American folk monsters. Additionally, one of the main themes in steampunk, besides the steam and gear-powered technology, is the idea of an alternate, fantastical past. This also provided me with the opportunity to include a diverse cast. Though, sadly, the reality is that a diverse cast such as the one depicted in the story would've never happened in the United States of the late 1800s, I can just imagine the possibilities! After all, it was this same embracing of diversity within humanity that provided our main character a chance to accept diversity in other creatures, mystical or not.

Question: What kind of steampunk weapon would you use if you were part of the Hunters?

CLAIRVOYANT LAW

The idea of a police force having psychic detectives or officers who would be able to use clairvoyance or telepathic powers to investigate crimes is nothing new. However, I wanted to bring in a master criminal with the same, or perhaps even superior, powers to even out the game. For *Clairvoyant Law*, I also thought deeply about the potential human limitations and physical implications and manifestations when using such powers. Making the main character epileptic made sense to me. I grew up with an epileptic brother and I witnessed firsthand the very real debilitations and dangers of seizures. We eventually lost my brother due to a seizure, which caused an accident that resulted in his death. I always wondered how this would impact any superhero – let's say, that Superman suffered a draining physical symptom every single time after using his powers. Would he continue to use them without measure? Would he chose to continue being a hero, or would this ultimately make him "selfish" and look after himself?

Question: If you had any type of psychic power, whether clairvoyance or telepathy, what would be your ideal profession?

METAMORPHOSIS OF AN ANGEL

Science Fantasy is perhaps one of my favorite genres in literature, as it combines two of my top preferred ones. I knew I wanted to include a science fantasy story in this collection, and I opted for *Metamorphosis of An Angel.* Even as a young child, I always wondered what it would be like if human beings transformed into angelic beings, just as caterpillars change into butterflies. I asked myself what it would take, and it dawned on me that perhaps some complex surgical procedure in the future involving an electro bio-chemical cocoon of sorts made sense. However, the reality is that there is always a danger to complex surgical procedures even now. I thought of memory loss as a potential side effect, bringing a heavy question for every potential client to consider.

Question: If money wasn't an issue, but you knew there was a big chance that you wouldn't remember anything about your current life, would you still undertake a human-angel metamorphosis procedure?

CONFESSIONS OF A LIFE WELL LIVED

If you haven't noticed yet, I like to write #ownvoices stories more often than not. To me, however, this means going beyond including characters of my own ethnic background and culture or making them the main characters. It also involves incorporating geographical places where I have lived or visited frequently. Not only does this provide much needed fresh characters of color in literature that are relatable, but it also allows me to write my stories, locations, and characters from firsthand experience. With *Confessions of A Life Well Lived*, which is probably one of my favorite stories in this collection, I wanted to visit my homeland and explore elements of my culture through the lens of a background story. At the end of the narrative, I wanted to leave the reader with the question of what is real and what is fantasy within the story. This one is in honor of those Latin-American writers of the 20th century who brought the beauty of magical realism into the world of literature.

Question: If you possessed a magical amulet which allowed you to accomplish anything you'd wanted in life, what things would you do?

PERPETUITIONOMY – A CASE STUDY ON THE CONTROVERSIONAL LONGEVITY PROCEDURE

In my first sci-fi collection, I included a piece that didn't read like a short story, but rather, as an article written in a tech magazine. For this fantasy collection, I knew I wanted to do something similar. *Perpetuitionomy* is what one would find written in an academic or scientific journal. Though (obviously) fictional, I wanted it to feel and read as legit as any other piece included in a any significant and respected journal, including having an abstract, instead of a typical short story. For mere practical design purposes, I decided to remove the footnotes and graphs that I'd originally included in this piece. I hope it doesn't take away from the journal article feel. Ultimately, I wanted to explore writing creatively without the archetypal plot elements found in fiction.

Question: If you could live forever, but in order to do so you had to endure constant controversial surgical procedures, would you do so?

THE PAPER CRANE

As a child, I was fascinated with origami. It was my mother who gave one of my brothers and I a book on origami and paper folding techniques. Soon after, we would create different paper animals and play with them, using our overactive imagination while pretending they were alive. Even as an adult, decades later, I can still remember the basic folding techniques. When learning origami, the paper crane is usually the piece that almost everyone learns to fold first. It is simply a classic. I originally wanted to write a story that reflected a child's imagination while using origami, particularly this bird. However, *The Paper Crane* developed to a full-on magical narrative as I wrote it. I decided to use this story as the centerpiece to this collection because it resonated with me in several ways – dealing with the recent death of close family members, growing up as a child with an overactive imagination, and having a fascination with fantastic elements. For these reasons, I hold this story close to my heart.

Question: Is there a tangible object that has special significance to you, either because it reminds you of something or someone?

DREAM FRIGHT

Insomnia is not joke. Over time, it will kill you, literally. The lack of sleep can cause anxiety, memory loss, mood swings, depression, anger, obsession, organ failure, mania, and in some cases, over long exposure, it can even trigger dissociative identity disorder or schizophrenia. In one way or another, many of us have experienced it. What most of us haven't experienced is having visions. Throughout human history, there have always been seers or prophets. But, though they argue that they are able to dream, see, hear, or experience that which others cannot, such as foretelling future events, instead of gifted, they are usually thought of as crazy. In *Dream Fright*, I wanted to write a psychological thriller in which the main character, who is a seer, has dreams and visions of the future, but these have a major impact on his psych. Just keep in mind that, sometimes, there are endings that not even a prophet could predict.

Question: I purposely left the ending of this story up to interpretation. What do you think the ending means and how do you interpret Ellie's actions in the end?

TATA'S SECRET

This story is another one I hold close to my heart. I consider *Tata's Secret* as one of my all-time favorites. There are so many elements of my identity engrained in it; but most importantly, it is possibly due to the fact that I wrote it right after my dad, who my children refer to as *Tata*, passed away. Dad was a great chef, and our family reunions have always involved gathering around a table full of "magical" food. I have countless memories of him working his miraculous wonders in the kitchen. Even as an adult, we'd continue to cook meals together at times, always creating something lovely. On more than one occasion, I witnessed people asking him what was the secret to his great cooking. "The secret ingredient is love," he would always reply. To him I owe much, including the love of food and cooking, as well as the love for fantasy. Though it doesn't reflect my views on the state of the dead, I still wrote this story for him and for my children to remember him. Oh, how I wish we could have just one more sweet *Mole* together with Tata.

Question: Cooking and the love of food is something that unites my family. What is something that connects you with your loved ones?

REPLICAS

Being couped in for a year due to the pandemic was no fun. Though it did provide me with plenty of quality family time and also with the opportunity for lots of writing and music composing, at the end of the day, I craved physical relationships with others and the outdoors. One other thing it did give me, however, was the idea for this story. I've always wanted to write a story about someone with agoraphobia, but this being the least of the things the character should fear. But it wasn't until the pandemic that it all came together in my head. *Replicas* is my attempt at horror, though still with a magical realism feel.

Question: What are some folk horror stories or scary cultural characters that you grew up with, and how did they impact your upbringing?

MIRAGE

A mirage, by definition, is an optical illusion caused by special conditions, something that appears real or possible but is not in fact so. Light and atmospheric conditions are involved in the appearance of this illusion. Keeping that in mind, know that *Mirage* is symbolical for so many things; though I leave that up to you, the reader. Sometimes in life we must ask what is real and what is not. And as we grow older, our perception of things changes. Perhaps there are mirages in our lives that help us through difficult times and we are simply not aware of them.

Question: What is something that has help you get through a difficult time in your life, whether tangible or intangible?

THE ORPHANAGE

I have to be honest. *The Orphanage* originally started as something completely different. It was meant to be a cute story about an orphan kid who had the ability to bring his toys to life. This ability helped him and those around him survive challenging situations as they navigated the system. However, sometimes stories begin to tell themselves as you write them. That was the case here, and a charming children's story turned into something much darker. I allowed it, simply because at the time, I hadn't written any monster stories yet. I included this story in this collection because it was my first attempt at monster writing, and I found it interesting.

Question: What is one magical ability you wished you had during childhood?

OTHERWORLDLY EXPERIENCE

I want to say a few things in relation to this story. First, I almost included this science fantasy story in my first collection. However, I decided to save it for this one because I felt it was somewhat heavier on the fantasy side than the sci-fi one. I feel it fits better. Second, just like our main character in *Otherworldly Experience*, I personally love escape rooms, and I can also say that I've had 100% success in escaping all of my attempts, which are quite numerous. I don't say this to boast, but simply to state the fact that I've always enjoyed a good challenge. You see, I worked at a university for ten years dealing with students on a daily basis. I got to witness firsthand the stress that students get and the temptation to rely on drugs in order to remain focused. So, thirdly, I challenged myself to write a story about college students using drugs and the potential ramifications of this. I thought about a psychedelic/hallucinogen high gone wrong as if it was an escape room that you're trying to escape. And that is ultimately how the idea for the story was born.

Question: Reality, the most fundamental thing in the universe, is everything that would remain even if we were not here to perceive it. What, if any, advantage(s) exist for altering reality in our brain?

THE BOY WHO WOULD BE ROBOT

This one is personal. As a school psychologist, I've worked with many brilliant, neurodivergent children—some of whom find machines far easier to understand than people. Aytor, the protagonist, came from those encounters. *The Boy Who Would Be Robot* is not a story about "fixing" autism. It's about honoring a different way of being, while still wrestling with the very real desire to feel safe and understood. At its core, this is a story about identity, acceptance, and the beauty of embracing one's own wiring—even when the world doesn't make it easy.

Question: Do you know anyone, or are you, neurodivergent? What challenges have you encounter because of this?

ACKNOWLEDGEMENTS

To my wife: You may be crazy (or drive me crazy). But even if I got to choose all over again, I'd still choose to be with you. Let's continue being crazy together and writing our own stories. I'll always be crazy about you.

To my kids: Without you and your continuous loving interruptions, this book would've been done ages ago. Hehe. Nonetheless, without you, life would make no sense. Always remember this – everything I do is for you, *pollitos*.

To my mom: Thank you for being the best mother, supporter, and beta reader I could've ever asked for. I am so lucky to have you in my life.

To my friends: Thanks for choosing to stick with this foo. You're all alright.

OBED OLIVARRÍA was born in Mexicali, Mexico and spent his youth as a fully bicultural transnational citizen. He has a passion for writing both fiction and nonfiction, public speaking, composing, arranging, and performing mostly jazz music, as well as traveling around the world. He loves the thrill of adrenaline-pumping activities, but also the quiet reflection he gets from writing and creating.

His love for books started at an early age, as his parents were eager readers and owned thousands of books. His passion for writing was born after winning a city-wide short story competition while in high school in Arizona. The publication of this in a local journal inspired him to continue creating worlds and characters in print.

Obed has worked as a youth and young adult pastor, as a freelance graphic designer, as a session musician, as a ministry consultant, and as university dean. Having worked at every level of the education system, from pre-k to university, has given him an expedition to the human psyche. He has a dynamic love of life and ministry, and he is a deep thinker, and an honest intellectual to the Christian gospel.

Obed lives in sunny Orange County, California with his charming wife and two energetic children, where he works as a school psychologist by day. In the future, Obed hopes to be able to continue to write inspiring books that entertain, but also challenge the status quo. On a personal level, he would like to visit every country in the world, perhaps drawing inspiration from these travels for another great story.

www.obedolivarria.com

www.ingramcontent.com/pod-product-compliance
Lightning Source LLC
LaVergne TN
LVHW041056080826
845145LV00007B/1596

* 9 7 8 1 9 6 6 1 7 9 0 5 4 *